Beloved Poison

Beloved Poison

E. S. THOMSON

PEGASUS CRIME

NEW YORK LONDON

BELOVED POISON

Pegasus Books, Ltd.
148 West 37th Street, 13th Floor
New York, NY 10018

Copyright © 2016 by E. S. Thompson

First Pegasus Books hardcover edition September 2016

ISBN: 978-1-68177-214-1

10 9 8 7 6 5 4 3 2 1

Printed in the United States of America
Distributed by W. W. Norton & Company, Inc.

For Guy and Carlo

Chapter One

⤫⤬

I stood on the threshold of my room, my hand on the door knob. A man was inside. He leaped to his feet, the long roll of paper he was holding open on the bed springing closed and tumbling to the floor. It was not *my* bed he was using – that remained where it was against the wall. The situation was far worse than that: the truckle bed that lay beneath it had been pulled out, and set up opposite. A mattress had been dragged up from one of the store rooms, and the bed neatly made. A stove-pipe hat, new, obviously, and precious, sat on the pillow.

The man who owned the hat was in his mid-twenties, with curly brown hair cut close to his head. I noted the ink on the fingers of the hand he held out to me, and on the cuffs of his shirt. I saw the sheen on his waistcoat from habitually leaning against a desk, or drawing board. His boots were beside the door, the clay-coloured mud of the infirmary's main courtyard drying on the soles. At five feet and eight inches in height he was no taller than I.

1

He had settled himself in nicely. An open carpet bag at the foot of his bed showed a clean shirt, collar and cuffs. Against the wall, beside the fireplace, leaned the neatly folded legs of a tripod, a small wooden instrument case tucked between them.

'Mr Flockhart?' he said, stepping forward. 'Mr Jem Flockhart?'

I nodded, my expression grim. I did not ask *his* name. There was no need, for I knew exactly who he was. I would have told him so but I was so surprised to see him in my room that, for once, I was unable to say anything.

He stepped neatly into the silence. 'Mr Flockhart,' he repeated, still holding out a hand. 'I am—'

'William Quartermain, junior architect for Shaw and Prentice.'

'Have we met before?'

'No,' I said. His voice had a pleasant West Country burr to it. Wiltshire, perhaps, or Somerset? London was growing at a prodigious rate and there were opportunities for incomers with ambition. A glance at the shiny brass plaque on his new theodolite case confirmed my thoughts: 'J. King and Son, 2 Clare Street, Bristol.' And yet he lacked any degree of urban sophistication – his outlandish stove-pipe hat suggested as much – and I was sure he was not a native of that city. He must be from some fearful yokel-infested backwater – Bath, perhaps, or Devizes – come to London to seek his fortune. I wondered how long he had been in town. His skin had the sickly pallor of all who had breathed in the city air for longer than a fortnight, though his cheeks still bore the traces of a provincial journeyman's tan. He smiled at me, his gaze trusting, as if he anticipated the start of a marvellous friendship. London would eat him alive if he was not careful.

I shook his hand, aware of the roll of thick paper that lay between us on the floor. It was a plan of the hospital – my hospital – that much I had glimpsed. How much did it show of the place? The cellars that had once belonged to the medieval monastery? The dark, sluggish watercourse that flowed beneath out-patients or the underground passage that led from the dissecting rooms to the church-yard? There was more to St Saviour's than any neophyte architect might see. But there was a more urgent matter to attend to, and I was obliged to put aside my curiosity.

'You can't stay here,' I said. 'This is where *I* sleep.'

His smile faded. 'But the apothecary said—'

'*I* am the apothecary.'

'What about that tall thin man downstairs? Isn't he also the apothecary?'

'Yes—'

'And senior to you?'

'I suppose—'

'Well *he* said—'

'Whatever he said, I doubt he meant that you should sleep *here.*' I had meant to sound calm but authoritative. Somehow, I had ended up sounding like an idiot, and an unreasonable one at that.

'The apprentice brought up the mattress on your father's bidding. The governors thought it best if I live within St Saviour's, to be close to my work, and there's nowhere else to stay.'

Nowhere else? Was there not space in the porter's lodge? Could the man not sleep beneath the deal table in the apothecary? I closed my eyes. My father was sick, that much was clear to anyone. Had his tiredness so befuddled his senses that he no longer knew the difference between appearance and reality? Had he forgotten who I was? All at once I felt naked, exposed, the clues to my secret identity shouting from every corner of the room. I had bought a screen from the auction house on Priory Street, and over this I had draped a pair of fine Paisley shawls. A small bottle of *Valeriana officinalis* tincture, which is good for menstrual cramps, stood on the shelf above my bed. Before the fire the rags from my monthly bleeds dried in a line of dismal greyish pennants. Oh, yes, I was unique among women. There had been an apothecary named Flockhart at St Saviour's Infirmary for over one hundred years and I was set to inherit my father's kingdom amongst the potions. But it took a man to run that apothecary, and so a man I must be.

I swept forward to gather up the rags from the fireplace. 'Dusters,' I muttered. I snatched at the Paisley shawls too – such feminine details would never do – and bundled them away. On the desk, a large hyacinth rose from its bulb in a defiant pink fist. William Quartermain regarded it, and then me, in silence.

'Excuse me, Mr Quartermain,' I said. 'But there must have been a mistake.'

Downstairs in the apothecary Gabriel Locke, our apprentice, was crouched goblin-like over the work bench, rolling out sulphur pills. A smudge of chalk on his nose gleamed white in the candlelight. 'I tried to tell you, Mr Jem,' he said, before I could speak. 'But you didn't listen. It was your father's idea.' Gabriel pointed.

My father was slumped in the wing-backed chair before the fire, his eyes closed. He was sitting so quiet and still

4

that I had bounded up the stairs without even noticing him. I chided myself inwardly for my selfishness. He was sleeping badly, I knew, and yet I had not even paused to look for him and ask how he fared. At my father's elbow, a stack of prescription ledgers teetered on a small table. Each ward in the infirmary sent its ledger down to us for midday, and we spent the afternoon making up the necessary prescriptions. There was much to do, even when my father was helping. Now, with him asleep, it was just Gabriel and I. And there was also the matter of the man upstairs.

But the man upstairs was now the man downstairs, as all at once I noticed that he had followed me in his stockinged feet, and was standing at the back of the apothecary, his face pale and earnest in the shadows. 'The Company sent me, Mr Flockhart. I believe I was expected,' he said. 'It was arranged with the governors, but I apologise personally for any inconvenience. I realise there are not many who welcome me at St Saviour's.'

'It's not your fault.' My father opened his dark-ringed eyes, looking from me to Mr Quartermain. 'Commerce will always come before health. We cannot obstruct progress – so called – or we will be crushed. There were a few who said as much at the meeting.'

'Dr Bain, yes, I heard him myself, sir. But there were many who wished to refuse the Company's offer. Dr Magorian was particularly vocal. And Dr Graves, well—' Mr Quartermain cleared his throat, and then added in an undertone, 'I thought he and Dr Bain were going to come to blows.'

'Not on this particular occasion, Mr Quartermain,' said my father. 'We must be grateful for that at least.'

'Your Company, sir, has offered less than half what the hospital and its lands are worth,' I said. 'St Saviour's has been here since 1135 and you expect us to go away just because your employers wish to build a railway into the centre of the city? Can they not build somewhere else?'

'It seems not,' he replied. 'But I'm merely the junior architect. I'm not one of the hospital governors, who agreed to the proposal, nor one of the railway company officials, who made the offer. The decisions to pull down the hospital, and to build the railway bridge in its place, were none of my doing. I'm simply tasked with organising the emptying of St Saviour's graveyard, as the Company cannot knowingly build on the bones of the dead. I'm also instructed to look over the rest of the place, and report my preliminary impressions.'

'Mr Quartermain is to stay with us while he . . . while he does what's required,' said my father. 'You are to assist him in any way he sees fit.'

'I? But I have work to do. Especially as you're so . . . so tired.' I chose my words carefully. To suggest that he was sick, too weak and ill to perform the duties he had attended to all his life, would be a mistake. And yet I had watched his recent deterioration with alarm. How might I raise the matter without provoking his anger? I had no idea. Perhaps I should speak with Dr Hawkins. The two of them seemed uncommonly friendly all of a sudden. 'And the physic garden requires my attention,' I added. 'I can't—'

'Yes, you can. Besides, no one else will look after the man. As Mr Quartermain says, he has few friends at St Saviour's.' He eyed the architect critically. 'Few friends in London, too, I should think – eh, Mr Quartermain? And

6

none at all at the Company, or at your firm of architects, for why else would they give you such a job as this?'

'But where will he stay?' I asked. 'We don't have room for him here.' I glared at William Quartermain. No one ever saw beyond my birthmark. A port-wine stain that covered my eyes and nose like a highwayman's mask, it was as though I was born for disguise. I felt safe – watchful, protected, anonymous – behind it. Mr Quartermain stared back at me. His eyes were blue and clear, his expression sharp, and curious.

'He'll stay in your room, Jem,' said my father. 'You're usually so observant. Hadn't you noticed?'

'But Father!' I heard my voice rising in shrill alarm. 'Where am *I* to go? And where am I to . . . to put all my books?'

'The room is easily big enough for both of you.' My father closed his eyes and sank back into his chair. 'As well as your books, and anything else you care to mention. Stop making a fuss. What's the worst that may come of it?'

❧

I stood with Will Quartermain in the courtyard. I had left my exhausted father and his apprentice alone in the apothecary. The statue of Edward VI that stood in the centre of the courtyard looked down at me accusingly.

'I have work to do,' I muttered. I glanced over my shoulder at the open door. Gabriel was changing the water in one of the leech jars. He would never manage it on his own. I turned away, expecting to hear the sound of breaking glass and the shouted curses of my father as Gabriel bungled the job, but there was nothing. 'You can

hardly be looking forward to your task, Mr Quartermain?'
I said.

'I'm not looking forward to it at all, truth be told,' he
said. 'But it has to be done. As I'm only recently qualified
my sensibilities are considered by my employer to be less
important than anyone else's. And so the job fell to me.'

I nodded. I knew what awaited him. How did I know?
Because I had seen it. One midsummer, shortly after my
tenth birthday, the rain had poured down for two weeks
without stopping. Beyond the west wall of the infirmary,
where the gardens of St Saviour's priory had once been
cultivated, long-buried watercourses materialised once
again. In the graveyard of St Saviour's parish church,
which lay adjacent to the infirmary, the waters boiling up
from the earth met those pouring down from the heavens.
The floodwaters passed through the western fringe of the
burial ground, scouring away the thin layer of soil that
covered the most recent incumbents, packed beneath,
one on top of the other, like kippers in a smokehouse.
Bodies were churned into view: skulls, limbs, ribs and
vertebrae sieved against the gates of the graveyard as the
waters rose . . . and receded.

Of course, it was impossible to get them all back into
the space they had vacated. The sight, and the smell made
it a matter of public health. That and the fact that a gang
of ragged boys from the rookeries of Prior's Rents was
seen using a human skull as a football in one of the filthy
courts that lay not far from the infirmary. Dr Magorian,
our most distinguished surgeon, had been quite insistent:
as soon as possible the skeletons were to be taken away
and buried somewhere else.

I had gone to have a look. Was one of them my mother?

She was buried against the wall of the church in a patch of ground warmed by the morning sun. Perhaps I might look upon her face at last . . . How foolish I had been to expect anything but the most appalling sight – yawning skulls, gaping, muddy eye sockets, bony hands reaching out at me through the gates. I ran back to the apothecary. Alone in my room I wept, wept for the mother I had never known, for my father grown so cold and sad, and for myself, alone and without comfort in the world.

A few months later, when the ground had been cleared, I visited the graveyard again. Apart from a muddy scar across the centre of the greensward, the place looked no different to usual. I found my mother's headstone untouched by the waters. I had never forgotten the sight of that filthy mass of bones and rags being carted away. And now the same job on a far greater scale had landed in the lap of this raw, rosy-cheeked country boy. 'Perhaps you should take a look around the infirmary first, Mr Quartermain,' I said, taking pity on him. 'The graveyard can wait. It's not as if the residents are going anywhere, is it?'

William Quartermain peeped at me from beneath the brim of his ridiculous hat. 'I'd be honoured to have your company. If you could show me St Saviour's – your knowledge would be invaluable. But could you call me Will instead of Mr Quartermain – so much easier. We're similar in age and rank. And height.' He grinned. 'Like brothers, almost. What d'you say?'

I hesitated, disarmed a little by his familiarity. St Saviour's was a deeply formal place; respect for tradition and the veneration of reputation were everything. Even my good friend Dr Bain did not allow me to call him anything but 'Dr Bain'. But it was not just convention that made me pause. I had lived in this place all my life. Did I really wish to share its secrets with a stranger? And yet, the destruction of the hospital was inevitable; it would be taken down, brick by brick, whether I wanted it to happen or not. And I was flattered too, by his gratitude and enthusiasm. All at once I was glad that Will Quartermain had come. Perhaps my final weeks at the hospital would not be as lonely as the great many that had preceded them.

'Tell me all you can,' he said, as we walked across the infirmary's principal courtyard.

'What do you wish to know?'

'Everything.'

Where might I begin? St Saviour's was one of the city's smaller hospitals, crammed into an acre and a half of land to the north of the river. The southern edge of the place, which looked out onto St Saviour's Street, was lined with tall flat-fronted town houses, built in King George's reign. These houses contained the lodgings of the wealthier medical students and of the less vainglorious medical men: Dr Bain and Dr Hawkins, men without the pretention to live in great mansions further to the west, among them. Dr Magorian kept a house here, too, though he lived at the farthest end of the street, so that the stink of the infirmary did not blow in at his windows. On the other three sides, we were surrounded by the buildings of the Empire – the railway station and its accompanying hotel, a tea warehouse, the offices of a shipping clerk – and the houses of the poor. They crowded close to our eastern wall like mushrooms beside a decaying tree, the smells of industry – from the tanning yards and the leather market

10

– mingling with the reek of putrescence and privies breathed from the open windows of our wards.

Was that what Will Quartermain wanted to know?

'Of course, it's people who interest me most,' he said, as if reading my mind. 'The men who work here, for instance. What are they like?'

I shrugged. 'Dedicated.' It was bland, I knew. And predictable. Should I tell him what I really thought? I had been schooled to revere them all, but I had formed my own opinions. I prided myself on never joining in the gossip, but I heard everything. Mrs Speedicut was the worst. *That Dr Graves . . . The way he boils up the bodies of the dead . . . Human broth, that's what's in that great copper cauldron of his, human broth. And don't he just stink of it? As for anatomy, I've seen them at Smithfield making a cleaner job of it . . .* I had heard it so many times, though I could not disagree. *And that old stick Dr Catchpole. Married to that young slip of a girl? There's trouble! I knew it soon as look at her. She was after Dr Bain quicker than a toddy-cat once he'd thrown her a smile . . .* On and on she went, sitting before the stove in the apothecary, her pipe clenched between her blackened teeth, her mug of gin and coffee in her hand. *That Dr Magorian, thinks he's God, so he does . . . That Dr Bain, you'll never imagine what he's come up with now . . .* Although I did not join in, I did not stop her either. Mrs Speedicut's observations were always perspicacious. Certainly there was little that happened at St Saviour's that she didn't know about. I could see her now on the far side of the courtyard, her great thick arms folded across her huge bosom, her matron's cap sitting drunkenly awry on her greasy hair as she whispered and cackled into the ear of one of the laundrywomen.

Will was talking again. 'And why is there a statue of Edward VI out here?'

'He reopened the place after his father, Henry VIII, closed it down.'

'Is that all? How dull.'

'Indeed he was.'

'Unable to live up to expectations.' Will slid me a glance. 'Like so many men. And yet his sisters were quite the opposite – always their own masters. Don't you agree?'

'I'm sure there's more to many women than meets the eye, Mr Quartermain.'

'I don't doubt it.' He grinned. 'And what of the other women here, at St Saviour's?'

'Other women?' I said. 'Other than whom?'

'I mean the women who work here. Other than you. That is to say, *in addition* to you.'

I stared at him through my devilish mask, unsmiling.

'Not that you're a woman, of course. I can see that *quite* clearly. What I meant to say was *other* than you, and the doctors, there must be women at St Saviour's—'

'Nurses,' I replied. 'Naturally. And the usual complement of domestics, cooks, cleaners, washerwomen. Women's work is done by women, Mr Quartermain, here as elsewhere.'

'Of course,' he said, his eyes now fixed meekly upon the ground. 'It is the natural way of things.'

'You think they're not capable of more?' I said. 'But of course they are! Give them an education so that they might think, listen to their opinions so that they might gain confidence, treat them as you treat a man and they'll succeed at anything. I have no doubt about it.'

At that moment we heard women's voices echoing from

12

the passageway that led to the governors' building. '"If anyone destroys God's temple, God will destroy him. For God's temple is holy, and *you* are that temple!" Ladies, where in the scriptures might we find those words?'

'Oh! Corinthians!' came the answer.

'Quite so,' said the first.

I groaned. 'Not them. Not now.'

Will grinned. 'Give them an education so that they might think?'

I laughed. 'Exactly my thoughts.'

'"A joyful heart is good medicine,"' cried the voice, '"but a crushed spirit dries up the bones". Yes, ladies, yes?'

There was a rustling of skirts, the sound of soft shoes in the passageway, and a trio of lady almoners swept into the yard – Mrs Magorian, her daughter Eliza, and Mrs Catchpole. The lady almoners were unstoppable. Their activities were endorsed by the hospital governors, who had quickly come to appreciate the healing qualities of the Scriptures. The evidence was clear: malingering had come to an end since the almoners had begun their Bible readings about the wards. Mrs Magorian thanked the Lord. I thanked the lady almoners, and their unbearable piercing voices.

'Oh! Proverbs!' cried Mrs Catchpole, clapping her gloved hands together. That morning she was wearing a long black coat, open at the front to reveal a gown of emerald silk – far too fine for skirting spittoons and chamber pots on a ward visit. She was hoping to impress someone, that much was certain. Her husband? It seemed unlikely. Her gaze swept the yard. 'Dear Dr Bain said he would be on the wards this afternoon. Monday afternoon, he said.'

'I do not see him.' Mrs Magorian, the tiny bird-like wife of the great surgeon, was their ringleader. She licked a forefinger and leafed through the large, dark-skinned Bible she always carried when she was about the wards. 'Perhaps he is inside.'

'But he said he would come. I expected to see him today.' Mrs Catchpole looked about as she spoke, as though at any moment Dr Bain might burst out from behind a door, like a partridge flushed from a thicket.

'Eliza!' cried Mrs Magorian. 'Carry those flowers with their heads up, my dear. Up and proud. That's it!'

Eliza glided toward Will and me, a tattered bunch of pus-coloured chrysanthemums carried stiffly in her arms. 'Good afternoon, Mr Jem,' she murmured.

'Miss Magorian, what a pleasure to see you.' I meant it too, despite my more general view of the lady almoners. 'This is Mr Will Quartermain,' I said. 'The surveyor. Mr Quartermain, this is Miss Magorian, Dr Magorian's daughter.'

Will gave a bow, and swept off his tall hat. 'Will Quartermain, junior architect for Shaw and Prentice.' I could see that he was unable to take his eyes off her. And no wonder! She was so beautiful today. Her mouth as red as berries, her hair curled into shining ringlets. Her skin was white, almost translucent, her eyes dark and huge. I had known her all my life and I knew she was as spirited as a boy and tough, tougher than any of them.

'I see you have become a lady almoner, Miss Magorian,' I said.

'Yes.' She sighed. 'It was my mother's idea. Mrs Catchpole and I are her new recruits. We are to start off with the less gruesome wards.'

14

'The Magdalenes?' The Magdalene ward was Mrs Magorian's favourite.

'Of course.'

'Mrs Catchpole is not really dressed for the occasion,' I murmured.

'On the contrary,' said Eliza. She plucked a petal off one of the chrysanthemums the way a schoolboy might tweak the wings off a fly, and released it into the air. 'She's dressed *exactly* for the occasion. She's in love, you see. But not with her husband, though one can hardly blame her for that. He's an old brute.'

'Dr Catchpole is very distinguished.' I glanced at Will, alarmed by Eliza's reckless heresy. Would he disapprove? For a lady to express an opinion about a man's character – but if he was surprised by her unguarded comments he did not show it.

'He's a beast,' Eliza continued undaunted. 'He told my father I would become barren if he allowed me to read anything more stimulating than *Blackwood's Magazine.*'

'*Blackwood's*?' I said. 'How very modern! I would have drawn the line at *Household Words.*'

'She despises him.' We watched as Mrs Catchpole sneaked a mirror out of her pocket while Mrs Magorian was examining her Bible.

'How can you possibly know that?' I said.

'Because she told me. And because he has hair up his nose. Surely every woman hates that?'

'One cannot judge a man by the content of his nostrils.'

'And he smells of old books and stale things.'

'Unlike Dr Bain, I presume?'

Dr Bain.

15

'*There's* Dr Bain!' It was Mrs Catchpole's voice. Dr Bain had emerged from the doors to the lower operating theatre, carrying what looked like a bucket and stirrup pump. He glanced up. Apprehending Mrs Catchpole hastening towards him, he bounded through another doorway, vanishing into the darkness of the male surgical wards.

Eliza Magorian regarded me over the shaggy heads of her chrysanthemums, and raised an *I-told-you-so* eyebrow. Then, when Will was not looking, she winked. The blood rushed to my face, my birthmark throbbing in time with the violent beating of my heart. Could she hear it? Did she feel as I did? And yet how could she? How could anyone? Instinctively I put my hand to my eyes, shielding my hideous face from her gaze, and looked away.

❧

I had hoped to show Will around the place without the whole of St Saviour's knowing what I was about, but it seemed my luck was out that day, for hardly had the lady almoners disappeared up the staircase to the Magdalene ward when a shadow fell across our path.

'Good afternoon, Mr Flockhart.' Dr Magorian, St Saviour's most revered surgeon now stood before us. The man was tall and well built, with broad shoulders and long muscular arms, but his stride was quick and silent, and I had not heard him approach. His face was gaunt, his eyes pale and blue above a hawkish nose. He was always perfectly dressed, from the shine of his top hat to the red silk lining of his coat. He leaned on his stick, blocking our way – though seeming not to – and staring at my companion with a belligerent expression. 'St Saviour's is not a place for sightseers.'

Will bowed an apology. 'I realise that, sir—'

'I am to perform an operation at two o'clock. Amputation at the hip. Perhaps you would care to join us, since you're here. I have been a surgeon at St Saviour's for almost twenty years, and other than Dr Syme in Edinburgh, there is not a man alive who can excise a hip joint faster.' Dr Magorian slipped long, thin fingers into a pocket of his waistcoat, and drew out a small silver case. Prising open the lid, he selected a large chunk of lump sugar from inside, and popped it into his mouth.

As a child I had been intrigued and excited by Dr Magorian's sugar box, though he had never given me a piece. He did not give his sugar to anyone – apart from those who were his special favourites. As assistant surgeon, principal anatomist and chief sycophant, Dr Graves was the most regular recipient. He collected them like treasure, ostentatiously emptying his pockets during lectures to allow students to see how often the great Dr Magorian had bestowed upon him this sugary benison.

Dr Magorian snapped the case closed, and stowed it back in his waistcoat pocket. He crunched his sugar lump noisily, with a sound like the distant march of boots on gravel. 'Yes,' he said. 'You must come and watch, sir, since you insist on being here. It's Quartermain, isn't it?'

'Yes, sir,' said Will. He looked up at the clock tower that projected from the sagging roof of the men's foul ward. It was almost one o'clock.

'I performed this very operation on a Quartermain in

17

1830. I remember all my cases, you know. Tricky job, I seem to recall. Any relative?'

'My father, sir.'

'Oh! And is he well?'

'He's dead, sir.'

'But not killed by his amputation, I hope. Though there is a tendency to suppuration and gangrene.'

'He did not survive it,' said Will.

Dr Magorian licked his lips. 'Oh. Well, one does one's best. Afterwards it's in God's hands. And now *you* must tear *us* limb from limb, eh?'

'Hardly, sir,' said Will. 'The demolition men will do that. I'm merely here to take some preliminary measurements of the body, so to speak.'

Dr Magorian's face grew stony. 'And will you be plundering her, too?' he said. 'Stripping her corpse of anything useful or valuable?'

'No, sir.' Will coloured. 'I'm here to empty the graveyard. But I hope for work more worthy of my skills and knowledge when the time comes.'

'Do you?' said Dr Magorian. 'Well, I shall put in a good word for you. Your master, Mr Prentice, was a patient of mine. Lithotomy. 1838. His gratitude was extraordinary.' The doctor's laugh was spiteful and joyless. 'I'm sure yours will be too. I will do what I can to ensure you are *correctly* employed in future. But if you wish to see St Saviour's, what better place than the operating theatre? I shall expect you there at two o'clock, sharp.'

Dr Magorian's voice was loud and arrogant, and a small crowd had gathered as he talked. On the edge of the group I saw the great bulk of Mrs Speedicut, a pair of underlings by her side, all three of them grinning like gargoyles. Dr Graves too had emerged from the shadows, his habitual crouching gait giving him the air of a burglar creeping along a garden wall.

'Ah, there you are, Graves,' said Dr Magorian. 'This is Mr Quartermain. He is coming to see me perform this afternoon.'

'Is he?' Dr Graves smiled. 'Good.'

I looked at Will. His face had turned a sickly greenish colour at the very mention of the word 'amputation'.

'My principal dresser is absent this afternoon and Dr Graves has been kind enough to take his place,' continued Dr Magorian.

'I consider it an honour,' said Dr Graves, as unctuous as ever. His grin grew wider. A brown snuff-laden droplet hung from his left nostril. On more than one occasion I had seen such a droplet plop directly into a patient's open wound.

'Don't worry, sir,' cried Mrs Speedicut, noticing Will's luminous pallor. She exposed her long peg-like teeth, one of which was missing, giving her a hungry, piratical air. 'At least it's not you what's having your leg amputated.'

'Not today, at any rate, eh, Mr Quartermain?' Dr Magorian and Dr Graves laughed. Mrs Speedicut and her harpies nudged each other and cackled.

Should I have stopped their game? Was it wrong of me to allow them to sport with him? After all, not moments before I had decided that I liked the man. And yet I did nothing to save him from his fate. Perhaps I was annoyed that he spoke about the rape and demolition of St Saviour's so glibly. I was not usually so irrational – it was only a building, after all. But it was too late now.

Behind us, the students were gathering outside the

doors to the men's foul ward. Dr Bain appeared amongst them. He said a few words, and smiled, and there was a gale of laughter.

In the passage that led up to the Magdalene ward something caught my eye. There was a movement in the shadows and I saw the flicker of a pale face staring out of the gloom. Mrs Catchpole. She was watching Dr Bain with wide, anxious eyes, her face white as the dial of a clock. She wanted to speak to him, that much was clear, but she was held back by the presence of so many others, so many men.

Dr Bain came over to us, his students trailing in his wake. St Saviour's was a grey world – grey blankets on the beds, grey blinds at the windows, grey food on the plates, the patients' faces grey with pain and sickness. Into this gloomy monochrome strode Dr Bain in his midnight-blue frock coat and azure watered-silk waistcoat. He was half a head taller than anyone else, with broad shoulders and thick dark hair. His eyes gleamed with mirth, and his whole frame seemed to radiate energy. The students loved him. 'Sir,' he said, addressing Dr Magorian. 'I believe you're operating today? If I might trespass upon your good nature, I have something I would like to try—'

'*I* am assisting Dr Magorian this afternoon,' interrupted Dr Graves.

'Quite so, Richard,' said Dr Bain, patting Dr Graves on the shoulder. 'I hope you might also—'

'I think not.' Dr Graves's voice was sharp. He gave a thin smile. 'What is it this time? Using maggots to clean a wound? Scrubbing the operating table with carbolic like a cabin boy? And you need not *pat* me, sir, as though I were a dog to be pacified.'

20

Dr Bain looked surprised. 'I'm sorry, I—'

'Yes, yes, you *say* you are sorry. One day perhaps you will be.' Dr Graves shook his head, and turned to Will Quartermain. 'This is Dr Bain,' he said. 'Dr Bain, this is Mr Quartermain – he represents our nemesis.'

'The railway company, yes, I know. Welcome amongst us, Mr Quartermain.' Dr Bain shook Will by the hand. 'Come to pull us down, I hope? Can't happen too soon.'

Dr Magorian, suddenly finding himself eclipsed, spoke up irritably. 'Well, Dr Bain,' he said. 'What is it this time? I'm hoping for a quick excision. Under fifty-five seconds, if possible. I don't want to be hindered.'

'A new idea, sir,' said Dr Bain. 'Simple measures, but ones that should make all the difference. No hindrance at all.'

'In the operating theatre? During the procedure?'

'Yes, sir.'

'Well.' Dr Magorian looked thoughtful. He waited for the students to fall silent before he answered. 'Come along and we will see what you have.'

'Dr Magorian, I must insist—' Dr Graves's pale cheeks darkened with indignation.

'Must you, Graves?' Dr Magorian sighed. 'Give the fellow a chance, eh?'

'Thank you, sir.' Dr Bain inclined his head. 'Now, if you'll excuse me, I must prepare.'

He bounded off to where the laundry girl waited with a bundle of clean washing. Her arms were bare, her cheeks ruddy from the warmth of the ironing room. The neck of her dress was open, and her flesh was pink and white beneath it. I could not hear what he said as he bent his head to hers, but she nodded, and leaned back against

21

the wall, smiling lazily as she offered him her pile of folded linens. I could see Dr Bain's hands amongst the laundry. Partly concealed by his bundle, Dr Bain tweaked the girl's nipple through her bodice. I saw her gasp and blush, and then he had taken the linen, and was carrying it off towards the operating theatre.

The exchange had been quick, and furtive. But not quick and furtive enough, for it was clear that Mrs Catchpole, desperate and vigilant in the shadows, had seen it too. She staggered back, her hand to her breast as if reeling from a pistol shot. I saw her face crumple in anguish, stunned by his betrayal. Had she really thought she was the only one? She stumbled out of the doorway, calling his name. 'Dr Bain!' But her voice caught in her throat and he did not turn around. At the same moment her husband, Dr Catchpole, emerged from the library. He wore a long dark cape, like a European aristocrat, as though he were going to the opera, rather than the operating theatre. Above its tall collar his face was tragic. Mrs Catchpole took one look at him, and fled back into the shadows.

'Two o'clock,' muttered Will, as Dr Magorian and his followers walked on. 'Two o'clock.'

'Yes,' I said. 'Still, it gives us a bit of time for me to show you the place.' I looked about. Where should I start? The brewery? The laundry room? The cook house? Such dull places. The post-operative ward, with its stink of pus and gangrene? Or the general ward, perhaps? The general ward offered less of an olfactory assault than some of the other wards, though it was still suffocating with the reek of dirty bedding, recently emptied chamber pots and exhaled breath. As an apprentice on the wards I had quickly learned to breathe through my mouth, as one could hardly mince between the beds with a clove-stuck orange held to one's nose, though I generally disliked doing this as there was always a risk of looking doltish. As for opening a window, I knew Mrs Speedicut shut them again the moment I left the place. There was the men's foul ward . . . But he would never have the stomach for that. Granted, it would be dark – the foul ward was always dimly lit. Faces suppurating with chancres, teeth loose and black, all these might be less visible in the gloom. Nonetheless, the foul ward was, at times, unspeakable.

On the far side of the courtyard I noticed Dr Catchpole standing in the shadows. He was joined by Dr Graves, and together they vanished into a doorway. 'Come along, Mr Quartermain,' I said, starting after them. 'Let's start over here.'

The anatomy museum was on the top floor of a tall building, built during the reign of George I and accessed by a winding stone staircase. Above us, though out of sight, I could hear Dr Graves and Dr Catchpole still ascending.

'Damn the man,' I heard Dr Graves say. 'Damn the man and his damnable arrogance. Speaking to me like that in front of Magorian. In front of students! Last week he wanted to coat the amputees' stumps with tar. Tar! Magorian was all for it! Confounded arrogance. Can't think why Magorian panders to him.'

'Can't think why anyone panders to him,' replied Dr Catchpole. 'Can't see his appeal at all.'

'There must be *something* we can do.'

'I can't think what.'

'*I* can,' muttered Dr Graves.

'Hoots toots mon!' said Dr Catchpole. 'Will ye no try ma tarr mixture on yer amputations, the noo?' He tittered. Dr Bain had done the first year of his medical education in Edinburgh. He had not the slightest trace of a Scottish accent, but Dr Catchpole seemed to think it witty to pretend that he had.

Dr Graves said nothing.

'Oh, come now, Graves,' said Dr Catchpole. 'Magorian is not as enamoured of him as you seem to think.'

'Isn't he?' Dr Graves spat out the words. 'He seems to be happy to accommodate Bain's ideas, even if it means making me look foolish. I've not done Magorian's bidding for all these years to be made to look stupid in front of my own students.'

'You can't blame him—'

'I don't. Bain chose the moment. He has a habit of humiliating his colleagues in the most unassuming ways. You know *that* much yourself.'

'Yes,' Dr Catchpole sighed. 'I live with the consequences every day.'

'You're still suffering?' asked Dr Graves.

I did not hear Dr Catchpole's reply.

'There's no shame in it,' said Dr Graves. 'What you did that night, Catchpole, you did for science. For medicine. You did it to find out the truth.'

'I did it without thinking,' said Dr Catchpole. 'Just as Bain knew I would.' His voice was bitter. 'I made a mistake. He knew I would react as I did. He was so provoking! And now, now—'

'Now he has ruined your life.'

'And there is also the matter of my wife. She is besotted

with him—' Dr Catchpole broke off. I could hear the wretchedness in his voice. And, for all that I disliked him, I could not help but feel sorry for the man.

The door to the library slammed closed, and they were gone.

'It seems Dr Bain has something of a reputation,' said Will. 'I couldn't help but overhear—'

'Oh – yes,' I said, embarrassed to be caught eavesdropping so blatantly.

'Has he ruined Dr Catchpole's life?'

'In a manner of speaking.' We entered the anatomy museum. The room was large, illuminated by a long glass skylight overhead. Before us stretched row upon row of bottles and jars, inside each, a flabby-looking lump of flesh – organs, limbs, heads, eyeballs, ears – growths and deformities of all kinds, all with that pale, uncooked look that all specimens get once they are bottled in preserving fluids.

'How?' whispered Will, staring round in disbelief at this silent, globular audience. 'How has he ruined Dr Catchpole's life? Is it because of Mrs Catchpole's infatuation?'

'Partly,' I said. But Dr Graves had also been referring to something other than Dr Bain's dalliance with Mrs Catchpole.

It had occurred at a meeting of the St Saviour's Medical and Chirurgical Society. The society met once a month, in Dr Magorian's anatomy museum, lecture theatre and meeting room – a suite of chambers on the top storey of Dr Magorian's town house. One evening, some two years ago, I had been helping Dr Bain prepare a specimen – a two-headed puppy which the dog catcher (knowing Dr

Bain's interest in the macabre) had brought to the doctor's house.

'Well,' Dr Bain had said, once we had prepared a satisfactory cross section of the beast. 'Shall we take the product of our labours to the Society tonight?'

The place was lively. All St Saviour's physicians and surgeons were present that evening, as well as a number of students, and the two-headed dog we had brought was admired by everyone. But the main debate of the evening had concerned venereal diseases. Dr Catchpole had prepared a specimen of a severed finger blighted by a large syphilitic chancre. He had also brought with him a monkey with a globular sore upon its testicles, and a costermonger exhibiting the first signs of syphilis. The question being addressed was whether it was possible to inoculate against the pox.

'Dr Hunter's ideas concerning syphilis have long been discredited,' Dr Bain remarked. 'There's no link between pox and clap. The one is unrelated, as a disease, to the other. Ricord's ideas on the matter were little better. Inoculation is impossible – it cannot be done.'

'Perhaps you should try it for yourself?' Dr Catchpole's voice had a mocking edge to it, but Dr Bain remained unperturbed.

'We stand on the shoulders of giants,' he replied. 'But I don't claim to be a giant myself. I'm not heir to the likes of John Hunter.'

'And you, Dr Catchpole?' cried a student. 'Do you follow Hunter's methods of experimentation? You knew him, did you not?'

'I'm not *that* old,' cried Dr Catchpole.

'But your ideas are,' said Dr Bain.

The students had sniggered. The doctors had smiled. The monkey had screamed and bounded up and down in its cage, rattling the bars and showing its teeth, as though it too were laughing. All eyes had turned to Dr Catchpole. His face was furious. 'You, sir, would do well to listen to those with experience. I have seen inoculation against syphilis with my own eyes.'

'Then your observations are flawed,' said Dr Bain. He sat back in his chair and folded his arms. 'You may well have mistaken a chancrous lesion for true syphilis. Your reasoning is logical, but it is unsound.'

'Unsound?' Dr Catchpole's countenance turned thunderous. Before us, the syphilitic patient was still sitting with his genitals exposed. All at once Dr Catchpole snatched up a surgical blade from the table top and sprang towards him. Before the man could react, Dr Catchpole had seized the fellow's penis between his finger and thumb and scraped the side of the blade against the moist and seeping chancre that blighted the soft skin of the glans. Holding the scalpel, glistening with the offending matter, between his teeth, Dr Catchpole unbuttoned his own trousers.

'There is but one way to prove the truth,' he cried, now waving the blade in the air. 'As you rightly say, Dr Bain, the way forward is through experiment and observation.'

'But, sir—' Dr Bain raised his hands. 'As cowpox may be used to inoculate against the small pox, it may be that a similar, chancrous disease from an animal might cause an inoculation against syphilis. But *directly* from the human chancre? It's not possible. It's the *monkey*, Dr Catchpole. We might use matter from the sores of the *monkey*—'

27

He leaped forward to seize hold of Dr Catchpole's wrist, but Dr Catchpole danced free.

'I apologise, sir, if my humour was misplaced,' said Dr Bain. 'It wasn't my intention . . . Please, Dr Catchpole, think what you're doing!'

'Ha!' cried Dr Catchpole. He pulled out his penis, and stabbed the blade bearing the syphilitic matter into the end of it. There was a gasp, as everyone in the room drew a sharp breath, and then complete silence. The students exchanged appalled glances. Dr Graves and Dr Magorian stared at Dr Catchpole in disbelief.

Dr Catchpole flung down the knife and dabbed at his bloody genitals with his shirt tail. 'I shall report my findings regularly to the society,' he said. 'And you'll see that I'm right. The matter from the primary lesion will inoculate me from the disease.'

In fact, as Dr Bain predicted, we saw no such thing. I did not attend subsequent meetings of the society, but Dr Bain informed me that a week later a large globular gumma had appeared at the site of infection. Some weeks after that, Dr Catchpole vanished from public view. He was attended by Dr Graves, I assumed to be dosed with mercury until his symptoms had abated.

I told Will this as we slowly circled the exhibits in the anatomy museum. Will's eyes were glazed, his face drained of colour, though whether it was from the tale I had told, or the sight of so many anatomical specimens, I had no idea. We walked over to the window and looked down at the courtyard, the statue of King Edward, and the grey walls of the ward building opposite. At first, Will said nothing. He opened the window and breathed in the cold damp air. Then, 'This is a most peculiar place,' he said.

'And the people in it are driven by the most extraordinary motives to do the most deplorable things.'

Later, when the storm was upon us, I had cause to remember his words. The time was soon to come when I would wish with all my heart that we might return to such innocent times.

⊗⊗

I took Will to the counting house, the governors' hall and the out-patients' waiting room. He wandered about, his hands in his pockets, clearly relieved to be away from the rows of pickled organs and bobbing chunks of diseased viscera. Occasionally, he ran a hand across the lime wash, or tapped and pulled at a section of wooden panelling. He poked at damp patches in the wall of out-patients with his pen knife and dug out a lump of plaster.

'You can't do that!' I said, alarmed that the place appeared to have no more structural integrity than a piece of rotten cheese.

'Damp,' he replied. 'And evil-smelling damp, at that. What runs beneath?'

'A watercourse.'

'A sewer, I should think. A brook once, but culverted, built upon, and now so full of effluent that it is fit to burst.' He sniffed, and wrinkled his nose.

Beside us, the patients waited, sitting side by side on long wooden benches. The air was warmed by the dismal smouldering of cheap coal in the grate, and by the great mass of people crowded together in so small a space. The place was so damp and vile it would have been impossible to detect the smell of bubbling sewage, even if it had risen up through the cracks in the floor boards and lapped about our toes. I sighed. I could remember when the air was sweeter, the roof tops that surrounded us were fewer and less ramshackle. Time brought change, and St Saviour's had lurched along in the wake of progress like an old woman trying to pursue a wayward child. Her wards were filthy and crowded, out-patients packed to bursting, the mortuary, dissecting rooms, lecture theatre, all too small and cramped for the requirements of the times. Beside me, an old man coughed, and spat onto the floor. The phlegm quivered beside my boot like a great blob of raw egg.

'For God's sake, man.' I pointed to a sign on the wall. 'Can't you read?'

'No, sir,' he said. He drew a hand across his glistening nostrils and sniffed.

I could bear it no longer. 'The chapel,' I said to Will, 'and the herb drying room will clear our heads.'

I led him across the courtyard. 'Five hundred years ago we were surrounded by gardens and small holdings,' I said, as if talking about it might somehow invoke the fresh scents of the countryside. 'Originally we were a part of the Priory of St Saviour's. London was miles away, though it's hard to imagine as we are suffocated by it now. There's little left of the medieval religious house other than the crypt of the old church – which now does office as a mortuary – and the chapel. No one uses the chapel now; they go to St Saviour's parish church, which is just beyond that wall.' I pointed. 'Your work lies that-a-way too. You can see the place more clearly from the herb drying room, upstairs.'

The door of the chapel swung closed behind us. It had not been used for prayer for decades, and was now little more than a store room, filled with the accumulated lumber – chairs, bed frames, old account books – of St Saviour's long existence. A battered human skeleton minus its arms stood in one corner, a wooden coat-stand in another. The place was no more than thirty feet by forty, its ceiling curved in a barrel-shaped vault.

'We have a ghost, you know,' I said.

Will dusted a veil of cobweb off the brim of his hat and peered into the gloom. 'A ghost? I'm surprised you give such tales credence, Jem.'

'But St Saviour's is ancient. It was here during the Black Death, the Reformation, the Civil War. Can you not imagine a Protestant martyr burned alive, who cannot rest? A medieval prior done to death by drowning in mead? Did you never read the penny bloods when you were younger?'

'No,' he said. 'I read *Richmond's Elements of Surveying.*'

'Much more edifying, though not half as exciting.'

He sat down on a dusty pew and held his arms wide. 'Go on then. Entertain me!'

In fact, I had not thought about it since I was a child – my father always dismissed such stories as the idle chatter of credulous simpletons. I had to agree, though there was some amusement to be found in the tale. I lowered my voice, so that it caught the chapel's echoes in a conspiracy of whispers. 'So, you have never heard of the Abbot?'

Will shook his head. I saw him shiver as a draught blew under the door. 'You see?' I said. 'You feel him pass this way!'

He laughed. 'Get on, Jem. Who was the fellow?'

'No one knows. They say—'

'They?'

31

'Mrs Speedicut for one. And the man at the pie shop on Fishbait Lane, Mr Sorley from the chop house, the nurses – all the most rational and reliable of witnesses . . . They say the Abbot is only abroad when it's dark and foggy – a shadow in a hood striding down St Saviour's Street. No one knows who he was – perhaps one of the medieval monks of St Saviour's who sold his soul to the Devil. They say he wanders the streets around the infirmary. If you see the Abbot, you don't have long to live. Mrs Speedicut's husband saw him—'

'And died soon after?'

'Apparently. But I would doubt the existence of "dear Mr Speedicut", as much as I would doubt the existence of a ghostly abbot.'

'Where did he see it?'

'Heading into Wicke Street.'

'Wicke Street!' Will grinned. Wicke Street was infamous, even to an incomer like Will. 'Perhaps he was looking for a trollop.'

'The Abbot or Mr Speedicut?'

'Both!'

We laughed. 'I'm afraid I'm not much of a storyteller,' I said. 'There's little call for ghostly tales at the apothecary – so my father says at any rate. He used to throw my penny bloods onto the fire. He does the same to Gabriel's – that's until I told the lad where to hide them.'

'You just need to learn how to embellish,' said Will. 'That's all.'

He climbed onto a tea chest and smoothed the building's great pale stones with his hands. Painted corbels studded the seam between walls and ceiling, onto which were carved the wings and faces of angels.

'This one is sad,' said Will. He put up a finger, as though to brush a tear from its cheek. An ancient fleck of white paint drifted to the floor. 'And that one is singing. See the lute below?' The colours were faded but beautiful, ghostly against the dim diamonds of light that filtered through the harlequin windows.

He jumped down and came over to me. His face was suddenly serious as he put out his hand. 'Thank you, Jem,' he said. 'Thank you for bringing me here, for showing me everything. For being my friend, despite the task I'm here to complete.' His fingers were warm against my own, his grasp firm, reassuring.

We grinned at one another as we shook hands. 'It's a pleasure,' I said. And I meant it too.

I turned to leave; the cold of the place was eating into my bones. But Will did not follow. 'What's this?' He was pointing to a wooden panel, no more than eighteen inches square, that was embedded low in the wall beside the altar. It looked to be made of oak, and was dark and pitted with age. It had slipped a little in its casing, and behind it we could glimpse a dark, rectangular space. Other than a small cross-shaped hole cut into its centre, it was quite unmarked. I had never noticed it before. 'May I?' Without waiting for an answer, he hooked his finger into the cross and gave a tug. It lifted out easily.

Within was a cavity, dark and cobwebbed. I crouched down, and squinted inside. 'There's something in there,' I said.

As I crouched in the dusty stillness of St Saviour's derelict chapel, peering into the shadows of that dusty hole, an icy dread seemed to grip my heart. I could not account for it, though after the bustle and din of the infirmary the air of the place felt dead, its silence and shadows oppressed me, and its atmosphere was as cold as the grave. It was a building I rarely entered, and one in which I never lingered. But we had started now, and there was no going back. I stretched my hand into the cavity. Something wrinkled and papery shifted beneath my fingertips. Was it parchment? Dried flesh? I could not quite get a purchase on it, and it moved away from my grasp like a live thing recoiling from the light. But I was curious now, and I thrust my hand in further.

The object I drew out was dusty and mildewed, and blotched with dark rust-coloured stains. It smelled of time and decay, sour, like old books and parchments. The light from the chapel's stained glass window blushed red upon it, and upon my hands, as if the thing itself radiated a bloody glow.

'What is it?' Will's voice was a whisper, though he could see as well as I what it was that we had found. No more than six inches long and three inches wide, it was a coffin, small and dirty, the signs of the knife that had created it visible in crude hack-marks at its edges. I could feel something moving within, and it was all I could do not to drop the thing onto the floor in horror. What did it signify? Were there more of them hidden in that dark, forgotten space? I stooped down, and slid my hand back into the opening.

Chapter Two

~~~

The herb drying room was a small, woody attic in the roof space above the infirmary's abandoned chapel. Warm and fragrant, away from the noise and stink of the wards and more private than the apothecary, it was my favourite place. Its gabled window looked out across the crooked rooftops of the city to the stubby panopticon of Angel Meadow Asylum, the dome of St Paul's and the possibility of countryside far beyond. Or one could forgo the view and look down into the infirmary's central courtyard. I looked down now, and saw Dr Magorian and Dr Graves walking towards the operating theatre. The infirmary clock indicated that we had twenty minutes until it was two o'clock.

I put our finds on the table, lining them up side by side. 'Six,' I said. 'All more or less the same size but crudely manufactured.' I pointed to the smallest. It had a dusty, cobwebby look. 'This must have been the first. It's dirtier than the others, the execution is clumsier, and the whole thing held together more crudely with glue and paper.'

'No doubt the maker got better at it with practice.'

'Or they started to use a template. Perhaps, after the first, it became clear that many more would be required.' The thought made me uneasy.

'Required for what?' said Will.

'I don't know,' I said. 'But consider the location: the chapel, the altar – this is a ritual. A ritual that took place time and again.'

'But why six times? What's the significance of that? Is there something – some event or happening – that occurs six times?'

'Nothing that I can think of. Perhaps there was meant to be more. Perhaps someone, or something, brought the practice to an end.'

'Perhaps the maker died.'

'Or an objective was achieved.'

'Such as?'

'I don't know.'

'What's inside?' said Will.

'We're due in the operating theatre in ten minutes.'

'So, we have ten minutes to look. What are you afraid of?'

I shivered. I did not know why – there was no door or window open, no draught blowing over me. And yet somehow his words filled me with disquiet. *What are you afraid of?* Was I afraid? If I had known what secrets we were to uncover, I would have answered with confidence. *Yes, I am afraid. I am afraid for myself, and for all those who are dear to me.* I would have acted upon my instincts and told Will Quartermain to leave, to find another commission, another Master, *anything* just so long as he was away from us, and the evil that lay hidden might remain where it was – lost, forgotten, undisturbed. But I said nothing.

I used a scalpel to slit the paper that sealed the boxes closed. One by one we took off the lids.

Inside each was a handful of dried flowers. Beneath them, a bundle of dirty rags swaddled a tiny human form. They had an ancient, frayed look and the faint musty smell of mouldering cloth. I took one out and laid it on the work bench. The bindings were made of coarse cotton, torn into thin strips and wrapped around and around, until the object beneath was no more than a formless kidney-shaped package. They were stained a dark blackish-brown. To me, the colour was unmistakable.

'Blood,' I said.

'Are you sure?'

'I've worked at St Saviour's all my life. I know dried blood when I see it.' I took up the smallest of the bundles. Beneath the binding I could feel something hard, almost bony. I began to unwrap it.

'What is it?' whispered Will. 'Is it . . . Is it a baby? A foetus?'

I knew it wasn't that. It was too hard to the touch, and I had seen enough dead babies, enough foetuses and aborted matter to know. I pulled the last fold away, and put the thing on the table.

Before us, lay a tiny doll. At least, 'doll' is perhaps the best way to describe it though it was hardly such a thing at all, and one would never show it to a child. It appeared to be made from a small piece of kindling, a shard of wood no more than four inches long and an inch and a half wide. It had been rudely shaped; the corners ground away by rubbing them against a rough surface – stone, perhaps, rather than a file, or a carpenter's tool, as the abrasions were clumsy and ragged. The 'face' was white, as though daubed with flour or chalk, and into this someone had gouged two misshapen eye holes. The dab of black ink that had been applied to each socket had leeched into the surrounding wood, so that the eyes had a grotesque lopsided appearance. Half an inch down from these, a crude gash did office as a mouth, and below this a clumsy nick on either side gave the thing the semblance of a neck. It had neither arms nor legs, but from the 'neck' down had been tightly bound, wrapped like a bobbin on a loom, in coarse greyish yarn. The whole impression was of a tiny swaddled baby.

Will swallowed. 'What devilry is this?'

'I don't know.' I peered at the thing through my magnifying glass. Its eyes drew me even as they repelled me. What tool had been used here? A bodkin? Too fine. A knitting needle? Too blunt. The slim end of a finger-saw? The point of a surgical hook? The tip of a short-bladed amputation knife?

One by one we unwrapped the bundles. Each was the same – the same tattered and bloody bandages, the same repulsive black-eyed doll, the same scattering of desiccated petals.

'These are mostly rose petals,' said Will, poking the rustling fragments with a pencil. He picked one up. It was as dry as dead skin.

'I think these are petals from a black rose,' I said. I examined one through the glass. 'No rose in nature is truly black, but there are some exceptionally dark red varieties, fed with ink, that purport to be so.'

'How contrived,' said Will. 'D'you know anything about the language of flowers?'

But I had already been thinking about that pastime of the vain and idle, and had been trying to recall the meanings attributed to various flowers. Eliza Magorian, the Great Surgeon's daughter, had been schooled by her mother in these obscure codes of middle-class sentiment, and she had once insisted on giving me a lesson. Drifting through the physic garden, she had made me an eccentric posy of purple-tufted lavender and fuzzy-stemmed borage.

'Lavender for devotion, starflower for courage.' Then, wrapped in a handkerchief to prevent its poison from touching my skin, she had given me the beautiful white and yellow flower of the bloodroot. 'Celandine,' she said. 'A symbol of the pleasures yet to come.' She had not smiled as she spoke, but had looked me directly in the eyes, so that I was almost sure that she knew my secret; almost sure that she was speaking about me, about both of us.

Almost sure.

Now, I reached across the table for my tweezers. Between their pointed tips I plucked up a small, fist-shaped seed capsule. 'This is rue.' I pinched at a withered shred of vegetation. 'Here are the flowers that go with it.'

'Rue,' said Will. 'Even I know what that means.'

'Regret,' I said, 'is what it means. What it *is* is a herb that promotes menstruation and uterine contractions. The oil is a known abortifacient.'

'The taking of a life before it is even born,' said Will. 'The law would call it murder.'

'The law is made by men for their own ends,' I replied.

'Besides, I doubt these flowers are the fragments of a misplaced prescription.'

'Can you identify any of the others?'

'Hops,' I said, pointing to a browny-green cone. 'We use hops to improve the appetite and promote sleep, and as a liver tonic. In the language of flowers it signifies injustice.'

I picked up a small, hard, triangular nub. '*Artemisia absinthium*,' I said. 'Also a medicinal herb. There's undoubtedly meaning here, but why go to such lengths? Why bother with meaning if the flowers are hidden? What use is a message if it's so obscure, and so secret? And was there more than one person involved? A language, even if it's the language of flowers, is meant to be spoken to others.'

'So what's artemis absinthum?' said Will.

'*Artemisia absinthium*,' I said. 'Also known as wormwood.'

For a moment, there was silence between us. I heard Will swallow. Then: '"*The third angel blew his trumpet, and a great star fell from heaven, blazing like a torch, and it fell on a third of the rivers and on the springs of water. The name of the star is Wormwood.*" Revelations, chapter eight—'

'Quite so,' I said. 'But in the language of flowers, wormwood means "bitter sorrow". My father planted wormwood on my mother's grave – at first, anyway. But nothing else would grow – it poisons the earth, you know – so I took it out. There are daffodils there now.'

'Oh,' said Will.

I could tell that he was puzzled by my matter-of-fact tone. But my mother's death had changed my life forever in the most unexpected way. I could not resolve my feelings of sorrow and perplexity, and time had done little to appease me. All my life I had hidden these emotions from my father. I could easily hide them from Will as well. 'It's also a herb,' I said. 'For worms.'

'And the black rose? Is that a remedy?'

'The black rose?' The withered petals were as droplets of dried blood on the work bench. 'The black rose means death.'

❧

The lower operating theatre was as noisy as a cock pit. Wooden balconies, buffed to a dull shine by cuffs and elbows, circled the walls from sawdust to skylight. They were crowded with medical students, row upon row. These galleries were accessed by almost vertical staircases, up which still more of them climbed, and the walls were alive with chattering faces and flapping coat tails. Dr Magorian pointed Will to a chair overlooking the operating table. I sat down beside him. There was no better view in the house.

Two o'clock was Dr Magorian's favourite operating time – the light was not too bright and not too dull – though his audience had often been to the alehouse at lunchtime and the place was sometimes less than gentlemanly. Dr Graves and Dr Magorian stood in their shirt sleeves. Against the wall hung their operating coats. I heard Will take a sharp breath at the sight. 'My God!' he whispered. I saw his fingers tighten around the neck of the sack he held, and into which we had put the six small coffins. I took it from him and put it beneath my chair. I did not want him to crush them when he fainted.

'Dr Graves has performed ninety-nine operations in that coat,' I said. 'Today is the coat's centenary.'

'An auspicious day,' said Will, weakly.

Stiff with old gore, Dr Graves's coat had a thick, inflexible appearance, and a sinister ruddy-coloured patina like waxed mahogany. Dr Magorian's was worse, being as dark and lustreless as a black pudding. No one knew how many times he had worn it to amputate. It was said that he had stopped counting when he reached two hundred, but that had been some years ago now.

At that moment the door swung open and Dr Bain appeared carrying an enamelled bucket. He was dressed in white from head to foot.

'Avast there, Dr Bain!' cried Dr Graves. He tittered. 'Have you come to scrub the decks again?' The students laughed.

'What in heaven's name are you wearing, man?' said Dr Magorian.

'It's his nightshirt,' said Dr Graves. 'Are you playing Wee Willie Winkie?' The students laughed again, louder this time.

'What's going on?' whispered Will. He had perked up, now that something dramatic was afoot, and he was watching Dr Graves and Dr Bain with interest.

'Oh,' I said. 'Where Dr Bain is to be found, Dr Graves is never far behind – usually with a criticism or a caustic remark.'

'I met Dr Graves at the governors' meeting, when the demolition of the hospital was decided upon. He appeared . . . well,' Will hesitated. 'I don't wish to sound disrespectful—'

'Oh, you don't need to be diplomatic with me,' I said.

'At least, not where Dr Graves is concerned. He appeared resistant to change. Any kind of change. Is that what you wanted to say?'

'Yes,' said Will. 'Though his master, Dr Magorian, was equally vocal. Look at his face!' Dr Graves's smile was now a grimace, his teeth bared like an angry dog. 'Is he frightened, d'you think? Frightened of change? Or perhaps frightened of appearing foolish when confronted with circumstances he does not understand—'

'It's easy to ridicule what appears new and peculiar,' I said. 'Easier than learning how to think differently.'

'I agree,' whispered Will. 'And yet it's Dr Bain who intrigues me. He's standing before a crowd of medical students wearing what does indeed look like a nightshirt. Does he enjoy provoking his colleagues?'

'Sometimes,' I said. Indeed, now I thought about it, it was hard to think who Dr Bain had *not* provoked at some time or other. Not ten days earlier he had riled Dr Magorian by daring to disagree about the merits of pus in a wound. ('There is nothing laudable about pus, sir!')

'How fascinating,' said Will. 'And what d'you think is happening here?'

'I think Dr Bain is out to make Dr Graves appear a fool.'

'Oh?'

'Yes. Though I admit that at first glance, the odds would seem to be the other way around.'

Before us, Dr Bain was holding up his hands for silence. When he spoke, his voice was low, but clear. 'I have a suggestion, sir, if you will hear me.'

Dr Magorian, perhaps able to read the situation better than Dr Graves, waved a gracious hand. 'Proceed, Dr Bain.'

'I've been thinking about dirt.'

'Dirt?' Dr Graves gave a bark of derision, as if the subject were irrelevant. 'Ha!'

'Dirt, sir,' said Dr Bain. 'Put simply, dirt must be avoided. Especially when there's an open wound.'

'Well, I'd no more rub dirt into an open wound than you,' said Dr Graves. 'Nor would any doctor. Not even the young gentlemen of the audience would do *that*!' There was a murmur of laughter.

'Neither would I expect them to,' said Dr Bain. 'But there is dirt which we *can* see, and there is dirt which we *cannot* see. I advise that we must try to *see* dirt at all times, so that we know where it is. Only then can we avoid it. To wear these dark old coats is to hide it. To wear a white coat is to make it plain to see.'

'But you look like a baker,' cried Dr Graves. 'Or a half-dressed lunatic!'

'A baker wears white because he is dressed in old sacks. And it also happens to hide the fact that he is covered in flour. You wear a black frock coat because you are a gentleman, and also to hide the fact that you are covered in—'

'Blood,' interrupted Dr Graves. 'Of course!'

'No!' cried Dr Bain. 'When it flows through the veins, *then* it is blood. When it has left the place where it is *meant* to be, *then* it is dirt. But we *must see the dirt*! For this reason I urge you to put away your operating coat, and wear one of these.'

'Excellent logic,' murmured Will.

'Rational, yes,' I replied. 'But I think it would take more than a white smock to show where the dirt lies.'

But Dr Bain was speaking again. 'I'm aware, Dr Graves,

that you're about to undertake your one hundredth surgical procedure in that coat. But the greater the degree of cleanliness, the greater likelihood that suppuration of the wound can be avoided.' At this point Dr Bain produced from his bucket a brass spray pump. I recognised it as the one I used in the small glasshouse at the physic garden. He turned to Dr Magorian. 'I have made up a 2 per cent solution of pine tar oil. If you will permit me, sir, I would like to mist the site of the operation during the procedure. Miasma, sir. Need I say more? The miasma too contains dirt, I am sure of it. It must be cleansed from the area!'

'Good.' I nodded, impressed by his thinking.

'What!' cried Dr Graves. 'Are we to be sprayed like aphids on a rose bush?' He looked about, expecting to be supported by the mirth of the students, but now they were silent. Dr Magorian, the great man, was about to speak.

'Miasma?' he said, raising a shaggy eyebrow. He sniffed deeply. 'I must agree that the river is at its worst today.'

'If we can prevent the miasma from entering the wound then the likelihood of suppuration is sure to be reduced still further,' said Dr Bain.

'We close the doors,' said Dr Graves witheringly. 'The miasma is kept out that way.'

'But we always close the doors,' said Dr Bain. 'And yet the place still stinks, and the patients still die.'

'Miasma,' repeated Dr Magorian. He stroked his chin, and waited for the silence to deepen. 'It is a curse upon us. I am willing to try your ideas, Dr Bain.'

A student leaped forward to help Dr Magorian out of his famous blood-blackened coat and into the white linen smock. Dr Bain held out the other. 'Dr Graves?'

45

Dr Graves snatched hold of the smock and dashed it to the ground. 'No!' he snapped. 'I am a surgeon, and a gentleman, and I will wear the coat that has served me well for so long.'

'But it has perhaps not served your patients well,' said Dr Bain. 'Will you not help us to see whether we can improve a man's chance of surviving the knife?' He lowered his voice. 'Come on, Richard! Experiment and inquiry is the life blood of our profession. What *seems* right may well be wrong. We must test alternative ways of doing things, no matter how absurd they may seem. Change is good. We cannot fear it or we must give up!'

Dr Graves looked up at the students. They had heard every word. Not one of them was smiling now. Nor could they bring themselves to look at Dr Graves. He turned around on his heel, peering up into the galleries, searching for someone, anyone, who might meet his gaze. 'What, no laughter now, gentlemen?' he shouted, 'No questions as to why or how this theory has been arrived at?'

The students looked down at their hands. Dr Graves took a step backward. But one of his boots had become tangled in the folds of the smock he had flung to the ground and all at once he lost his balance. He made a desperate bid to stay upright by grabbing hold of the table upon which rested Dr Magorian's surgical cutlery, and then, with a great clatter, down he went, to sprawl upon the sawdust amongst a confusion of knives, saws, hooks and clamps. A mass of sugar lumps spilled from his pockets onto the floor.

There was a moment of appalled silence, and then a great shout of laughter erupted from the audience. 'Silence!' bellowed Dr Magorian.

Dr Bain went to pull Dr Graves up off the ground, but the man staggered to his feet unaided. Sawdust covered his coat and trousers. His face was almost purple with rage, and in his hand he gripped a long curved boning knife.

Will clutched my arm. 'The knife!' he whispered.

'This is a hospital. Men hold knives all the time here.' I saw no reason for hysteria, despite the heated exchange taking place before us.

Dr Graves was panting hard; his hair was awry and his voice trembled with fury. He pointed the boning knife at Dr Bain. 'You!' he shouted. 'It's always you! You could just as well have presented your absurd ideas in private but no, you must have an audience. You are a maverick, sir, and you jeopardise the gravitas of our profession with your persistent nonconformity!'

'Dr Graves—'

'And when I do not choose to follow your lead in these clownish activities, you see fit to scoff at me beneath the gaze of my students. What professionalism, what courteousness is there in that?' Sugar crunched beneath his heels. 'Dr Magorian,' he cried, 'you asked me to assist you, and I would be honoured to do so. But I will not do so if you continue to allow our noble profession to be ridiculed by *this man.*' His knuckles turned white as he jabbed the knife in the direction of Dr Bain. 'He will be asking you to wear your nightcap next!'

'An excellent idea, sir,' said Dr Bain.

Dr Graves made a choking sound. The students hooted. 'Gentlemen, will you *be quiet!*' shouted Dr Magorian. He motioned to me to pick up the utensils that lay scattered in the sawdust.

The uproar continued, but Dr Graves had now fallen silent. He was holding the knife tightly, his fingers wrapped around the top of the blade, so that his hand was cut and bleeding, though he appeared not to have noticed.

'Look, sir,' I murmured, hoping to help him save face, even a little. 'You've cut your hand. You can't possibly operate without first attending to this.'

I took the knife from him and pressed my handkerchief against the wound. Dr Graves gaped at me. His eyes were vacant, his face slack and defeated. He looked different, somehow. I stared at him. Something cold and hard, something dark, and filled with hatred seemed to be stirring at the back of his blank, glazed eyes. He blinked, and cocked his head as though he were listening, listening to a voice deep within himself that he had not understood before. Then he turned, and stumbled out of the operating theatre. The door crashed closed behind him. No one followed. No one spoke. I had been acquainted with Dr Graves for years, and yet, at that moment, I realised that I did not know him at all.

But the spectacle was set to continue, and the next moment the door opposite burst open and a pair of orderlies marched in. Between them they carried a stretcher, upon which was strapped a tall thin man of about fifty years. He lay still as he was carried forth, but on apprehending his two white-clad surgeons and possibly thinking he had arrived early at the celestial gates, all at once he burst into violent activity.

'Calm down, man,' roared Dr Magorian. 'Do you not recognise me?' He kicked the blood box around the operating table until it stood below the place where the patient's hip would be once he was in position. The patient was now wild eyed. He had been dosed with opium and alcohol, but he had caught sight of the table of knives and fear at what was about to happen seemed to have rendered useless all attempts to stupefy him.

There was a cry of 'hats off' so that those at the top-most standings could see. The patient gave a muffled gurgle. Dr Bain offered him a leather strap to grip between his jaws, and this he did, an involuntary moaning sound coming from behind his clenched teeth. The orderlies – burly men with hairless heads and giant hands – lashed the man's body to the operating table with thick, buckled straps. One of Dr Bain's dressers donned Graves's discarded nightshirt and took hold of the pine tar spray. Another eager student sprang down from the standings to man the pump in the bucket. Dr Magorian picked up a knife. A saw waited its turn. Beside me, Will was now as limp as a rag doll. He moaned faintly.

'Sniff this,' I said. I passed him a handkerchief. Hidden in it was a bottle of salts.

Will buried his face in the linen folds. 'Oh!' His head snapped back, his eyes streaming.

'Easy now,' I whispered.

'Oh!' cried Will again. 'Oh!' His voice echoed round the theatre.

'Mr Quartermain, if you could restrain yourself,' said Dr Magorian. He leaned forward

'Mist!' cried Dr Bain. The students began working the pump and the aphid spray.

49

I saw the flash of the blade as the white flesh parted and a crimson flood poured onto the operating table. The students craned their necks to see. Dr Magorian's voice boomed out instructions, drowning out the dreadful muted screams of the patient, which soon evaporated into a whimper as the man lost consciousness with pain and fear.

Dr Magorian clamped the knife between his teeth like a pirate and plunged his fingers into the wound. The patient's blood stained his lips and cheek; his hands were coated in the stuff, his new white smock soaked from the waist. There was a glimpse of bone and gristle and red glistening tissue. There came the sound of the saw, and the *thunk* of Dr Bain's boot as he kicked the blood box forward, the better to catch the thick streams of scarlet that dripped over the lip of the operating table.

Will's face was as white as a corpse. Would he attempt an undignified exit, or simply crash sideways off his chair onto the floor? The first time I had witnessed an operation I had brought salts in my handkerchief and a pin in my pocket, just in case. I would not have had any of the medical men think I could not bear it. In the event I had not needed them – after all, was not blood and pain a woman's lot? Beside me, Will began to sway. I put my arm about his shoulders but he shook me off and staggered to his feet. He took one step in the general direction of the door, and then collapsed, dropping to the ground like a wet sack, recumbent in the bloody sawdust at Dr Magorian's feet.

'Get rid of him,' snarled the surgeon, his boning knife still clenched between his teeth.

I seized hold of Will's legs and dragged him aside. 'Mr

Quartermain,' I hissed. 'Will!' I jammed my salts beneath his nostrils. And all the while came the rhythmic rasp of the saw and the faint *psst . . . psst . . . psst . . .* of Dr Bain's spray pump.

Then it was over. Dr Bain held the leg as it was finally severed, flinging it aside into the sawdust. Dr Magorian knotted the arteries, stitched the flaps of skin and removed the tourniquet. He stepped back from the table. 'Time, gentlemen?'

'Sixty-two seconds, sir,' cried a voice. There was a cheer. Dr Magorian acknowledged the enthusiasm of the crowd with a wave of his bloodied hand, though I could see he was disappointed. He had hoped for less than fifty-five seconds. Still, the extra seven might easily be blamed on Dr Bain.

I dragged Will to his feet and slung his arm about my shoulders. Like a pair of drunkards we lurched out of the operating theatre and into the courtyard.

'Breathe!' I ordered.

'When I close my eyes I can still see it,' he cried, gulping down air. 'I can hear it. The screams! The saw! Oh!'

'Then don't close them,' I said. 'Don't think of it.'

'I can think of nothing else. So much blood!' He slipped from my grasp, sinking down until he was on all fours, his head lowered, and his stove-pipe hat rolling in the dust. I picked it up. There was a blob of red-stained sawdust on the rim. I wiped it off with my cuff. 'Keep your head down and it will pass,' I said.

At last, Will rose to his feet. 'Well,' he said faintly, 'perhaps I didn't acquit myself too badly, all things considered.'

'Perhaps,' I said. 'Though there is some ignominy

attached to fainting at the surgeon's feet and being hauled aside like a Smithfield carcass.'

We grinned at one another, though I could see he was still shaken. 'But I'm new to the business of blood and bones, so you must excuse me.'

'You'll have to grow a stronger stomach if you're to exhume the contents of the graveyard.'

'I'd rather we didn't talk about that at the moment.'

I steered him towards a bench in a patch of sunlight against the wall of the women's surgical ward. 'Here,' I said. I took a poke of eucalyptus drops from my pocket. A powerful blend I made myself out of sugar, lime, eucalyptus and peppermint. 'Take a piece. It helps, believe me.'

We sat side by side in silence, the watery sun warming our faces.

'The operation was . . . interesting,' said Will after a moment. He wiped his eyes, which were watering from the eucalyptus. Across the courtyard Dr Bain and Dr Magorian had emerged from the operating theatre. They were surrounded by students. 'He seemed very emotional.'

I remembered Dr Graves's face as he stumbled from the operating theatre and I could not answer.

'And Dr Magorian?' Will buffed the nap of his hat with his coat cuff. 'I was surprised he wore the smock. Had he not done so things would have turned out differently. Your friend Dr Bain took a gamble.'

'Dr Magorian is very highly regarded,' I said. 'Though if you ask me he cares for little but lopping off limbs as fast as he can. The cheers of his students and the obsequiousness of his colleagues are as important as the air he breathes. If Dr Bain's idea works then Dr Magorian will share equally in the glory. If it fails, he will say he was merely pandering to the whim of a colleague.'

'Ah, reputation. Often a man's most prized possession.'

'It is certainly Dr Magorian's. His reputation and his wife – upon whom he dotes with a sugary fondness. His daughter, though—' I stopped. I had said too much already. And yet, how good it felt to talk.

'Yes?' said Will. He put his hat back on. 'Does he not dote upon her too?'

I shoved my hands into my pockets. How much I longed to say and how little I was able to explain. I thought of Dr Magorian standing beside the operating table, his face yellow against the grey cobweb of his hair, his pale eyes plunged into shadows on either side of his proud, beaked nose. He looked dried out and cadaverous. And yet his hands were strong, the long bony fingers powerful from years of gripping limbs and holding down screaming patients, from wielding knives and saws. And I thought too of Eliza. Her hands were small and soft, but tanned like a gypsy's from being outdoors in the garden.

Eliza loved to be outside. When she was little she had been allowed to play beside me while I worked in the physic garden. I planted and pruned and gathered; Eliza flitted in and out of the herbs like Titania, the rank weeds of the poison beds dancing about her.

'Come out of there,' I would say as she pranced amongst the nodding purple purses of wolfsbane. 'If you so much as touch the leaves of the wolfsbane you will die.'

'Like this?' the little minx had cried, and she flung a handful of leaves into the air. A moment later she gasped, and coughed, and then sunk out of sight beneath the thick foliage.

I remembered bounding forward amongst the herbs. At twelve years old I was already tall and strong, and I picked her up and carried her out of the poison bed. I knew the game well enough, and enjoyed it as much as she. The leaves she had tossed were plantain and dandelion and had been hidden in the pocket of her apron (she knew better than to touch the wolfsbane). She lay limp in my arms, but I could see her eyelids fluttering, and her mouth curved in a smile. All at once she sprang back into life. She threw her arms about my neck and kissed my cheek. 'Can you make me a mask, like yours?' Her voice that day was close, her breath warm, and sweet from the mint leaves she had nibbled. She put her hands to my face, over my birthmark. 'Let me take it from you,' she said. 'I know it makes you sad, but I would be glad of such a disguise.'

'Why would you hide such a pretty face?' I had asked.

'So that no one will know me,' she replied. 'Who I am, and where I come from can be my secret.'

I knew people looked at me with pity and disgust, but Eliza never did. For that alone, I would always love her. Now, I put my hand to my crimson face, touching it where she had touched it. Will was watching me, waiting for my answer, but my thoughts were my own, and they were precious. I would not share them with anyone.

We sat for a while, watching as the students gradually dispersed. I saw Dr Graves skulking in the shadows beneath the archway that led through to the mortuary. He scowled as Dr Bain moved off, surrounded by his students and dressers. Some of those young men were Dr Graves's students. Dr Bain's laugh echoed from the walls. The students laughed with him. They were all off to Sorley's for ale and chops before the afternoon lecture – which was to be given by Dr Graves. There would be some rowdiness in the lecture theatre that afternoon.

'Oh, no,' murmured Will. 'Here he comes.'

Dr Magorian was walking towards us. He had changed his shirt and wore his frock coat and hat once more. Apart from a spot of dried blood on his cheek one would never have guessed that he had just cut a man's leg off. I stood up as he approached. No doubt he was looking for an apology, though from what I had seen it was he who should be apologising to Will – forcing a layman to watch an amputation . . . 'Sir—' I began.

Dr Magorian held up a hand. Instinctively, I fell silent. He looked down at Will. 'Don't get up, Mr Quartermain,' he said, though Will had made no attempt to do so. From behind his back Dr Magorian drew out the sack containing the six small coffins. In the drama and kerfuffle of the operating theatre, I had forgotten all about them. 'You left this, I believe?' said Dr Magorian after a moment.

'Oh,' I said. 'Yes.' I put out my hand to take hold of it, but the doctor snatched it away. He held it, swinging gently, just out of my reach. Had he looked inside? I had tied the top with string, but it might be undone, or severed, quite easily. I squinted up at him, but his face was deep in shadow, and the sun behind him hurt my eyes.

Later, I often wondered what would have happened if Mrs Magorian had not appeared at that moment. Would her husband have asked me what was inside the sack? No doubt had he seen them, he would have kept them for himself. Perhaps he would have thrown those wicked-looking objects onto the fire, and everything that

happened would not have taken place at all. But such
questions serve no purpose. The past cannot be altered,
no matter how much we might wish for it, and the fact
remains that, at that moment, Mrs Magorian came out of
the apothecary. She saw her husband, and scampered
over to him directly, her small frame childlike.

'So you operated today, my dear?' Her tiny fingers
dusted imaginary motes off the great man's shoulders.
'*Such* an honour for the students. And the man, will he
live? But of course he will! Another life saved! They must
be so grateful.'

'Now, my love,' Dr Magorian tossed me the sack, so that
he might take hold of his wife's hands. He kissed her
fingers and smiled down at her. 'You oughtn't to spend so
much time here, you know. It's not good for your health.'

'Oh, but I want to!' she cried. 'It's where *you* are. And
the lady almoners do such *good work*. Oh, and cook says
she has pheasant for dinner. I have asked her to make it
with oysters, the way you like it.'

Dr Magorian stroked her cheek. 'Well, poppet,' he said.
'I will be sure to come home early, then.'

'Eliza is with us now too,' said Mrs Magorian, simpering
up at him. 'She is quite a tonic on the wards, Dr Bain says.'

Dr Magorian looked over at his daughter, who had
followed her mother and was standing a few feet away. His
face was impassive. Eliza did not meet his gaze.

Chapter Three

❧

I took Will to Sorley's. The place was full of medical students, as usual, but we found a booth in the corner and settled ourselves in. I ordered chops and a glass of porter each, for I could see Will needed something to thicken his blood. I was not very hungry, and pushed the food about while Will ate. In the end I called Sorley's dog over and fed the creature what I had left.

'What is it, Jem?' said Will.

'Not much,' I said. The sack containing the coffins lay on the table beside us. The crude, lumpen bulk of the thing unsettled me, so I turned my back on it, stretched out my legs towards the fire and pulled out my pipe. On the other side of the room Dr Bain was talking to a group of students. Every now and then there would be a burst of laughter. I felt sure they were talking about the day's events, about Dr Graves as much as about the rationale behind Dr Bain's experiment. But when I thought of Dr Graves's face as he left the operating theatre I could see no cause for laughter.

'So, your father was one of Dr Magorian's patients?' I said.

'Yes. My father was a stonemason. There was an accident, his leg was crushed and he was taken to St Saviour's. Until today I had no idea what he had actually endured on the operating table.' Will closed his eyes. 'Perhaps the ordeal turned his mind – I would not be surprised – but his wound did not heal and he said he'd sooner die at home than in a stinking hospital bed. Apparently they were quite happy to let him go.'

'The governors don't like the patients to expire on the wards,' I said. 'It affects the subscriptions.'

'Yes, well, he died a week later.'

'I'm sorry,' I said. I had seen death by septicaemia and gangrene a hundred times and it was both brutal and wretched.

'Thank you. I was just a boy, of course, but I remember it clearly. How could I forget? Afterwards we went to stay with my mother's family in the West Country, though I always knew I'd come back to London. I'm not sure why – the place is far less pleasant than I remember it – colder, dirtier. More cruel.' There was a moment's silence. I found I could not disagree. Then, 'And what about *your* father? What ails him?'

'Mine?' I blew out a thin plume of blue smoke, watching as it curled and eddied into a hazy question mark. 'I don't know. He's been sleeping badly these last weeks but won't say why.'

'Have you asked?'

'Yes, but he won't tell me. Something is wrong, though.' I leaned forward. I knew Will would not have any answers for me, but was simply sharing my troubles – 'He goes out,' I said. 'At night. Two nights ago I followed him.'

'Where to?'

The story, as I told it then to Will, did not show me in the most positive light. Spying on my own father? I had told myself that I was staying up that night so that I might write up the prescription notes – a job I always found tiresome. But I knew I was waiting for him. I was sitting in the old wing-backed chair, Culpeper's *Herbal* open on my lap, when I heard the scuttling of mice. Something must have made them run, and I was sitting too still and silent to disturb them. From behind me came the faint creak of the wooden stair. The embers in the grate flared briefly and a shadow leaped against the wall, a giant spindly-legged golem, poised as if to spring. I held my breath. The latch made a faint 'clack' in the darkness as the door opened . . . then closed.

Peeping out of the window, I saw my father. He was walking towards a cloaked figure waiting beneath the archway that led through to the infirmary's main gates. The two of them disappeared without even a word or a nod of greeting. I opened the door a little and sniffed the night air. Beneath the familiar reek of the tannery and the hospital latrines, I could distinguish the faint aroma of lemon geranium. Dr Hawkins, superintendent physician at Angel Meadow Asylum often smelled of lemon geranium. He said it reminded him of the warmth and brightness of India – a necessary antidote to the stinking squalor of the infirmary – though I found it hard to believe that the sun-baked hospitals of Calcutta were any less foetid than ours. Should I follow them? Why else had I been waiting?

By the time I emerged from the infirmary gates my father and Dr Hawkins were already half-swallowed by the dark, and the rising fog. They walked briskly, heading north without once looking back, so they had not noticed me stealing through the shadows behind them. Soon, a towered and crenellated building, tall and dark as Newgate, rose up before us. I heard the dull rap of the doctor's stick against the wooden panels of a door. A grimy smear of yellow lantern light flickered through the fog as the door opened, and then they were gone.

The dark walls of Angel Meadow Asylum gave nothing away. The door they had entered was tightly locked, and no window looked out. I had tried to stay close as they hurried along, desperate to catch the odd word from their whispered conversation. Now, as I told the tale to Will, I wished once more that I had crept closer. Might I have discovered what terrors made my father so lean and fearful? What compulsion drove him to sneak out at night to attend someone, or something, inside that terrible Bedlam?

The following morning I asked him myself. For a moment he looked at me, appalled. 'You followed me?'

'You and Dr Hawkins.'

'And you heard us? You heard—'

I hesitated. 'I heard nothing.' He sighed then, as if he had been holding his breath, the expression of horror on his face dissolving into relief. 'But you must tell me,' I said.

'Not now.'

'Then when?'

'Soon.'

'*When?*'

Will was sitting forward in his chair, listening. His gaze was fixed upon me, his eyes grave. 'And he would not say?'

'No,' I said. 'He will not admit to being ill; he will not tell me what business he has with Dr Hawkins, and he is silent about whatever reason he has to go up to Angel Meadow at night. When I pressed him he said that it was better that I didn't know. That hopefully I would never *have* to know.'

'And Dr Hawkins has said nothing?'

'He would not break a confidence.'

'Then you can do nothing but care for your father and be patient, and hope for the best.' Will took up the sack of coffins. 'I was going to suggest that we showed these to him—'

I shook my head. 'I think not. He is not . . . not what he was.'

'It might take his mind off his troubles.'

'I fear it would only add to them,' I said. 'Hops, wormwood, rue . . . The only place where all three might be found is the apothecary.'

'But anyone at St Saviour's might have access to that place. And what of the black rose?'

'I don't know. But there's something else too. You recall the material they're made from—'

'Thick board, covered in a fine, grey-coloured fabric.'

'I didn't mention it earlier,' I said. 'But I recognised it instantly.' Even as I spoke I wondered at the wisdom of sharing what I knew. Will was right, anyone with regular access to St Saviour's might be able to procure any of the materials that had gone into the making of those six small coffins. Was it absurd to be concerned that those materials pointed to the apothecary? In reality they were no more than a collection of poorly executed boxes, foolish totems that may well have been made and hidden away by a child, their significance at best random, and most likely meaningless. And yet I knew, in my heart, that these were spurious arguments. 'That grey-coloured material, Will,' I said. 'The stuff used to construct those coffins, it comes from the apothecary too.'

❧

Gabriel was surrounded by an explosion of chalk dust, senna leaves and cochineal powder. There was a sticky pool of glycerine oozing from beneath one of the ward ledgers, and iron tonic was splattered down his apron front and across the apothecary table. The air reeked of sulphur, and I could see a broken bottle of the stuff beside his feet. The prescription ledger stood open in the middle of the table. I reached out and closed it, running my hand over its dull, grey-green binding.

'Look,' I said to Will. 'You see? It is the same.'

'See what?' said Gabriel. 'Same as what? I ain't done nothing to that ledger, Mr Jem. Them stains were already there!'

'Where's my father?' I said, looking round for him.

'Dr Hawkins came,' Gabriel wiped his nose on his sleeve. 'I don't know where they went. I've been on my own for ages.' He blinked at us, his gaze lingering on the sack I held, his expression wary. 'What you got there?'

'Nothing,' I said. I put the sack onto the table. 'Can't you clear up as you work?' I said. 'My father hates this mess.'

'He ain't here to say anything,' replied Gabriel.

'Have you taken the medicines up to the wards?'

'I ain't had time.' Gabriel sounded tearful. 'And Mrs Speedicut came. She said she'd be back later.' He looked up at the clock fearfully. 'It's almost time!'

As Gabriel spoke there came a thump at the door. I turned, expecting it to crash open, and a furious Mrs Speedicut to burst in – she hated it when we were tardy with the ward rounds. Nothing happened. I clicked my tongue. Could the woman not just come in, like everyone else, and say what she had to say? I marched across the apothecary and flung open the door.

On the ground, not two steps from the threshold, lay my father. All at once Gabriel was clinging to my arm, crying; Will was kneeling beside me as I pressed my fingers to my father's neck. The pulse was no more than a flicker. 'Father!' I said. 'Father!'

'Jem.' Will's voice was calm. He laid his hand on my shoulder. 'I'll help you to carry him.'

We laid my father on a blanket before the fire. Between us, Will and I removed his coat. When I saw what lay beneath, I could not help but draw back.

'Blood!' said Will.

'Who did this?' I whispered.

My father's eyes flickered open. 'Nathaniel?'

His mind was wandering. 'Uncle Nathaniel has gone,' I said. 'It's Jem.'

We had no family, my father and I. My mother had no relations; my father one brother, a surgeon on board an East Indiaman. I met him only once, when I was no more than eight years old – a tall thin stranger who looked just like my father, but for his neat brown beard and his weathered face. 'Are you a pirate?' I had asked, my

imagination excited by his nautical appearance, his tales
of wild weather and strange cargos.

'Would you like it if I were?' My uncle's eyes had
twinkled. My father's never did.

'Yes!' I cried.

'Well then, so I shall be!' He slapped the table top.
'Nathaniel Flockhart, Cap'n o' the *Bloody Hand*, forced to
roam the seven seas for ever and a day.'

'Why?' I had asked, jumping up and down beside him.
'Why, "forever"?'

'Why?' He lowered his voice to a whisper, and leaned
close. 'Because o' the curse o' the Flockharts, that's why,
my lad!'

I thought he was going to wink, but he didn't. I thought
he would give me a grin, but he didn't do that, either. In
the silence that followed, I laughed, and looked at my
father. But my father was not laughing.

My uncle left that afternoon. He never returned. I
wondered why my father chose to remember him now.

We pulled off his shirt. The crooks of his arms were
bandaged; the bandages too were soaked with blood.
'Jem?'

'Yes, Father.'

'Don't speak of this to anyone.'

I was prepared to say anything to keep him calm. To
excite him, to stir his pulse now, might be fatal. I nodded.

He closed his eyes. 'Good. Now, let me sleep.'

I unwrapped the bandages. Beneath, at the bend of
each elbow, was a hole. Blood oozed out, the way a leech
bite seeps long after the leech has been removed. And yet
I could not detect the characteristic three-sided bite of
the leech, nor the tell-tale cut of venesection. It was as

though he had been punctured, and the blood drawn off.

'He's been drained,' whispered Gabriel, his eyes wide with horror. 'Drained of blood.'

'But who, or what, would do such a thing?' said Will.

I was about to speak, when I noticed something amongst the folds of my father's discarded shirt. It was bright, almost luminous, against the white cotton. I held it up between finger and thumb: a single yellow rose petal.

'Dr Hawkins,' said Gabriel. 'He always wears a rose. But he's kind. He'd not do this.'

'Whatever happened here was by consent, Gabriel,' I said. 'See how tranquil he is? How at peace? If this had been the work of a fiend he would most likely be in a state of terror.'

'A fiend?' whispered Gabriel. 'At St Saviour's?'

'You read too many penny bloods,' I said. Poor boy. He would be little use to me amongst the powders and pills that evening. But there were tasks he could do, and I knew the familiar would be comforting. I patted his head. 'Make us some tea, Gabriel, there's a good lad.'

I bandaged my father's arms once more and dressed him in a clean nightshirt. I made him comfortable beneath a blanket in his chair beside the fire. Behind me, I could hear Will sweeping up the mess. He worked with Gabriel, setting bottles in their rightful place, clearing up spilt tinctures and powders, following the lad's instructions to keep his mind occupied. 'Where does this go, Gabriel?' and 'Can you show me how to tidy these away?' But I saw the boy peep in the sack where the coffins were hidden, and his cheeks turned paler still. 'The work of a fiend,' he whispered. His hands trembled as he placed the jar of burnt alum back onto the shelf.

Gabriel fell asleep at my father's feet, his mop of dark hair glinting in the firelight. Will slipped a cushion beneath his head and covered him with a blanket. The boy should have accompanied me on my final rounds later that evening, but I hadn't the heart to bother him. I was tempted to go out to Angel Meadow there and then, and demand that Dr Hawkins tell me what was going on. But I did not want to be away from my father for long, and so I put the thought from my mind as best I could and went out to the wards.

After the silence of the apothecary, the hospital was a pandemonium. The doctors had finished their rounds long ago, and the place was now the domain of Mrs Speedicut and her minions. I went from ward to ward, my lantern in my hand, the mutterings of the patients and the observations of the nurses as commonplace and boring as ever.

'Oh yes, Mr Flock'art, he's been purged reg'lar this past week. Feels all the better for it,' and 'Dr Catchpole do love his leeches sir. Worked wonders he has!' and 'Blue Pill, sir, same as usual.'

Leeches! We went through thousands of them. Why, the previous year alone we had spent two hundred and fifty one pounds, nine shillings and sixpence on the things. 'Where would St Saviour's be without blood!' Dr Graves had cried when I dared to object. As for Blue Pill . . . There was not a doctor in the place who could see it for what it was: mercury bound with chalk and as poisonous a substance as you might wish to find. It was

66

used on the most persistently costive patients – which included pretty much all of them. I had fallen out with Dr Catchpole on the matter of its use on many occasions. Could they not see that a similar effect might be produced with psyllium husks or a bowl of stewed rhubarb? I had told Dr Catchpole the same that very morning. 'Good lord, Mr Flockhart,' he had bellowed across the ward. 'I am a physician, not a gardener, and this is a hospital, not a pie shop!' The patients themselves were no better. 'Dr Catchpole says I must 'ave the calomel,' one of them had remarked as Dr Catchpole turned away. Already he had the black teeth and copious saliva characteristic of mercury poisoning. 'Dr Catchpole's a proper doctor. I'll not 'ave no fruit. And no seeds, neither!' Dr Bain was the only man there who saw sense. Leeches and Blue Pill indeed. Some of them were still cupping too!

There was nothing remarkable on any of the wards, which was just as well, as that evening my mind was elsewhere. All at once the ordered and predictable world of St Saviour's seemed to be coming apart at the seams. I had not realised how unsettled it had made me feel. But what better remedy for disquiet than the routine of the evening ward rounds? I stalked between the beds, allowing the noise and stink of the place to wash over me like a soothing familiar balm. The reek of vomit and effluent took its effect upon my spirits almost immediately. Purged, for the moment, of any sense of regret that we would soon be obliged to leave the place, I paused at a window and flung it open. A cold blast of night air, laced with the whiff of the tannery and the brewhouse blew in from the east.

'Please, sir,' a voice quavered from beneath a mound of

frayed blankets beside me. 'No air, for pity's sake! You'll kill us all!'

Out in the corridors the night nurses chatted and cackled. They were a different stock to the nurses who worked the wards during the day – less biddable, noisier and rougher in their manners and habits. They fell silent as I approached, but I knew they were a raucous lot when left to their own devices. In the wards, the inmates tossed and moaned, hunched beneath their blankets, coughing and farting in the gloom. Usually, I was accompanied about the infirmary by Mrs Speedicut. There was no need for her to come with me, but she insisted. She still remembered me as a child – how she had enjoyed walloping me through the wards when I was an apprentice! That evening, however, she was nowhere to be seen.

'She's out, sir,' said the nurse. 'She went down to the apof'cary a while ago and I ain't seen her since.'

'I was in the apothecary a while ago,' I said. 'I didn't see her.'

'That's where she went.'

'And where is she now, pray?'

The woman shrugged. ''Oo knows, sir?'

'Sweep the floors, can't you?' I said, suddenly irritated by her insolence. 'I saw a rat earlier.'

'I can catch it for you, if you like, sir,' came the reply. 'Dr Graves gives me a shillin' for every half dozen.'

I went up to the surgical ward. The night nurse was dozing on a chair in the corridor. Her mouth hung open, as brown as the inside of a tea pot. She reeked of gin, her nose bluish in the light from the lantern, the blood vessels on her face standing out against her sallow cheeks like red pin worms. I left her where she was. I knew her for a sharp-tongued gossiping ninny, and as much of a trollop as any of them. I was glad not to have her braying in my ear as I walked amongst the beds, though I'd be sure to give her chair a good kick as I walked past later.

Most of the patients were drugged with laudanum and seemed to be sleeping. I checked Dr Bain's amputee. Dr Bain had given instructions for the man's wound to be dressed every day. New, clean lint and linen were to be used and the area washed out with a weak carbolic acid solution. The patient was still and quiet. I pulled back the dressings. The wound was clean, and there was no sign of suppuration, though it was too early to comment on the success of the operation. I would check again in the morning.

The night nurse had not drawn the blinds and, for once, the moon was as bright as a new shilling. It shone full into the ward, painting the patients' blankets silver. But even the moonlight could not impart glamour to the scene, and the place resembled an overcrowded church-yard: the beds the mounded graves, severed stumps projecting like the bony remains sometimes visible in the workhouse burial ground – a place where a good many of them would end up.

I stood at the window. Below me, in the main courtyard, Edward VI's shoulders were cloaked in silver. Beyond him, I could see the dim yellow squares of the apothecary windows. I wondered whether I had been rash to leave my father in the care of Will Quartermain. After all, before that day I had never met the man. Now I was entrusting him to look after my only relative. And yet there was something about the young architect that I had liked immediately. He did not try to prove himself a better man than I. He did not question my knowledge and authority. He made me laugh. His curiosity matched my own. I wondered whether he would prove so agreeable if he knew who I really was.

On the opposite side of the square the eight tall windows of the Magdalene ward gleamed as black as onyx in the moonlight. I caught a movement at one of them. Was a patient out of bed? The night nurse should be on hand to prevent such wanderings. No doubt she was cackling with the rest of St Saviour's midnight coven out in the corridor. I cupped my hand about the glass, pressing my nose to the cold pane. All at once a white face appeared, emerging from the darkness of the opposite ward the way a drowned corpse might rise up from the black depths of a mill pond. Mrs Magorian! Her small, round face stared down, the bottle-green ribbons on her bonnet hanging limp against her cheeks like strips of weed. Beside her, tall and slim, stood Mrs Catchpole.

I clicked my tongue. What in heaven's name were they doing on the wards so late at night? I had not noticed them when I had passed through the place not half an hour earlier, and it was far too late for a Bible reading. I knew that I should go over there directly and tell them to go, but I had no stomach for a pair of lady almoners that evening and no wish for a confrontation. I waited for one or other of them to look up and see me. But neither of them did. They seemed to be engrossed by something at the far end of the courtyard. I followed their gaze.

Eliza had her cloak pulled close and her hood up, but her small quick figure was unmistakable. She was in the shadows with somebody, a man, though from that distance in the darkness I could not be certain who it was. All at once she ran across the courtyard and disappeared out into St Saviour's Street. Behind her, in the doorway to the library, her companion watched her go. He shifted in the shadows, his face suddenly visible in the moonlight.

Dr Bain.

For a moment he stood there. Mrs Magorian stared down, her expression unreadable. But Mrs Catchpole was not so guarded. Even from the opposite ward I could see her lips twist as she struggled to master her sense of betrayal, her hand clutched to her breast, her face frozen in a mixture of such pain and fury that I felt myself blanch.

As the clock above the hospital struck the half hour, the door to the laundry opened. Within I could see great bales of bedding illuminated like mounds of pale flesh – limbs, arses and torsos. The laundrywoman appeared, her arms folded, and leaned against the door-frame. Dr Bain hesitated; but not for long.

My skin grew hot, then cold. How could he court Eliza and then go immediately to a great fat trollop like that? Not two months ago I had come across him in the ironing room, beached on a dune of sheets, the laundrywoman stripped to the waist and sitting astride him. 'What can I do for you, Mr Flock'art?' she'd said. She had lifted up a great swaying breast in each hand, the way a baker might weigh up two lumps of dough before flinging them into the oven.

Later, Dr Bain had begged me not to tell anyone. 'A man has needs, Jem,' he'd said. 'At least until he's obliged to marry – and even then there are passions that fall beyond the compass of a wife. But perhaps you'd care to come along with me one night? Mrs Roseplucker in Wicke

71

Street has some new girls. Clean too. What d'you say? A young chap like you must have something of an appetite, eh? And we've not been there together for a while.'

But I knew about men's needs well enough: did I not visit the foul wards every day? Now, I wished I had not been so easily persuaded to say nothing. Dr Bain was my friend, but Eliza deserved better. And now Mrs Magorian, and Mrs Catchpole, had seen them together. Dr Bain, I knew, could look after himself, but Eliza? *Damn the man*, I thought. Could he not be content with whores and doctor's wives?

I was about to return to the corridor and wake up the night nurse with a kick and a bellow, when I heard a noise. At first I thought it was Mrs Speedicut come to find me, but there was no laboured breathing and no rustling skirts. Had the night nurse woken up? And yet I could still hear her snores out in the corridor. I was hidden from view by a cupboard, and was invisible to anyone coming in at the door. I could not tell who had entered, but I saw a shadow, tall and thin as a scarecrow, rearing against the walls. Perhaps Dr Bain had not stayed in the laundry after all, but had come to check on his patient. He was curious and diligent as a doctor, whatever his faults might be as a man.

I had left my lantern on the table in the middle of the ward, but the visitor seemed not to have noticed. He had his own lantern and he raised it now as he stood over Dr Bain's patient, looking down. Dr Graves. His face was white, almost greenish in the light, his eyes two dark hollows. He put his lamp on the table beside the patient's bed, and began gently to open the man's bandages. The patient did not move. The sleeping draught he had

been prescribed had been a powerful one. Dr Graves
slid a hand into his pocket, and produced a small glass
phial.

'Good evening, Dr Graves,' I said, stepping into view.
'The patient is healing well, is he not?'

Dr Graves cried out and sprang away from the bedside.
He tried to slip the phial back into his pocket, but in his
haste the thing fell to the floor.

'Let me help,' I said.

'No!' Dr Graves plunged beneath the bed. The phial
had not smashed, but had rolled away from him. I too
dived beneath the bed. There was a scrabbling of fingers.
My fist closed about the phial but Dr Graves clawed the
back of my hand with his long brittle nails. 'I do apologise,'
he said through clenched teeth as he seized the glass from
my slackened grip.

We stood up, both of us panting. 'Thank you, Mr
Flockhart.' Dr Graves grinned at me, a trickle of sweat
running down his temple. He plucked a handkerchief
from his breast pocket and swabbed at his face.

'Think what you're doing, sir.' I nursed the back of my
hand, wet with blood. 'Consider your reputation—'

Dr Graves said nothing. His face twitched.

'And your conscience,' I added.

Dr Graves looked at me, his face blank. A dry rattling
sound came from his throat and his eyes bulged. He put
out a hand to steady himself as I started forward. Had he
somehow managed to slip himself some of his own poison?
I had been able to do no more than glimpse the contents
of the phial in the dim light beneath the bed – a white,
crystalline powder. What was it? Arsenic? Oleander?
Cyanide? All were fast acting and quite deadly.

And then I realised that he was not dying at all. He was laughing.

≫

I was awoken by the sound of someone moving about the apothecary. I had slept on Gabriel's bed beneath the table, while Gabriel remained in his blanket at my father's feet. Only Will Quartermain had spent the night in the space he had been allocated: the truckle bed in my room. I was glad to have been spared that forced intimacy, at least for another night. Still, the sight of him pottering about the apothecary was most welcome. He had poked the fire back into life, and on the stove top sat a large, fat-bellied flask, dark flecks eddying in the amber-coloured liquid. Will seized the neck of the thing with a pair of tongs.

'What's that?' I said. I used the large flask for collecting the distillate of plant oils, though I was sure I had not undertaken any such procedure the day before.

'Tea,' said Will. 'I couldn't find the tea pot. Don't you have one? And where's the maid?'

'The maid?' I laughed. 'Why would we need one of those? We can look after each other.'

'Cups then. Do you have cups?'

'The cups are in the dresser.' I looked over at my father.

'He seems rested,' said Will. 'Was he quiet during the night?'

I had slept heavily, my dreams filled with bloodied bandages, blotch-eyed dolls and dead flowers. 'Yes,' I said. In fact, I had been so tired that my father might have risen up and danced a jig on the table top and I would not have

74

noticed. 'At least, I think so. Gabriel!' I threw a shoe at the recumbent form on the hearth rug. 'Get up!'

Will and I sat side by side staring out at the thick brown fog that rubbed against the windows. I had smelled it on the air as I walked back across the courtyard the night before. Now, not even the sun could be distinguished. Behind us, Gabriel began scrubbing the table. My father remained, unmoving, but breathing steadily, in his chair. I spooned some tea between his lips and was reassured to see him swallow the stuff. His face was grey and still. Beneath his lowered lids, however, I could see his eyes moving, restless and wakeful despite everything.

'This tea tastes of lavender,' I said.

There was one thing I wanted to do before the day began in earnest. 'The wrappings around those dolls,' I said to Will. 'We must test to see whether it's blood or not.'

'You have doubts?'

'No. But I'd like to be certain. What if it's no more than, say, vegetable dye? The objects themselves would become quite harmless.'

'And if it's not?'

I did not reply.

Will and Gabriel watched in silence as I took one of the coffins from the sack. Gabriel's eyes grew wide, and his lips began to tremble when he saw what was inside – the dried weeds, the bloodied rags, the hideous peg-like doll. To my surprise, however, he said nothing. I snipped off a piece of the blood-coloured wrappings and put it onto a glass saucer. Potassium chloride dissolved in ice vinegar was the necessary reagent. 'Now,' I said. 'If we drop the acetic acid mixture onto the cloth and then gently heat it . . .' I used a glass dropper to cover the material with fluid, and then carried the saucer over to the stove. Other than the ticking of the clock, and Gabriel's gormless breathing, the room was silent. We stood there, Will and I, watching while the saucer and its bloody mixture grew warm. Too much and the test would not work. Too little and we would see no change. It was anyone's guess. At length, I extracted a drop of the heated, loam-coloured liquid with my pipette, and plopped it onto a glass slide ready for the microscope. I loved that microscope, a brass beauty made by Leitz of Wetzlar that I polished every week until it gleamed like gold. I had bought it some years ago, under Dr Bain's advice, and it sat in the window, the best place in the apothecary to catch the light, where it was regarded jealously by Dr Graves, Dr Catchpole and Dr Magorian, all of whom though it scandalous that a mere apothecary should possess such a mighty scientific instrument.

'Well?' said Will as I peered into the Leitz's brass eye-piece. I turned the knobs, my heart suddenly racing, waiting for the microscopic construction of the droplet to become visible. 'Is it—'

I felt my skin grow cold. Caught in that icy gaze was a tell-tale ring of rhombic crystals, what Dr Bain called the 'hematin derivative'. There was no doubt about it. 'Blood,' I said. 'These rags are soaked in blood.'

❦

I went out to get some bread. When I came back, Dr Hawkins was there. He was holding my father's wrist, his pocket watch open in his hand.

'I hear he's been sleeping,' he said.

'He's been unconscious, certainly,' I replied. 'But that's not the same as sleeping, is it? His eyelids might be closed but beneath them his eyes move constantly. It's as though he's searching for something even though he cannot see. I would not describe such a state as "sleep" any more than you would.'

'But his enervated condition may give him some rest,' said Dr Hawkins. The rose on his lapel that day was white – a dense creamy head of thickly curled velvet petals. Flawless. Beautiful. And in the language of flowers? It meant silence, I thought bitterly. Silence and secrecy. Eliza had taught me well, that day in the physic garden.

I clamped my hand about his wrist. 'What have you done to him?' I whispered. 'You've bled him until he can hardly stand.'

'I'm trying to help him, Jem.'

'But what's wrong with him?'

'It's not for me to explain what ails him. He must do that himself. And he *will* tell you. He'll have to. But it'll be in his own time. All you can do is wait. Wait and hope.'

Tears stung my eyes. I could not reply. I could only stare at my father, at the dark rings that circled his eyes. 'But look at him,' I whispered. 'He's as empty as a glove. And for what?'

'I hoped we had taken enough to weaken the system. To make sleep, or at least unconsciousness, inevitable.'

'But he does *not* sleep. You've made him into a living corpse.'

'We had to try. He insisted that we try. If you knew, you would understand—'

'But I *don't* know,' I cried. 'You won't tell me. *He* won't tell me. How can I understand?'

My father stirred. 'Jem.' I crouched down and took his hand. 'Don't shriek,' he whispered. His fingers were cold and limp, and did not respond to my touch.

'You can't help him like this, Jem,' said Dr Hawkins.

'But I *can* help him,' I said. I pulled my coat off and fumbled with my shirt cuff. 'Here,' I cried, exposing an arm and thrusting it towards Dr Hawkins. 'Take *my* blood. Take it and put it into him.'

'No!' My father's voice was sharp, his expression irritated, as if he wished I would just shut up and go away. But I would not shut up. And I would never go away.

'Father—'

I watched him struggle to control his annoyance. 'No.' He attempted a smile, but looked away from me. 'I think a dose of iron tonic would be useful, don't you?'

I knew when I had been dismissed. I fetched the bottle in silence.

❧

When I returned from the morning ward rounds my father had the out-patients' ledger open on his lap. He had the long-stick ruler in his hand and was using this to direct proceedings.

'There, Gabriel,' he said, jabbing the air in the direction of the top shelf. 'The powdered clove is up there. Seventy-seven grains, as I showed you. Come along, lad!' He looked exhausted, and I could see that even wielding the ruler was an effort.

Gabriel scaled the ladder against the shelves like a sailor amongst the rigging. He was glad my father had recovered sufficiently to order him about the place. He was also pleased that there was now someone at work in the apothecary who knew even less than he did about medicinal matters, for with my father incapacitated, Will had offered to help us. Was he not supposed to be making a survey of St Saviour's churchyard? He was stalling, I knew.

'*I* know what you can do,' Gabriel said. 'You can polish the brass scales and weights. Then you can scrub all the glassware and dust the bottles on the top shelf and take the hops up to the drying room and then change the water in the leech tank—'

Will gazed at the leeches. 'Do I scoop them out first?'

'Forget the leeches,' I said. 'I need you to grind, and measure.' I pointed to the scales, and the pestle and mortar. 'Follow my instructions exactly.'

As usual, people came and went. At ten o'clock I sent Gabriel to take the medicines to out-patients. He returned some time later with a bag of buns (cadged from the baker on Priory Street who was sorry to hear of my father's ill health) and bearing news of Mrs Speedicut's brutality – she had caught him by the fire in the out-patients' waiting room and had boxed his ears for 'lolling about'. 'I weren't lollin' anywhere,' said Gabriel, rubbing his ear. 'I were *standin'*.'

The ward sisters brought down their prescription ledgers; a group of students came in looking for Dr Graves, who was due to operate and could not be found anywhere. Mrs Magorian came in on her way to the almoners' meeting, asking for the tincture of St John's wort my father had made up for her. Everyone seemed to know about the coffins, and we were asked about them again and again. The nurses looked at them askance; the students laughed and shrugged and turned away.

'It makes me feel quite faint just to look at them,' said Mrs Magorian, who had indeed turned rather green. She fluttered a small silk handkerchief in front of her face. I caught a whiff of lavender and sal volatile. 'Where's Dr Bain?' she added, her voice suddenly sharp. 'Have you seen him?'

'Gabriel,' I said, as the door closed behind them. 'Have you told the entire world about these boxes?' I stowed them back out of sight beneath the work bench.

'No, Mr Jem,' he said. 'At least, not the *entire* world. Perhaps if you showed them to me, prop'ly, rather than just letting me peep into that sack . . .' Only my father seemed uninterested. He looked at them and shrugged, his face registering neither surprise nor recognition. I could not help but feel relived, though it was clear his indifference was due to other, more pressing preoccupations.

Not everyone who came in went away again so promptly. Mrs Speedicut appeared looking irritable. She was breathing heavily, as though from some recent exertion. She wore the same cuffs and apron as the day before, and I noticed that her skirts were singed slightly on the right hand side. Clearly, she had fallen asleep before the fire. Perhaps that was why she had missed the ward rounds the night before. She had been conspicuous by her absence that morning too. She sat down in the chair opposite my father and peered into the blackened bowl of her pipe. Finding it empty, she contented herself with sucking on the stem. I heard the sound of tar gurgling. I had made a pot of coffee, and I handed her a cup. My father winced as she slurped the bitter black brew. I was determined not to show her the coffins unless she asked.

80

Dr Bain and Dr Catchpole arrived at the apothecary at the same time, and were obliged to enter together. Dr Catchpole looked dejected, his eyes red rimmed, his gaze hostile and ill tempered. Dr Bain affected not to notice Dr Catchpole's black looks. He winked at Will and me, ruffled Gabriel's hair and made Old Mother Speedicut an elaborate bow. 'Dear lady,' he said. He turned to my father. 'And how are you, Mr Flockhart? Dr Hawkins tells me you're feeling the benefit of his treatment.'

My father nodded. He was lying back on his cushions again. 'You know of it?'

Dr Bain glanced over at me. 'I know . . . something of it,' he said. I was about to object, to ask whether everyone but me was privy to my father's health concerns, but Mrs Speedicut had fixed her gimlet eye upon me, so I said nothing.

'Well now,' said Dr Bain. 'What's all this about coffins?'

'Coffins?' said Dr Catchpole.

'Clearly, Dr Catchpole, you are not quite as devoted to listening to the gossip of the hospital's servants as Dr Bain,' said my father.

'I dare say you're right, Mr Flockhart,' said Dr Bain. 'Oh!' he added, turning to his colleague. 'How is Mrs Catchpole? I heard she fainted yesterday while she was with the lady almoners. Feeling better, I hope?'

'She has taken to her bed, sir. She is—' Dr Catchpole breathed deeply. 'She is not herself.'

'I'm sorry to hear it,' murmured Dr Bain.

'No doubt you are,' snapped Dr Catchpole. 'My wife is pregnant.' He glared at Dr Bain. In his left hand he held a pair of dogskin gloves, so that for a moment I thought he was going to slap Dr Bain across the face

81

with them, or at least throw one to the ground and demand satisfaction.

Dr Bain looked at Dr Catchpole warily. Then, when nothing more seemed to be forthcoming, he leaped forward to seize the doctor's hand. 'Congratulations, my dear fellow.'

Dr Catchpole snatched his fingers away.

Dr Bain pretended not to notice. 'So, Jem,' he said, rather too brightly. 'Where are they then? These coffins young Master Locke has been telling me about?' Did his cheek turn pale as he spoke? Was his smile forced? I saw his eyes flit nervously across the bottles and jars set out on the table top, as if searching for something he did not want to find. At the time I made nothing of it.

'I see no coffins, Dr Bain,' said Dr Catchpole. 'If you want coffins I suggest you try the undertaker, rather than the apothecary.'

'It's the Devil's work,' cried Mrs Speedicut.

'How do *you* know what it is?' I said. 'You've not even seen them.'

'Yes,' said Gabriel. He rubbed his ear. 'I *told* her about them, and she boxed my ear. Boxed my ear, for *nuffink!*'

'What are you doing here anyway?' I added, wishing now that I had not given the woman some coffee. She was taking an inordinate length of time to drink the stuff. 'Don't you have work to do?'

'I'm here for ars'nic,' said Mrs Speedicut. She looked at my father. He had closed his eyes, so she leaned forward and jabbed his shoulder with the stem of her pipe. 'There's rats again, Mr Flock'art. Rats!'

'There are always rats,' I said.

'Got any ars'nic?' repeated Mrs Speedicut.

'Of course I have arsenic,' I said. 'This is an apothecary. We have no want of poisons here.'

'You should try some yerself, Mrs Greedigut,' said Gabriel. 'Just to make sure it works.'

Mrs Speedicut rose from her chair, her cheeks quivering with fury. 'You young tyke!' She flung her pipe at Gabriel's head, but he had already scuttled up the wall-ladder. Quick as a monkey, he mounted the half-empty top shelf and crawled along it.

Mrs Speedicut seized the broom and jabbed the end of it towards his retreating arse. 'You come back!' she shouted, her cheeks trembling with fury. 'Come back this instant!' She began mounting the ladder, her great bulk swaying from side to side, her chubby, mottled ankles exposed for all to see. The rungs groaned beneath her as she tried to swat Gabriel off the shelf with the broom-head. A jar of sulphur crashed to the ground.

'Mrs Speedicut, *I* shall discipline the boy,' I said.

'Dr Bain,' whined Gabriel as the broom swooshed past his ear. 'Get her off me!' But Dr Bain merely grinned and folded his arms.

'Ha!' screamed Mrs Speedicut, still clinging to the ladder. 'Your beloved Dr Bain, he don't care about you! He don't care about anyone or anything except himself. He's no different from any man – selfish to the bone. He shags his wick – yes, my lad, don't you turn away from me with your blushes. I knows you've seen him yerself. Not that he cares *who* knows, or who sees, or what the consequences might be. Well *you're* a consequence and he don't care a fig about *you* neither. Nor about your mother.'

The room fell silent. Exhausted, Mrs Speedicut slid to the floor. Her face was crimson, her lips moist and quivering, as though her words had coated them with bile. It was true that Dr Bain paid Gabriel's apothecary fees. Dr Bain said it was merely an act of philanthropy for the benefit of a poor orphan boy, but we all knew better. After all, did the lad not look exactly like Dr Bain? As for Gabriel's mother, I would never forget the day, some fourteen years earlier, when she had handed me a bundle containing the infant Gabriel, and vanished into the infirmary's chapel.

What had happened next I could no longer recall in detail, though I know that some moments later I had been distracted by a sound high above. I looked up to see the woman emerging from the topmost arch of the bell tower. She did not hesitate, did not cry out or cling to the stonework in fear. Instead, she ducked her head beneath the arch, and stepped forward, black skirts flapping crazily as she plummeted into the courtyard below.

Dr Graves had been the first to appear, brought to the window of the out-patients' dispensary by the terrible sound of the girl's body striking the courtyard. In his eagerness to get to the corpse he clambered out of the window, and within moments was upon her, swathing her limp and bloody remains in a bed sheet he had brought with him for the purpose and carrying her off in the direction of the dissecting room.

A cursory attempt was made to find the girl's origins, but no likely answer was found. Pointing to the poor state of her clothing, Dr Graves observed (rather conveniently, I thought) that she clearly came of low birth (and therefore was hardly worth the trouble she was causing everyone). As she had chosen to end her life in the hospital grounds, he said, it was only right that her remains should be devoted to the advancement of medicine.

Dr Bain came into the hospital later that day to find the girl's brain bobbing in a jar of preserving fluid. Her body had been eviscerated, her organs bottled and labelled for the museum. Her face, which had remained untouched by the ordeal, had been photographed and a plaster cast taken of its features. Dr Graves's microscope had winked its knowing eye at me as I gathered up the empty carboys of formaldehyde from his work bench.

'Better than burial at a crossroads, with a stake through the heart, what?' Dr Graves laughed as he packed away his knives.

Dr Bain had said nothing. He stared at the dead girl's unpacked body, and at the cast of her face, for a long time. Then he bent to remove a stain from his boot with his handkerchief.

I never told Gabriel that I had witnessed his mother's leap from St Saviour's bell tower. I did not tell him that every day his feet passed over the flags where her body had lain, or that if he stood on his tip toes and peered behind the bottles laid out in the anatomy museum he might see her brain floating, like a sponge in a jar of dirty bathwater. No one had ever told him anything. Until now.

'Mrs Speedicut, please—' Dr Bain stepped forward, his face white.

But Mrs Speedicut had not finished. 'D'you know what happened next?' she cried. 'Once she were dead, he cut her up for all those young medical men to look at. She were your mother, an' he did *that* to her!'

'No, he didn't,' said Gabriel. His face was ashen. 'Dr Bain wouldn't do that—'

85

'It was Dr Graves who performed that post mortem,' said Dr Bain in a low voice. 'As you are well aware.'

'Yah!' cried Gabriel. He pulled off his shoe and flung it at Mrs Speedicut. She ducked, and it clipped Dr Catchpole on the ear.

'Confound it,' cried Dr Catchpole. '*Mr* Flockhart, this apothecary is no better than a bear pit. And in front of strangers too.' He glanced at Will who was standing beside the condenser, a beaker of cough syrup in his hands. He was wearing one of Gabriel's aprons, his ridiculous hat was crooked on his head and his expression was so startled that I could not help but laugh. The sound only enraged Dr Catchpole further. 'The governors shall hear of it.'

'Get off!' shouted Gabriel as Mrs Speedicut plunged forward to jab at his backside once more.

'Can't you control that boy, Mr Flockhart?'

'Can't you control your wife, Dr Catchpole?' said Gabriel.

Dr Bain gave a bark of laughter.

'Master Locke, come down this instant,' I cried, as the place erupted once more. 'Mrs Speedicut, step back, if you please. And put that broom down, woman!'

'This is intolerable!' shouted Dr Catchpole above the din. 'Mrs Speedicut, I am surprised at you – such vulgarity has no place here! And *you,* master apprentice!' His voice trembled with fury. 'I cannot even begin to think what Mr Flockhart means by allowing you to speak so to a physician. *And* to assault me!'

'Come, Dr Catchpole,' said Dr Bain. 'Can't you see Mr Flockhart is not at his best today?' We all looked at my father, who was sitting back in his chair, his eyes closed, while the hurly-burly went on around him. The noise abated. 'It was a moment's hot-headedness, that's all. I dare say Mrs Speedicut was provoked, though her exposition was certainly unwarranted. But the lad is young, he didn't mean to harm anyone—'

But Dr Catchpole had not finished. 'As for *you*, sir,' his fingers flexed about the silver knob at the head of his walking stick. '*You* are an insult to this hospital.'

'I?' Dr Bain blinked. 'But I have only just come in!' He attempted a smile, his teeth white between his dark curly side-whiskers. He looked at Dr Catchpole – old Dr Catchpole, absurd in his theatrical cape and frothing white regency neckerchief – and his contempt was plain. 'My dear fellow—'

'Don't you patronise me!' cried Dr Catchpole. 'I am not your "dear fellow". I am *forced* by professional etiquette to tolerate you. You and your . . . your . . . *behaviour.*' Suddenly Dr Catchpole raised his arm and struck out at Dr Bain with the knob of his stick.

Dr Bain staggered backwards, reeling against the shelves. He stared at Dr Catchpole in surprise, blood pouring down his face and seeping into his emerald waistcoat in an ugly dark stain. He sank to his knees.

At that moment the door opened and Dr Magorian strode in, his wife at his side. Dr Catchpole made a choking sound. He pushed past Dr Magorian and vanished into the fog.

'There he is!' Mrs Magorian pointed at Dr Bain. 'The defiler!'

'What?' Dr Bain staggered to his feet. The handkerchief he was now holding to his brow was almost as bloodstained as his waistcoat. He put out a hand to steady himself and brought a jar of powdered senna pod crashing to the ground.

'You and my daughter,' said Dr Magorian. 'Last night.'

Dr Bain shook his head, a look of pain and confusion on his face. 'Dr Magorian, I—'

'Don't trouble to deny it. I have witnesses. My dear wife for one. Mr Jem Flockhart for another.'

'I admit that I saw someone in the courtyard last night,' I said. 'But it was too dark to see precisely who it was.' I might still be angry with Dr Bain, but I would not hand him over to his enemies.

'Dr Catchpole appears to have meted out just punishment already,' said Dr Magorian. He loomed over the bloodstained Dr Bain, swinging his stick in his hand. 'Which saves me the trouble.'

'Sir, I—'

'You have despoiled her!' cried Dr Magorian.

'I've not touched her!'

Mrs Magorian wrung her hands together, and shook her head. '"*Whosoever looketh on a woman to lust after her hath committed adultery with her already in his heart*",' she whispered. 'Matthew, chapter five, verse twenty-eight. Oh!' She dabbed at her lips, as if overcome by nausea.

'Quite so, my dear,' said Dr Magorian. She looked up at him and nodded, as if giving her consent, before turning her head away. Dr Magorian took hold of one of Dr Bain's lapels and leaned forward. 'I don't need the Bible to tell me what sort of a man you are. You may do as you please with other men's wives and daughters, but you will not do as you please with mine.' He pressed the head of his cane hard into Dr Bain's crotch. 'I think you understand me.'

‏❦

'Well, Jem, I deserved that, didn't I? Who'd have thought old Catchpole had it in him.'

'Why must you be so provoking?'

'I don't know.' Dr Bain winced as I dabbed at his head with a cotton pad soaked in witch hazel. 'Thank God they've all gone.'

After the excitement and violence of the morning, I too was glad to have some quietness. Dr and Mrs Magorian had swept out into the fog. Mrs Speedicut had gone off to the laundry room; Gabriel had gone to the cook house. My father had asked to be helped upstairs to his room 'to get some peace from this infernal madhouse'. Only Will remained, poring over his plan of St Saviour's while he waited for the kettle to boil. After his morning in the apothecary I wondered whether the excavations of the churchyard had taken on a more appealing aspect. At least the incumbents did not fight amongst themselves.

'And now you've got Miss Magorian in trouble,' I said.

'Yes.' Dr Bain sighed. 'And I'm sorry for that. But it was her idea that we meet. She said she had something she wanted to speak to me about. But then when she came she didn't say anything much. She seemed rather nervous, in fact.' He grinned. 'D'you think she's in love with me?'

I exchanged the witch hazel for a wad of gauze soaked in alcohol and pressed it to the wound above Dr Bain's eye. 'Ow!'

'Serves you right. But it's a shallow cut. It could have been much worse.' What game was Eliza playing? I resolved to find out, one way or another. 'It's just as well that her father blames you for the meeting.' I wrapped a bandage about his head to hold the gauze in place. 'Now, take a look at these, if that's what you came for, and then go home. We've seen more than enough of you for one day.'

Before him, on the table top, I placed the six small coffins. Dr Bain looked at them in silence. He did not move, he did not touch them. 'Where did you find them?' he said at last.

'In the old chapel.' All at once his face appeared paler than ever, the blood draining from his lips. I started forward. 'Are you feeling unwell?'

'What? No, no,' he said. 'It's just . . . just my head.' He unwrapped one of the bundles and stared, appalled, at the rags, and the hideous blotch-eyed doll within.

'It's blood,' said Will. 'Each one of them is soaked in blood. Or at least, the bindings are.'

Dr Bain seemed not to be listening. 'Look, Jem,' he said suddenly. 'Would you mind if I took these away with me? Just for a day or so.'

Will and I exchanged a glance. 'No,' I said. 'Of course not.' What else could I say? I could hardly refuse. After all, it didn't matter who had the coffins, not really. And yet why did I feel that they should remain here? Why did I feel as though it was up to me – up to Will and me – to find out where they came from and who had hidden them away? I thought of the six crudely shaped dolls, their six ragged screaming mouths and six pairs of black misshapen eyes. They had seen something. They *knew* something. It was something monstrous, I was certain. And they would yield their secret – if we asked the right questions.

'Why not come for supper tonight?' said Dr Bain. 'You and Mr Quartermain? Perhaps we might examine these peculiar little relics together. The light is better in my study. Besides, I have something else I need your help with. You'll understand when you come. But I'll take them now, if I may.'

Without waiting for my answer, Dr Bain took a sack from beneath the apothecary table and loaded the coffins inside. Suddenly he seemed anxious to be gone. He glanced at the window, as though distracted by a movement, but there was nothing to be seen but brown fog, as thick and dense as the flank of a giant beast. 'Pity about that fog,' he muttered. 'Can't see a damn thing. Still, can't be helped.' He adopted a brisk tone that was at odds with his obvious feelings of unease. 'Come over directly after your rounds, Jem. Earlier if possible. You too, Quartermain. We shall uncover the secrets in these boxes before the night is out.'

Chapter Four

⁂

By the time my evening rounds were over the fog was so thick that we could barely see to the ends of our noses. We had a lantern each, but it made little difference. Once we were outside on St Saviour's Street it was as though we were walking along the bottom of the Thames. I could feel the squelch of ordure beneath my feet and the rustle of refuse though I could not see where to step that I might avoid it. We had covered our mouths and noses with scarves, but still the fog tickled our throats and coated our tongues with the taste of sulphur and effluent. Beside me, I heard Will retch and cough. I was glad that Dr Bain's house was so close to the infirmary, as it was not a night to be out.

It was peculiar for a gentleman to open his own front door, and I could see Will's surprise, but Dr Bain was not a slave to etiquette. When he wished to have an evening of experimentation he would send the servants out for the night. It was easier than having to explain the smells and noises, and servants, once acquired, were hard to keep even in the most respectable households. Supper would no doubt be some cold meats and cheese, set aside by the housekeeper before she went out, though Dr Bain may well have forgotten about supper altogether, and we would end up going to Sorley's chop house.

Dr Bain shook me warmly by the hand. 'Good to see you, Jem,' he said. 'And you, Quartermain. You'll be glad to hear that I'll not be excising any hip joints tonight. Just a little taste of something to see what its actions might be. Jem knows the drill. We've done it before, haven't we, Jem?'

Dr Bain led us down the hall and into the drawing room. I saw Will wrinkle his nose at the smell of the place – the ammonia reek of rats' piss and spirits – and stare in surprise at the scorch marks on the carpet, the table covered with glass retorts, beakers and condensers, crucibles . . .

Unrestricted by the expectations of a wife or the demands of propriety, Dr Bain conducted his life as he chose. If he wanted a laboratory in his sitting room then he could have one. If he wanted to keep a cage of rats on the floor there was no one to stop him. And yet, his mode of living was not without difficulties: he was forever looking for a new housekeeper, as they appeared unwilling to preside over so unorthodox a household for long. Servants too were in short supply, and Dr Bain was obliged to turn a blind eye to all manner of insubordination, laziness and pilfering, simply so that he might have someone to kindle his fire and get him his breakfast in the morning. It always surprised me how well turned out the doctor was, given how often he had no one to clean his shoes and brush his clothes for him.

'Dr Bain and I are working on a treatise on poison to rival Christison's,' I said.

'Oh?' Will raised his eyebrows.

'Yes,' said Dr Bain. 'The art of the poisoner has become quite the fashion – if the penny broadsheets are anything to go by. More favoured by women as a means of murder than the knife, the bludgeon, or the pistol.'

'Are you including physicians and surgeons in the tally?' said Will. 'I'm sure your fellow medical men are most adept.'

'Oh indeed,' I said. 'With a death rate at St Saviour's of ten patients in every one hundred, the men here show an unusual degree of expertise in the use of physic as a means of despatch.'

Dr Bain laughed. 'How dare you deride my brilliant and gifted colleagues, Jem Flockhart,' he said. 'And you a mere apothecary. As for you, Quartermain – I can't imagine who you might be referring to.'

'I would not presume to name names,' said Will. 'The question was general, rather than specific.' He looked askance at the cage of seething rats. 'But what of this evening—'

'Well.' Dr Bain rubbed his hands together. 'I thought we might examine the actions of spindle tree bark. I believe it may have tonic and diuretic effects. I tried a little yesterday – no more than five grains. But we need a proper experiment. I have a dog at the ready and have prepared a decoction—'

'Dr Bain, I am always telling you.' I sighed. 'You will kill yourself and I will have no way of knowing what finished you off.'

Dr Bain appeared not to have heard. 'We tried

bloodroot last week,' he said, addressing Will. 'The tubers weep sap like blood. Quite alarming to see – especially for a chap like you, Quartermain. Good job we did it last week and not tonight – might have had you fainting at the sight of a severed tuber! Ha, ha!

'But one can't allow oneself to be deceived by appearances, can one? The thing might look like something from the Devil's banquet, but we are men of science here and as such we grasp superstition and turn it on its head. We had a right old time of it, didn't we, Jem?'

'Yes, Dr Bain.'

'Of course, I gave the stuff to a dog first—'

'A dog?' said Will.

'Christison tells us that the responsiveness of dogs to medicines and toxins most closely resembles that of man,' I said.

'The streets are full of stray dogs,' said Dr Bain. 'What better use for them than to be the assistants of scientific inquiry? There are suggestions that bloodroot might exert a powerful effect on the heart and lungs.' He shrugged. 'How else might we find out more unless we try the stuff? But most physic is poison, Mr Quartermain. Did you know that? That's where the dogs come in.'

'And so the dog was given fifty grains of powdered bloodroot,' I said.

'It died, of course,' said Dr Bain. 'When we cut the beast open we found its heart and liver engorged, the blood thick and sluggish, and copious in the heart chambers – just what we expected—'

'I think Mr Quartermain has heard enough,' I said, perceiving Will's growing pallor.

Dr Bain blinked. 'Oh! Yes, well . . . Well, after that I *had* to try the stuff. Took half a drachm.'

'Far too much,' I said.

'I nearly died,' said Dr Bain.

'You *did* die.' I turned to Will. 'There was no evidence of pulse or breath. I had to beat the life back into him. Thumping on his chest like a monkey on a drum . . .' I stopped. I did not like to think of it. Dr Bain was my friend. Time and again I had sat with him while he spewed and retched, his bowels gurgling, his skin sweating, my fingers clamped to his pulse. And always we were observing, noting down, comparing – how else might medicine move forward? That evening, however, he had gone too far. I had forced an emetic between his lips; blown lungfuls of my own breath into him, sobbing as I applied my lips to his, my face salty with snot and tears, willing to try anything to bring him back. How we had clung to one another when he had finally gasped and coughed back into life, asprawl on the floor of his drawing room surrounded by mess and filth, our arms around each other like lovers.

'An exciting evening, what?' cried Dr Bain now.

'You shouldn't make light of it,' I said. 'I saved your life that night, and not for the first time. You should treat it with more respect.'

Dr Bain seized me by the hand, his expression suddenly serious. 'So you did, Jem, so you did. And I thank God for your prompt action that night.' He wrung my hand. To my surprise, his eyes shone with tears. 'You're a true friend. God knows, I don't have many of those at St Saviour's.'

'Well then, perhaps you will do as I ask, for once.'

'But of course—'

'And tonight we will examine the coffins Will and I found, as we agreed.'

'Oh.' Dr Bain's glance strayed to the sack containing the coffins which lay on the table top. For a moment, I thought I saw a look of apprehension cross his face. 'Is that what we agreed? But I already have the dog.'

'The dog can wait,' I said. It was only afterwards that I had cause to reflect upon his reluctance. But by then it was too late.

❧

I cleared a space amongst the books and papers on the table top. Dr Bain rummaged in the drawer of the desk and produced a large ebony-handled magnifying glass. 'You've already looked at them?'

'Yes,' I said. I told him what we had found – the blood, the flowers.

'I doubt there's much else to see.'

'I wanted to look at the lining paper,' I said. 'Some of them are lined with notepaper, foolscap – something. There's writing.'

'Mm,' said Dr Bain. He poured himself a glass of Madeira.

I opened the first of the coffins – the smallest and most crudely formed – and emptied the contents onto the table. I took the magnifying glass and peered at the paper. There was definitely something written there. A phrase? A name? Perhaps a date? I handed the glass to Will.

'The words are back to front,' he said. 'On the other side of the paper. Far too faint to read. And the paper is too old to peel away.'

'Ah, well,' said Dr Bain. 'Shall I get the dog—'

'Steam?' I said.

'But the paper is too thin,' said the doctor. 'Too brittle.'

'What about oil?' I said. 'Oil changes the properties of paper, so that it doesn't reflect the light. The paper becomes translucent. It might be possible to read the words on the other side of the page.'

'The writing would still be back to front,' said Dr Bain.

'Then we must use a mirror.'

'Dr Bain,' said Will. 'Do you have any oil?'

'No,' said Dr Bain.

'Turpentine?' I asked.

The doctor rubbed his chin.

'Dr Bain?' I said.

'Yes, yes.' He went to a glass-fronted cabinet that stood against the wall. We heard the chink of glass as he searched amongst bottles and jars. I knew the turpentine was in there. Was he about to say he did not have any?

'It's at the back,' I said, determined not to be forestalled. 'I saw it last week.'

'Oh, yes.' He held up a bottle containing a brownish coloured liquid. 'There's not much of it.'

'And a mirror,' I said, plucking a pipette from amongst the table-top apparatus. 'Do you have a mirror?'

'I don't think I do.'

'You must have!' I cried.

'Perhaps upstairs.' He vanished into the hall. We heard his heavy footsteps on the stairs.

Will was regarding a pair of wing-backed armchairs, one on either side of the fireplace. Both of them were blighted with scorch marks and loaded with books and papers. 'Why does he bother to have chairs if he has no intention of sitting on them? Why not simply get another book shelf? I don't know how he lives like this.' He looked in distaste at a pair of bloody aprons draped over a brocade-covered screen that was folded against the wall. 'Is this his drawing room?'

'I suppose it is rather disorganised,' I said. The room was furnished as one might expect, with well-stuffed chairs and an ottoman, and a fire burning in the grate. There was a heavy Persian rug on the floor, and framed paintings on the walls. But the paintings were indifferent – dark and formless landscapes, chosen to fill up the walls rather than to reflect taste. The hearth was littered with clumps of dried masticated coca leaves and the mantelpiece home to an eclectic mixture of medical paraphernalia – a gas jar, a phrenology bust, the skull of an ape. In the corner beneath the window a cage of rats squeaked and rustled.

Will ran a finger across the rim of a picture frame. 'Dust an inch thick,' he muttered.

'So?'

'And what are these black blobs on the hearth?'

'I can't remember,' I said.

We heard Dr Bain thumping about overhead. I began to wonder whether he would return with a mirror after all. Perhaps he was preparing for bed. Will went over to the cupboard beside the fireplace and looked along the shelves, peering at the exhibits in their dusty jars. He held up a large, wide-necked bottle filled with a viscous yellow fluid. Inside, something bobbed, grey and wrinkled. 'A brain?' he whispered.

'Of course it's a brain,' I replied.

'Whose?'

'It belonged to the last person who looked through Dr Bain's things, and asked too many questions.'

'Ha ha,' said Will. He put the brain back on the shelf. He crouched down, and lifted a flap of old sacking. The sack had been on the bottom shelf of the cupboard for as long as I could remember. I never looked at it. I was always too busy. But now Will had extracted from it something I had never seen before – at least, not in a doctor's rooms.

It was a large curved hook, smooth and sharp, the handle ending in a rounded, wooden 'T' shape. 'What's this?' A long iron jemmy followed it, black and oily looking in the lamplight. There was also a mattock and a thick coil of mouse-nibbled rope. 'And these? What are these for?'

I ran my hand across the cold iron of the hook. The worn wooden handle fitted comfortably against my palm. 'I'm not sure,' I said.

'I've seen hooks like this before,' said Will. 'Butchers use them to haul carcasses.'

I had seen them too, but I didn't acknowledge it. 'Well.' I took the hook and the jemmy and put them back on the bottom shelf. I covered everything with the sack, just as it had been. 'That sack has not moved from that spot for ten years, at least. The dust down here tells us as much. I imagine Dr Bain can hardly recall what he used these things for.'

I dusted my palms and stood up, just as we heard Dr Bain's boots upon the stair. 'And we've more interesting things to attend to this evening than to waste our time speculating about Dr Bain's gardening tools.' But I knew, in my heart, that those tools were not used for gardening. I glanced at Will out of the corner of my eye. I was sure, almost, that he too knew their purpose.

Dr Bain appeared. He was holding a small, circular mirror, edged in gold and backed with mother of pearl – the kind a lady might carry in her reticule. It was quite at odds with the brutal, iron instruments we had just been looking at, and it appeared small and fragile in Dr Bain's large brown hand. The hook, and mattock, I could imagine would look far less incongruous.

'This mirror belongs to Mrs Catchpole,' I said. I had seen it in her hand many times, as she pored over her complexion when she thought no one was looking.

'Does it?' Dr Bain grinned. 'Never mind. I'm sure she has others. Now then, let's get on with it, shall we?'

I looked down at the six rectangular boxes, lined up before us on Dr Bain's work bench. "*These six things doth the Lord hate:*" I said, "*yea, seven are an abomination unto him. A proud look, a lying tongue, and hands that shed innocent blood—*"

'You sound like a lady almoner,' said Will. He put his hand on my shoulder. 'Shall we continue?'

I sucked a droplet of turpentine into the pipette and held it over the corner of the coffin where the writing was faintly visible. Slowly, gently, I squeezed the rubber teat. For a moment a muddy golden tear hung from the crystal tip. It swelled and trembled, and then it fell, spreading a perfect circle of oil into the parched paper lining. 'Pass me the mirror,' I said. 'Quickly now. And the magnifying glass.'

❧

The coffins yielded no more to us that evening. The bandages remained nothing other than strips of dirty cloth; the boxes that held them no more than a crude assemblage of roughly cut boards; the dolls slivers of kindling wrapped in string. Once we had read the words, revealed by a single droplet of turpentine, I had not the heart to look at them further. Dr Bain seemed relieved; Will perplexed.

'But there's another box,' he said. 'Another box with writing inside. Fragments, admittedly, but words nonetheless. Aren't you curious?'

I shook my head. 'Not now, Will.'

'I think it's time for Sorley's,' said Dr Bain briskly. 'Come along, gentlemen.'

I nodded. My mind was filled with only one thing: the name, and the date, which we had found in the coffin.

'*Elizabeth Maud*,' said Dr Bain, pulling his coat on. 'Who might that be?'

'And the date,' said Will. '*18th July 1822*. I can think of no significant event that occurred on that day. Does it mean anything at the hospital? Or would we be correct to assume that it was torn from some old case notes?'

'The latter, I think,' said Dr Bain.

'1822. That was a long time ago.'

'Twenty-four years.' I was determined to say something, even though my throat was dry, and my words felt strange in my mouth. *Elizabeth Maud. 18th July 1822. Elizabeth Maud* . . . I could sense Will's gaze resting upon me and I glanced up. He smiled, his blue eyes grave, worried. I looked away and caught sight of myself in the over-mantel mirror. My eyes were bloodshot, my cheeks like whey, my birthmark a gash of strawberry-coloured skin about my eyes. Once, when I was young, I had tried to rid myself of that hideous stain. Whilst my father was on the wards I had attached half a dozen leeches to my face in an attempt to drain the area white. He had returned to find me crouched behind the apothecary table. The leeches, speedily engorged, had slipped off. But the bites had continued to ooze, as they always did, so that the blood ran in thick crimson ribbons down my cheeks, over my fingers and onto my collar.

My father's expression was stony. 'Clean yourself up, Jem,' he had said. 'Before someone sees you.'

But no one had seen me. No one ever saw me. I was hidden from the world behind that birthmark as surely as if I had died on the day of my birth and someone other substituted in my place. My nativity was a source of sorrow and regret, never to be acknowledged or noted. But I knew its date, and I alone had marked its passing for twenty-four years. The 18th of July 1822 was a day I would never forget. It was the day I killed my mother; the day she exchanged her life for mine. Her name was Elizabeth Maud Flockhart.

❈

I had no memory of my mother, and there was no portrait, no miniature or sketch, to allow me to trace my features in hers. But where art failed, science succeeded: an image of her pregnant belly graces the pages of Dr Sneddon's anatomical paper on the *gravid uterus* like a ripe pear in a recipe book. Sliced open, a dead baby is visible curled within. She was sketched by Dr Sneddon himself – a fat apoplectic surgeon with meaty fingers and a surprisingly light touch with the ink and watercolours – and published for all to see in the *London Chirurgical Review* the autumn after she died.

The babe in her womb was my brother. No one could say when, or why, his tiny heart stopped beating, but it was clear that I had grown alongside his corpse for months. Beside my brother, who looked as pale and shapeless as a nub of coral, the doctor had drawn a large tear-shaped void. This space *I* had occupied, lying back on crimson cushions getting as fat as a grub.

Appalled by the living succubus fate had handed him in exchange for his wife and son, my father sent me to a wet nurse in the country. The woman looked after me well, and the time passed quickly enough. When I returned some seven years later, Dr Sneddon was dead. In my absence, I had been referred to only as 'the child', so that no one could remember which of us had survived, or what my name was.

'Jem,' my father said when, at last, he summoned me home. 'That's your name.'

'Jemima,' I corrected him. '*You* are Jem. Mr Jeremiah Flockhart, Apothecary to St Saviour's Infirmary.'

He shook his head. 'Jem,' he repeated. '*That's* your name now, mind you remember it. It takes a man to run this apothecary, and man you must be. You'll have cause to thank me one day.'

Apart from my eyes, which they say are green like my mother's, I looked just like him – I had his coarse hair, large bony hands and square shoulders. Over time I developed his mannerisms – if I was anxious I tugged my ear as I talked; I stood straight as a reed and walked with a long stride; and in the evening I sat before the fire with my legs stretched out before me. I became tall and lean. I was without grace or beauty; I had no use for the former, and the latter was never my prerogative.

Why did my father not marry again? Why did he not start another family to get the male heir all men want? I asked him many times. The answer, when he gave it, was always the same, though I could make no sense of it. It was because he was afraid. I should be afraid too, he said, though he would never tell me what I should fear, or why.

❦

Walking to the chop house on Fishbait Street I had little to say. Dr Bain too appeared preoccupied. He seemed nervous, repeatedly glancing back the way we had come as though expecting at any moment to feel a hand upon his shoulder. I saw him put his fingertips to his forehead, gingerly touching the moist cut at his hairline and its surrounding bruise. No doubt his run-in with Dr Catchpole and Dr Magorian had unsettled him. But his uneasiness was infectious, so that in the end I too turned and looked back. I stopped. Was that a shadow I could see at Dr Bain's door: tall and black and hooded with darkness? But then the fog ebbed and billowed, and the shadows swirled – and dissolved.

Dr Bain and I exchanged a glance. 'Were you expecting someone?' I said.

He shook his head.

We passed the wrought iron gates to the hospital, the

grubby yellow glow of a candle visible through the window of the porter's lodge. Further along, a line of ragged children were huddled together against the infirmary wall, beneath them the iron ventilation gratings of the furnace room. There were often children lying on the gratings. They slept there, wrapped up in sacks and old newspapers like bundles of rubbish. The porter tried to move them along, but they always came back again. Dr Bain knew each of them by name. He was often seen with a line of them following him down the road to the pie shop at the end of St Saviour's Street. Dr Magorian was not so charitable. It threatened to engulf us all, he said, that tide of human misery and degradation. To leave them to die of cold and hunger would be a kindness, as the poor were so numerous that it was impossible to go anywhere without, quite literally, falling over them. Not two streets away from St Saviour's lay the children's neighbourhood: Prior's Rents, a savage colony of blackened decayed tenements teeming with the most wretched examples of humanity. Their corpses filled St Saviour's churchyard to bursting, and provided Will Quartermain with his ghastly work.

The children's ringleader was a lad called Joe Silks – a snitcher of handkerchiefs by trade. He had appeared amongst the ragged children about two years earlier, and, after a series of scraps and brawls, had succeeded in assuming a leadership role. 'Dr Bain!' Joe's rough-edged voice cried out from amongst a mound of greyish rags as we drew close. 'Dr Bain, there's a man what's lookin' for you.'

'But I've been in all evening, Joe,' replied Dr Bain. 'I didn't hear anyone at the door.' He rooted in his pocket and tossed a shilling towards the bundle of rags. For a moment it glittered as it spun, caught in the lamplight like a moth in the moonlight. And then a bruised and bony arm flashed out, and deftly snatched the coin from the air.

'No,' said Joe, more vocal now that he had been rewarded. 'No one *knocked* on yer door. But 'e looked. Looked right in! I seed 'im with my own eyes, just *lookin'.*'

'Who was it?' I said.

Joe shook his head. 'I din't see *that,*' he said. 'But the fog's up, so small wonder. Night like this? P'raps it were the Abbot.'

'The Abbot?' said Will. 'The ghostly Abbot?' The dampness of the night must have been eating into his bones for I saw him shiver. 'Where? When?'

'Lookin' in Dr Bain's window, like I said,' said Joe. A cab rattled past. The fog was lifting, and despite the darkness of the night we could now distinguish the outline of the houses on the opposite side of the road.

'How did you see anyone at Dr Bain's window when the fog was so thick?' I said.

'I were walkin' past, weren't I?' said Joe. 'I were just comin' back from mindin' me own business and I passes the doctor's gaff an' I sees 'im there. Standin' outside, 'is face pressed almost to the glass. You 'ad the shutters open, din't you? Don't know 'ow you din't see 'im yourselves.'

'Then what happened?' said Dr Bain.

'Saw me watchin' 'im and 'e scarpered. Quick as you like.' The boy's eyes were sharp in his dirty face. 'Worth another shillin', ain't it?'

'Two shillings if you saw where he went?' I said quickly.

'Easy.' Joe grinned, and gestured up at the great dark edifice of St Saviour's wall. 'He went in there!'

❧

It was after eleven by the time we emerged from the chop house. A plate of lamb cutlets and a few glasses of ale had restored Dr Bain's mood, and he winked at me and clapped his hands. 'Well, Jem,' he said. 'Fancy a little trip to Wicke Street? And how about you, Quartermain? Are you up for some entertainments? There are a few hours still left of the night.'

I had made my excuses so often, but tonight Dr Bain was not prepared to accept my refusal. 'If it's money you're worried about then don't. Don't worry. Tonight, it would be *my* pleasure to pay for *your* pleasure.' He clapped an arm about my shoulders. 'Come along now, gentlemen. Quick march!'

And that's how I found myself walking down Wicke Street arm in arm with Dr Bain and Will Quartermain. I had been to Mrs Roseplucker's with Dr Bain on a few occasions, though I did my best to avoid it. There were many such places nearer the hospital, but for some reason – familiarity, economy – this one was Dr Bain's favourite.

'Are you not tempted to look for a wife, Dr Bain?' said Will as we marched brothelwards through the thinning fog. I was surprised by his familiarity, but the ale and the darkness, and perhaps our destination, lent our little group an unexpected intimacy. 'A man of your age and profession usually is.'

'Are *you* not tempted, Mr Quartermain?'

'I'm only twenty-five,' said Will. 'I have plenty of time yet.'

'Whereas I am forty-five, and feel every day of it in my

bones.' Dr Bain sighed. 'Yes, sometimes I do think it might be time to settle down. Besides, Mrs Roseplucker has put her prices up, and I fear Mrs Catchpole may be developing expectations.' He smiled. 'And Eliza Magorian would be worth the sacrifice, don't you think?'

'Her father would never allow you near her,' I said. 'Not now. Have you forgotten already? Besides,' I added, 'you might have the pox.'

Mrs Roseplucker's house was at the top of Wicke Street. It was a tall town house, built during the Regency and plastered in a scabrous layer of peeling white stucco. A lamp burned in a downstairs window but the rest of the place was engulfed in smoggy darkness. At the far end of the street I could make out the shape of a stationary hansom, but, despite the usual popularity of the establishment, other than that there was no one about. Gentlemen customers came in through the front door, but were let out at the back, so that there was little chance of them meeting one another.

The door was opened by Mr Jobber, a gross, silent man with flabby cheeks, who rarely stepped out of the shadows long enough for one to appreciate anything more about him than his air of menace and his gigantic size. He sat in a curtained cubby-hole little bigger than his own dimensions, located behind the door. His purpose was to let men in, to ensure there was no trouble upstairs, and to make sure they left quickly via the back entrance once they had done what they came to Wicke Street to do. And no one ever argued about payment when Mr Jobber could be heard breathing in the shadows.

'Good evening, sir!' cried Dr Bain. He stepped swiftly past the vast bulk of Mr Jobber's greasy waistcoat, and

strode down the hall into the parlour. Will seized my arm
in the gloom.

'I have never been to a . . . a brothel,' he hissed. 'What
shall I do?'

'You're a man, aren't you?' I said. 'I'm sure you'll think
of something.'

'But what about you? What in heaven's name do *you* do
here?' He looked at me strangely. I could see that he was
still a little drunk. All at once I was certain that he knew
who and what I was. He *knew*! How could he?

'What's it to you?' I snapped. 'I do as I please, just like
any other man.'

'Of course,' stammered Will. 'I didn't mean—'

'Come along,' I said. Then I saw his face. He looked
almost tearful. I knew I had looked the same on my first
visit to such a place. But we were here now, and were
both obliged to disport ourselves as best we could. 'Since
you ask,' I muttered, 'I don't especially want to be here
either.'

Will followed me into the parlour. Before us, sitting by
the fire in a straight-backed chair, was Mrs Roseplucker.
She was reading a greasy, well-thumbed copy of *Crimes of
Old London*, and appeared not to have noticed our arrival,
though I knew from experience that very little escaped
her notice. She was well over fifty years old but she was
powdered and rouged like a Regency courtesan. Her
dress was a brazen crimson monstrosity, ragged with torn
lace and blotched here and there with sinister dark stains.
Her head was crowned with a giant wig of dark frizzy curls,
upon which her widow's cap was jauntily perched, like a
crow caught in a thicket. The creases in her face had
caught her powder in floury drifts and the vermilion

grease she applied to her lips had leeched into the surrounding wrinkles, so that her mouth looked as though it had been darned onto her face with coarse red wool. The room was lighted by dim yellow lamps, the walls painted a visceral plum colour and hung with crude paintings depicting scenes of elaborate congress. The place was boiling hot – perhaps as an incentive to go somewhere else and remove one's clothes – the atmosphere musty and sweetish. I recognised the reek of opium – along with some other things: cardamom and cloves, and an underlying whiff of camphor, against the moths.

There were two girls lolling on chairs, one dark, one red-haired. Their dresses were low on their shoulders, as though the merest yank at the hem would cause the flimsy garments to slip to the ground. They stood up as we walked in, and I watched them in the mirror over the fireplace as they dragged the smiles onto their faces.

Dr Bain greeted Mrs Roseplucker cordially enough. She knew his requirements by now, even if she pretended not to know his name. 'Any of the girls available, Mrs Roseplucker?' he said.

Mrs Roseplucker indicated the two young trollops. 'New girls, sir. Virgins.'

Dr Bain smiled. 'They will be perfect for my companions. But where's Lily? I would like Lily tonight.'

Mrs Roseplucker nodded. She reached out and tugged on a bell-pull. Then she turned to me, her loose-rimmed eyes taking in my stony expression, my dusty clothes and red mask, and her smile vanished. She remembered me, I could tell. How could she forget?

I stared closely at the two girls. Neither of them displayed any obvious signs of disease, though what might lie beneath their skirts was another matter. I already knew about Mrs Roseplucker – the fix of her eye, the gentle rhythmic nodding of her head from the flaccid heart valves of advanced syphilis. 'The madam has the pox,' I had whispered in alarm to Dr Bain the first time he brought me to the place. 'Did you notice?'

'I'm not interested in the madam,' he had replied. 'I'd no more have her than I would Dr Graves.' He laughed. 'But what's life without a little risk?'

Now, one of the 'virgins' approached me. 'Would you like to come through?' She smiled, revealing crooked teeth. She must have been no more than sixteen years old and although her mouth was painted and her cheeks were rouged it was clear that she was tired out. Dark circles were visible beneath her eyes, even under her white make-up. She put up a hand to tweak her curls. Her fingers bore calluses – old ones, gradually softening, but calluses nonetheless. She had been a seamstress once, perhaps not all that long ago. I turned to speak to Dr Bain, but he had paid Mrs Roseplucker, and was being led towards the stairs by a tall blonde girl who had been summoned by the bell.

Beside me, Will was sitting stock still, his stove-pipe hat on his knees, his eyes fixed fearfully on the carpet in front of him. The red-haired virgin came over to sit beside him. I caught a whiff of sweat and, beneath the scent of cologne that still clung to her from the previous customer, something more briny and visceral. I saw Will's nostrils flare as he smelled it too. He squeezed his eyes shut, and I saw his knuckles turn white as he gripped the rim of his hat. Perhaps, by the time I saw him next, he would have torn it clean off.

'Never mind 'im,' whispered the ex-seamstress. 'Annie'll look after 'im.' She took my hand and led me to the stairs.

✦

Outside, the fog had closed in on us once more. The window of the girl's room was loose and I was sure the air within had a brownish tinge to it, as though the fog had somehow managed to gain ingress. I stood for a while, the dusty crimson curtains drawn back, looking out at the night. Sometimes I could distinguish a lamp, a dim beacon in a great grey-brown ocean, sometimes I could make out nothing. It was as though we were lost inside some gigantic liquid organism.

'I hope you clean yourself out afterwards,' I said without turning round. 'Between customers, I mean.'

'Course.' She sounded bored. She probably was.

'What do you use?'

'Soap an' water.'

I shook my head. 'That's not enough.' I pulled a scrap of paper from my pocket and a stub of pencil. 'Can you read?'

'More or less.' She lay down on the bed, her head propped on her hand. She saw my gaze drift down to where her breasts bulged above the rim of her corset and she ran her fingers across the white skin of her décolletage. I could not help but follow the gesture with my eyes. With a quick movement, she pulled out both her breasts. She was slim and dark-haired, like Eliza, her breasts small and pointed. All at once my breathing felt shallow, constrained. What would happen if I touched her? What if I ran my fingers across her soft, warm flesh, took her nipple in my

113

mouth or buried my face, my ugly blighted face and my loneliness, between her thighs? Would she laugh? Would she push me away? She would do anything I asked, I knew, for Dr Bain had paid Mrs Roseplucker well. All at once the atmosphere in that small dark room seemed to be made up of nothing but the panted breath of a hundred fucking men. Was I no better? I closed my eyes. 'You wantin' somethin' or not?' she said.

'No,' I replied. 'But thank you.' I handed her the piece of paper, upon which I had written the following words:

2pt hot water
Half pt vinegar
Tablespoon each of:
Peppermint
Comfrey
Camomile
Wintergreen
Sage
Pennyroyal

'Make it up, as if it were tea,' I said.

'I drink it?' She looked appalled.

'You clean out your cunny with it,' I said. 'It'll wash everything away, and soothe the skin. You've got something to use, I suppose. A rag, or a sponge or something?'

I was surprised to see her blush. 'Yes. Mrs Roseplucker makes us plunge. She wants a clean house.'

'Mm,' I said. I snatched back the paper and scribbled a few more words onto the list. 'I can give you some wild carrot seeds too.'

'What for?'

'To eat. You don't want a child, do you?'

A smile ticked at the corners of her mouth. 'Carrots don't stop babies.' She spoke slowly, as if talking to an idiot.

'Not *carrots*,' I said irritably. 'Wild carrot seeds. They can prevent conception. I'm assuming you'd rather not ply your trade with a baby at your breast?'

She held up her hands and gestured about her at the lurid wallpaper, the ghastly prints – copies of those downstairs in the parlour – the greasy-looking bed sagging in the centre of the room like a foundering ship. Her smile had vanished. 'Bring a child into this? No, sir. Not ever.'

'Well then. I'll give you the seeds, and you must chew them well. You must make up the rest of the ingredients into a wash and keep it beneath your bed. Use it after every man.'

'An' how much will all this cost?' she said. 'Mrs Roseplucker ain't *that* gen'rous. Got to pay for the room an' the sheets bein' washed and keep myself nice for me gentlemen.'

'Well, you won't be making Mrs Roseplucker any money at all if your face is eaten away with the pox,' I said. 'Come to the apothecary, St Saviour's Apothecary, and I'll give you the stuff myself.' I wondered what my father would say if he found that I was inviting prostitutes to the place and handing out prophylactics for free. I sighed. Why was I bothering? There were so many of them, Mrs Magorian never tired of telling me, so many girls who had 'fallen'. It was a hopeless situation.

'Is there no other work you could do?' I said gently. I knew the answer already.

'What? Like bein' stuck in a fact'ry, or spending all day

workin' me fingers raw stitchin' up gowns for rich ladies?'
She snorted. 'There's not much leisure in *that*, and less
money too.'

'I suppose so,' I said. The girls in the foul ward said the
same, even as they spat a tooth, and a mouthful of
blackened saliva, into the ward privy. What choice did
they have? Virtue was a useless ideal, and those who
espoused it would never be obliged to trade theirs in.

The girl grinned up at me. How young she was. Little
more than a child, really. 'You're nice,' she said. 'You're
not like most of 'em. But you're almost out o' time. D'you
want a go? Take it slow, like. No extra charge.'

I shook my head.

'No?' she looked surprised. 'But you must want
somethin'.' And then, almost to herself: 'They always want
somethin'.' She frowned, as though suddenly afraid she was
being gulled into trustfulness prior to some monstrous
violation. 'Who are you anyway?' she cried, rearing up
before me on the bed.

'Me?' I laughed, and slipped my coat back on. 'You'd
never believe it.'

At that moment there came a great banging from
downstairs. I listened. I recognised that voice. Surely it
wasn't—

'Thank you for your time, miss. And don't forget to
come for your herbs.' I flung open the door and burst out
onto the landing.

A familiar figure was standing at the top of the stairs.
Her eyes were red rimmed; her hair and dress beaded
with moisture from the fog. She looked about, staring at
one door, and then another as though hoping she might
see through them. Most unexpected of all, however, was

the fact that in her hand she carried a heavy stick. I recognised it as the same stick Dr Catchpole had used earlier in the day to beat Dr Bain over the head. As I appeared before her she flinched and raised it as if to strike me too. Her expression was wild, and despite my singular appearance – there was no one else in London who looked quite the way I did – it was clear that, for a moment at least, she had no idea who I was.

Behind her, at the foot of the stairs, a commotion had broken out. I peeked past. Mr Jobber was stretched out before the front door like some monstrous draught excluder. He appeared to be quite insensible. I could hardly believe it – had the gigantic Mr Jobber been felled by the diminutive Mrs Catchpole? Mrs Roseplucker was crouched over Mr Jobber's recumbent body, jabbering incoherently through her loose crimson lips, and fanning his face with her dog-eared copy of *Crimes of Old London.*

'What did you do to him?' I whispered.

'Who? That fat man?' Mrs Catchpole frowned. 'He wouldn't let me in. Said I had no business here. So I struck him on the jaw with my husband's cudgel. Down he went.' Mrs Catchpole giggled. '*All the king's horses and all the king's men, couldn't put Humpty together again.*' She turned her empty blue eyes upon me, her expression suddenly appalled. 'What place is this?' she cried. 'Is he here? Is Dr Bain here? You are keeping him against his will, he'd never come to a place like this himself. James!' she cried suddenly. 'James!'

'You know exactly what sort of a place this is, madam,' I said. 'And you know that Dr Bain it quite capable of making his way here without my help.'

'And where is he? I know he's here somewhere. I followed him. I followed you all!'

'Dr Bain is behind one of these doors,' I said. I wondered whether to add the word 'fornicating' but decided against it. Instead, I said 'Mrs Catchpole, are you sure you want to see him now?'

Mrs Catchpole crept closer. She licked her lips with the tip of her tongue. 'He loves me,' she whispered. She giggled once more and her fingers flew to her mouth, as if she were a child who has uttered a secret. 'He's going to take me away with him. Somewhere far away. I have packed my trunk. It's downstairs.' She stared down at her arms in surprise. 'Where's my coat?' She frowned. 'Did I leave it at home?'

Downstairs I could hear shouting now. Mr Jobber had regained consciousness and was rising to his feet. Mrs Catchpole looked behind her as, goaded onwards by a jabbering Mrs Roseplucker, the gigantic Jobber began mounting the stairs. His breath gusted in and out like a labouring steam locomotive. Suddenly, there came the sound of something being thrown violently at the front door. The entire house seemed to shake beneath the blows, until all at once the door burst open. Outlined against the fog was a tall thin figure with a frothing white neckerchief. Dr Catchpole stalked into the house. He pushed past Mrs Roseplucker, and Mr Jobber, and bounded up the stairs.

'Annabel,' he said, approaching his wife. 'Come home, my dear.'

'You!' Mrs Catchpole swiped her stick through the air. Her husband neatly side-stepped her (somehow managing to avoid falling back down the stairs) and seized her wrist.

In a moment he had removed the stick. He tossed it aside, swept her up into his arms and began to carry her back down towards the open front door.

'Get out of my way, you fool,' he cried to Mr Jobber. There was a moment of burlesque upon the stairs, as Mr Jobber attempted the impossible and tried to flatten himself against the wall to allow Dr Catchpole to pass. Mrs Catchpole's shoe became caught on Mr Jobber's waistcoat and her head banged against the wall. Dr Catchpole swayed upon the stairs. There was a great creaking of aged treads and the banister groaned. One of the pornographic prints was swept aside by Mr Jobber's massive shoulder, and sent crashing down the stairs. And all the while Mrs Catchpole was talking and talking, how much Dr Bain loved her, how they would go away together, how she had packed her trunk . . .

The front door banged, and there was silence.

Chapter Five

❧

The morning was fair – clear and bright with a stiff breeze blowing. It came from the east, gathering with it the stench of the vinegar works and the brewery, though the yeasty acidic reek was better than what usually passed as fresh air. The sunlight streamed in through the apothecary windows. My father seemed stronger. I had made him drink plenty of water, and had dosed him with iron tonic. He was at the work bench, seated (his only concession to poor health) with the pestle and mortar before him. Mrs Speedicut was sitting beside the stove, her mug of coffee in her hand.

'Out late were you, Mr Jem?' she said.

'Where's Will? I mean Mr Quartermain?'

'Oh, "Will", is it?' said Mrs Speedicut. 'Very familiar, aren't we? Very friendly with one o' them what's going to raze us to the ground.'

'It's not his idea, Mrs Speedicut,' I said. How tedious she was.

'He's gone out,' said my father. 'Said he had something he wanted to speak to Dr Bain about, but Dr Bain's not usually in today.' He shrugged. 'He went out anyway.'

'Did he?' I said. I wondered what was on Will's mind. Last night, after we left Mrs Roseplucker's, he had been very quiet. He had not spoken all the way back to St Saviour's, and then had got into bed with barely a word. Despite my original resentment about him sleeping in my room, I had to confess to being rather disappointed. Had he not wanted to go over the events of the day? What we had found in the coffins? The dramatic appearance of Mrs Catchpole at the brothel? I had scrambled down the stairs and thrown open Mrs Roseplucker's door just in time to see Dr Catchpole trying to stuff his wife into a carriage. But she had twisted out of his grasp and bounded off into the fog. Where had she gone? Had she been located? Where was she now? I found I was excited to be sharing, and had pushed back the screen in order to facilitate the anticipated whispered conversation. But Will had turned his face to the wall and said nothing.

'I see Mrs Catchpole's been taken to Angel Meadow Asylum,' remarked Mrs Speedicut, as if reading my mind.

'What?' I gaped. 'But I—'

'Saw her meself this morning.' Mrs Speedicut shook her head, and rammed a wad of baccy into her pipe. 'Could hardly believe it. Her face at the window of that carriage, all wild and bloated, and her hair all over the place, and the screaming and crying and Dr Catchpole trying to keep her calm. They were driving that fast—'

'Perhaps you were mistaken,' I said. 'If they went by so fast. Perhaps it was someone else—'

She looked at me strangely then. 'I know who I saw.'

'I'm afraid it's true, Jem,' said my father. 'Dr Hawkins was in earlier. He confirmed it.'

'Course it's true,' said Mrs Speedicut. 'And you know who's to blame, don't you?' She clamped her jaws about her pipe and drew in a cloud of smoke. The bowl gurgled. 'The truth will out,' she muttered. 'Sooner or later. And *then* you'll see.'

❦

When I came back from the morning ward rounds Will was still not back. My father was still at his work bench, the leech tank and a series of glass jars before him. 'Can't you stop, Father, even for a minute?' I asked.

'No.' He looked up at me over the rim of his glasses, a pair of leech tongs in his hand. 'Gabriel has vanished. Have you seen him?'

'Not since yesterday,' I said.

'Hm.' He watched me for a moment. 'You look tired,' he said. 'Are you? Did you sleep?' His voice was sharp.

'I have no trouble sleeping, Father,' I replied, though, truth be told, I had had a restless night. 'What was my mother like?' I said suddenly. 'You never speak of her.'

My father stared at me for a moment. 'She was nothing like you, you may be sure of that.'

'I know,' I said. 'I know that.'

He plucked a leech from the tank and plopped it into a glass jar. 'Then why did you ask?'

I cleared my throat. Should I tell him that I had found her name, and the date of my birth, written inside a model of a coffin? Should I say that I feared he might die, and then the only person who knew her, the only person who could tell me who she was, would be gone and I would never know? I shrugged, feeling my father's gaze resting upon me. Should I ask how she died? Whether she had known she'd had a daughter? I had so many questions, and yet I had never asked them. I felt the blood beating in my face. Before me, my father seized another leech. It writhed, black and shining in the sunlight, caught between the dull metal tips of the tongs.

Once, some years ago, I had crept into my father's room. The bed he had shared with my mother, the bed I had been born in, was against one wall. He had few clothes, other than a weakness for silk neck ties, and there was little else there but a marble-topped washstand set out with soap and razor, ewer and basin; a chest of drawers and a tall mahogany-framed dressing mirror. Beneath the window was an oak trunk. Inside it, folded neatly on a bed of lavender, was a dress. It was made of a heavy cotton fabric, olive green in colour, sprigged with cream and red and flecks of blue. In the drab, comfortless walls of my father's room the colours of that dress had glowed like springtime. It had belonged to my mother; the only thing of hers that he'd kept. Her locket, and wedding ring, had been buried with her.

My father never mentioned the dress. *I* never mentioned it, but I had always known it was there. The purple bracts of lavender had scattered about the floor as I lifted it out of its hiding place. The dress had smelled of flowers, and slightly of mildew, and I held it against myself and stood before the mirror. How small she had been – no bigger than Eliza. No wonder the act of giving birth to one so tall and spindly as I had ripped her insides apart.

I had pressed the fabric to my face. Could I smell her?

Could I imagine her arms about me? Would she have loved me for what I was – her daughter, no matter how disfigured, no matter how ugly, how blemished beyond repair by that hideous scarlet mask? But what purpose was there in such thoughts? I had taken her life – and perhaps my brother's too. My father had decided on the punishment: I must live out my life as a man in a woman's body.

I sat on my father's bed then, the dress crumpled in my lap, staring at my own reflection in the mirror. Who was I? I was no woman, with my short hair and long stride, but I was no man either. What joys were denied me? Childbirth and motherhood? The care and comfort of a man? But childbirth brought with it the risk of death. And as for a husband – who would have me, so unsightly as I was, and so schooled in the freedoms and sovereignty of men? Nor could I be a husband, that much was clear. But there was one person whom I loved with the strength of man and woman combined. I knew I would never be able to tell her. I folded the dress as neatly as I could, and put it back in the chest.

My father still watched me, his face stony, the leech in his hand squirming from side to side. *Was she anything like me, Father? Would she have been proud of me? Did she hold me in her arms?* But I said nothing.

He plopped the leech into another glass jar and turned back to the tank. 'Go out, Jem,' he said, his voice expressionless. 'Go out and find your Mr Quartermain and leave the past where it is.'

❧

I found Will sitting on the roof of the brewhouse, looking out across the churchyard. The brewhouse was a low, single-storey building that backed onto St Saviour's churchyard. The roof was flat, and the chimney provided protection from the wind. I often went up there myself when I wanted to get away from the hospital but still be in the midst of everything. The mounded greensward of the churchyard gave the illusion of countryside, as long as one did not turn one's head very much.

'You were out early,' I said.

'I wanted to speak to Dr Bain.' His back was against the chimney stack so that he was sheltered from the wind, his face towards the graveyard. On his lap, he had a sketch book. He had drawn the church – a low-slung building whose porch and nave appeared to have sunk into the earth. The place had once sat proud of its surroundings, but over the centuries the ground had gradually risen up; packed with the numberless dead, until it was no more than twelve inches below the windows. These days, parishioners entered the church by descending a short flight of steps, cut into the corpse-filled earth.

'I thought I should make a sketch before the job begins,' he said.

I sat down beside him. 'There are fewer bodies in there than you might think,' I said. I told him about the rains and the terrible tangle of bones caught at the gates. 'They were taken away. More have been added since, but not so many as there were.'

'I fear your childish memory deceives you,' he replied. 'What seemed like a multitude was, in fact, no more than a dozen or so, so the sexton told me. How many might be left beneath the earth? Two hundred? Five hundred? A thousand? Perhaps even more than that. The dead have been shoved into that patch of ground for seven hundred years.' He shook his head. 'I can think of no worse undertaking than this. And the ground is largely clay. That alone leads me to suspect the worst. Thank you for your attempts to make the task seem more . . . agreeable, but it's still a ghastly job.' He shrugged. 'Anyway, I went to see Dr Bain, and then I came here to take a look at the place.' He put his face up to the sun. 'It's warm on this roof, and quiet. I got up by climbing on the churchyard wall.'

'I know,' I said. 'It's my place too. Why did you want Dr Bain?' I added. I knew I was intruding, but I couldn't stop myself. 'Is it about last night?'

Will blushed. He rubbed his inky fingers on his lapel.

'You went with that girl, didn't you? The red-haired one who looked like a consumptive?'

He nodded. 'But I couldn't—' He closed his eyes. 'I don't know why. I felt nothing at all. Nothing. I was . . . repelled. Is that . . . is that usual?'

'I don't know,' I said. 'But I spent twenty minutes looking out at the fog and advising mine how to avoid the pox. What do you make of that?'

Will laughed. He sounded relieved. 'I ended up showing mine card tricks,' he said.

'Did she enjoy it?'

'She seemed to.'

'I believe they always do,' I said. 'It's part of the job, to seem to enjoy anything.'

'Oh, this one really *did* enjoy it,' said Will.

'There!' I laughed. 'You sound *just* like a man now!'

Will's smile wavered. 'But I still couldn't bear to . . . So

I thought I might ask Dr Bain. He seems very experienced, and he's a doctor. He might know what's wrong.'

'There's nothing wrong,' I said. 'Not everyone's like Dr Bain, you know.'

'You, for instance?'

'Yes,' I said.

'But no one's quite like *you* though, are they?'

I said nothing. Then, 'So, did you see the doctor?'

Will turned back to his sketch. 'He wasn't in. The housekeeper said his bed hadn't been slept in either. She said he was probably out seeing a patient.'

'Well,' I said, 'perhaps he's back now.' I sprang to my feet and held out my hand to him. 'It's almost midday. Let's find out.'

❧

The clear skies and sharp wind were a relief after the thick brown fog. But whereas the fog concealed every-thing, the sunlight and the wind served to draw attention to the dilapidation of St Saviour's Street. Straw, grit, rags, dust, all blew from west to east past the infirmary gates and along the thoroughfare. The stuff that was too heavy to blow away – offal, vegetable matter, ordure – clogged the street, churned into ridges of putrescence by the wheels of passing vehicles. Each ridge was home to a fizzing cloud of flies, which rose when disturbed by the traffic. Maggots crawled lazily amongst the debris, and I was forever finding them on my boots. Still, I thought, at least the wind meant that the flies were less bothersome that day.

Dr Bain's house faced north. Even in the midday sun

the building was a tall, dark cliff face. I pulled the bell and waited. The room we had been in last night looked out at St Saviour's Street, the tiny rectangle of grass beneath its window a tangled patch of dandelions and plantain. The weeds were crushed: the plantain leaves hanging by their threads, the hollow stalks of the dandelions snapped and broken.

The door jerked open. The housekeeper was as tall as a man, and thickset like a prizefighter. She folded her wrestler's arms across her broad bosom. 'Doctor Bain's not in, sir. He sent me out last night and I've not seen him since.'

'Oh,' I said. And yet, if the doctor was not in then we might as well pick up the coffins and take them back to the apothecary. 'Well, might we come in, please? Mr Quartermain and I left something important in Dr Bain's front room last night.'

'That front room's locked,' said the housekeeper.

'I have a key. I would be grateful if you would let us through.'

The woman stared at me. I knew she wanted to say 'no'. She had never liked me – my birthmark unsettled her, I could tell. She looked at it continually, her face set in an expression of pity, disgust and horror. But I could also see that she was curious. Perhaps she might get to see what was in that locked room, with its shuttered windows and its strange sounds and smells. 'Well, Mr Flockhart, since it's you.'

She led us down the hall to the drawing room door. I could hear the rats rustling within, and I turned the key in the lock, and ushered Will inside as hastily as I could. 'We'll show ourselves out, thank you,' I said, and I closed the door before the woman could stick her nose in.

Dr Bain's parlour laboratory was as dark as a tomb. Last night we had worked with the shutters open. Clearly, Dr Bain had come into the room again after getting back from Mrs Roseplucker's as the shutters were now closed. The air felt cold, with the wind moaning in the chimney and the fire long since burned out.

I locked the door behind us. I knew my way around the place well enough and I negotiated the table, the piles of books and the cages to arrive at the window without falling over anything. Other than the anxious rustling of the rats, the room was eerily quiet. I folded back the shutters. A shaft of dusty yellow light sliced through the darkness.

Afterwards, I wondered whether I had paid enough attention to the state of the room. It was as muddled as ever – the screen against the wall hung with bloodstained aprons, the table littered with glassware and papers, the floor mounded with books – so that any additional disorder was hard to apprehend at a glance. Later, when I tried to visualise the room, my mind seemed powerless to focus. I was able to recall nothing but that dark shape, head thrown back, lips and teeth stained red, that lay before us on the hearth rug.

His eyes were open, and glassy; his skin livid, his expression rigid. His lips were uncommonly bright, tainted by the tincture of bloodroot, the residue of which coated the bottom of the glass that lay at his side. I lurched past the table and flung myself to my knees beside him. What had happened? What had he done? I tried to speak, to say his name, but my throat seemed to have constricted. My breath rasped. I was no stranger to death – I saw it every day and I knew it to be both brutal and commonplace

– but to find it here, now? If only I had come back with him after we left Mrs Roseplucker's. Dr Bain's mood was bleak when we left him. The appearance, and removal, of Mrs Catchpole had shaken him. He had slunk out of Lily's bedroom as the front door slammed, and I knew he had heard everything. He hardly spoke as we walked back to St Saviour's Street. If I had stayed with him, would things have turned out differently? What if we had not gone to Mrs Roseplucker's at all? But such thoughts are as pointless as they are wretched. Time moves forward, not back, and here I was, crouched in the half-light in Dr Bain's front room, Dr Bain's corpse before me. I felt the tears hot against my cheeks, and I could not stop them.

And then Will was beside me. He pulled me to my feet, and put his arms around me. My body felt rigid. Not since I was a child at the wet nurse, crying for the mother that would never come, for the father that didn't want me, had someone held me close. He smelled of pencil shavings and draughtsman's ink, and very faintly of spike lavender, against the moths. It brought me comfort, and for a moment I thought I understood why Dr Bain had so often hired the affections of Mrs Roseplucker's girls. I rested my head against his shoulder and closed my eyes. Perhaps, when I opened them, everything would be back to normal. But it wasn't. I looked down at Dr Bain.

'Who did this?' I whispered.

'Why, he did it himself,' said Will. 'Look at the glass. Look at his lips.'

I put my hands over my face. I could not bear to think of him dying, alone and in pain, perhaps calling out for me. For all his faults, Dr Bain had been a good friend. He had treated me as an equal. He had taken my part against

Dr Graves and Dr Catchpole many times; he had asked my advice, and sought me out as his companion. But those characteristics in him that I had loved – his irreverence, his lack of prejudice, his kindliness – had been over-shadowed in the minds of others by his vices – selfishness, venality, intellectual arrogance. How lonely I would be without him. How dull St Saviour's would seem. And how would I tell Gabriel? The lad would be distraught—

I took a deep breath to steady myself. All my life I had been master of my emotions, I would not let them get the better of me today. Besides, would crying bring Dr Bain back? Would such a display undo what had been done? Will's words circled in my brain. *Look at the glass. Look at his lips.* But the Dr Bain I knew would never make such a mistake. He would never experiment alone, could not possibly have drunk the stuff unwittingly, and would not dream of taking his own life. I took my hands from my face and surveyed the room.

'What is it?' said Will. 'What do you see?'

'Look,' I said. 'Look at the chairs.' I pointed to the chairs on either side of the fire. 'Do you notice anything about them?'

Will shrugged. 'They're just chairs. They were there yesterday. I assume they are always there.'

'Yes, but last night they were not quite as they are now. Don't you remember? You commented on them, in fact. "Why does he bother to have chairs if he has no intention of sitting on them?" They were loaded with books and papers.'

'Oh, yes,' said Will. 'Last night the papers and books were on the chairs. Now they are on the floor.'

'*Hastily* put on the floor. Almost flung there, in fact.

But look! One chair was cleared hurriedly, the books dumped onto the floor. The other—' I looked about. 'The other stack of books has been placed carefully on the table.'

'Meaning what?' said Will.

'Well, why might he do such a thing?'

'To sit down?'

'But the chairs were always stacked with books. He never sat in them.'

Will said nothing. I could see by the way he was looking at me that he thought I was mad. Dr Bain had inadvertently poisoned himself. Did not everything point to such a conclusion?

'It seems to me that Dr Bain tossed his books aside because he was anxious to make someone comfortable as soon as possible. The man had many faults, but he did not have bad manners. He had a guest last night, after he returned from Wicke Street. A guest he was at pains to seat quickly, and comfortably.'

'A woman?'

'Perhaps we can assume so. He might have been not quite so hasty to accommodate a man. But the *second* chair . . . If we follow our reasoning it was not so important that the second person be seated so hastily, so he put the books on the table.'

'Perhaps a man?' said Will.

'But then where would Dr Bain have been seated? Might we assume that the second chair was for the doctor himself?'

'What woman would visit a man, alone, in the dead of night?' said Will. 'A prostitute?'

I shook my head. 'He had just been to Mrs Roseplucker's.

And besides, would he throw his books to the ground for a trollop? No, Will, I think we might assume it was a respectable woman whom Dr Bain entertained last night, and a respectable woman who comes alone to a man's house late at night is a desperate one.'

We looked at one another. Mrs Catchpole? I could think of none more desperate. And yet, the last time we had seen her she was being bundled out of a bawdy house by her husband. I had seen her run away from him into the fog. Mrs Speedicut had seen her being dragged into Angel Meadow Asylum at dawn. Where had she been in the hours between?

'Look!' said Will suddenly. He bent down and plucked something from the ashes in the grate. It was one of the horrible dolls. Protruding from a mass of blackened rags, its face was even more hideous now that it was scorched and smeared with soot. Before us, the hearth was scattered with dried flowers. 'Why did he throw these onto the fire?'

'Perhaps he knew their meaning.'

'He said nothing about it last night.'

'And yet there *was* something bothering him. He knew *something* about them, and yet he would not say. You recall how obstructive he was?' I forced myself to look at Dr Bain's face. His lips were rigid, drawn back over his red-stained teeth, the flesh at his cheeks taut and waxy. There were signs of *rigor mortis*, that much was clear from the degree of rigidity in the limbs, but it was not yet widespread. He had been dead no more than ten hours, I was certain. The position of his arms – held close, as though he had died in some sort of paralysis, hands claw-like, the skin mottled pink and blue – spoke of asphyxiation, the failure of the internal organs, and a congestion of

133

the heart. Perhaps, if we cut him open as we had the poisoned dog, we might find a similar pathology. And yet there were no signs of the emetic and purgatory effect one might expect from bloodroot poisoning. I peered into his glassy eyes. The pupils were fixed, dilated, the whites tainted with purple splotches. I picked up the glass that lay against the edge of the hearth and held it up to the sunlight. Inside, the crimson residue glittered like rubies.

Chapter Six

⟡

A pair of orderlies loaded Dr Bain's corpse onto a stretcher and carried him across the road to the mortuary at St Saviour's. The police inspector came. On hearing that it was customary for the doctor to try out poisons on himself, and having seen the bloodroot tincture in the bottom of the glass, he asked no more questions.

I had my own ideas about Dr Bain's death, though I shared them with no one at St Saviour's. What could I do? There was a murderer amongst us, that much was clear. The less I said about it – at the moment at least – the better. What I had seen of Dr Bain's corpse told me that whoever had killed him had done so not on the spur of the moment, but with a calculated plan of action, and a will to deceive that had gone unnoticed by everyone but Will Quartermain and myself.

Dissection of the corpse was inevitable. Dr Bain had always claimed that anatomy was the first and most important means of medical inquiry and training, and, in the absence of any relatives or next of kin, Dr Bain's colleagues were keen to stress how certain they were that he would have donated his body to medical science. With ill-concealed relish, Dr Graves elected himself to perform the task. I asked if I might be present. The doctor made no objection. 'Dead, he is no better than anyone else,' he said. 'I hope you will not take it too badly to find it so.' The grin was back on his face. I could not bear to look at him.

As much as I felt that the world should stop and mourn its loss, everything continued as usual. The patients came and went, the ward rounds took place three times a day, the routine of St Saviour's did not alter. Will could no longer avoid the subject of his commission and the exhumation of the churchyard was scheduled to begin the following day. We walked in the sun across the uneven grassy mounds of the place. Here and there, the stones had sunk into the earth as the cheap wooden coffins and their occupants decayed beneath, causing the ground to sag. On occasion, the grass bowed slightly as we walked, as if the turf were laid over boards only inches below the surface.

I led him to the south side of St Saviour's church. Against the wall of the nave a crowd of daffodils jostled one another in the breeze. 'My mother's grave,' I said.

'Luckily for her she will not be dragged from the earth and taken off to some other place. The excavations will not come this close to the church building.' Will stepped up to the daffodils, and bent down to take a closer look. The headstone was blackened with soot, as was everything in the city, and the words hard to read. Nonetheless, her name, and the date of her death, could be made out easily. *Elizabeth Maud Flockhart. 18th July 1822.* He looked up at me. 'But that's—'

'I know.'

'You didn't say?'

'I didn't want to say. I have no idea why her name was in one of those coffins. I didn't want to talk about it. I don't want to talk about it now.'

'Did you recognise the handwriting? You must know the hand of every doctor in this hospital,' said Will.

'I do,' I replied. 'And I don't believe it was written by anyone currently at St Saviour's.'

'It was not your father's?'

'No.'

'The answer must lie in one of the other coffins,' said Will. 'There was writing inside another of them, as I recall.'

'It's a pity Dr Bain or his lady visitor – whoever she might be – threw them on the fire.'

I closed my eyes. For once, the sun was shining. Suddenly, I did not want to think about death, for all that we were crouched at my mother's graveside talking of Dr Bain. I knelt down and plucked a dandelion from amongst the daffodils. I had covered my mother's resting place with flowers, cramming the scanty earth with bulbs – snowdrops, crocuses, narcissi, tulips. In summer, the place was a bright tangle of herbaceous perennials; in winter, I had pansies, sweet William, polyanthus and Christmas rose. I paid no heed to the language of flowers, that maudlin and spurious search for meaning; instead, I sought nothing but life, bright and unstoppable, in every season.

Once, as a child, I had stretched out upon her grave, my eight-year-old limbs half hidden in the daffodils. How far beneath the ground was she? Did she know I was there? Was she looking down upon me from heaven? With the questions tumbling in my mind and the clouds racing overhead, I had fallen asleep in the sun. I woke up in my own bed, carried home – I assumed – by my father, though neither of us ever mentioned the subject. I knew he attended her grave, though I saw him rarely. I was sure he came only when he thought he might be alone. The following Saturday I had come across him on his knees there, plucking weeds from amongst the nodding blooms. He had seen me out of the corner of his eye, I was certain, but he did not speak to me. Instead, he put his back to me, turning his face to the earth where my mother lay, a silent rebuke for disturbing his solitude.

❧

A team of men arrived to begin work at the graveyard. The sharp, bright weather vanished and a cold persistent drizzle seeped from the leaden skies. The world was leached of colour, becoming a drab mixture of grey and black – black clothes, grey faces, sooty walls, dark pools of glistening mud reflecting the slate skies. Everything was blurred at the edges, as though the places we knew were somehow disappearing, being rubbed out, like a faulty drawing on an architect's plan.

Will assisted us as best he could in the apothecary in the morning, and then disappeared to St Saviour's churchyard to supervise the excavations. He directed the proceedings with accuracy and precision, marking out the ground with pegs and string, paring back the scanty grass as an anatomist peels back the skin of a corpse, scraping away the miserly top soil and mounding it up at the side of the path. The gravestones were plucked from the earth and stacked against the church wall. And all the while the rain poured down, drumming on the church roof, gurgling along gutters and spouting from drains. Under such a deluge, that half of the churchyard upon which Will and his team of labourers were working soon became a foul-smelling mire. The first layer of rotten coffins was no more than six inches below the surface, visible now, and projecting from the reeking mud like the timbers of a wrecked ship. Periodically, the earth belched wearily as its contents eased and shifted, forcing bubbles of stinking gas to the surface.

With the coming of the rain, the weather turned a little warmer. It was vital that the dissection of Dr Bain took place as quickly as possible. And so it was that two days after Will Quartermain and I had found Dr Bain on the hearth rug in his laboratory-parlour, his body was anatomised by his most jealous rival in front of a room full of students.

The air in the dissecting room was damp and chilly. As usual there was no fire – the last thing the dead needed was to be warmed up, and the living had to endure the cold if they did not want to be driven from the place by the stench of putrefaction. The room was north-facing, which allowed us to make the most of the brightness of the day without the heat and glare of direct sunlight. We wore coats and caps set aside for the purpose, with brown aprons on top. The smell of decay pervaded everything, leaching into the clothes and hair of those present, occupying every inch of space, so that even when there was no corpse in the room the place reeked of rotting flesh, of bowels and viscera, preserving spirits and the smells of sickness and disease. Only Dr Graves didn't notice or care. He wore the same clothes whether he was working in the anatomy room or not. The smell followed him everywhere.

That day, Dr Graves was ecstatic. He rubbed his hands together greedily and sharpened his knives with the relish of a butcher about to carve a Sunday roast. His face, usually so pale, was ruddy with excitement; his grin wider and more gleeful than ever. He moved quickly, bounding from one side of the slab to the other with such speed that some of Dr Magorian's uneaten sugar lumps sprang from his pockets and scattered about the floor. He did not even pause to pick them up.

I looked down at Dr Bain's body with sorrow. Not two days ago he had been full of life and joy, enthralling the students with his new and peculiar ideas, laughing at Dr Catchpole and Mrs Speedicut, welcoming Will and me into his home. He had been, to me, a genius, a rogue, and a friend. Now, he lay naked before those same students, their knives poised to slice him apart. Oh, how blithely we go about from day to day, with little thought to the miracle of life that allows us to do so; and how little dignity there is in death.

'The guts are the first to putrefy,' cried Dr Graves. 'We must remove them at once.' He took up his knife and slit Dr Bain from throat to navel. The students leaned forward, the wooden benches creaking beneath them.

Dr Graves was both thorough and speedy. In no time at all Dr Bain's head had been sawn off and set aside. The lips and tongue, still stained red with the sap of the bloodroot, gave it the appearance of a grotesque carnival mask. I noted down a number of interesting observations. Not least of them was the relish with which Dr Graves was undertaking his task. I had helped him at the dissecting table before – my knowledge of the human body, my attention to detail and my slim, strong fingers had been invaluable to Dr Graves in the preparation of numerous specimens. But today he worked like a maniac. It was as though he had resolved to obliterate Dr Bain, and was determined to slice him into his constituent parts as quickly and as definitely as possible.

I stepped forward. 'Dr Graves,' I said, hoping the interruption would stop his morbid gusto, at least for a moment. 'Are you happy with the verdict of bloodroot poisoning?'

'What?' Dr Graves paused in his labours about the rib cage. Sweat dripped from his brow. 'Oh!' he said. 'Yes, bloodroot it is.' He gestured at Dr Bain's severed head with the end of his bloody knife. 'There. You see? The tongue.' He bent to his task once more. 'The stuff is in the oesophagus too.'

'May I look?'

'By all means.' I heard the sound of ribs splintering, and he stood back from the corpse. He wiped his forehead with the back of his hand and beckoned the students. 'In fact, you may all come closer.'

One by one, Dr Graves asked the students to step forward so that they might peer into Dr Bain and admire the arrangement of his internal organs: the liver, heart, kidneys and spleen, the delicate bags of the lungs, the smooth slippery yards of intestines. Then, he selected certain individuals to remove those organs. The liver was placed in a bowl; the heart in another. The lungs, blackened with pipe smoke and years of city air, occupied a third. He asked them to touch and feel, to smell and taste. 'Use every sense,' he cried. 'Only then can you truly understand.' They gathered round to peer at the membranes, ligaments and musculature of the body cavity. Hidden from view for a moment, I slipped from my pocket a bundle of surgical knives Dr Bain had once given me. Removing the smallest and finest of these I set to work.

The heart was congested, choked with thick dark blood, which I knew to be a possible symptom of bloodroot poisoning. And yet still I was not convinced. There were other poisons that would result in the same congestion. And there was still the appearance of Dr Bain's face when we had found him – the paralysis about the lips, the dark splotches in the eyes. I *had* to be sure . . .

'Let us examine the brain,' cried Dr Graves. 'If we take the skull—'

I closed my eyes at the sound of the trepanning knife, trying to blot from my mind the knowledge of what was taking place at the dissecting table. While everyone was distracted, I slit open the pale muscular bag of the stomach.

They worked upon Dr Bain diligently. St Saviour's anatomy museum was extensive, and there was little in Dr Bain's corpse that was worth preserving for posterity. But his body parts were useful for the purpose of instruction and practice, and a number of students were keen to keep some of his organs for their own collections. Dr Graves wiped his hands on a dirty towel and rinsed his knives in a bowl of muddy red water as he handed Dr Bain over to the students. Soon, there would be nothing left of the man at all: the veins and arteries of his major organs

would be injected with coloured wax; the flesh stripped
from the muscles; the brain put into a jar of preserving
fluid, or sliced up like a cooked cabbage and divided
between the students so that they might each preserve a
cross-section. Finally, his bones would be boiled in a
gigantic copper vat Dr Graves kept for just such a purpose,
and strung together with wire. I was glad not to have to
stay in the place any longer. I had seen what I needed to
see, had proved what I wanted to prove. I excused myself,
and went to find Will.

He was standing on the top of the brewhouse, looking
out over St Saviour's churchyard, watching the excavations.
I climbed up to stand beside him. 'Dr Bain's lips and
tongue were stained with bloodroot tincture,' I said. 'The
tumbler at his side suggested that it was the last thing he
had touched. And yet, Dr Bain and I had already tested
the actions of the bloodroot. Why on earth would he
choose to test it again, and do so when he was alone? Last
time he tried it the stuff had almost killed him.'

'But he was *not* alone,' said Will. 'There was another
person with him.'

'Nonetheless,' I said. 'It still doesn't explain why he
would down a tumbler of bloodroot tincture all over
again. Besides, although it was on his lips and tongue, and
from what I could see it was also present in his throat and
the upper part of his oesophagus, I detected none of it in
the stomach. The stuff is clearly visible. I would be able to
see it if it were in the stomach.'

'Meaning what, exactly?'

'Meaning he did not *swallow* it,' I said. 'It was *introduced*
into the area – presumably by his executioner. Bloodroot
is highly visible. It would look like accidental death

– accidental bloodroot poisoning – if it were found in his mouth and throat. After all, the last notes Dr Bain made in his ledger were about the actions of bloodroot. But it was not accidental at all.'

'You mean he was already dead when the bloodroot was poured down his throat?'

'Dead or paralysed.'

'Paralysed?' Will looked alarmed. 'By what?'

'Something fast acting. Something that would have rendered him insensible, or at least unable to move or call out. Cyanide, perhaps, though I could smell nothing of bitter almonds when we found him. Aconite is more likely. It has no smell. It causes paralysis. It kills as soon as it is ingested and one doesn't need a large quantity of the stuff to achieve a result. It can even be absorbed through the skin.'

'And who might have access to such a substance?'

'Anyone, of course. This is a hospital. We're surrounded by surgeons and physicians, all of whom have access to it and are aware of its uses and applications. The apothecary, the herb drying room, the physic garden . . . it might have been got from any of those places, by almost anyone who was of a mind to find it.'

'Why on earth do you keep it,' said Will, 'if it's not a medicine?'

'But it is a medicine,' I said. 'In small doses, at least. Medicine and poison, life and death, the point at which one becomes the other isn't always easy to command.'

'Though there are plenty here who claim to have that skill,' said Will. He looked out at the graveyard once more. Already, the excavations had produced a great many corpses. How glad I was that the wind was blowing from the east that day. 'All these bodies,' he muttered, shaking his head. 'D'you think most of them spent their last days in St Saviour's Infirmary?'

'A good many.'

'Makes me wonder how many of them were killed by your so-called doctors.'

'Yes,' I said. 'As for our murderer, well, we are looking at the work of a doctor there too, I'm certain. The whole crime is too methodical, too clever, the knowledge required to kill, and to deceive in the killing—'

'Can we find out who? And why?'

'I'm sure we can,' I said. 'We are dealing with someone quick and clever, but they're not as quick and clever as you and I.' I meant what I said. And, even now that everything is over, and despite the terrible events that occurred, I still believe I spoke the truth that day. But confidence breeds complacency, and my assumption that we could not fail to uncover the truth, that we could outwit anyone, was callow and foolish. What a price I was to pay for my arrogance.

Chapter Seven

❧

Dr Bain's will was simple and straightforward: his property should go to Gabriel, once the lad was of age and had finished his apprenticeship; his library, and his anatomy museum, was left to me. But what was I to do with such a superabundance of medical books and museum pieces? I had no room for them at the apothecary. In the meantime, everything stayed where it was.

I went to look for Gabriel. I found him in the herb drying room, curled up on a blanket on a high shelf amongst the hop sacks, his face turned to the wall.

'Gabriel.' I put out a hand and touched his shoulder. He shuffled forward, moving away from me. 'I've brought you some food. Bread and cheese. And some of those pickled oysters you like from the whelk stall on Fishbait Lane.

'And look,' I said. 'I've brought you a treat.' I produced a large orange from my pocket. I pulled out my knife and began to peel the thing, slicing the skin from pole to pole. The oil burst from the ruptured pores in a zesty mist.

Gabriel sat up. His face was red and puffy, his eyes bloodshot. He sniffed, and wiped his nose with the cuff of his coat. His nose was raw from the piece of sacking he had been using for the same purpose. 'Don't you have a handkerchief?' I said. Standards had to be maintained, despite the forces of grief overwhelming us. I handed him mine. 'Keep it.'

We ate the orange sitting side by side, looking out of the gabled window at the city. The sky was an inky blue-black, flat and featureless. Before it, illuminated by a shaft of sunlight, the roofs shone black and silver, picked out sharply against the lowering rainclouds.

'You know you will still be our apprentice, Gabriel,' I said. 'You're part of our family. You always were, you know.'

Gabriel sniffed. 'Is it true what ol' mother Greedigut said? Is it true that Dr Bain was my father? I always thought he was, but I never liked to say it.'

'I think there's little doubt about it.'

'And about my . . . my mother.'

I could think of nothing to say. 'Well,' I said, hoping comradeship might serve, 'I didn't know my mother either.'

'But mine's all cut up,' said Gabriel. 'Mrs Speedicut said. How will God know where to find her, when the trumpet sounds, if she's all in bits in jars?'

'Look,' I said, wondering where on earth he had got such nonsense – the lady almoners, no doubt, 'everyone's in bits in the end. D'you think they're all waiting below ground, nice and clean in their Sunday best?' I shivered at the thought of that growing mound of stinking corpses excavated from the churchyard. 'She's better off in bits in jars, if you ask me.'

For a while we sat in silence. 'I saw the Abbot, you know,' said Gabriel. 'I saw the Abbot and I knew Dr Bain was goin' to die. I told him too and he took proper fright.'

'What?' I turned to the lad and seized him by the arm. 'What did you say?'

'I went to speak to Dr Bain after ol' Greedigut said those things,' said Gabriel. 'I tried to forget what she'd said, but I couldn't. I pretended I didn't mind, but I did. I wanted to know about my mother, what were she like? Did he love her? Did he care about her? Greedigut said he didn't care. I just wanted to know. So I went out when you and Mr Quartermain came back that night. It was late, but I knew Dr Bain would be back too. I was going towards Dr Bain's house when I saw this man—'

'Man?' I said. 'How do you know it was a man? Did you see his face?'

Gabriel shrugged. 'Who else might it be? You don't get women out at night in St Saviour's Street, leastways not respectable ones. Not when the fog's up neither. I didn't see his face, but I knew it was the Abbot – the one what Mrs Speedicut talks about.'

'That's a ghost story.'

'Is it?' Gabriel turned to me with sorrowful eyes. 'Well, I saw someone in a cloak and a hood in the fog. Standing outside Dr Bain's house. Still, and quiet. Just looking. *Watching.*'

'And then?'

'Then nuffink. I came along and he just vanished.'

'Vanished where?'

Gabriel shook his head. 'I didn't see.'

'And you saw Dr Bain? You spoke to him?' My voice was sharp, almost accusatory. Poor Gabriel, he was no longer enjoying the interview, but I could not stop now. 'Did you see Dr Bain the night he died?'

'Yes, yes, I saw him.'

'Did you go inside?'

'He wouldn't let me in. Said he didn't have time. Said he would talk to me in the morning, and I was not to listen to what Mrs Speedicut said about anything. Then I told him about the Abbot. Proper angry I was, and upset. I was *glad* to tell him the Abbot was watchin' him.' Gabriel looked at me, his face awash with tears. 'I told him he would die. That the Abbot was after him, and that meant he were a goner. I said I were *glad*—' he gave a muffled sob.

'I'm sure Dr Bain took it in his stride,' I said, more sharply that I intended. 'What happened next? That's more important.'

'He looked up and down the street, but there was only fog, thick as porridge. Told me to go home. Said he'd speak to me proper in the morning.' Gabriel blinked tearful eyes. 'Gave me a shillin' too. Even though I said those things.'

'What time was it?' I said. 'Did you see?'

'It were too dark and foggy to see, but I know it was after midnight. Dr Bain told me. "Go home, Gabriel," he said. "It's after midnight. Far too late for a lad like you to be out." I ran straight home.' He shivered. 'That night – the night Dr Bain died – the street was so cold. Soon as I was out in it I wanted to be back home.'

I knew what he meant. It was the sort of cold that made your bones ache; made you long for a warm fire and company. The fog seized your throat so you could hardly breathe and drowned the world in brown. Familiar streets were filled with fearful shadows, inexplicable noises and disembodied footsteps. It came too regularly to surprise anyone, but one never got used to it. For me, it always brought a terrible sense of loneliness, as though I had been deserted by the whole of humanity, even as I stood in the centre of the world's greatest metropolis. Anything might happen, anything might befall me, and no one would have any idea about it.

That fear crept up on me now, as I sat beside Gabriel in the herb drying room. I had once felt safe at St Saviour's. Life was always the same for us, circumscribed by ward rounds and prescription making, by the gathering of herbs and the preparation of tinctures, pills and salves. There was comfort in that routine, for all of us, and pleasure in doing it well. How quickly things had changed. People and places I had once regarded with a rather bored familiarity had taken on an unkind aspect. Our world, once so ordered and predictable, now seethed with jealousy, resentment and murderous ambition. I wondered why I had never noticed it before. Perhaps I was not as worldly wise as I thought I was.

I opened the window. Looking down, I could see the men toiling in St Saviour's graveyard. Coated in the mud in which they worked, it was as though the earth itself had come alive. Beside them, at the edge of the workings, stood Will, his tall hat chimney-black against that world of brown. From being quite unknown to me, he had, in the space of a few days, become the one person I felt I could rely upon; the one person I was sure, in my heart, was a good man. I had known those who worked at St Saviour's for my entire life. And yet could I say the same about any of them? Could I say that I knew for certain they were good men? Behind Will, in the shadow of the graveyard wall, three dark figures watched. Even from my eyrie in the herb drying room above the old chapel, I could recognise them well enough: one tall and proud; one powerfully built and crouched, always, as if to spring; one weary, stooped beneath a weight of resentment and melancholy as though he carried his troubles upon his own back. Dr Magorian. Dr Graves. Dr Catchpole.

❦

The funeral was speedily arranged. The executive committee had decided to honour Dr Bain's commitment to the hospital and the medical profession with a commemorative service, and a brass plaque inside St Saviour's parish church. The plaque was to be engraved with his name, the dates of his life, and a quotation from the Bible: '*Have mercy upon me, O LORD, for I am weak: O LORD, heal me, for my bones are vexed. Psalm 6, verse 2.*' I had chosen it. No one else had suggested anything, and I liked its combination of meekness, disgruntlement and understated vengeance.

'He *was* weak,' Mrs Speedicut had said. 'Weak as water.'

'His bones have been wired together into a skeleton and are going to stand in the dispensary,' said my father. 'So they'll be pretty vexed too, I should think.'

Gabriel gave a muffled sob.

'Let us hope the words are prophetic,' said Will.

151

'My thoughts exactly,' I replied. 'D'you know the rest of Psalm six, Gabriel?'

Gabriel shook his head.

'"*Let all mine enemies be ashamed and sore vexed: let them return and be ashamed.*"'

The event itself was, in every sense of the word, economical. As there was nothing left of Dr Bain once Dr Graves and his students had finished their work, there seemed little point in bothering with a coffin. And there was no family to object to the thriftiness. The service was brief, the church cold, the afternoon so dark that candles had to be lit. The wicks had not been trimmed and streams of sooty smoke trailed upwards to mix with the smell of tallow and mildew, and the reek of the open graves outside. Dr Bain's colleagues were in attendance in the front pews. I sat at the back, with Gabriel, my father, and Will. Will had given the workmen outside the afternoon off, so that the sound of the excavations did not impinge upon the service. Instead, the funeral – if one might call it that – was conducted to the thunderous accompaniment of the rain drumming on the roof, and the hypnotic *plop* . . . *plop* . . . *plop* of some invisible ingress of water.

But the indignities accorded Dr Bain in this final acknowledgement of his life did not end there. The chaplain was suffering from a cold, and his words were, more often than not, obliterated by a volley of sneezes, or muffled by the folds of a handkerchief. The organist had sprained his wrist and was obliged to play using only one hand – a performance that could have been bettered by any street musician's monkey. Dr Magorian read the eulogy. The candlelight threw his proud beaked nose and

152

deep eye sockets into ghoulish chiaroscuro, and as he
stood at the lectern I was reminded of an ancient woodcut
I had once seen that depicted the Devil emerging from
the depths. He spoke for no more than three minutes. It
was an insult, and we all knew it. I had heard him talk for
longer on the matter of emptying the ward spittoons.

I was wondering whether I should step forward and
offer my own celebration of Dr Bain's life, when there was
a great rattling at the door. The candles shrank and
guttered and a gust of malodorous wind billowed up the
aisle. We heard the moist slap of bare feet running, and a
woman's voice cried out.

'Where is he? Do you have him here?'

The rows of black-clad backs, the bowed shoulders and
heads, slowly turned around. Faces, pale as mushrooms in
a dung heap, peered into the gloom, looking back towards
the door. I could see frowns of disbelief, hear the clicking
of tongues. 'This is no place for a woman,' someone
muttered. 'Who is it?' But I knew who it was. I recognised
the voice – ragged with emotion, and taut with grief and
desperation.

Mrs Catchpole moved swiftly up the aisle. Her hair was
undone, plastered to her head and hanging about her
shoulders in lank, dark strips. Her feet were bare and
covered in mud. She was dressed in only her shift – had
she run all the way from Angel Meadow dressed like that?
Once white, it was now ragged and filthy. Her hands were
caked in mud from finger tips to elbow. Her face was
streaked with clay, two pale rivulets scoured through her
muddy cheeks by her falling tears.

I dashed forward and slung my coat about her
shoulders. 'Mrs Catchpole,' I whispered. 'What are you

doing? You should not have come here. Not like this. Your husband—' I recoiled. I could not help it. She stank of putrid flesh. 'Where have you been?' I said, pulling a handkerchief from my pocket to cover my nose.

'I've been looking for him,' she whispered. Her eyes darted here and there, searching for a beloved face. 'Where is he? Why does he make me hunt for him? They say he's dead. But he isn't. He can't be!' She peered up at me, her eyes glassy and unfocused. 'I looked in the churchyard. But none of them were him.' Her sudden smile was wild, crazed. Her voice was hushed, her words tumbling from her lips. 'He wasn't there at all! I knew he wouldn't be. He's alive, you see! They lied to me to keep me quiet, to make me say nothing, to keep us apart from each other. But I know better. I looked everywhere and he's not there at all. Where is he? You're his friend, I know. You'll tell me. Where is he?'

I realised then why she reeked of death; why her hands, clasping and unclasping, were slathered with brown; the sleeves and hem of her shift all caked in the stuff. I imagined her outside in the rain, amongst the excavations, sifting through the churchyard mud, prising up bodies, the sucking earth plucking the shoes from her feet as she floundered and fell – against a decaying coffin, into a pool of ancient slime – searching for her dead lover.

Her teeth were chattering now, despite my coat. Where on earth was Dr Catchpole? He seemed to be taking an age to extricate himself from the congregation. 'I looked and looked. Out there in the graveyard.' She smiled again, and then she laughed gleefully, the sound ringing against the walls and rafters. 'He has tricked them all,' she cried. 'He's not dead at all. He was sleeping, only sleeping.

I saw him, and I . . . I *knew*,' she sank her voice to a whisper. 'I saw!'

There was a movement behind me and Dr Catchpole appeared at my side. 'Annabel,' he said. 'My dear—'

Mrs Catchpole drew back at the sight of him, and her expression was suddenly furious. 'Where is he?' she said. All at once she darted forward, pushing past her husband's outstretched arms. 'James!' Her voice rose to a shriek – 'James! James!' – on and on, until the place echoed like a madhouse with her cries. Hands reached out to seize her, but she slipped past them all and dashed free. She turned about, still calling his name, her shift clinging to her legs like a winding sheet, her hair wet and dirty about her shoulders. On all sides now the granite faces of St Saviour's medical men closed in on her – grey cheeks, glinting spectacles, long fingers. And amongst them, taller and thinner and more aghast than all the rest, was her husband. He put out a hand to her, his lips drooping in despair as he mouthed her name. Mrs Catchpole screamed and reeled away from him. She attempted to run, to flee back down the aisle the way she had come. But her bare foot caught in the torn and trailing hem of her wet nightdress. The sound of her head striking the stone floor rang out like a pistol shot.

∞

I came back from the ward rounds to find that the world appeared to have returned to normal: Gabriel was making worming lozenges; my father was examining the account books. Outside the rain had stopped, though the clouds were so low that they seemed to be wiping themselves across the rooftops. The apothecary was a warm and cosy cave in a dark and dreary world. I was glad to slam the door behind me, but not so glad when I saw who else was there. Dr Graves and Dr Magorian. Dr Graves was talking – as he usually was.

'Due to Dr Bain's death, his cases have been redistributed amongst us remaining surgeons.' He made it sound as though Dr Bain's death had been both selfish and deliberate. 'I have taken the liberty of overseeing the recovery of the patient whose hip you and he excised, Dr Magorian. I know you already have your hands full. I am the same, but who else might attend to the man?'

Dr Magorian nodded. He pulled out his sugar box and offered it to Dr Graves. 'How is the fellow?'

'In great pain.' Dr Graves selected a lump. 'There's evidence of suppuration. I've drained the area and packed it with gauze. Let us hope Dr Bain's ridiculous behaviour with the aphid pump has not done lasting harm.' He slipped the sugar into his pocket.

I opened my mouth to speak. Then I caught Dr Graves's eye, and I closed it again. I had nothing to gain by provoking those I now believed to be our adversaries. Far better if I watched, and listened. I wanted to speak up, to defend the ideas of my friend, but I knew there was more at stake than the intellectual honour of a dead man. Dr Bain's approach to cleanliness – the spray, the white smocks – was persuasive, but without Dr Bain himself to advocate such ideas there was no chance they would gain common currency amongst his colleagues. I wondered whether Dr Graves had sabotaged Dr Bain's experiment after all, rubbing something toxic into the patient's severed stump to make it weep. And yet it hardly mattered now (as long as the fellow did not die as a result). It was clear that the subject was closed, and that surgical procedures would be undertaken as always – with dirty instruments and filthy coats.

I saw Eliza and Mrs Magorian pass by. Would they come in? Eliza glanced in at the window. She saw me, and smiled. I bowed my head in acknowledgement. But then she realised that her father was inside too, and the smile dropped from her face. Dr Magorian bounded to the door. He flung it open, and drew his wife and daughter inside. 'Dear me, dear me,' he scolded. He took his wife's hand and steered her towards the warmth of the fire. 'You should not be out in this weather, my love. You know you have a weak chest. You must have my umbrella and take a cab home directly.'

'But I feel quite well,' replied Mrs Magorian. The rain dripped from her bonnet. She smiled up at him and patted his hand. 'It was my idea that we come out. And the rain has stopped now.'

'Please,' he said. 'Come closer to the fire. The warmth will do you good.' He chafed her tiny fingers between his large strong hands. 'How cold you are. Your hands are like ice. Eliza!' He turned to his daughter. 'You should not let your mother come out in such weather. And without her gloves too!'

'I'm sorry, Father,' said Eliza. She did not look at him. Her skin had a dry, greyish appearance and she looked tired. Her fingers, I noticed, plucked restlessly at the cuffs of her coat. Her hair, which I could see beneath her bonnet, was dull and lustreless, her ringlets limp and unravelling in the damp. I wondered what the matter was. Was she ill? But the crowded apothecary was no place to ask.

'Miss Magorian,' Dr Graves smiled. He removed his cloak – perhaps to show off the new Dr Bain-style emerald-green waistcoat he was wearing underneath. The reek of the dissecting rooms billowed from its folds. Eliza recoiled, though Dr Graves did not appear to notice. 'You're looking pale,' he said. 'The wards are no place for a lady. I have always said as much.'

'Tea,' said Mrs Magorian brightly. 'That's all you need, my dear, a hot cup of tea. And then we shall go directly to the Magdalene ward. They value our Bible readings, I know, and I don't like to disappoint them.'

'This is an apothecary, not a tearoom, Mother,' said Eliza.

'Tea leaves are both a diuretic and a stimulant,' I said. 'We always have them in. It's no trouble, Miss Magorian. There's a pot on the stove already. Gabriel!'

Gabriel vanished into the scullery. He reappeared with a tray, upon which was our best china – cups, saucers, milk jug, sugar bowl, silver sugar tongs. I stared at them in astonishment. Those were my mother's things. We never used them. None of us was even allowed to touch them. I expected my father to say something, but when I looked over to his chair, he was no longer there. I had not noticed him go out.

Eliza took her cup of tea. And then something curious happened. I could make no sense of it, not then, and not later, when I went over in my mind what I had seen – or what I thought I had seen. Her father was standing beside her, and as I put the tea tray on the table, he rested a hand upon her shoulder. Was it my imagination, or did Eliza's face seem to close over, shutting in upon itself? She put milk in her tea, her expression stony. It was as though I were watching an automaton. I had seen such things in the museum of curiosities in Vauxhall Gardens, lifelike, robotic figures driven by clockwork, which moved their arms and heads like real people. Her father's hand seemed peculiarly large, white and bony in the dim light of the apothecary. It was as if she were shrinking beneath it, recoiling, and yet not moving a muscle. She dropped a sugar lump into her cup, picked up a tea-spoon and began to stir, round and round and round, making the tea whirl. And yet Eliza did not take sugar in her tea; she had always told me she despised the stuff – the smell, the taste, made her sick, she said. I could not make it out.

And then the door to the apothecary opened, and the spell, or whatever peculiar enchantment it was that had stolen over me, was broken.

Dr Magorian turned to his colleagues. Mrs Magorian, oblivious, was holding out her hands to the fire and humming a snatch of *Lead, Kindly Light.*

Eliza stared down at her cup, her expression one of confusion and surprise, covering her nose with her hand as she tried not to gag at the smell of the sugary steam.

Then I noticed who had come in. Dr Graves said, 'Out-patients is on a Monday morning, madam.' He sniggered. 'And the lock ward is across the courtyard. This is the apothecary.'

'I know what it is,' came the reply.

'Good afternoon, miss,' I said. It was my ex-seamstress from Wicke Street, come for her prophylactics. She had done her best to look respectable, with a closed bonnet and a shawl drawn tightly around her shoulders. But her profession was plain to anyone who cared to look – in the

159

directness of her gaze, the sway of her hips as she walked, the way she trailed her hand against the table top. The wink and the grin she gave me didn't help. But she had little reason to appear demure, and had probably forgotten long ago how to ape the coy mannerisms of respectable girls.

Dr Graves looked her up and down and shook his head. 'I see Dr Bain's influence has taken root here too. Is our apothecary to become a trysting place for prostitutes and their *clientele*?'

'Our relationship is purely professional,' I said.

Dr Graves sniggered again. 'Undoubtedly.'

I steered the girl away from him, though the apothecary was so crowded now there was nowhere for us to go to speak privately. 'Don't mind him,' I said.

'I don't,' she replied. 'I don't mind nuffink from any of them. Not even him, though there's many of the girls that won't go with him. Smells something awful, he does. Like as though you've got the Reaper himself on top o' you . . . *inside* you.' She raised her voice and looked over her shoulder at Dr Graves. 'You gets used to anything, but not that smell. He's as strong as the Devil,' she whispered. 'Hands like whip-cord.'

'Tea?' I said. I could tell by the mud that coated the hem of her skirt that she had walked all the way from Mrs Roseplucker's.

'I ain't got time for tea.' She looked longingly at the delicate cup resting in Eliza's saucer.

'I have just poured this one,' said Eliza. 'Please, take it.' She pushed the fine bone china cup and its filigree silver spoon across the counter. 'It'll warm you up a little.'

'Thank you, miss.' The girl sipped the sugary brew. 'I've

come for those herbs,' she said. 'Against the pox. The others wants some too.' She lowered her voice. 'And whatever you have to bring a girl on. You know what I mean?' She slid a few coins onto the table.

'No, no,' I said. 'You keep that. I know exactly what you require. Now then, peppermint, camomile, sage, wintergreen – was there something else on the list?'

She handed over the list of herbs I had given her that night at Mrs Roseplucker's. How long ago that seemed now. The world had become a much darker place since then. I reached for the pennyroyal.

'That doctor you came with that night,' she said. 'Dead, ain't he?'

I nodded. 'How d'you know?'

'Whole district knows,' she said. 'Everyone knew Dr Bain, and now everyone knows he's dead.' She leaned towards me across the counter, and spoke in a conspiratorial whisper. 'He came back, you know. Later. After you'd gone. Came back to see Lily. Said he had something for her to look after. Told her to give it to you as soon as she could if he didn't come back for it himself, but she knew I were coming here so she gave it to me to pass on. Nasty, queer thing it is. Can't think what it means.' She opened her bag, and placed a small, cardboard coffin onto the table.

Hideous, battered, dusty, it lay amongst the shining glass retorts and gleaming bottles like a lump of earth amongst a cache of gemstones. I felt my flesh prickle, as if someone had whispered in my ear. But there was no sound at all, other than the snap of the coals in the fireplace. Behind us the apothecary had fallen silent.

꧁

'Why did Dr Bain save this particular coffin?' I said. 'How can my mother be connected with these horrible things?'

Will had returned from St Saviour's churchyard. He could not have been wetter if he had fallen in the Thames. He sat before the fire, wrapped in a blanket whilst his clothes steamed on the pulley overhead. He sipped at the cup of tea I had given him. 'If we knew the coffins' purpose—'

'But we *don't* know their purpose.'

'I don't think the connection can be found in the present,' said Will.

He was right. The past was the only place where answers might be found, and yet I could not determine how to get there. I flung the coffin back onto the table in frustration. The hollow-eyed doll, the torn and bloody strips of fabric, the dead flowers – they were all things we had seen before. The words on the scraps of paper that lined it were painfully familiar: *Elizabeth Maud. 18th July 1822.*

'We need to go back to Mrs Roseplucker's,' said Will. 'We must speak to the woman who was Dr Bain's companion than night. Lily, I think her name was?'

'Yes, I'm afraid we must.' I clapped him on the shoulder. I could see from his face that he did not relish a return to the place. Poor Will. The city was draining the life from him. He was a country boy, as I had guessed, from Wiltshire. His work at St Saviour's was his first commission – I had been right about that too – and he wanted to impress his Master. But it was clear to me that Will's task

amongst the corpses was consuming his soul. Every hour
he spent at the churchyard made his cheeks paler, his eyes
more sorrowful. Even away from the excavations, death
seemed inescapable – Dr Bain's demise, the knowledge
that there was a murderer somewhere at St Saviour's. As
much as he was intrigued and curious, he was also
sickened and dismayed. I could see it in his face. The city
was ugly and cruel and filthy, the hospital dark and
morbid, the people he met ambitious and spiteful. And
the coffins, the grim *memento mori* whose appearance
seemed to have precipitated such unspeakable events . . .
I could think of only one remedy.

The physic garden was half a mile from the infirmary, at
the western end of St Saviour's Street. It was set back from
the road, bordered by a high stone wall. Next door was Dr
Magorian's primped and preened garden, and his soot-
blackened villa. There was a gate that led from Dr
Magorian's property into the physic garden, though I had
never seen anyone use it. Dr Magorian ensured that it was
locked at all times. He kept his own botanical specimens
in his own garden and his own hot house. Perhaps he did
not trust me to keep them. Perhaps he did not want me to
see what he had grown.

'Do the medical men come here? Dr Graves? Dr
Catchpole?' said Will as I pushed open the heavy wooden
side-gate and led him into the garden.

'No,' I said. 'Not even Dr Bain, though he charged me
with growing some of the poisonous plants. Only Eliza –
Miss Magorian – comes. Sometimes.' In fact, I had not
seen Eliza in the physic garden for months. When she was
a child she had come all the time, scrambling over the
wall from the garden next door, holding out her arms as

she asked to be lifted down. She would make herself a crown out of the bindweed I had pulled up, or crouch in the rhubarb like a pixie, one of the giant leaves upturned on her head. I had made her a swing on the apple tree and helped her to make a den out of birch twigs. Such adventures seemed a long time ago now.

'Have you been naughty?' I had once asked when I had not seen her in the garden for weeks. 'You are always kept inside.'

'My father says so,' she had replied. 'Though he will never tell me what it is that I've done.'

Will and I sat on an iron bench in the sun, our legs stretched out before us. We were sheltered from the wind, and far removed from the sights and sounds of St Saviour's Street. Before us, bushes of wintergreen and box, rosemary and spike lavender filled the air with their perfume – astringent, woody, cleansing. The fogs that plagued the city blocked out the feeble March sun and chilled the earth, so the plant beds were still ragged, waiting for the warmth of the spring to call forth green shoots and new growth. But the place was more pleasing on the eye than the dreary walls of the ward building or the dissecting rooms. Will gave a sigh of contentment. He bruised some lavender leaves between his fingers and breathed in their scent. 'Do you tend the place alone?'

'There's a gardener,' I replied. 'And a boy. I come when I can.'

'I'm surprised you have the time.'

'I don't. And with my father's illness – we may need to consider getting another apprentice.'

'Really?' Will sounded surprised.

'I know,' I said. 'They're so slow, and have to be taught,

164

and disciplined, and shown how to do everything. At first anyway. Hardly a help.'

'I didn't mean that—'

'Oh? Then what did you mean?'

'Only that . . . that your household is less than orthodox. Your father. You.'

'Me?'

'Yes.'

'Yes,' I said after a moment. 'There's that too.'

There was silence between us. Then, Will reached forward and plucked a single flower from a golden crown of early daffodils that grew beside the lavender bush. He handed it to me, the gesture shy and hesitant. I took it, surprised and a little puzzled. 'Narcissus,' I said.

'You know what it means?'

'What it means?'

'Yes.'

I glanced at him sideways. 'Yes, I do,' I said. Surely he didn't mean . . . He couldn't . . . *Could* he? 'It means "unrequited love".'

His cheeks flamed crimson. 'Does it? I thought . . . I thought it was something else.'

'What?'

'I don't know.' He shook his head. 'New beginnings, perhaps? Optimism? Looking to the future?'

'Oh.' Now it was my turn to look discomfited. 'I'm sorry.'

He spoke softly then, peeping up at me from beneath the brim of his tall hat. 'Are you, Jem?'

'Well,' I said. 'I mean . . . I think . . .' But I did not know what I meant, and I did not know what to think. I fell silent.

He sighed, his gaze now fixed upon the ground. 'I understand. I just . . . I just thought you might like it. A flower the colour of sunshine.'

'I do.'

'Well there it is then.'

He looked downcast. Had I offended him? I could not bear to leave it that way; could not bear to have anything come between us. 'But you know,' I said, 'to give only *one* narcissus is considered unlucky.'

'Is it? Good Lord! Well *that's* no use! No use at all.' He reached forward and with one swift movement ripped up the whole bunch. 'Here,' he thrust them towards me, twenty golden trumpets tumbling into my lap. 'Then take them all, every last one. For luck – lots of it – and anything else you care to add into the bargain.'

I laughed, gathering the flowers in my arms. 'Thank you.'

'My pleasure.' He sat back and closed his eyes, the moment and whatever awkwardness it contained dissolving in a brief shaft of sunlight. 'Well,' he said. 'I suppose it won't be long before the hospital moves to new premises. Who knows what might happen then. Perhaps the governors will provide you with a new physic garden. And a new apprentice.'

I knew he was trying to be reassuring, but I felt despair creep over me once more. All at once the daffodils I held seemed garish and artificial, their brightness obscene, their petals cold and thick as dead flesh. I thrust them aside. What, indeed, might happen then? And *before* then? I looked up. I could see dark clouds gathering. It would not be long before the rain found us.

'What do you grow here?' said Will, looking about.

'Lots of things,' I replied. 'The poisons are my speciality. We have *Aconitum lycoctonum, Cimicifuga racemosa, Atropa belladonna*—'

Will covered his ears. 'In English,' he said.

'Wolfsbane, black cohosh, deadly nightshade, poison hemlock, opium poppies – of course, by poison I don't necessarily mean deadly poison. Some of the plants will just make you ill. In small amounts they can have medicinal properties. Others have parts we might eat without much caution, and parts that might kill us – rhubarb, for instance.'

'It's a poison?'

'The leaves.' I held out my arms, embracing the green sweep of the garden. 'This is the most comprehensive poison garden in the city. I've been working on it since my apprenticeship. I've even devoted a section of the glasshouse to cultivating those species that don't tolerate our climate well, though I've had limited success with that. One simply can't recreate South America in a London glasshouse, no matter how hard one tries.'

I could have talked about the poison garden all afternoon, but I could tell that Will's interest was waning. 'Who has access to the poison plants?' he said.

'Anyone who climbs over the wall or comes in through the gate. But not everyone knows which plants are which, and how they might be used. Some specialist knowledge is required—' I sat up, peering down the garden. 'Who's that?' I shaded my eyes with my hand and stood up. At the far end of the garden, beyond the glasshouse, someone was moving about, crouched behind the yews.

'Who is it?' said Will. 'The gardener?'

'No,' I said.

'I'll sit here.' He leaned back and closed his eyes. 'And chew on a mint leaf while you go and find out. I assume you have some edible herbs here too?'

She had her back to me, and was bending over a small, creeping plant. I could smell the pungent mintiness of the leaves she had picked from it, even before I saw who she was. 'Good afternoon, Miss Magorian.'

'Oh!' She spun round, dropping the leaves she had gathered onto the path. Sage, pennyroyal, peppermint, camomile, wintergreen. 'Jem – Mr Flockhart – I didn't hear you.' She fell into a guilty silence, looking down at the scattered herbs. 'They're not for me,' she said at last.

'Of course.' I waited.

'My maid—'

'Is in trouble?'

She nodded.

'You should have spoken to me sooner.'

'But you're never alone and I couldn't speak in front of anyone else. And your father's ill. I didn't want to bother you.'

'And Dr Bain?' I knew every shadow, every expression of her face. Blindfolded, I could have drawn her likeness. I regarded her now, watching her countenance for signs of the truth. But her face had taken on that closed look I had seen earlier in the apothecary. Her eyes were downcast, her face blank and impenetrable.

'I met Dr Bain,' she said. 'The night before he died. I was going to tell him – To ask him—' She bit her lip so hard that a pinprick of blood appeared.

'About your maid?' I said.

'Yes. But then when it came to it, I couldn't—'

The silence gathered about us, tense and charged, as if we were counting the seconds between lightning and thunder. 'I'm surprised your father allows you to keep such a girl in your employ,' I said at last.

Eliza said nothing.

'Well.' I stirred the fallen herbs with the toe of my boot. 'What you have here will never do. And you have no idea about the correct quantities, nor how to prepare it.' I waited. Still she did not speak. 'Will you tell me what's going on?' I said. I spoke sharply. All at once I hated Dr Bain. Was he not content with Mrs Roseplucker's girls, with Mrs Catchpole, that he must have Eliza too? For a moment, a single crimson second, I was glad he was dead. He had taken Eliza, and he had treated her no better than the laundry maid, Lily the whore, Gabriel's mother . . . But fury, I knew, was a destructive emotion. No good ever came of it. No one could help her but I, and I would do anything I could. 'Eliza—'

'I cannot tell you,' she said. 'You mustn't ask.'

'But how else can I help?'

She drew back, her face hard, her eyes downcast. 'I must have the herbs,' she said. 'It's all you can do. Please, Jem. No one else can help.' She glanced up at me. 'And then you must forget. Forget what I've just asked, forget this conversation. And when you think of me, think of me as I once was, as I used to be when I was in this garden, with you.'

I tried to look at her, but I could not. I put my hand up to my face, to my eyes, covering my ugliness with an instinctive gesture. She reached up and took my hand.

'Don't hide,' she said. 'Not from me.'

I could not speak. I tried to turn away; I would not be

scrutinised, or pitied. I knew I could never be loved or touched by anyone.

She dropped my hand with a sigh, and turned to go.

I could not allow it. I could not permit her to leave with nothing. 'Wait here,' I said.

I moved quickly. I knew what I needed and where I could find it. I took up a fork and dug up roots. I gathered handfuls of leaves – some dried and hanging in bunches in the hot house, some fresh and growing.

'Blue cohosh root, pennyroyal, camomile, tansy,' I said. I wrapped them in muslin, and pressed the packages into her hands. 'Two tablespoons each of cohosh and tansy, three of pennyroyal and camomile. Pour on two pints of boiling water. Leave it to steep for three hours. Strain it. Heat it up again and drink a cup every four hours, day and night, for five days. No more than five days, d'you hear? I have given you enough for that.' I took her wrist. 'No more than five days. And tell your maid to be careful with this formula. I would not lose her for the world.'

'Will it work?' she whispered.

'I've nothing else if it doesn't.'

She nodded, and took my hand. She looked into my face, searching my expression for – what? I lowered my gaze, my feelings visible in the heat of that scarlet, heart-shaped mask. 'Will you not look at me?' she whispered. 'Jem?'

'Eliza?' Mrs Magorian's voice came from the other side of the wall. 'Eliza!'

'Quickly now,' I said. 'Put those herbs in your pocket and over the wall with you.' I dragged her over the beds to where a lawn roller rusted amongst the ivy against the wall – it had always been her route out of the physic garden.

'Let me check,' I whispered. I stood on the roller and peeped over. I saw Eliza's mother vanish behind a beech hedge.

'Quick!' I sprang down. 'Over you go.' I helped Eliza onto the roller and over the wall, unapologetic as I shoved her arse up with the heel of my hand. She glanced back, her curls an auburn halo about her face. It was how I would always remember her, innocent, blameless, an angel looking down at me from heaven. And then she was gone.

Chapter Eight

❧

Wicke Street had once been a proud terrace of sugar-white stuccoed town houses, though it had been half a century since anyone had felt the need to patch or paint the plaster on any of them. Years of smoky rain had covered the once-gleaming edifice with a layer of sticky black soot. Here and there chunks of filthy plaster had bubbled like the pox on the smooth cheeks of the buildings, or fallen away in great chancres to reveal the stone beneath.

Mrs Roseplucker's house looked far worse in the daylight. The windows were dark with grime, the gutters drooped; the drainpipes leaned like drunken men, bearded about the knees and elbows with green stains. We mounted the steps and scraped the mud and horse dung off our boots while we waited at the door.

'What a wretched place this is,' muttered Will. 'I hardly noticed how bad it was when we came here with Dr Bain.' He sniffed. 'And the air is abominable.'

'The city is full of such houses; some *far* worse. It'll never change.'

Will sighed. 'Well, I for one am not resigned to it, even if you are.' He closed his eyes and lifted his face as a shaft of sunlight shot through the rainclouds. How young he looked. With his cheeks hardly whiskered, his narrow shoulders, tall hat and broad-shouldered top coat, he looked like a boy dressed up in his father's clothes. 'This city is drowning in filth,' he said. 'Its houses are crowded and decayed, its citizens sick, diseased and grubby. But whereas you accept it, and work within those constraints, I hope for better things.' He smiled. 'I hope for drains and sewers and culverts. I hope for clean, new buildings and wide, airy streets.'

I shrugged, cross that he had made me sound so uninspired. 'Rebuilding the city won't get rid of venality.'

'No.' Will dragged his shit-caked sole across the metal rim of the broken boot-scraper. 'But it might make the place smell better.'

Mrs Roseplucker was sitting beside the fire. She looked no different to the last time we had seen her: in the same dress, the same pose, the same chair. In the grimy daylight her elaborate coiffure of ringlets was dull with dust, her red dress gathered about her in folds and ruffles of lace and rumpled, water-stained taffeta. Her lips moved soundlessly as she turned the page of a greasy-looking penny blood. Beside her chair more of the same were scattered: *Ramona and the Bloody Hand*; *Dick of Old London*; *Lady Elvira's Secret*. I plucked *Lady Elvira* from the wreckage and flicked through its pages. The story of a wealthy heiress locked away in an asylum while her fortune was squandered by a theatrically nefarious husband, it had kept Gabriel enthralled for weeks. But I knew for certain that there were far more men than 'ladies' shut up in asylums. A lady might behave erratically and it would be passed off as 'nerves' or 'feminine weakness'. For a man, the bar was set far higher. There was no domestic sanctuary to hide in, no boudoir door to weep behind, no sofa to droop upon. There were no excuses, and no quarter. For every wrongly imprisoned heiress or pregnant unwed girl locked away there were a hundred broken down fathers weeping or raving beside them. I could guess which version of events fiction – and posterity – would choose to remember.

I flung the paper down. Mrs Roseplucker watched me, with watery, malevolent eyes. There was no sign of any of the girls. Instead, the daylight revealed a slovenly domesticity, the dusty mantel, the threadbare furnishings, a chipped plate of congealed kipper bones on the hearth. Despite the fire, the room felt damp, and the red walls had a moist, spongy look to them, as though the place was located within a gigantic bodily orifice. I pushed the image from my mind and tried to concentrate on the task in hand.

'I'm looking for Lily,' I said.

'She ain't up.'

'But it's after three o'clock,' I said. 'When does she get up?'

Mrs Roseplucker licked her finger, and applied it to the crumpled corner of a page. 'You can go up, but not before you've paid. Both of you. Double, each, seeing as there're two of you and it's not even tea time.'

'Madam—' Will began to protest.

At our back, I heard the creak of a chair. Mr Jobber was sitting behind the parlour door. It was unusual to see him out of his cubby-hole in the hall and I had not heard him come in. His waistcoat bore the signs of a recent breakfast: a drool of egg yolk and a gleaming circle of bacon fat. He cracked his knuckles with a sound like marbles rattling in a sack. Will and I reached into our pockets.

❧

Without her covering of powder and rouge, Lily looked no more than eighteen years old. She pulled a shawl about her thin shoulders. 'Not two at once,' she said. 'Not at this time of day.' Then she noticed the red splash across my eyes and she opened the door wide. 'You're Dr Bain's friend.'

I nodded. 'And this is Mr Quartermain.'

Will took off his hat and held out his hand. 'Good afternoon, Miss Lily.'

The shadow of a smile passed across her face. 'Show me that card trick? The girls have been doing it ever since you showed it to 'em, but I can't work it out.'

'It's the ace,' said Will. 'Keep your eye on it.'

Lily sat on the bed wrapped in her shawl. Her knees were drawn up to her chin, her thick yellow hair about her shoulders. Her room was the master bedroom of Mrs Roseplucker's seedy old town house, furnished with only a bed, a washstand, a wardrobe and a screen. It depressed me more than I could say. How could she bear to spend her life inside that room, reamed and rogered over and over again by a succession of strangers? Will had pulled out a pack of cards and was amazing her with his 'magical bending card' trick. Lily's eyes sparkled. She clapped her hands like a child.

'You're clever,' she said. 'Can you teach me?'

'You know Dr Bain's dead,' I said.

She shrugged. 'Course I know.'

'He left something for me.'

'Yes,' said Lily. 'Ain't you got it? I didn't want it here. Horrible thing. He said I weren't to look at it, but o' course I did. It were like a doll in a box. A coffin.'

'Have you seen anything like it before?'

'No. Why would I?'

'What did Dr Bain think of it?'

'Don't know.' Lily shuffled Will's cards. 'Didn't say much. Seemed a bit worried about something. Scared almost. He gave it me wrapped in a sack, and said I was to keep it hid till he came back. Then I heard he was dead. Course, when I knew one of the other girls was going to see you, I just gave it to her. I weren't wanting to go out and it didn't seem to matter. It were only an old box and Dr Bain dead so not likely to say much.'

'Dr Bain was a good man,' I said.

Lily sighed. 'P'raps he was. He din't deserve to die. Some of them I'd wish dead a hundred times over. But Dr Bain, he weren't so bad. Treated me nice. Normal. You know.'

I was glad to hear that Dr Bain was 'normal'. I wondered what the opposite might be. I shut my mind to thoughts of outsized cocks, screaming mouths and violent, wrenching hands. 'What was he like last time you saw him? What did he say and do?'

'Not much,' said Lily.

'Come on, Lily.' I began to feel exasperated. 'Can't you tell us anything? He's not just "dead", you know. Someone killed him.'

'There's nothing to tell,' said Lily. She pointed to a threadbare armchair in front of the fire. 'He sat on that chair. Looked rather untidy, considering how smart he usually was. Didn't say much to me, not really. Kept running his hands through his hair and muttering to himself.'

'Muttering? Muttering what?'

'"Not again. Not this again." At least that's what it sounded like.'

'Not what again?' I said.

'Didn't say what.'

'Did you ask?'

'Why should I care what it was?'

'Well was there anything else?'

'Nuffink.'

'But what did you talk about? What exactly did he say? Did he give you the coffin and walk away? Did you have . . . congress?'

'Did we have what?' Lily grinned.

'You know what I mean.' I glanced up. Will was watching me, his expression unreadable in the dismal afternoon light. All at once I wanted to get out of the place. It was so hot, and the smell – the stink of sweat and hot chafing bodies, of skin and hair, was thick and heavy about us. I could only assume that the men who came here were so intoxicated with lust that their olfactory senses were dulled to the point of uselessness.

Lily sighed. 'Dr Bain came back about an hour, an hour and a half after you'd left the first time. He seemed – different.'

'How "different"? Agitated? Anxious? Afraid?'

'All those things. I never seen him like it before. Usually he din't seem bothered about nothing. He sat in that chair and said "Not this again," and I said "What?" and he shook his head and said "Never mind what." Then he went all silent and just stared at the fire. Well, I wondered what were the matter. It were a bit peculiar. So I gets up and I goes to the window and looks out at the fog and just to be sayin' *somethin'* I says "Look how thick its getting! Mrs R says it's a night for the Abbot when it's like this," an' ain't I glad not to have to go out to look for trade on such a night—'

'You told him a tall story?' I said.

'It ain't a story,' said Lily, 'it's the truth. And *I* didn't tell it. It's Mrs Roseplucker's story and *she* told it. She remembers it. Just you ask her. She'll tell you. She were *there*, back then when the Abbot was abroad.'

'What's this got to do with Dr Bain?' I snapped.

'That's what I'm tellin' you,' said Lily sulkily. 'I'm tellin' you what I said to Dr Bain. I happened to mention the Abbot—'

'And did Dr Bain ask?' said Will. 'Did he ask about the Abbot too?'

'Seemed mighty interested,' said Lily. 'Asked me all about it. But I said it was for Mrs Roseplucker to tell, not me. Then he gives me the coffin and says "Look after this for me. Keep it hid and don't show it to no one till I come back for it. Unless anythin' happens to me."'

'Like what?' I said. 'Did he say what he was expecting to happen?'

'No. Just said that I were to give it to "young Mr Jem at St Saviour's Apothecary".' She shrugged her thin shoulders. 'I thought it were a bit peculiar like, but there's many a gentleman what's odd in his ways. It's best not to ask 'em too many questions, so I just smiles and says "Yes, sir, o'course I will, sir."' She got off the bed and crossed the room to fling another lump of greasy coal onto the fire. 'P'raps he thought the Abbot were after him, too.'

Lily turned to me. 'Look, I know he were your friend, and it's sad to lose friends.' She smiled, but her expression was bitter. 'I should know. There's not many what lasts long in this game. If the pox don't get you first there's only the streets once you're too old for a house like this. So I'm sorry he's dead – sorry for you.'

I nodded. But they were just words, and Dr Bain simply another customer. 'Did he pay you to look after the coffin?' I said.

'A thick 'un,' said Lily with a grin. She plunged a hand into her pocket and drew out a sovereign. 'I'd not do nothing for nobody otherwise.' I nodded, and handed her a shilling. It was all I had left in my pocket. Lily looked at it in disgust. 'P'raps you ought to save *that* for Joe Silks.'

'Joe Silks?' I said. 'Why?'

'He's got the other one.'

I frowned. 'What other one?'

'The other box. There were two. Dr Bain said the other one was with Joe Silks. Lives in Prior's Rents—'

'I know where he lives,' I said.

'Well then,' said Lily. She turned her back, her expression sulky. 'You know where to go then, don't you?'

As patrons of Mrs Roseplucker's, we were supposed to leave by the back door. But I was not yet ready to go, and I led Will back towards the parlour. The place was warmer than ever. The virgins had appeared and were sitting side by side, slumped on the ragged brocade sofa in poses that suggested a complete absence of stays. Their legs were parted sloppily beneath their skirts, and their expressions were bored. Both held a pamphlet. One had folded hers into the shape of a bird, the other, the girl who had brought the coffin to the apothecary, was using hers to fan her face. It was one of Mrs Magorian's favourites: WHAT IS WOMANHOOD?

'Has Mrs Magorian been here?' I asked.

'You mean that interfering doctor's wife?' said Mrs Roseplucker, staring at me accusingly over the top of her penny blood. 'She was here all right. Her and her little troupe of ladies. Telling me how to run my own house.' She shook her head. 'They should come in the evening and hand out them leaflets to the gentlemen upstairs. They might find they knows one or two of 'em quite well.'

'And Eliza? Was Eliza with her?'

'That pretty girl? The young one?' Mrs Roseplucker's horrible old lips parted in a leer. 'Worried what she might say if she knew *you* was here?'

How glad I was that Will and I had been upstairs. Eliza thought well of me, she trusted me and loved me like a brother. Imagine if she had found me in a brothel! I would appear brutish and hypocritical, no better than any other man she knew. And yet I was not like them. I was not like any of them. All at once I wanted to shout it out, to declare myself to anyone who would listen – but I didn't.

'Eliza. That her name, is it?' Mrs Roseplucker frowned, and put down her dog-eared copy of *The Vampyre Returns*. 'Looked just like one o' Mrs Goldberg's girls,' she said. 'I never forget a face, though there's been many what's paid me to pretend otherwise. Fanny Bishop, that's it! Mrs Goldberg died a long time ago and I don't know where

young Fanny ended up but she looked just like your Eliza.'
She laughed, a peculiar rasping sound, like the scratching
of a yard brush. Then she added, 'She'll never have *you*,
you know.'

'I know that,' I muttered. 'And she's not *my* Eliza. She's
not anyone's.'

'*Ain't* she?' said the old madam. 'That's what *you* think.
She's bin plucked, that one, you can tell it a mile off! Din't
you know?' She leered. 'You ain't as clever as all that then,
are you?' She sat back, shaking her head. 'Fanny Bishop,'
she murmured. 'Why, I ain't thought about her in years.
Pretty girl. Leastways she was till she got her teeth bashed
in one night. Mrs Goldberg weren't quite so partic'lar as I
am about what sort o' gen'lemen she let into her house.'

'Perhaps it was the Abbot,' I said.

'The Abbot?' Mrs Roseplucker turned her watery eyes
upon me. 'Well now, why'd you go and mention *him*, I
wonder?'

'Can you tell us about him?' said Will.

'Oh, yes, tell us about the Abbot,' cried one of the
virgins, sitting up. 'There's nothing else to do and you tell
such a good story, Mrs R. Go on. Please.'

'It makes me shiver,' said the other. 'Even if I've heard
it a dozen times. Tell us again.'

Mr Jobber, who had been sitting motionless behind the
parlour door, clapped his hands like some gigantic village
idiot. The girls pulled their chairs closer.

'Ten shillings,' said Mrs Roseplucker.

'Ten shillings?' I said. 'For a story?'

'It was worth that much to your dead man.' Mrs
Roseplucker looked at me and grinned. Her wig, that
tangled nest of ringlets, had slipped back. The scabs on

her scalp matched her scarlet dress. 'And you wants to know what I told him, don't you?'

'Well, it's not worth ten shillings to me,' I said.

'Ain't it then?' Mrs Roseplucker licked her lips. 'Don't you be so sure o' that, *Mister* Jem.'

She leaned forward in her chair, and waited; her scarlet skirts smouldering in the heat of the fire. Silence fell. No one sniffed or coughed, no one fidgeted. All eyes were fixed upon her. In the grate, a lump of coal shifted and a belch of yellowish smoke rolled out. I had no money at all, other than the shilling Lily had refused. I turned to Will. He was already rummaging in his pockets.

Mrs Roseplucker grabbed at Will's half-sovereign, stowing it away in some secret nest beneath the tattered frills and flounces of her dress. 'It was a long time ago now, my dears,' she said, settling back on her cushions. 'But no one knows better than I what terror the Abbot brought to St Saviour's parish. They said he was a ghost, a spirit tormented by the wretchedness that had come to these once-proud streets; streets that ladies and gentlemen had once walked down and where fine carriages had passed; where orchards and gardens and fields had been laid out, as rich and green as Eden itself.

'But those places had vanished beneath the city. They were rendered foul and pestilent, filled with stench and decay, the residents given over to lust and greed. The Abbot of St Saviour's, so they said, turned in his grave to see his beautiful grounds so despoiled, and he rose up from his tomb to walk the earth, weeping for those lost and innocent times.'

Mrs Roseplucker's small moist eyes were fixed upon me. She spoke to the room, but I knew she was telling her story to me. And she had chosen that time and place, that audience, for a reason. After all, she could quite easily have refused to say anything.

'What was he looking for, this ghostly abbot? Some said he was driven by sorrow to walk the parish until he found innocence and truth.' Mrs Roseplucker gave a grin, and a gentle wheezing laugh. 'Well, my dears, he'd be looking a long time before he found much of that around here. And those who thought it were fools.' Her voice grew harsh. 'For the Abbot of St Saviour's was as wicked as the rest of them, and he was lookin' for a young girl to slake his appetites. Yes, missy, you might well gasp, though I know you've heard it a hundred times. For the Abbot was no more a ghost than you or I, though it suited him well enough to let others think so. An' sure enough he seemed like a ghost to those what saw him. Fast, he was. Flittin' through the fog without a sound, silent as the night itself.'

'He weren't a ghost at all, then?' whispered one of the virgins.

'That's right, my dear,' said Mrs Roseplucker. 'They saw him from afar, a dark, hooded shadow drifting through the fog and so he seemed a ghost more than a man. They said those who saw him hadn't long for this world, as the Abbot had seen their sinful ways and had marked them out for death.'

I recognised Mrs Speedicut's version of the tale, and thought of my own bald and colourless rendition, delivered to Will in the chapel beneath the herb drying room. But Mrs Roseplucker's adaptation was vividly coloured by the bloodthirsty realism of Reynolds' Penny Weeklies. A mere ghost story would never do. I glanced at

Will. Were we wasting our time here? But he was listening intently.

'Carry on, Mrs Roseplucker,' he said. 'You are quite the Scheherazade.'

Mrs Roseplucker frowned. 'The what?'

'Do get on,' I said. 'The Abbot. You say he wasn't a ghost at all?'

'Who was 'e then?' cried the other girl. 'Who was 'e, Mrs Roseplucker?'

'Nobody knows,' said Mrs Roseplucker. 'But he were a man right enough. And he liked young girls too. How do I know? Cause I were one of 'em, that's how!'

'*You?*' The word burst from me before I could stop myself.

'I weren't always like this,' snapped Mrs Roseplucker. 'I were a beauty once. Men called on me day and night. The King himself asked who I was!'

There was a moment of silence while we all looked at the wretched pox-ridden Mrs Roseplucker and tried to imagine beauteousness. It was too much for the imagination.

'Never mind about that,' thundered Mrs Roseplucker. 'I were a beauty and that's all you need to know.'

'So what happened?' I said.

'I was walking towards Fishbait Lane. It was dark that night, dark as pitch. No moon, and the fog was up, thick as you like – great curtains o' the stuff, sometimes lifting a bit, then falling thicker than ever. It choked me to breathe and neither light nor lantern made no difference to how far you could see.' Her voice dropped to a low and husky whisper. Her eyes were wide in her skeleton face, her arms stretched towards us, bony hands projecting from the stained flounces of her crimson sleeves as though she was back in the past, groping fearfully through the Georgian fog. The effect was both unnerving and dramatic. 'I was lost,' she whispered. 'Lost in the very streets I knew as well as I knew my own body.

'I stopped and waited for a moment. Perhaps the fog would lift and I would be able to get my bearings. But it was too thick. And cold! Cold as the grave.' She shivered. 'And that's when I felt it.'

The clock ticked. Mrs Roseplucker looked around at the faces turned towards her, allowing the questions to grow in our minds.

'Felt what, Mrs R?' cried one of the virgins, unable to bear it any longer. 'Felt what?'

'I knew there was someone nearby,' whispered Mrs Roseplucker. 'I could feel him. And if I listened hard enough I could hear him too. *Breathin'*. In and out. In and out. In . . . and out. Close, but invisible. And his breath was shaking, like from excitement, or fear. And I heard his steps. Quiet, they were, and slow; creeping footsteps as though he were walking on the very edges of his shoes. Coming closer? I couldn't tell. Behind me? I couldn't tell that neither. I cried out. "Who's there?" No answer came. But I weren't alone any more. I knew it from the chills on my neck and the feel of my hair standing on end.

'I waited. Nothing happened. No one came at me, and after a while I says to myself "Well, my girl, are you going to stand here all night like a dog tied to a tree? Get home to your bed right this minute!" I took five paces – and as soon as I did, I knew he was there. I heard those footsteps again. Faster now and nearer, nearer all the time, no

matter how I ran. Behind me!' Mrs Roseplucker's voice
rose to a shriek. 'I turned, and there he was. Tall and
black as night, cloaked from head to foot, bearing down
on me in his terrible dark hood.'

'It were the Abbot,' shouted Mr Jobber suddenly. It was
the first time I had ever heard him speak. His voice was a
great, deep bellow, his eyes wide with horror as he rose to
his feet. 'Run, Mrs Roseplucker! Run for your life!'

'I tried to run, my dear,' said Mrs Roseplucker. 'I tried
to run but it was too late. He had his hands on me, round
my throat, then over my mouth and nose. But I was young
and strong then and I'd been expecting him, and, bless
you, but it weren't the first time I'd had to fight a man off.
He held me tight, but I wriggled like an eel. I stamped my
feet and jabbed my elbows. I had a hat pin in my pocket
and I poked 'im, *hard*! Lord knows but that ghost could
scream, and scream he did. He let me go just a bit and I
got away, and I've never run so fast in all my life. I ran and
ran, and as soon as I saw the infirmary lights I knew where
I was.'

'So who was he?' I said.

'No one knows,' said Mrs Roseplucker. 'They kept
seeing him, though, when the fog was up. For years he
came and went. And the girls disappeared. Street girls.
No one cared whether they lived or died, and maybe
they're alive still, somewhere about, but they disappeared
from St Saviour's parish all the same.' She shrugged.
'Then he vanished.'

'When did he vanish?' said Will. 'Can you remember?'

'Years ago now. Some says they see him still. When the
fog's up. But I don't believe it.' She shook her head. 'No
one's seen the Abbot for twenty years or more.'

'*I've* seen him.' We turned, all of us. Lily stood on the threshold in her shift and shawl, her face pale as a corpse beneath her tangled yellow hair. 'I saw him,' she said. 'The Abbot. Out in the street. That night Dr Bain came.'

Chapter Nine

❦

'Why didn't Dr Bain come to me if he was worried about something?' I could not help but feel jealous. 'Why did he choose a whore and a street urchin over his closest friend?'

'Maybe there were things he didn't want to talk to you about.'

'That doesn't make me feel any better,' I said.

'Well, as he's not here to explain himself, perhaps, as his closest friend, you should do him the courtesy of trusting his motives.'

I fell silent. He was right, of course. How foolish I was to feel snubbed by a dead man.

'So,' said Will. 'We must try to follow Dr Bain's way of thinking.'

'He might not have wanted to speak to me about his fears. I accept the point. But what other reasons might there be for his behaviour?'

'Perhaps he was afraid that he would put you in danger

if he told you anything,' said Will. 'So he took some precautions. He may well have resolved to explain himself the next day – I doubt he expected death to come quite so promptly, even if he was afraid of something, or someone.'

'Mm.' I was still not convinced.

'You said it yourself,' said Will. 'A whore and a street urchin. Who would guess that a doctor might entrust anything to such an unlikely pair? Who would ever find out but you – assuming Dr Bain was not able to reclaim his secrets for himself.'

'It makes sense, I suppose,' I said.

'I think we can assume Dr Bain found something in the coffins when he returned from Mrs Roseplucker's. Then he split up his discovery, and deposited the knowledge with two separate people, so that if anything *did* happen, he might trust *them* to tell you, and trust *you* to figure it out.' He shrugged. 'Not that I had anything more than the most slender of acquaintances with Dr Bain, but despite his flaws he struck me as a good man – a good friend – and an intelligent one.'

For a while we walked together in silence. We were the same height, and our stride measured the same distance. We were hardly ever out of step when we were together. I said, 'The woman who visited him the night he died – I wonder how on earth she got him to ingest aconite?'

'Are you sure that's what killed him?'

'The signs are unmistakable. Surely he would not be so naive as to eat or drink anything she had given him. Unless he had no suspicions.' I shook my head. 'But perhaps we are trying to run before we can walk. The question is, who was she?'

'She was Mrs Catchpole,' said Will. 'Remember what

she said at Dr Bain's funeral? "He has tricked them all. He was sleeping, only sleeping. I saw him, and I *knew*."'

'Yes,' I said. 'I heard that.'

'Perhaps Mrs Catchpole killed him. She loved him. Obsessively, it would appear. Obsession is closer to madness than it is to sanity. You saw her that night at Mrs Roseplucker's. And at Dr Bain's funeral. She was capable of anything. Her actions might be motivated by love, certainly, but they were rendered murderous by obsession.'

'Yes, yes,' I said. 'But your explanation also tells us why that was *not* what happened. A jealous rage, especially one that borders on madness, is a spontaneous eruption of feeling and action, as violent and passionate as it is unexpected. But there's nothing violent or unexpected about poisoning. It's an act that must be coldly calculated and meticulously planned. Oh no, Will, Mrs Catchpole didn't murder Dr Bain, though it's quite possible that she knows who did. Did you notice that the grass outside the laboratory window was trampled?'

'No. Was it?'

'It was quite clear. Someone had been standing there. And more than one person, judging by the way the weeds were crushed. Joe Silks said there was a man, outside the window, while we were inside with Dr Bain examining the coffins, d'you remember? That was long before Mrs Catchpole appeared. And according to Gabriel a man was there *again* at midnight. At that time Dr Bain was still alive to answer the door and send Gabriel on his way. Unfortunately I could not make out the shape of his footprints, as the ground was too hard for the mark of a man's heels.' We turned out of Wicke Street. On either side, the houses grew more and more dilapidated, though it was nothing compared to where we were headed.

'But a *lady's* heels are smaller and sharper,' I continued. 'I could see indentations in the ground beneath Dr Bain's window that I dare say would match the heel marks left by a fashionable button-sided ladies' boot, not unlike those habitually worn by Mrs Catchpole.'

'So we can be certain where she stood and looked in,' said Will. 'But if a woman was with Dr Bain that evening, is it not logical to assume that it was Mrs Catchpole?'

'And yet the facts suggest quite the opposite.'

Will looked puzzled. He removed his tall hat and wiped his forehead with a large handkerchief of the kind favoured by Joe Silks. 'But she had walked all the way from Wicke Street to find him,' he said. 'She may well have been at large in the city for hours after her escape from Mrs Roseplucker's. Surely she *would* go inside.'

'But if she had gone inside she would have discovered that Dr Bain was dead,' I said. 'When she barged into Dr Bain's funeral she said that he was "only sleeping". Unless she was simply raving – there is always that possibility – my feeling is that she spoke the truth, as she saw it when she looked through the window. She *thought* he was sleeping. If she had gone in, she would have *known* that he was not.' I smiled, pleased by my own perspicacity. 'It's quite clear that Mrs Catchpole was not the lady visitor, and did not go into Dr Bain's house. In fact I'll wager she didn't even knock on the door.'

'Why?'

'Think, Will! What might she have seen that ensured she did not – *would* not – knock on her lover's door?

191

Despite her desperation, despite her hours spent in search of him across London?'

Will stared at me, his expression blank. 'Ah!' Comprehension flooded his face. 'She didn't knock because she saw that there was already someone in there.'

'Yes! But who?'

'The woman,' said Will, his cheeks turning pink with excitement. 'The woman who sat in the chair before the fire. The woman Dr Bain moved his books for. Dr Bain's lady visitor. We must ask Mrs Catchpole who—'

I shook my head. 'But if it were a lady, would Mrs Catchpole not barge in and demand an explanation? She has already attempted to flush Dr Bain out of a brothel. She has wandered about the city for hours, and now she finds him with yet *another* woman? Would she really just creep away again? She was only prevented from breaking down his bedroom door at Wicke Street because her husband arrived and carried her off.'

Will began to look exasperated. 'A man then?'

But I was determined to make him find his own way to the truth. 'One she is too frightened to confront? Earlier that evening she had rendered the doorkeeper of a whore house completely unconscious with one blow from her husband's walking stick. One can only wonder what sort of a man might so frighten Mrs Catchpole as to stop her from knocking on her lover's front door.'

'Well, *I* don't know!' cried Will. 'If it was not a woman, and not a man, I can't begin to imagine who else might be left. Neither? Both? Who do *you* think it was?'

'Oh, perhaps it's all just conjecture.' I rubbed my eyes wearily. '*Is* it deduction, or is it simply guess work? I'm not sure I can tell the difference any more.' I sighed. The steps we had followed were logical, based solely on the facts we had before us. And yet there was something about it all that didn't seem right. Was there a dimension to the problem that I was not seeing? Some part of the puzzle I had missed? Common sense told me who it was that Mrs Catchpole had seen through Dr Bain's window, and I was certain I was right. But was that person really Dr Bain's murderer? It was possible. But was it also probable?

Will seized me by the arm and pulled me to a halt. 'Who did she see? Who stopped her from going in? It was a man, wasn't it? You said it wasn't a woman but you *didn't* say it wasn't a man.'

'Think, Will,' I said. 'Who is the only man who could make a deranged wife hesitate about entering her lover's front room?'

He stared at me. And then all at once his look of irritated perplexity vanished. 'Of *course!*' he cried. 'Why, it has to be – oh, well done, Mr Flockhart.' He seized me by the hand. 'Well *done!*'

'D'you see?' I said.

'It's obvious!'

'We don't know who Dr Bain's late-night lady visitor was, but we *do* know who Mrs Catchpole saw. It could be none other—'

'—than Dr Catchpole.'

❧

Where was Joe Silks? I had not seen him outside the infirmary that morning. If he had gone to ground, hiding somewhere in the great rotting hulks that made up the rookeries to the east of St Saviour's, then we would never find him. Still, we had to try. We turned out of Fishbait Lane into St Saviour's Street. The sun was warm now. The vapours were putrid, and there was no breeze to drive them away. I began to wonder whether Will's utopia of sewers and drains might well be beneficial to the outlook and disposition of the city. I could feel my mood darken as the atmosphere thickened.

The stretch of wall above the gratings where Joe Silks and his gang usually sat was unoccupied. No doubt the ragged children were somewhere about the city, picking pockets or sliding their skinny arms through pantry windows. But I knew where Joe Silks lived when he was not on the grating. We would look for him there, though the fact that he preferred to spend his nights shivering beneath a pile of sacks outside the hospital said much about the place he came from.

The streets leading in the direction of Prior's Rents grew narrower and darker the further we walked from the infirmary. The houses were ramshackle, crooked tenements thrown up to house the poor. Over time they had been divided and subdivided to accommodate more and more people, until it seemed as though the fabric of the buildings themselves was shored up with humanity. Men loitered in doorways, pipes in their mouths and bottles in their hands; women squatted on steps, babies half forgotten in their laps. Packs of children ran in and out of the filthy refuse-choked alleys. The usual flotsam of straw, manure, dog shit and vegetable matter littered the ground. We skirted a pool of brown, lumpy water, and turned into a dismal court.

The sun seemed to vanish as we entered the place. Windows without glass punctuated the black edifices that reared on either side of us – some boarded over, others bearing a fluttering pennant of ragged grey curtain. Flies hummed in the air. Voices – a crying baby, a shouting drunkard, a pair of women arguing – were audible, and below this, a constant underlying clamour. No one who was not a resident had any business amongst those foul, narrow streets, and I felt eyes – hostile and predatory – staring at us from windows and doors. I glanced from side to side at the slimy black walls. Were the shadows creeping closer?

'We're being followed,' said Will.

'I know.'

'Since we left Wicke Street.'

'Do you think it's time to find out who he is?'

'He? Are you certain?'

'Undoubtedly.' I took Will's arm and bundled him into a doorway.

For a moment, we could see nothing at all. The place stank like a sewer – indeed, it may well have been used as such for beneath our feet the ground was sticky and gave off a fearful stench. Our footsteps echoed off black walls, iridescent with moisture. I stopped. Will slithered to a halt beside me. His face was visible in the darkness like a painted mask, his features set into an expression of such mingled alarm and disgust that I almost laughed. Behind us, further up the passage and somewhere out of sight, there came the sound of grunting and rustling.

We stood, side by side, just beyond the reach of the light at the passage entrance. All at once a shadow appeared. For a moment it stood there, outlined against the light, a tall hooded figure. And then it was gone.

'Quickly!' I bounded back towards the main thorough-fare, my feet skittering on the muddy cobbles. He couldn't have gone far. I sprang over the fly-blown corpse of a dead tom-cat and plunged down the street.

'Where is he?' Will was at my side. 'Where did he go?'

'Look!' I pointed. Moving swiftly along in the deep shadows on the north side of the street, a cloaked figure was gliding away from us.

I tore after him, Will close behind. Clouds of furious flies rose about us. 'Faster!' I said. 'We mustn't lose him!'

We were heading into unfamiliar territory now, moving further away from the reassuring noise of St Saviour's Street and deep into the twisting maze of slums. Even Dr Bain, with all his familiarity with the area, his fearlessness and audacity, had not ventured down these streets. Would we be able to find our way out again? The figure ahead had a long and confident stride. Behind me, I could hear Will panting.

'Jem,' he said. 'D'you know where we are going? D'you know the way back? Jem!' He sounded worried and afraid. I knew he would follow me wherever I went, that he would not let me head off alone into such evil streets, no matter how anxious he was. But I would not ask that much of him. I would not have to – we were sure to catch the man at any moment. I ran faster, my arms pumping.

Ahead of us, the street narrowed, the houses on either side tall and black, leaning towards one another as if eventually, one day, they would slump together, and the thin strip of sky would be blotted out completely.

'Come on!' I cried. 'We almost have him!'

Our quarry turned right, sprinting up a flight of steps and beneath a crumbling archway of blackened bricks. I followed, heading deeper into that dark, uncharted labyrinth of streets and courts. All at once we emerged onto the crumbling edge of a narrow waterway, a filthy canal tributary, no wider than a barge. It was barricaded at one end by a giant wooden lock-gate, its sheer walls some twenty feet deep, brick-lined and coated with green and black slime. The filthy waters at its foot had a thick, lumpy texture, like boiled mince. Here and there the bloated flank of a dead animal broke the surface. The smell was intolerable.

Hardly visible in the shadows, the cloaked figure raced along the slippery stones of the canal bank, heading towards a single narrow plank that traversed the chasm in a makeshift bridge. He dashed across, and plunged towards the warren of tenements on the opposite bank. And yet if we were quick, if we ran that bit faster – I bounded after him. The plank bridge was barely wider than the sole of my boot. I felt it bow beneath my weight, but I did not hesitate and was across in an instant.

Behind me, I heard Will cry out. I muttered a curse and turned to urge him on. If he could just keep up—

Will was standing, motionless, in the centre of the slimy plank. His arms were outstretched, his knees bent, his gaze fixed in terror on the stretch of brown water some twenty feet below. 'Jem!' he screamed, his arms windmilling. I stopped. Up ahead, the figure in the cloak stopped too, and looked back. For a moment, he stood there, watching us, his face hidden in the shadows. He knew, as I did, that the chase was over. Who was he? I *had* to know. I took a step towards him.

'Jem!' Will screamed again. I could see the plank rocking beneath his feet, no more than two inches of rotten wood balanced on the lip of the canal-side. When I looked back, our quarry had vanished. We had lost the game – for the moment, at least.

I stood on the great stone slabs at the edge of the canal and held out my hand, trying not to look down at that yawning pit and the ribbon of effluent at its foot. 'Take my hand, Will,' I said. 'Two steps and you'll be safe.'

'I can't,' whispered Will. The plank rocked violently as his knees trembled. 'I can't move.'

'Stop looking down,' I said. 'Looking down makes it worse.' He looked up at me. His face was frozen in terror, his eyes staring, his breathing shallow. I held out my hand. 'Now,' I said, gently this time. 'Just walk forward. Two steps.'

And then I realised that he was not looking at me at all. Instead, he was looking at something over my shoulder.

Behind me, where the buildings throttled the street into a narrow passageway, two dark figures had appeared. They were short, wiry men with dirty caps and ragged greasy coats. Between them, a scrofulous, one-eyed dog bristled and growled. One of them pulled an iron bar from behind his back and held it like a cudgel in his hand. The other swung his arms, ape-like.

I turned back to Will, still poised and trembling on that rotten plank above the stinking stretch of effluent. 'Go back,' I said. 'I'll follow.'

'Go back?' cried Will. He was looking down again now, trying to turn, slowly inching his feet around. The slimy wood beneath his feet bowed and rocked as he moved. His arms flailed. All at once he was crouching down, holding onto the rotten timber with both hands. 'I can't!' he screamed. 'I can't move.'

'Will,' I said. 'You have to.' The dog was barking now, the men coming closer. They might kill us and rob us and fling our bodies into the canal and no one would ever know. I took one look at them, and stepped onto the plank.

'You have to move, Will,' I said. I tried to sound calm, as though we were merely standing on a pavement having a conversation. 'Stand up. Keep your eyes on the other bank, and walk over to it.'

What happened next is fixed in my mind like a series of random photographs. I can remember Will's terrified face, and the yawning pit at our feet. More clearly than anything, I can recall the strip of blue sky visible between the black, crooked rooftops, bright and hopeful, like a child's ribbon fluttering overhead. I know there was movement – a footstep, a stumble – and then Will was across and I close behind him. And then I slipped, and the world dropped away beneath my feet.

I remember rushing air, a shriek, the clawing of hands as I fell . . . I flailed my arms, trying to grip something – anything – and then I was hanging there, my fingers scrabbling to hold on, my feet scraping impotently against the slimy bricks of the canal wall. The smell of shit and decay was all about me, the metallic taste of blood on my lips was the taste of fear. I dangled there, clinging to an iron ring fixed into the canal-side, my legs kicking, the air about me echoing with the bark of a dog and the shouts of men. I looked down. Beneath me, far below, the plank was already sinking out of sight beneath the reeking brown sludge. I heard screaming, and with the ragged pain in my throat realised it was my own voice. And then Will was gripping my hand, his fingers clamped about my wrist as he hauled me upward.

We lay there for a moment, side by side on the greasy refuse-strewn paving slabs beside the canal. I could taste blood from where I had bitten my own tongue. My arm felt as though it had been almost torn from its roots, my knuckles were bloody where I had grazed them, and my coat was smeared all over with black slime. Will's arms were around me, his grip still tight as though he feared I might slip out of it. I could hear his heart racing, thudding wildly against his ribs in counterpoint to my own. But we were in no place to linger. We had run deep into the rookeries and I hoped we could find our way back out again. Without a word to one another, we got to our feet and began to retrace our steps. To the left, I heard a low whistle. Up ahead, another answered. I looked back. The two men and the hideous dog had walked along the canal and were making their way across the lock-gates at its head. They would soon be upon us, and from the sound of it there were others just like them lurking all around.

'Keep walking,' I hissed.

'Look!' Will bent down. He plucked something from the thick layer of slimy refuse that covered the ground, and held it up.

'What is it?' I said. 'Did he drop it? The man we were following?'

'He must have,' said Will. 'It's clearly been on the ground for only a moment.'

'What is it?' I said again. I could not make it out. 'Let me see.'

Will didn't answer. He looked at me strangely, and then held out his hand. On his palm was a small piece of lump sugar.

❦

We ran back towards Prior's Rents. I felt no shame in it – far better to be thought scared and get away from the place, than to be foolhardy enough to stroll homewards, and be murdered into the bargain.

Joe's building was a corner tenement, dark and derelict. It was quite possible that Joe would not be there, though there was some comfort in the knowledge that if we could not find him then it was unlikely that anyone else would. There were any number of places he might be hiding in that great ants' nest of tumbledown buildings.

There was no door, just a flight of stone steps leading up into the groaning darkness. Here and there a mound of rags told where a human being lay – dead, perhaps, or insensible, brains and organs poisoned beyond redemption by cheap gin. Higher and higher we climbed, at length passing a window, the shattered panes sharp against the mocking blue of the sky. In the light it threw onto the stair a pair of sunken-cheeked children sat, their faces black with dirt. They looked up at us with exhausted indifference. One of them stuck out a hand. I continued on. What use was a coin to such as they? They would only use it to buy gin. Or the coin would be extorted from them by violent family members, reluctantly exchanged for a bloody nose and another broken tooth. Behind me I heard Will stop. I turned, and saw him pressing a shilling into the grubby outstretched hand.

'You lookin' fer Joe?' The child's voice was sharp, its eyes suddenly bright and hungry looking.

'Yes, please,' said Will.

'He's not up here?' I said, turning back quickly. 'He used to live at the top.'

'He's not there now,' said the child. I had no idea whether I was addressing a boy or a girl. The face looked familiar, though lack of food gave them all the same pinched, sepulchral appearance.

'Where is he?' I said. 'Can you take us to him?'

'Joe said you'd come. The one with the red mask and the one with the 'at, he said. Said the one with the 'at was soft as butter and like as not'd give us a shillin' just for lookin' sad.' The child winked. 'Easy to look sad in this place, ain't it?'

'Will you take us to Joe?'

'Course!' Quick as ferrets both children sprang up and vanished through a hole in the wall behind.

'Well,' said Will. He looked at my filthy coat, and then down at his own scuffed and shit-caked boots. 'It can't get much worse, can it?'

The further we followed those two ragged children, the more uneasy I felt. We crawled through a jagged gap in the wall, clambered up a tall rickety ladder, and tiptoed over a dozen or so worm-eaten rafters. Here and there the lath and plaster had fallen through and dark holes gaped at our feet, the abyss below unfathomable. A draught of foetid air, and the sound of rustling and muttering voices, drifted up from the depths. The place was dark, the only light coming from holes punched in the roof where the slates had tumbled down. We ducked below a wooden beam, upon which, inexplicably, the bodies of dead rats had been pinned, lined up in a row – some curious tally of the city's most populous and execrable vermin. There were four score at least, all dangling by their tails, all in various states of desiccation, dried like kippers in the warm draught that blew up from the tenement below. The first ones we passed were now no bigger than tobacco pouches, the last plump and oily-looking.

'What are these for?' said Will, appalled.

'Never mind, Will,' I whispered. 'Some things are best left unexplained.' We crawled behind a chimney stack and along a narrow passage directly beneath the roof. I was sweating with exertion. How quickly those children moved, scuttling before us. Behind me, I could hear Will gasping for breath. He kept knocking his hat on the overhanging rats and they swung gently on their dry tails as he shuffled past. All at once the child in front of me vanished through a hole in a wall beside the greasy black flank of a chimney stack. At first I could see nothing, but as my eyes adjusted to the darkness I noticed that the shadows beyond the hole were moving. The sound of smothered coughing was audible, and whispered voices. Then a match was struck and the darkness was interrupted by the feeble yellow glow of a cheap tallow candle-end.

'Mr Flock'art?' It was a whisper from the cave ahead. The smell of unwashed bodies and dirty clothes was pungent beneath the smell of smoke and burnt fat.

'Joe.' I kept my voice low. 'That you?'

Joe's face appeared, lit from below by the feeble yellow candlelight. 'You shunt o' come,' he whispered. 'I tol' the others to look out fer you in case you came but you shunt o' come.'

'Do you have something for me?' I said.

'It ain't here. I hid it.'

'Where is it?' I could hardly imagine a more well-hidden and repulsive hidey-hole than the one Joe currently occupied. Why on earth he chose to hide himself in one place and Dr Bain's missing coffin in another—

'You'd never find it even if I tol' you,' said Joe. 'No one can find it 'cept me. But I'll get it and bring it you. Tomorrow. I were goin' to do that, but I heard there's been someone lookin' for me. P'raps someone what saw Dr Bain give it me.' He shrugged. 'I don't know who.'

The building was suddenly eerily quiet, for all that it teemed with vermin and paupers. From somewhere – whether behind or below us I could not tell – came a scuffling sound, followed by the echo of cautious footsteps. Even I could tell that those footsteps were made by the sharp heels and supple soles of new, finely crafted leather. Had we been followed after all? I put my hand into my pocket and felt the rough surface of the sugar lump between my fingers. Then the footsteps stopped – there was only silence, and the sound of the wind rattling the rotten shingles above our heads.

'He's 'ere!' whispered Joe.

'It was probably just the wind,' I said. 'God knows, there's enough loose boards around here to squeak and bang and thump till you're half frightened out of your wits.'

'I know all the sounds o' Prior's Rents,' replied Joe. 'And them footsteps weren't none I've heard before.'

'Then you'll know when to run, won't you?'

Joe looked up at me, his face pinched, and frightened. 'Dr Bain's dead, ain't he?' he said.

'Yes,' I replied.

'I knowed it,' said Joe. 'I liked Dr Bain. I got no complaints about 'im.' He sniffed, and rubbed his eyes with hands black with soot and grease. 'Gave me a sov that day. Just for keepin' that box for 'im.'

'A small coffin?'

Joe nodded. 'Somethin' nasty lookin' inside it, but I seen much worse round 'ere. Said I were to give it to you if he din't come back for it 'imself. Trusted me to keep me word, Dr Bain did, and I will too.'

'Well, you bring me what Dr Bain gave you, and I'll give you half a crown.'

'Here's one for now,' said Will. 'Go and buy yourselves something to eat.'

The coin was hardly visible as he tossed it forward, but I heard the sound of Joe's grubby hand snatching it from the air. 'Now go away,' he whispered. 'I'll bring that thing tomorrow mornin', sharp.'

Chapter Ten

〜

We said little as we walked back to St Saviour's. Will had to go to the graveyard – he had spent too much time away from the place already – and I knew I had left Gabriel and my father alone in the apothecary for too long. How selfish I was, gallivanting about the city when my father was ill. I glanced behind us. Were we being followed again? But St Saviour's Street was thick with people, cabs, coaches, carts, and I could see no one in pursuit. I took a deep breath. After the stinking tenement of Prior's Rents the place was like a fragrant oasis.

I had not been in the apothecary five minutes when Dr Hawkins appeared. 'Where's your father, Jem?'

'Out-patients, with Gabriel.'

'Has he slept?'

I shook my head.

'Then he's no better?'

I thought of my father, gaunt and worried, directing Gabriel about the apothecary shelves, trying his best to pretend that all was well. But I knew from his face, when he thought I was not looking, that fear and sorrow were his constant companions. 'From what I can tell he's just the same.'

Dr Hawkins rubbed a hand across his chin. 'We're running out of time.'

'Running out of time?' I said. 'For what?'

He did not answer.

'Will he die?' I said.

'We will all die, Jem.'

'That's not the sort of sleep my father needs.'

Dr Hawkins shook his head. 'He may well beg for it before much longer.'

'What do you mean by that?' I said. 'What do you mean "beg for it"? Why would he do such a thing?'

'I'm sorry.' Dr Hawkins laid a hand on my arm. 'I spoke out of turn. He won't die yet, not if I can help it.'

'And in the meantime?'

'In the meantime . . . There is something—' He stopped, as though the words had stung his lips.

'What?' I said. '*What?*'

'Something we might try. We can't wait much longer. And this time I will need your help.' He clapped me on the shoulder. 'Tonight, Jem. I will come for you both.'

❧❦

My father and I attended to the ward rounds together that evening. I knew the seven o'clock round was his favourite. The physicians were seldom on the wards at that time, the nurses behaved themselves and it was too early for them to be noticeably drunk.

I had told him that Dr Hawkins had been, that we were to go to Angel Meadow together that evening, and he lingered over his duties about the wards as though it might be the last time he ever saw the place. We passed from bed and bed. He stopped and spoke to every patient who was still conscious. 'You'll need another apprentice when I'm gone,' he said as we left the surgical ward.

'Gone?' I said. 'You'll not be away for long, surely?'

He smiled, but his eyes were grave. 'You know what I mean.'

When we got back to the apothecary my father went upstairs to gather whatever personal items he might need for his sojourn at Angel Meadow. I waited downstairs, staring into the fire. Will had taken Gabriel out to Sorley's for supper, and the place was silent. I wondered when Joe Silks would come. We had learned little from the coffin brought to us by the girl from Mrs Roseplucker's. Perhaps Joe's would be more illuminating.

At that moment Dr Catchpole came in, Dr Magorian and Dr Graves in his wake. I was surprised to see them at the hospital so late – why were they still here? But then I remembered that there had been a meeting of the Building Committee over in the governors' hall to discuss St Saviour's relocation south of the river. They would not have missed the chance to opine about the new hospital.

'I cannot bear to be at home without her,' said Dr Catchpole as he entered.

'But it is for her own good,' said Dr Graves. 'Dr Hawkins concurs. Angel Meadow will provide her with a refuge from the world.'

Dr Catchpole shook his head. 'She will not see me,' he whispered. 'I cannot put that knowledge from my mind.

I've been in the library all evening trying to distract myself but I have failed. I stepped in to see whether Mr Flockhart would give me something to help me sleep tonight.'

'Surely you have laudanum?' said Dr Magorian. He rested a hand on Dr Catchpole's shoulder. 'I'm sorry for your troubles. A wife should be a support to her husband. A helpmeet in all he does.'

'You are lucky, Magorian,' said Dr Catchpole. 'Your wife is an angel.'

Dr Magorian smiled and nodded. He slipped a hand into his pocket and drew out his silver sugar case. 'Mr Flockhart,' he said. 'Do you have a moment to prepare a draught for Dr Catchpole?'

'If you're not too busy running about doing *other* things.' Dr Graves grinned. He watched me reach up for a jar of powdered valerian. I winced, as my shoulder burned from my escapade at the canal side. 'Something troubling you, Mr Flockhart?' he said.

'What *have* you been doing, man?' murmured Dr Magorian. He peered at the grazes on my cheek, before offering his sugar case to Dr Graves.

I looked from one to the other. Both were tall, both were wrapped in cloaks. I looked at their boots, searching for the distinctive filth of Prior's Rents, but both men's boots had recently been cleaned.

'I have the same draught I make up for your wife, Dr Catchpole,' I said.

Dr Catchpole closed his eyes, pressing his folded handkerchief to his lips. 'Have you nothing stronger?' he whispered.

'Yes,' I said. 'If you wish it.' I reached for a bottle of tincture of *Cannabis sativa*. 'I'm going to Angel Meadow shortly,' I added. 'May I take Mrs Catchpole something? A salve, perhaps, for her head?'

'You're very kind,' said Dr Catchpole. I could see I had disturbed him by even alluding to her. His chin trembled. 'Oh, Annabel.' He dropped onto a chair, his spirit broken, the tears running down his face. Dr Graves and Dr Magorian cleared their throats and looked out of the window at the night, embarrassed by the sight of such weakness.

I decanted the *Cannabis* tincture, and sealed the bottle with wax. I had made some lavender and oatmeal soap, which I sold to the ladies' committee for sixpence each, and I put one aside for Mrs Catchpole. I filled a pot with salve made from beeswax, olive oil, calendula, lavender and comfrey. The comfrey would reduce the bruising to her head, and help the skin to heal, the lavender was astringent and would ease any inflammation, the calendula would soothe.

I handed Dr Catchpole his tincture. He slipped it into his pocket with hardly a nod of thanks.

'Come along, sir,' said Dr Graves gruffly. 'Let's find you a cab.'

I held the door open for them as Dr Graves and Dr Magorian helped Dr Catchpole out into the courtyard.

Later on, when it was all over, I looked back at those moments with Dr Catchpole, Dr Graves and Dr Magorian and I was amazed at my complacency. I prided myself on my powers of observation, and yet I could not have paid less attention to what was said and done if I had been deaf and blind. My mind was filled with my own worries – about my father and what might happen to him that evening; about Eliza and the herbs I had given her. And yet such excuses only serve to reveal my imprudence further. It was clear that it was either Dr Magorian or Dr Graves who had followed Will and me through the rookeries of St Saviour's earlier that day. And yet still I was convinced that I was one step ahead of them. Was I not going to speak to Mrs Catchpole that very evening? Would I not then discover who, or what, she had seen as she looked through Dr Bain's window? And did I not have one of Dr Bain's coffins? Joe would deliver the other soon enough, as promised. We had yet to uncover their secrets but it would be only a matter of time and then we would know everything. Oh, how arrogant I was! And how greatly I underestimated our adversary. It was to prove my undoing. After that night, nothing would ever be the same again.

Chapter Eleven

W e walked up to Angel Meadow in silence, Dr
Hawkins, my father and I. The evening was chilly,
and I could feel the familiar lick of damp against
my skin as a brown fog drifted up from the river. The air
had an opaque, grainy look to it. In an hour's time we
would hardly be able to see to the ends of our noses. My
father was too tired to speak. Dr Hawkins was deep in
thought. And me? I would, at last, discover what made my
father so sick, so unable to sleep that even laudanum
appeared to have no effect on him, and he rose from his
opium-induced stupor worse than when he lay down. I
wondered what Dr Hawkins's plan might be, and what
role I would play that evening. I wondered whether I
would see Mrs Catchpole and what she might say.

Angel Meadow was a dark fortress of a building. More
like a prison than a hospital, at least from the outside, it
was built of the same dark stone that had been used in the
construction of Newgate. Once, like St Saviour's, it had

been situated outside London. Fresh air was considered beneficial to the inmates, and besides, who in the city wanted to be reminded of their relations condemned within? Far better to forget such tainted individuals, to condemn them to a life of incarceration in the country, out of sight, and, quite literally, out of mind. But the city had grown, and now, like our infirmary, Angel Meadow Asylum was surrounded on all sides by the houses of the poor. Slick with moisture from the rising fog, and coated with coal dust and soot, it had a black, sweaty appearance. There were only two small windows in the northern wall. Situated high in the brickwork, they glittered in the darkness like a pair of tiny yellow eyes. The main entrance was a large arched gateway to the west, through which secured coaches and padded ambulances rattled during the day, but which was closed, locked and bolted during the night. It was through those gates that Mrs Catchpole had been brought, her dress torn and soaking, her face streaked with mud and blood, crying and sobbing for Dr Bain.

Below the yellow eyes was the small door through which my father and Dr Hawkins had vanished on the night I had followed them. As I expected, Dr Hawkins knocked three times upon it with the head of his stick. Behind the door a man in a leather apron held up a lantern. Beyond, a low whitewashed passage plunged into the heart of the building. Dr Hawkins nodded to the man, but said nothing. He led us into the passage and the door closed silently behind us. There came the sound of keys jangling, of locks turning and bolts shooting home, and then the sound of footsteps – my own, Dr Hawkins's and my father's. The man in the leather apron moved noiselessly behind me.

'Dr Hawkins,' I said. 'Is there time for me to see Mrs Catchpole?'

Dr Hawkins spoke to the silent turnkey, then he turned to address me. 'Mrs Catchpole is an interesting case,' he said. 'I think you'll be surprised at what you find. She's found Angel Meadow to be a refuge from the world. The effect on her mind has been remarkable.'

'And Dr Catchpole?' I said. 'Has he been to see her?'

'She won't see him. I've advised him to stop coming – for the time being at least.'

Dr Hawkins and my father vanished through a doorway. The attendant led me further into the building. He said nothing. He was no taller than I, but he was broad. His forearms bulged below his rolled-up shirt sleeves, his skin etiolated and as pale as fat. No doubt most of his muscular activity – which presumably involved restraining mad people – took place in dark cells or dimly lit wards, far from the hope of sunlight and rescue.

We ascended a long flight of stairs until we reached a heavy metal door. The man produced his great bunch of keys, selected one of them with the precision of a master safe-cracker, and inserted it delicately into the lock. All at once the place was illuminated by the warm glow of lamps. The floor beneath our feet was carpeted with drugget, the walls lined with pictures – soothing landscapes mostly, or images of trees and flowers. I noticed they were screwed tightly to the wall in their frames. Through a door to our right, I saw a room filled with large comfortable chairs. Attendants waited in the shadows.

'Do you have wards?' I asked.

'Yes, sir.' It was the first time the man had spoken to me.

His voice was low and soft. 'But not in this wing of the building. This is the east wing. The ladies have rooms to theirselves here. Your Mrs Catchpole's on her own. The ladies don't get wards. At least, not at first.' He grinned. 'But time changes everything at Angel Meadow. Ladies included.'

'I assume she's calmer than when she first came?'

He nodded. 'She spent a night in the basement when she were brought back from Dr Bain's funeral – shrieking and crying, wouldn't change her clothes, wouldn't get into bed, wouldn't eat. Mud everywhere. Then Dr Hawkins saw her. She were calm after that.'

'What did he do?'

'Nuthin'. Spoke to her, that's all. She's been better since then.'

'And has she had visitors? Her husband?'

'He came with Dr Graves and Dr Magorian, but she went hysterical again and we had to ask them to leave. Later it were Mrs Magorian and her daughter.' From somewhere at the far end of the gallery, the sound of one of Chopin's nocturnes echoed. 'Opus nine,' said the man. His apron creaked as he moved. 'Number two.'

'Very soothing,' I said. Music, heavy food, warm baths, were all part of Dr Hawkins's therapeutic regime. I had to admit, the place seemed to be a model of order and tranquillity. Nonetheless, not everyone could afford such treatment. I wondered where the ladies were sent when their families could no longer afford to pay for them to be kept in such luxury. I doubted there were comfortable chairs and Chopin in those places.

We stopped at an open door, and the attendant stood back. 'Don't look at her for too long,' he whispered.

215

'Don't look her in the eye. Stick to simple questions, like as though she's a child.'

'Another visitor for Mrs Catchpole?' said the female attendant standing sentinel on the threshold. She raised an eyebrow. 'At this time! Well, one more won't make much difference. But you've not got long. It's bedtime in half an hour.'

'I only need half an hour,' I said.

Mrs Catchpole's room was about twenty-feet square. Its window was high in the wall, the shutters had yet to be closed and I could see that six white-painted bars covered it on the outside.

Mrs Catchpole was sitting in a chair beside the bed. Her hands moved in her lap, as though at work on some invisible knitting. Her blue eyes were focused on a spot on the floor, about a yard from the edge of the carpet. She smiled slightly, as though her own thoughts brought her amusement. Her hair had been pinned up inexpertly by hands that were neither her own nor her maid's. Other than a deep purple bruise over her right eye, with a crimson cut at its centre, there was no sign at all of her recent escapade in St Saviour's parish church.

'Good evening, Mrs Catchpole,' I said.

She looked up at me then, her eyes dull with grief. 'Hello, Mr Flockhart,' she said. I was glad to see that her mind was clear at least. 'Have you come to ask me about Dr Bain?' She tried to smile. 'You were his friend, weren't you?'

'Yes,' I said. And then: 'Mrs Catchpole, I have to ask you . . . did you see him before he died?'

Mrs Catchpole sighed. 'I feel better if I pretend that he loved me, though I know he didn't.' She turned huge, sad eyes upon me. 'Am I mad to say such a thing?'

'No. At least, I don't think so.' I did not know what else to say.

'He *said* he loved me. But he was lying. I know that now. I didn't believe it at first, but Dr Hawkins assures me that it was the case.' Her hand fastened about my wrist, the circling fingers drawing tight as a wire. She pulled me down so that her face was close, her lips almost against my ear. Her breath was stale, and tainted with a whiff of laudanum. 'I know he's dead,' she hissed. 'And I know I am not to have his child, not any more.' Her eyes filled with tears. 'Dr Hawkins says I should be glad that scandal was so quickly and easily averted. But what do I care about scandal?'

'But you *should* care, Mrs Catchpole,' I whispered. 'Your husband has many friends. He can make your life very difficult should he choose it. He can lock you up in a place far worse than this.' I took her twitching hands in mine, and forced them to be still. 'You must calm yourself,' I said. 'Don't let him see you like this.'

'I will not allow him to see me at all!' cried Mrs Catchpole. 'He says I might go home, but I'll not go there. I'd rather die than go back to his home ever again.'

I looked into her thin face, the flesh sunken with worry and sadness, the skin stretched over her bones like white silk, her eyes dark and frightened. But behind them there was a calmness, and a serenity. There was nothing deranged about Mrs Catchpole, I was certain. I handed her the soap, and the pillow of lavender I had brought with me. I produced the pot of salve I had brought too. 'It will help your head. Will you let me apply a little? It's comfrey, rose water, beeswax, olive oil—'

She shook her head, but took them from me all the same. They lay in her lap, untouched.

217

'Who did you see that night, Mrs Catchpole?' I said. 'You remember coming to Mrs Roseplucker's? To Wicke Street?'

Her eyes darted to the door, and then back to me. She nodded.

'You remember striking Mr Jobber – the fat man at the door?'

She nodded again.

'Do you remember anything else? Did anyone follow you when you left, when you escaped from your husband? Was anyone waiting outside?'

Mrs Catchpole shook her head. She put a finger to her mouth and nibbled at the nail. I could see then that all of them were bitten down to the quick.

'Your husband carried you out. Tried to bundle you into the carriage but you escaped.'

'He wanted me dead,' she said. 'Dr Graves was with him, in the carriage. Did you see him?'

I shook my head. I had seen only the outline of the carriage, the blinds drawn, and Mrs Catchpole's petticoats, her legs waving wildly as she struggled.

'I pretended I had fainted,' she said. 'When he relaxed his grip, I struggled free.'

'And you ran,' I said. 'You ran away from them.'

'He followed, of course, and the carriage came after. But I ran too fast. There was fog. They couldn't see me. I had no idea where I was and I took a wrong turn. I don't know how long I wandered, but I was cold, so very cold. And then,' she smiled. 'All at once there were the gates to St Saviour's, and the light from the apothecary window visible inside beneath the archway. I went down the street to his house and looked through the window.'

'The shutters were closed,' I said.

'Yes,' she said. 'But I could see through a crack between the boards, and there they were!'

'Who did you see?' I held my breath. 'Who?'

Mrs Catchpole's eyes were fixed upon the door. 'Is someone there?' she whispered. 'Someone outside in the corridor?'

I looked up. The door was open, and the lamplit gallery outside was visible. Shadows moved against the wall, but no one passed by. Other than the attendant who had brought me, there was no one there.

'I thought I saw—' a frown creased her brow. She produced a silk handkerchief and dabbed at her lips. 'I seem to see him everywhere.'

'Dr Bain?'

'My husband. Dr Magorian. Dr Graves.'

'You saw your husband,' I said. 'Didn't you? You saw him at Dr Bain's house.'

She nodded. 'He was crouched over Dr Bain. Dr Bain was in a chair before the fire.'

Her voice was faint, as if she were reluctant to talk about it, but I pressed on anyway. 'And did you see anyone else there? Did you see anything unusual? Anything out of place?'

'I don't know,' she said. 'It was always a mess in there.'

'Always?' I said. 'Have you been in Dr Bain's house before?'

Mrs Catchpole sighed. 'I suppose it hardly matters now,' she said. 'Yes, I'd been there before. I'd followed him too. I knew he went to that horrid house in Wicke Street. They all go there. That's why I knew where to find him.'

'And there was nothing different about the room the evening Dr Bain died?'

'Only—' Mrs Catchpole frowned. 'Only the screen. It was usually folded back, but it had been opened.'

'The screen?' I said. It had been folded when Will and Dr Bain and I were there. And it had still been folded when we found the doctor, dead. But Mrs Catchpole had seen it *un*folded.

She shrugged. 'Well, I can't think it means anything.'

'It means that there was someone else there, Mrs Catchpole,' I said. 'Someone who didn't want your husband to see them. Perhaps if you close your eyes and try to visualise the room, visualise what you saw—'

'But it was the same as ever.'

'No!' I said. 'No, it wasn't! Come, Mrs Catchpole. Close your eyes and think of the room.'

She withdrew her hand from mine, and covered her eyes. 'But I can only think of him. I can only see him, slumped in that chair, his book in his lap. I thought he must have been reading and had fallen asleep, that my husband was about to wake him—'

'A book?' I said. 'He had a book in his lap?'

'Yes, I saw it slip to the ground.'

'What kind of book?'

'I don't know,' she said.

I nodded. Dr Bain had lots of books. It might have been any one of those that was in his lap – and yet, when we found him there was no book beside the body – no book on the floor, or nearby. What book was it? It was clear to me that Dr Catchpole had disturbed the murderer. Was Dr Bain dead, or dying when Dr Catchpole stood over him? Had Dr Catchpole taken the book? I resolved to ask him myself.

I sensed a movement behind me. Mrs Catchpole saw it too and she rose to her feet, her hands flying to her face. 'He is here!' The jar of salve fell from her lap and rolled across the carpet.

But it was not Dr Catchpole. It was Mrs Magorian and Eliza. I was always glad to see Eliza, but at that moment I felt a flutter of irritation. Confound the lady almoners and their Bible readings! Could they not just go home and sit still?

Mrs Magorian fluttered forward. 'My dear Mrs Catchpole, please forgive us for coming so late. But I said we would visit you every day until you were better, did I not? We would not desert a friend in her moment of need.' She picked up the salve. 'What's this?'

'Salve,' I replied.

'Oh, how kind,' she said. 'How *very* kind of you, Mr Flockhart.' She put it on the washstand beside the soap I had brought.

Eliza smiled at me. 'Hello, Mr Flockhart,' she said. She had regained her complexion and curled her hair. I could not take my eyes from her.

'I have brought you a Bible, Mrs Catchpole,' said Mrs Magorian. 'And a bunch of chrysanthemums – Eliza, my dear, put those in some water.' She pulled up a chair and sat down at Mrs Catchpole's side. 'Perhaps if I were to read one of the psalms, to calm your raging spirits before bed?' She flipped it open. '"*Blessed is the man that walketh not in the counsel of the ungodly, nor standeth in the way of sinners, nor sitteth in the seat of the scornful*",' she began.

At that moment there was a scuffling sound out in the passageway. We heard voices raised, and all at once Dr

Catchpole burst in. 'Annabel!' he cried. 'Why will you not see me?'

Mrs Catchpole sprang to her feet. 'You!' she cried. 'You killed him!'

'No!' Dr Catchpole fell to his knees in the middle of the carpet. 'No, I swear it.' Dr Graves stood behind him, his smile ghastly in the lamplight.

'Ladies,' he said, bowing. 'Miss Magorian.' Eliza backed away. Dr Graves stepped closer. 'What lovely flowers,' he said. The chrysanthemums Eliza was holding were dark red shot with yellow – the colours of blood and bile. They were the lady almoners' usual choice, and I could not see that there was anything beautiful about them. Dr Graves made a show of plucking one, and placing it in his button hole. 'That I may think of you,' he said to Eliza.

'Gentlemen,' I cried. 'Dr Hawkins asked you not to visit. Not until Mrs Catchpole is more settled.' All at once the room was crowded with people and ringing with voices.

'"*And he shall be like a tree planted by the rivers of water, that bringeth forth his fruit in his season; his leaf also shall not wither*",' cried Mrs Magorian.

Dr Catchpole shuffled towards his wife, his hands together in supplication. He had aged, even since I had seen him in the apothecary that afternoon, and his face was as drawn and sunken as a corpse's. His nostrils, brown with snuff, were the only marks of colour in his face. I caught a whiff of spirits from him as he inched forward. Was he drunk? I looked at Dr Graves. He appeared to be quite sober. He affected to sniff his button hole whilst leering at Eliza.

'Come home, my darling,' cried Dr Catchpole.

'Get away from me!' screamed his wife.

The attendant who had brought me downstairs reappeared, drawn, no doubt, by the din. He grinned, and pulled a lever at the side of the fireplace – I assumed it would summon assistance. I had expected him to wrestle Dr Catchpole out of the room, but he appeared to be enjoying the spectacle, and he did nothing more.

Dr Catchpole was now on his knees at his wife's feet. She scrambled onto her chair so that he would not touch her skirts but he lunged forward with a sob and seized her foot. Mrs Catchpole's arms windmilled as she tried to stay upright. She kicked out at her husband, the point of her shoe causing his spectacles to come loose and swing down across his face. Mrs Magorian, still sitting beside Mrs Catchpole with the Bible open in her lap, froze in her chair as Dr Catchpole grovelled before her. Eliza looked on, ignoring the glances of Dr Graves, her expression almost gleeful at the sudden uproar.

Two orderlies burst in. They seized Dr Catchpole by the arms and manhandled him back towards the door. 'Annabel!' he cried. At first he resisted, struggling to escape and come back into the room. And then all at once he sagged between his captors, as if his limbs had turned to liquid. 'You are my wife,' he sobbed. 'You cannot leave me.' The orderlies hauled him away down the corridor.

I dashed out after them. 'This gentleman is one of St Saviour's most respected physicians,' I cried. 'You will treat him with respect.'

The orderlies stopped. Dr Catchpole dangled hopelessly between them, his spectacles awry, his face wet with snot and tears. 'Let him go,' I said. 'He won't give you any trouble now.'

Dr Catchpole sank down onto one of the numerous chairs that were bolted to the floor at intervals along the corridor. He put his head in his hands. I crouched before him. I knew I would not get the chance again. 'Dr Catchpole,' I said. 'I know you went to see Dr Bain the night he died.'

He clenched his fists on either side of his head. For a moment I thought he was going to assault me, but he did not move.

'I didn't kill him,' said Dr Catchpole. His voice was low and furious, so that I had to lean in close to catch his words. 'I only went there to speak with him. To reason with him.'

'And he would not listen?'

'He would not answer the door!' Dr Catchpole sat up, his face furious. 'I knew he was in,' he said. 'I could see the light. I could see a shadow moving. So I went around the back. The kitchen door was unlocked.' He sighed, and sagged once more. 'I went through and I found him in his chair.'

'Was he dead?'

'He was not.'

'So what did you do?'

Dr Catchpole smiled. When he spoke, his voice was low and soft. 'I did nothing.' He pulled out a handkerchief and wiped his face. Then he folded it and slipped it back into his pocket. I could see he had mastered himself completely. He stared at me over the rims of his spectacles, his eyes cold and hard and blue. 'I did nothing,' he repeated. 'I found him in his chair before the fire. I saw he was not long for the world. He tried to stand up, but I pushed him back. I watched him for a little, perhaps five minutes? I could not tear my eyes from him. I wanted to see his pain, his impotence, his fear.' His voice was scalpel-sharp. 'And then I left. I would not help him. Even if I had known how to, I would still have left him there.' He laughed. 'D'you know, he slid onto his knees before me, as if begging for my forgiveness. But I would not forgive. I was glad to see him suffer. There was nothing I could do; nothing I *would* do.' He shrugged. 'He fell forward onto the hearth rug, and there I left him.'

'And that's all?'

'That's all.'

'Did you take the book?'

Dr Catchpole frowned. 'What book?'

'The book he was reading.'

'I didn't go there to borrow Dr Bain's books, Mr Flockhart.'

'And the poison. Was it bloodroot?'

'Dr Graves says so. I hardly care. I only know that I left him there, gasping for breath, unable to move a muscle to save himself. There was no dignity for him, just as he accorded me none.' He stood up, and brushed a fleck of lint off his sleeve. 'And if I could relive that evening, I would do exactly the same thing again.'

❧❧

Dr Graves appeared at Dr Catchpole's elbow and steered him away down the hall. Some minutes later, after doing their best to calm Mrs Catchpole (but merely, in my view, inflaming the woman further), Mrs Magorian and Eliza left too. On her own at last, Mrs Catchpole paced her room. She refused camomile, laudanum, any sedative at all. I could see that rest, and quietude, would serve her best, and I abandoned her to the care of her attendant – a pinch-faced woman with hard bony hands. I felt uneasy about leaving her, though I could not say why. But Dr Hawkins and my father would be waiting and I could stay with her no longer.

The attendant and I walked back along the carpeted corridor. 'I'm surprised to see that she doesn't want to rest.'

'She's always up,' he replied. His face was expressionless. Above his white slab-like cheeks, his eyes shifted. 'But not as late as some of them. Them what never sleeps.'

'I beg your pardon?' My voice was sharp. 'You have patients who never sleep?'

'One of 'em, at any rate. *Never* sleeps.' The attendant was old – perhaps sixty years – a relic from the days when Angel Meadow Asylum was a place where one might come to gawp and jeer at the mad. I knew what he was going to say next. 'Want to see him?'

I could not look at the man. I felt suddenly breathless and anxious and my heart was thumping. The smell from his leather apron nauseated me and my guts squirmed. No doubt he was merely being fanciful, exaggerating to impress me. A man who never slept? Surely that was not possible. I should not pander to the fellow, I thought. My father was waiting. My father. 'Show me,' I said.

The attendant reached, unlocked a door. I followed him down a flight of uncarpeted stairs. 'The basement is where we keeps some of the bad cases. The ones what can't be cured, or what upsets the others.'

'And the one who never sleeps?'

'Down here.' He did not meet my gaze. 'God save us all from such a fate.'

❧

The basement was a dismal low-ceilinged corridor. There were no floor coverings, and beneath our feet were cold, stone slabs. My footsteps echoed, no matter how hard I tried to walk silently. Ahead of me, the attendant moved without a sound. The corridor was lined with heavy wooden doors, riveted with iron, each with a sturdy lock and a small sliding panel for viewing the occupant. No windows looked onto that subterranean passage, and the place seemed to stretch on and on into the dark bowels of the earth. From the other side of a door came the sound of low and rhythmic moaning. From behind another I could hear sobbing, and from behind a third a voice spoke over and over again: 'Where's Papa? Where's Papa? Where's Papa? . . .'

There came a sigh from somewhere deep in the shadows. I could see a glow in the darkness, up ahead around a bend in the passage. The sound of a dragging footstep, the rattle of keys, and a hollow cough spoke of the approach of the warden. He wore an old top coat, with wide lapels and a high shawl collar, of the kind that was fashionable some thirty years earlier. It was green with age, shining with greasiness and spotted here and there with mould. He looked to be about eighty years old, and a fine scattering of scalp flakes clung to the verdigris shoulders of his coat, as though he were desiccating before my eyes. I wondered how long it had been since he had climbed the flight of stairs out of that basement burrow, how long since he had felt the sun and wind on his face, though he was so old and dry I was not sure he would survive very much of either.

'This gentleman's come to see Macbeth.' My guide addressed the warden.

'Macbeth?' I said, hopefully. 'Is that really his name?'

The warden laughed – a sound like wind passing through the dried keys of a sycamore. 'Naw,' he said. '*That's* not 'is real name. I just calls 'im that. I'm *edge-akayted*, see?'

'"Macbeth doth murder sleep."' All at once I felt sick and dizzy. I closed my eyes. 'Show me,' I whispered. I heard the sound of the keys, the scrape of a lock, the scream of an ancient iron hinge. Inside, was darkness. Beside me, the warden held up his candle.

The room was small, no more than eight feet by twelve. It was upholstered in its entirety with tough cotton padding, riveted to the walls and floor. The door too was lined with the stuff. It had a waxy sheen in the candlelight, and an oily brownish patina. High in the wall, a small barred window, no more than eight inches square, allowed the moonlight in.

On the floor, sitting against the far wall, was a man. He was on his knees, and he rocked back and forth, his head in his hands, making a low moaning sound. I realised now that I had been listening to him even before the door was opened, so demented and pitiful was the sound. I could not see his face for his hands were held over it. White hair straggled over his fingers. He wore a tattered shirt and a filthy pair of navy blue britches. He rocked without stopping, as though the act and the sound had a rhythm and sonorousness than comforted him.

'Does that all the time,' said the warden. 'Rocks and rocks like that. Never any bother. Poor devil.' He shook his head. 'Thought I'd seen everything, but I ain't never seen this.'

'And this is the man who never sleeps?' I whispered.

'Used to sleep, so I were told. But not now. Did sometimes when he first came. That were a while ago now, though. Can't remember when he last slept, but then I'm not watchin' 'im all the time. But the sound never stops. He hardly moves, just rocks. Hardly eats. Blind now too.'

The blind man's shoulders were skeleton-thin, his clothes hanging off him. Beneath he was little more than a living corpse, the flesh and muscle worn away so that he was nothing but bones and sinew. I closed my eyes, hardly able to look. I could feel the blood thumping at my temples. I put my hand to my head, as a low groan escaped my lips. The man before us fell silent. He had not noticed the opening of the door, but now his head snapped round and he turned towards us. His eyes were red rimmed and glassy, and he stared at the light without blinking. His skin was grey, the flesh cleaving to the skull in a papery layer. He stared at me, his eyes, once sharp and sparkling and blue, now milky and pale.

When I awakened I was lying on the floor of the basement corridor, the attendant looking down at me. The door to Macbeth's cell was closed, and I could hear once again that dreadful rhythmic moaning. I felt sick. My head ached from where I had struck it upon the floor and my guts churned within me, so that for a moment I wondered whether I had compounded the ignominy of passing out by soiling my own britches. I let out a great fart, and felt all the better for it.

'There you are, sir,' said the attendant, helping me to my feet. 'It's the shock, ain't it? There's not many that can look on Macbeth and not come over all queer. It ain't nat'ral, a human ghost.'

I nodded, licking dry lips. He did not meet my gaze as he turned away. 'Perhaps we'd better get you up to Dr Hawkins's rooms now.'

⁂

My father lay on a leather-topped couch, the size and shape of an operating table. His upper body was angled so that he could sit up slightly, and his head rested on a pillow. His eyes were closed. In the dim light, with his eyes in shadow, his resemblance to 'Macbeth' was more striking than ever.

'And you saw Mrs Catchpole?' Dr Hawkins was standing at a table, the surface of which was littered with scientific equipment – rubber tubes, syringes of varying size, beakers, clamps. His shirt sleeves were rolled up.

'Yes.' I did not want to talk about Mrs Catchpole. 'And then I saw someone else,' I said. 'In the basement. The attendant took me.'

For a moment, Dr Hawkins froze, a cannula and a large stoppered flask in his hands. My father's eyes opened.

'He had no business in the basement,' muttered Dr Hawkins.

'I'm glad he took me,' I said. 'As neither you nor my father saw fit to do so.'

'Macbeth,' said my father. 'That's what they call him, isn't it?' His lips curved in the faintest of smiles. 'But you and I know better, don't we, Jem? You and I know exactly who he is.'

'He is my uncle,' I said. 'Your brother, Nathaniel.'

Mr father nodded. 'I thought he was dead,' he said. 'We went our separate ways a long time ago. You met him, Jem, remember? When you were a child? I never saw him again after that, until Dr Hawkins told me—' He closed his eyes. The only sound came from the ticking of the clock, a reminder that every second that passed was a second closer to insanity, a second that advanced my father's illness and took him further from cure. Tick. Tick. Tick. Unceasing. Relentless. Inevitable.

Then, 'There was always talk of bad blood, tainted blood, running through the family. Our father's brother. A grandfather. A great-aunt as mad as King George. We vowed never to speak of it. But it was a constant shadow in our lives, like a storm on the horizon, and Nathan and I watching it, waiting for the wind to change direction and bring it home. There was always hope, always a possibility that the illness, the affliction, whatever it was, would pass us by – one of us at least, perhaps both, might be spared.' He shook his head, his grey hair straggling across the pillow like the ragged seeds of the fire-flower. How thin it had become and how old he looked; how tired and without hope. He turned his eyes upon me. 'Nathaniel, as you saw him, is what I shall become. Blind, insane, demented with exhaustion, my mind and body eroded from within by the very life force that sustains us all. It never stops, nor rests, nor leaves us be. It eats away at us, consuming us the way an engine consumes coal, faster and faster the less and less there is to take. And you? You can only wait, and hope. And pray. For my brother, and for me. And then, when I am gone, you must pray for yourself.'

It was no more than I had expected. The moment I heard mention of the man who never slept, I knew. When I saw him, I became certain. And yet the knowledge, somehow, seemed alien to me. I could not comprehend it. My father was to die, blind and raving? I was to live my life without him, hostage to a similar fate? I could not, *would* not believe it, even though I knew it to be the truth.

'Jem.' My father held out a hand. His fingers, always so strong, looked like the fingers of an old man. 'I'm sorry I didn't tell you. I'm sorry you had to find out this way. Seeing Nathaniel. I didn't tell you because I couldn't – I couldn't bear for you to live with the knowledge of what may happen, the possibility of madness, as I have done—'

'I know, Father,' I said.

'I was just a boy when my own uncle fell ill. We watched, Nathan and I, watched him slowly change. And then one day he was gone. He took his own life.' My father took a deep breath. 'He chose eternal damnation,' he whispered. 'At the time I could not understand how he could make such a choice, but now . . . now I pray that I will find the strength—'

And so, at last, I understood his loneliness and dread, his taciturn nature. He had been waiting, in fear, all his life. And now? Now he was more afraid than ever. 'There must be a chance,' I whispered. 'A hope.'

'My only chance lies with Dr Hawkins. We tried bleeding, tried weakening the whole bodily economy in the hope that new blood would be manufactured to replace the old, and that sleep would come.'

It had not worked, I knew that much. 'What happens now?'

'Dr Hawkins will remove my blood, and replace it with his own.'

'And you are here, Jem, because you must put your father's blood into my veins.' Dr Hawkins was standing with his back to the candlelight. His face was in darkness, but I knew there would be a gleam in his eyes. I had seen that light in Dr Bain's eyes many times. 'I know you understand,' he continued, as though reading my thoughts. 'Your work with Dr Bain – he told me what took place on those evenings you spent together. You understand the need to test, to experiment, to try for ourselves. It is only then that we can draw conclusions.'

'Yes, yes,' I said. I had heard it all before. If it was Dr Hawkins's wish to fill his own veins with my father's tainted blood, then I was not about to dissuade him.

'And how did Nathaniel find his way here?' I said.

'Your uncle was brought to me not four weeks ago,' said Dr Hawkins. 'But it was not the first time I had come across him. We had met in India, years ago, when I worked at the Calcutta hospital and he was surgeon aboard the *Admiral Greystoke*. The details are irrelevant, but we became friends. One day Nathan told me of his fear: the hereditary blood of the Flockharts. He was quite well at the time, and showed no sign of the illness that was later to leave him the wrecked and blinded wretch you saw.

'Sometime later I returned to London, but I told Nathan to look me up in that city if ever he was there, and to be certain to do so if the malady came upon him. Of course, once I met your father, Jem, it was quite clear to me that he was Nathaniel Flockhart's brother, and that he too might one day suffer from the same sickness. But it was not for me to break Nathaniel's confidence, and I said nothing of the matter. In time, I discovered that your father suffered from insomnia. Was it a mild form of the same condition? I could not be sure, but I watched, and listened, and waited.

'Eventually, though I had hoped it might take place in happier circumstances, one day Nathan Flockhart sought me out. He was already deep within the grip of that terrible illness – his eyesight was failing, and he was hardly able to speak. At first, he stayed with me, in my home. But he deteriorated quickly, and it soon became impossible to keep him there. It was then that he was brought to Angel Meadow, and here, eventually, he met your father once more.

'It appeared at first that your father remained free of the disease. I wondered whether there had been exciting causes that, for Nathan, had precipitated the illness, whereas for your father those stimuli had been avoided. The question was soon answered, as it became apparent that your father too was afflicted.

'Nathan is now blind, and quite mad. But your father? Your father is in the early stages, and perhaps there is some hope, even if it is just a little. These past weeks he has watched his own brother turn mad, and all the while he knows that he too will end up that way, unless we find a way to intervene.'

'And me?' I whispered.

'We don't yet know what your fate will be.' He patted my shoulder. 'But we must live in hope. I am convinced the environment has nothing to do with the appearance, nor the progress, nor the cure of the illness, and so we must try other means. Dr Bain was to have officiated at this evening's experiment. I suppose I might have asked

Dr Magorian, or Dr Graves, perhaps, possibly even Dr Catchpole, but they have their own preoccupations and somehow none of them seem . . . suitable. Dr Bain was fascinated, as you might expect. He offered to share his own blood, as well as mine, so that as much as possible of your father's might be drawn off.' Dr Hawkins sighed, and shook his head. 'But we will have to make do. We can do enough to make a difference, at least. And so, Jem, if you would be so kind? The collecting jar is here. This one is to gather my blood, the other is for your father's. And then we will replace my blood with his, and vice versa.'

My father shook his head. 'Dr Hawkins, I cannot allow—'

'Shush, man,' said Dr Hawkins. 'We have already discussed the matter, and my mind is resolved.' He sat on the couch and rolled up his sleeve so that it was above his elbow. 'This is an extraordinary opportunity. The disease is deep inside the system. But is it in the mind, or the brain? The spirit, or the blood? Sedatives are all useless; the mind seems still to race no matter that the body appears unconscious. If we replace the blood, then the taint may be eradicated, or at least diminished—'

He talked on and on, but I was hardly listening. The evening had taken on a peculiar, unreal feeling and I moved as though in a daze. I did as Dr Hawkins instructed, inserting the cannula, drawing off the blood, swapping the flasks, feeding Dr Hawkins's blood into my father, and my father's into Dr Hawkins. I felt as though I was hardly present, merely going through the motions. The blood that leaked out of my father's arm was no different to the stuff I took from Dr Hawkins: thick, scarlet, the colour of life itself. I thought nothing of it. I was numb, empty. I caught sight of myself in the mirror and I saw only a stranger: a madwoman disfigured by a red birthmark, with a flask of blood in her hands.

❧

When I arrived back at the apothecary, the place was in darkness. A single candle burned on the table top – a night light left for me by Will. Beneath the table, on his truckle bed, Gabriel snored. The table itself was laid out neatly for the next day – the prescription ledger tidied away, a batch of new-made pills drying, the condenser set up ready for the following morning. The place smelled of citrus fruit and lavender, with a faint, underlying aroma of hops – clean, homely, reassuring. I sank into my father's chair before the fire. I could not get the images out of my mind – the bottles of blood and the crimson connecting tubes; my father's veins, visible beneath the skin like earthworms. Nathaniel crouched against the wall of his cell, the noise, that droning half-moan, half-sob, over and over and over as he rocked himself; his eyes, empty of everything but desperation – blind and tortured. Already, I could see that my father's face had taken on the same gaunt and sunken look; his eyes, though still keen, had a gluey, viscous appearance. Would Dr Hawkins's procedure work? If not, how long before my father took Nathaniel's place? Before I met the same fate? Should I have to spend my days thinking about death? And yet, all at once it seemed as though I had hardly even lived. I put my head in my hands, and wept.

Chapter Twelve

※

Gabriel woke me at half past five. *Father.* I seized my boots and dragged my coat on. 'See to the morning purgatives, Gabriel,' I muttered. 'I'll be back soon.' I let the door slam behind me.

Mrs Speedicut accosted me at the entrance to the surgical ward. 'You been up to Angel Meadow this morning? How is he?'

'I'm going back there the moment I've been round the wards,' I said. I couldn't be bothered to ask how she knew. Perhaps, like Dr Bain, she had been in my father's confidence all along.

'And last night?

I shrugged. 'He seemed as well as might be expected, Mrs Speedicut. No worse. Let's hope for better things today,' I added. 'I'll send your good wishes.'

Mrs Speedicut's face was suddenly beet red. 'I've got something for him,' she said. 'Something I made. Can you take it to him?'

'Of course.' No doubt it was one of her dreadful pound cakes, so dry and musty-tasting that I suspected her of using the sawdust from the floor of the operating theatre in place of flour. 'Just leave it at the apothecary.'

'I've got it here.'

'Well, I can't very well carry a cake about the wards, can I?'

'It ain't a cake.'

'No?'

'No.' Her beady little eyes were tearful now. 'I don't know what ails him, Mr Jem, but I've seen him getting thin and pale and always in his chair. It breaks my heart to see him like he is. And then there were them coffins. And then Dr Bain.' She fell silent, swabbing her face with a square of cotton cut from an old hospital bed sheet. 'Well, I made him this. I thought it might be a comfort.' From behind her vast skirts, Mrs Speedicut produced a bundle, tied with string. She unwrapped it and drew out a heavy patchwork quilt. The colours glowed warm as summer in the dismal light.

I touched the rich fragments of fabric, stitched together with tiny, almost invisible, stitches. 'Mrs Speedicut,' I cried. 'I had no idea you were so skilled with a needle.'

Mrs Speedicut blushed. 'Who else might I do things for?'

'I can think of someone.'

'Gabriel,' she said. 'I were wrong to treat him so harsh, to say those things. He's just a lad, it ain't his fault where he comes from or what his parents did.' She looked left and right, and then leaned close to me. She stank of cheap candles, sweat and baccy. 'Don't you tell him.' She looked up at me coyly. 'I'm making one just the same for him.'

I tried to keep the surprise off my face. I failed. 'Really?'

Mrs Speedicut nodded. 'It ain't 'is fault 'e were born.'

'No,' I said. 'Look, you don't need to do the rounds with me, Mrs Speedicut. Why don't you go over to the apothecary? Take your quilt. Gabriel will have made some coffee.'

'D'you think he'll speak to me?'

'Gabriel?' I said. 'I sincerely hope so, or he'll feel the yard rule across his backside.'

'Oh, no, not that.' I must have looked astonished at such unexpected soft-heartedness, for she changed the subject abruptly. 'Think you'll find out who did it? Who murdered him?'

'You think it's murder?'

'Course it is. You know it as well as I do. That Dr Bain, he were too clever by half. And too clever to make a mistake like that. Poison himself? You watch your step,' she said. 'Doctors! They're all the same. They looks after each other.'

'I know that.'

Mrs Speedicut frowned. 'You don't know nothing! I've seen you, disobeying their orders with your rhubarb and your boiled water. *And* I've heard you too, answering back and showing them up an' making them feel stupid. Well they might well be stupid, but no one likes to be made to *feel* that way.'

'My dear lady—'

'Don't you dare talk down to me, Jem Flockhart!' she cried. 'You're not too big to feel the yard stick across your own arse. And you're not near careful enough, neither. Ain't you seen them? Whispering together? Looking at you?'

'Well,' I said. 'I suppose I have.'

'No you ain't.' She jabbed at my shoulder with the stem of her pipe. 'Think you're so clever, but you ain't *watchin'*. Not like you should be. You ain't one o' them – you never will be – and that means somethin'.'

'I'll find out who murdered Dr Bain, and then they shall hang for it.'

'Not if they get you first.' She backed away, her precious bundle now cradled in her arms. Her voice hissed out from the shadows. 'You watch them. Don't take your eyes off *any* of them.'

I left her then, to go about the wards. I was grateful for her warning. She was a busybody, and an eavesdropper, but her gossip's eye was sharp, and she noticed everything. She probably knew more about St Saviour's than anyone else. And yet still I paid no heed. I had worked with medical men all my life: I could see their weaknesses, I endured their arrogance and I knew they held no one in higher regard than themselves. But one of them, perhaps more, was a party to wilful murder. How long could they hope to hide such a secret? I had lived a lie for my entire life, I knew what it was to conceal, to dissemble, to pretend one was something one was not and all the time to be in fear of discovery. It was a difficult act to sustain. The urge to tell someone, to explain or justify oneself, was powerful and corrosive. They would make a mistake, I was certain, and I would see it instantly. None of them would get the better of me.

꧂

Nothing had happened on the wards during the night. The routine of the morning was a comfort, and I arranged for the usual bleeding and purging without thought. I felt calm by the time I left the place, and decided I would breakfast with Will and Gabriel, and perhaps Mrs Speedicut, when I came back from Angel Meadow.

My father was exactly where I had left him, sitting in an armchair in front of Dr Hawkins's fire.

'Did you sleep?' I asked.

'A little.' No doubt he had not slept at all but did not want to worry me further. I looked at Dr Hawkins. Had my father's raging blood, newly present in his veins, meant that he had paced the floor till dawn? If so, he looked remarkably fresh for it. The rose in his lapel was as yellow as clotted cream.

I did not linger. My father was no worse, and that would have to suffice. Besides, there seemed little to be said. Always taciturn, he was even more disinclined than usual to talk. Perhaps I might send Mrs Speedicut to see him. He always seemed to find her prattle soothing, and she was sure to be better company for him than me, with my searching gaze and bleak silence. His fate weighed heavily upon me so that I could think of nothing else when I was with him. What use was the present, when it would soon be gone? What use was the future when it held nothing but madness and death? And the past – we had neither of us ever had much cause to dwell upon that.

The attendant who led me away from Dr Hawkins's rooms was new to me. 'Might I see Mrs Catchpole?' I said.

'It's early for a visitor,' she replied.

'I'm the apothecary from St Saviour's,' I said, deciding that impatience and manly arrogance would serve me best. 'And a friend of Dr Hawkins. He says I may see the lady. The matter cannot wait.'

The attendant pulled out her keys. She did not care where she took me, and she did not want an argument. 'This way, sir.'

She led me down the stairs and into the ladies' corridor. In the morning light I could see that the tall arched windows I had noticed the night before looked out over a wide, well-kept lawn. The flower beds were filled with daffodils, the vegetable garden hoed and ready for spring planting. There were attendants everywhere; one of them at Mrs Catchpole's door, a kettle of hot water in her hand. She jangled her bunch of keys and smiled at me as I came up to her. 'Mornin' sir,' she said. 'Back to see Mrs Catchpole?' She knocked and listened, then opened the door, and stood back to allow me in.

What I saw within I will never forget: that close, darkened room, a single candle on the washstand, the shadows rearing and jumping as the flame guttered in the draught, and on the floor—

I cried out, and reeled back. How was this possible? Beside me, the attendant sank to her knees, her keys tumbling from her fingers. The woman who had brought me down from Dr Hawkins's rooms stood, transfixed, in the doorway, her mouth open, her fingers plucking at her lips. She struck up a terrible moaning sound.

Mrs Catchpole was lying on the floor in the middle of the room. Her head was thrown back, her eyes glassy and staring, her hands clutching at her throat as if in her final moments she had tried to unwind a scarf that was tied too tight. But there was no scarf, no assailant, no rope or cord; indeed, no sign that anything at all had touched her throat. I could not understand it. I had seen her myself before she went to bed. The door had been locked all night, surely? I looked about the room. The bed was rumpled and Mrs Catchpole was wearing her nightdress. Whatever had happened, it was clear that at some point she had been in bed. I looked at the candle – it was hardly burned down at all. Obviously recently lit, a box of matches was beside it on the mantle. Mrs Catchpole had lighted it no more than quarter of an hour earlier, I was certain.

I sprang across the room to crouch at Mrs Catchpole's side. Her eyes stared up at me accusingly, but there was no breath in her body. 'Have you been in here this morning?' I directed my question at the attendant with the kettle of water. She shook her head, her mouth hanging open. 'And you heard nothing? Nothing at all?' The woman shook her head again. She could not take her eyes off Mrs Catchpole's prostrate figure.

Then she said, 'She was in bed when I saw her last night. I checked them all before I locked up, I always do. She was in bed. I locked her in.'

'It's your practice to lock the patients in at night?'

'Of course. Some of them wander.'

'And no one came to see her after you had left her?'

'It was lights out. No one came. Not even Dr Hawkins, and he's the only other person with a key.'

'I think this woman needs a cup of hot sweet tea,' I said to the attendant who had brought me downstairs. 'Can you see that she gets it?'

'But Mrs Catchpole—'

'I'll stay with her,' I said. 'Dr Hawkins will be here in a moment, I will stay with her till he comes.' No one moved to obey my instructions. I had to get rid of them. I clicked my tongue, the way Dr Magorian did. 'For God's sake, take her away, woman!' I bellowed. 'And close the door when you leave. We don't want people traipsing in and out. Have a little respect.'

They bustled out of the room and pulled the door to. Had I been less absorbed, less stunned by what we had discovered, I might have paid more attention to them; I might have noticed the way they looked back at me, the way they looked at each other. But I was too engrossed by the conundrum of finding a corpse in a locked room; too determined to discover what I could before the place was filled with busybodies. By and by I was to remember it, and to wish I had acted with more caution.

But time was short, and I had to act quickly. Other than the limited number of furnishings I had observed the day before, the room was empty. I sprang over to the bed and slid my hand between the sheets. They were still warm, she had clearly been between them only minutes earlier. I flung open the shutters, though the morning was so dull and grey that the light was hardly improved by it. The window was closed, the bars and shutters meant that it was impossible that anyone had entered the room that way. I seized the candle and crawled quickly back and forth across the floor, looking for a vial of some sort – had it rolled beneath the bed, or into the corners of the room? I pulled open her clenched fingers but found nothing. I crouched beside the body, and sniffed. I could smell nothing – not vomit, not the mousy smell of hemlock nor the bitter almonds of cyanide. Was it aconite? Again? Possibly. But aconite must be ingested, the vial containing the poison, or whatever food or drink had been tainted by it, would be quite evident. And yet there was nothing. *Nothing.*

I squatted beside the body. The eyes were wide and glassy, the face curiously smooth. Beside her lay a hairbrush, perhaps knocked to the floor as she fell. Her hair was loose about her shoulders, and still tangled from sleep, so that it was clear that whatever had occurred, it had taken place almost as soon as she had washed her face. And yet – I looked at her face again – there was something about the eyes that unsettled me. She was not breathing, that much was clear. How long had she been dead? I put my ear to her chest – a heartbeat! How was it possible that she might be dead, and yet alive? That she might have a heartbeat, but no breath? Surely one was not possible without the other? Unless – I crouched down again, my own heart now so loud in my ears that I could hardly focus upon hers.

'Mrs Catchpole,' I whispered. 'Mrs Catchpole.' Was there a movement in her eyes? The skin had a rigid, unnatural look to it. I took a deep breath, and, holding her nose closed, I put my mouth over hers and blew. Her rib cage rose, and fell. I blew again. And again. I listened to her heart, still beating. But she would not, could not, keep breathing. Could she see and hear? Was she sentient, observing her own death, knowing her fate but able to do nothing about it? Again her lungs filled with breath – my breath – and emptied. Again she was still. I pressed my ear to her chest. This time, there was no heartbeat. Her eyes, I could see, were those of a corpse.

Her face was waxy; her eyes stared up at a corner of the ceiling; her tongue visible behind blue lips. I examined her throat and head. I opened her nightdress and surveyed her naked body. There was no sign of violence, no wound, no puncture, no apparent trauma to any part of her. There was no blood. The bruise on her head from

245

where she had struck it when she fell during Dr Bain's funeral was still dark and purplish, but fading already as the blood drained. The cut at its centre was still red, but granular, healing. I could see a greasy smear across the wound from where she had applied the salve – no doubt this had done something to help the bruising, though that hardly mattered now.

But Dr Hawkins would be there at any moment, and with him a horde of trampling, bustling attendants. I went to the washstand. There must be some clue as to what had happened. There was nothing on it but a selection of hair pins and a wedding ring. The soap I had brought was untouched, the bag of camomile tea still wrapped, the jar of the comfrey and camomile salve bore the imprint of her fingertips. I examined each item, but they told me nothing. The lavender-filled pillow was on the bed, the chrysanthemums were exactly where Eliza had left them. Mrs Catchpole's clothes had been taken away the night before and brought back that morning – they remained on the floor, where they had tumbled from the attendant's arms. *How* had she died? A stroke? A heart attack? But that would not account for the paralysis, for the fact that the heart had continued whereas the lungs were unable to draw breath – and yet . . . I looked about – the bed, the pillow, the hairbrush, the washstand, the body . . .

And all at once I knew. I knew how she had died, and why. It was murder, without a shade of doubt and, for the first time, I felt vulnerable, exposed. Why had I not been more cautious? I had led the murderer to Mrs Catchpole as surely as if I had pointed her out in a crowd, and in my foolish confidence I had set the scene for her execution.

❦

'Has Joe Silks been here?' I asked as soon as I got back to the apothecary. I wished Will was back, but he was still out at the graveyard. Gabriel was cleaning out the large leech jar. I did not tell him what had happened, that Mrs Catchpole was dead. I could not face a barrage of absurd questions and sensational speculations. He would find out soon enough anyway. But Gabriel knew something was amiss. He watched me, his expression wary. 'Well?' I said. 'Has he been?'

He shook his head. 'What you want him round here for?'

'He has something for me.' I looked out of the window, at the statue of Edward VI with his cape of bird droppings and the looming grey prison of the ward beyond. Where was Will? I needed to talk to him. I could not help but feel uneasy. Joe had said he would bring the coffin this morning. It was only eight o'clock but I knew the lad was always up early. Besides it had been quite clear that he had been anxious to get rid of the thing Dr Bain had entrusted him with. Why had he not appeared? Of course, he was a homeless boy, a pauper and a thief. There was always something he was up to. He was unreliable and unpredictable, and I should not be surprised if he was late – I should not be surprised if he didn't show up at all. And yet, his loyalty to Dr Bain was without question. I knew he would come. I glanced up at the wall clock. I pulled out the silver pocket half hunter watch my father had given me – once a gift from his own father – when I had finished my apprenticeship. Both dials told the same time.

'Breakfast time,' said Gabriel, seeing the object of my interest.

'Very well,' I said. 'Put a pot of coffee on the stove and go to the bakery.'

'Shall I get a currant loaf? Mr Flockhart always likes a currant loaf.'

'Mr Flockhart is not here,' I said. I thought of my father. I doubted very much whether currant loaf would be on his mind.

'I wish he *was* here,' said Gabriel, tearfully. 'I wish everything were like it used to be. But now Dr Bain's dead, and Mr Flockhart's ill and St Saviour's is to be pulled down. P'raps it's my fault. P'raps I bring bad luck.' He sniffed, pathetically.

'Of course it's not you, Gabriel.' I handed him a half crown. 'Look, buy a loaf, and some cheese and butter. And get the currant loaf too. Perhaps you can take it to my father directly. Have your breakfast with him.'

'Might I go and see him?' His face brightened, and then fell. 'Oh, but he's in Angel Meadow,' he whispered. 'I don't want to go in there.'

'It's not so bad,' I replied. 'Not like it used to be. Perhaps you would be so kind as to accompany Mrs Speedicut. I think she's as afraid of the place as you are.'

'Me!' cried Gabriel. 'I'll not go nowhere with her!'

'I'll not go *anywhere*,' I corrected. 'Gabriel, you must do as you're told. Mrs Speedicut will be in the matron's office, as she always is, no doubt planning on coming here, as she always does.' All at once I had to get rid of both of them. I had to *think* and for that I needed silence. 'Go and get her, and ask her to accompany you to Angel Meadow to see my father. You must take him a currant loaf and talk to him to keep his spirits up. Then come back and tell me how he fares.' I held up a hand as he opened his mouth to object. 'You will be polite and courteous to Mrs Speedicut at all times. Am I making myself understood?'

Gabriel nodded, his expression hostile. 'I'll do it for you,' he said. 'And for Mr Flockhart, that's all.'

'No,' I said. 'You'll do it for Mrs Speedicut. She's sorry for what she said, though she did no more than speak the truth, as unpalatable as that might be. Besides, we must take our friends the way we find them. The world's a cold and lonely place for orphans.'

I sat for a while in silence, glad to have Gabriel out of the way. I put my hand in my pocket, closing my fingers around what I knew to be the source of Mrs Catchpole's death. I had taken it from her room so that none but I should know of it. How was it that St Saviour's Infirmary had come to this? I might suspect who was behind the murders of Dr Bain and Mrs Catchpole, but why they had committed such crimes I could not possibly guess. And across all this, across every moment I was awake, my father's illness cast its long shadow. I was not so naive that I believed Dr Hawkins's exchange of blood would have any effect on him. I had spent my life amongst sickness and disease, surrounded by medical men, their various 'remedies' and 'cures', and I knew that, for the most part, they had nothing useful to suggest about anything. Anatomy and physiology had improved understanding of the body's functions, but the mind, and the brain, remained a mystery. As for sleeping and waking, why, we took it for granted that should we be able to do one, then the other would automatically follow. Dr Hawkins's idea was coherent – rational and logical – based as it was on an assumption that madness might somehow be carried by tainted blood, but if madness had its root in the mind, and the brain, what use was new blood? I closed my eyes. I understood why my father had not told me: now I too had to live with the knowledge that I might one day lie blind and deranged in the basement at Angel Meadow. I looked back on my ignorance with a grieving heart.

At half past eight I heard Will scraping his boots at the door. He hung his coat on the hook above the hop basket and removed his hat, examining it for blemishes and stains. He sniffed it, and wrinkled his nose. He washed his hands and face, working the pump vigorously in the vain hope that he might be able to remove the fearful smell that hung about him. Then he looked up at me, his face drawn and serious.

'How's your father this morning?'

'The same.'

'I'm sorry.' He dried his hands.

I could see he was troubled. Mrs Catchpole might wait another minute, and so I said, 'How are the excavations?'

'God help me, Jem,' he replied. 'The job will be the death of me.'

'No,' I said. 'You will complete the job in the best of health, though somewhat distressed by it, and then, after a while, you will never think of it again.'

He gave a faint smile. 'Never think of it again? I doubt that very much.' He sank into a chair. 'I don't believe I have the stomach to continue.'

'How long will it take?'

'Two months? Three? The Company have under-estimated the job, as there are many more bodies than they first thought. The parish registers told us as much, though no one but I thought to look in them. The number of corpses defies imagining. It's as though the entire earth is made of bones. It depends on the rain too – the place is a quagmire.' He shuddered. 'I cannot get the sight of it from my mind, nor the smell of it from my nostrils.'

I handed him a cup of bitter black coffee. 'Try this.'

Outside, the light grew dim. The sun had hardly risen, and already it was as dark as evening. The sky above the ward building opposite was the colour of slate. 'Rain again,' I remarked as the stuff sluiced down, battering onto the sodden courtyard. The drain outside the apothecary door gurgled. I said, 'Mrs Catchpole is dead.'

'Dead!'

'Murdered.'

'But how? Did you not see her last night when you went to Angel Meadow with your father?' He sprang to his feet, and began to pace up and down the apothecary. 'How can she be dead? It must have been an accident. Are you quite certain it was murder? But why would anyone do such a thing?' He put a hand to his head. 'What kind of a place has this infirmary become, that murder is commonplace?' He reached out to put his mug on the table, but in his agitation he missed. It crashed to the ground, and he was lashed from head to toe by a tongue of hot coffee. The shock seemed to bring him to his senses. He wiped his face with his handkerchief, and reached for a piece of sacking. In silence I watched him, down on his hands and knees, swabbing the pool of brown liquid off the hard stone floor. 'Poor woman,' he muttered. 'Perhaps she would still be alive if she had stayed away from Dr Bain.'

'Undoubtedly,' I replied. On the table beside his empty coffee cup I placed the pot of salve I had taken from Mrs Catchpole's washstand.

'What's this?'

I told him what it was and how I had come by it.

He opened the lid, and sniffed it. 'But it's only beeswax and herbs—'

'Careful!' I said. 'It's now poisonous beeswax and herbs.'

He froze, the pot held out before him. 'Poison? What—'

'Curare,' I said. 'Someone put curare in it.'

'But how could they have done that?'

'Easily enough. Dr Magorian, Dr Catchpole and Dr Graves all saw me fill the jar. They all knew I was going to Angel Meadow with it. And I had not been with Mrs Catchpole five minutes when Dr Graves and Dr Catchpole also arrived. Along with Eliza and Mrs Magorian.'

'Eliza?' said Will.

'Yes.' I looked away. 'Though she amongst them is without blame, I'm certain.'

'Of course you are,' said Will.

'What do you mean by that?' I retorted. 'D'you think I would excuse her simply because—'

'Yes?' Will let the silence speak for me. And then he said gently, 'I think you might not see her in the same objective light as you do the others.'

I could not answer. I had grown fond of Will, but he had no idea who I was. I was not about to discuss my feelings for Eliza. Not now. Perhaps not ever. But she was no murderer, I was certain, and so I said, 'Miss Magorian was nowhere near the washstand, and the salve. Neither was Dr Catchpole.'

'And who was?'

'Dr Graves. And he remained in the room when I followed Dr Catchpole out into the hallway.'

'And you're certain it's curare?'

'Yes,' I said. 'And a clever choice it was too. Curare works only when it enters the blood stream – it's the stuff of poison darts, made principally from the roots and stems of the *Chondrodendron tomentosum*, though often other plant matter is added, and the sweat from poisonous frogs.'

'How on earth might one make a frog sweat?' murmured Will.

'By holding it over a fire,' I replied. 'More important is the question how on earth it might be got into Mrs Catchpole's blood stream.'

'The salve.'

'Of course. The poison would enter the open wound immediately. And I believe that is exactly what happened. The steps she followed as soon as she awoke were plain to read. She lit a candle, and washed her face – the candle was hardly burned, the towel and the edges of her hair were damp. She applied the salve, and began brushing her hair – the bruise and the cut glistened, her hairbrush lay at her feet. Death came swiftly. The stuff paralyses, prevents breathing, so although her heart continued to beat, the lungs, the diaphragm, were unable to work to provide the body with air. And so she slowly suffocated to death, fully sentient, but unable to move, to speak, to let anyone know what was happening.'

Will swallowed. His face showed me that he could hardly believe such cruelty existed. 'And the antidote?'

'It hardly matters.' I said. 'She's dead, is she not?' I held up the pot of salve. 'And this is the cause.'

'And so you took it?'

'Of course,' I said. 'Everyone knew I'd given it to her. The real murderer is bound to point to the salve, and then they would assume that it was I who killed Mrs Catchpole. I could hardly leave it there.'

'I hope you don't come to regret taking it,' said Will. 'Far better to have left it were it was and see who drew attention to it as the likely cause of death—'

But I was not listening. I went over to the window, and looked out. Despite the rain, the courtyard was busy with people coming in through the gates to go to out-patients, with doctors about to begin their rounds and with all the usual people and activity of a busy infirmary. And yet out of all of those people, we had narrowed down Dr Bain's murderer, Mrs Catchpole's murderer, to only a handful of possible perpetrators. 'You can see how clever our killer is,' I said. 'And how knowledgeable.'

'But who might it be?' said Will. 'And why did Mrs Catchpole have to die?'

'I am convinced that Mrs Catchpole saw something that night when she looked through Dr Bain's parlour window.'

'She saw her husband.'

'That much is certain. But I think she might have seen something else too. It's clear from what she said to me last night that there was someone else in the room at the same time as her husband. Of course, she didn't stay to find out. Once she saw Dr Catchpole in there she ran away again. And when I asked, she was unable to recall any meaningful details about Dr Bain's room. But if she had thought some more, if she had been given time to think and reflect without being disturbed by so many people, then she might very well have remembered something. But she could not be *allowed* to remember. Even the possibility that she might recall something, *anything* that might point out Dr Bain's murderer, was enough to ensure her death. And so she was killed.'

'By whom?'

I held up the pot of salve between finger and thumb. 'Dr Graves,' I said. 'He had every opportunity. And there is the sugar lump, remember, from Prior's Rents?'

'Can you be sure?' said Will. 'Forgive me, Jem. I mentioned it earlier, I know, and I could see you weren't to be persuaded, but I can't help but notice that Miss Magorian . . . distracts you. You can't deny it. Can you be sure you were paying attention to what took place in Mrs Catchpole's room last night? Are you certain that it's not Dr Magorian, and that he might have a willing accomplice in someone?'

I opened my mouth to object, but I knew he was right. If I had not been so absorbed with looking at Eliza—

'Is Miss Magorian herself *really* above suspicion?'

I shook my head. Eliza had not been anywhere near the salve, had she? I was no longer sure. And had she been instructed to smile at me, so that I would see nothing else? I had taken her wink to mean that the herbs I had given her had proved to be efficacious. Perhaps I was simply a fool, one easily gulled into not noticing what she, or her mother, might be up to. Had she, and her mother, and Dr Graves, all deliberately remained in Mrs Catchpole's room while I had pursued Dr Catchpole out into the corridor? I felt my face flaming, humiliated by my own naivety. Mrs Speedicut's words, spoken in earnest that very morning, crept in my head: *you ain't one of them – you never will be*

255

– and that means somethin'. She was right. Will was right. I could not trust any of them.

Before I could say anything a face appeared at the window. It was a small, wizened face, with dirty hair beneath a greasy-looking bonnet. The eyes were large and dark ringed above hollow cheeks, the mouth small and downturned.

Relieved by the distraction, I sprang to the door and flung it open. Dashing outside into the rain I grabbed the girl before she could make off, and propelled her swiftly into the apothecary.

'Your clothes are soaking,' I said. 'Come over to the fire.' The girl twisted in my grasp. I turned her around so that she was facing me. I recognised her as one of the urchins who hung about above the heating vents outside St Saviour's laundry. 'You're Joe Silks's friend, aren't you?'

The girl nodded. She stood there miserably, her skirts ragged above bruised ankles and filthy feet. Even from two yards away I could see the lice crawling in her hair. She put up a grubby hand and raked at her scalp.

'You need new clothes,' said Will.

'She'll only sell them,' I replied. 'And then be colder and wetter than ever.' Even if she didn't sell them, I knew that she would most likely be beaten and stripped by her fellows, or by her own family (if she had any), and then *they* would sell them. The best we might do was to wash and dry what she had. Already the steam was rising off them. The smell was abominable.

'Take everything off,' I ordered. I tossed her a blanket. 'Wrap yourself in this.'

'I brought you summink,' said the girl. She rooted

beneath her tattered shirt and produced a parcel. It was about eight inches long, loosely wrapped in a piece of dirty sacking and tied up with a scrap of frayed string. 'Nasty fing it is,' she said. 'Don't know why Dr Bain gave it to Joe, but now Joe's gone so he can't say. He tole me someone were after him. Don't know for what – thievin' most like. Said he had to keep out o' sight a bit. Said I were to just give you this an' then run, run as far away as I could. I reckon Joe's den at the top o' Prior's Rents is far enough for anyone. I ain't got the strength to go no further 'n that. Not that Joe's there,' she added dismally. 'Don't know where he is.'

I took the sack-covered parcel and unwrapped it. I knew what it was. I could tell by the shape beneath its coarse grey shroud and the feel of something shifting within. Will and I exchanged a glance. Now we had both coffins, the only two that had not been destroyed in Dr Bain's fire; the two Dr Bain had hidden, to keep them safe. But safe from what?

I set the kettle to boil on the stove top, and flung the girl's clothes into the large brass cauldron I used for boiling up cough syrups. I added lemon oil and lavender against the smell, rosemary and thyme to kill the lice, and then the hot water. I wondered whether it was worth the bother. Perhaps it would be a better idea simply to throw everything onto the fire.

The girl sat, wrapped in a blanket, watching her clothes bubble. I wanted her to take a bath – there was no point putting her in clean clothes if she was still verminous – but she refused. I decided I would set Mrs Speedicut onto her: when Mrs Speedicut wanted you to take a bath, you took a bath. In the meantime, I gave her a cup of sweet milky tea and a plate of bread and cheese. She gobbled the food and glugged down the tea in no time, then curled up in the blanket on my father's chair, and fell asleep.

Will opened the coffin. Within was the familiar, hideous bundle. 'Do you have the other one?' said Will. I had hidden it at the bottom of the hop basket. I brought it out and laid the two boxes side by side. They were almost identical in size and shape: both contained the same mixture of dried flowers, the same rough, rag-swaddled doll. 'Whatever their secret is, someone considered it worth killing two people over,' said Will

'We need to examine them properly. To think about what they mean. But not here. Not at the apothecary, it's too public.'

'We might return to Dr Bain's laboratory? It's quiet and private. None but you has the key.'

'This evening,' I said. 'We can go there directly after my rounds.' It was a good suggestion, and I was glad to postpone our examination of those horrible objects, even for a few hours. Suddenly, our possession of them had become a huge and dangerous burden. Would Dr Bain have taken them if he had realised that he was forfeiting his own life, Mrs Catchpole's life, by so doing? I wished with all my heart that I had never seen them, that they had remained where they were, in the darkness under-ground, slowly decaying until they were nothing more than paper fragments, their meaning lost in time. I closed my eyes. I tried to be calm, to be focused and rational, but all at once I could not manage it; I could not step back from events taking place so close to my heart, events that were tearing apart the only world I had known. Even Eliza was implicated—

I put my hands to my face. I could not let Will see me crumble, not now. But he was there, beside me, as he always was. He put an arm around my shoulders. 'Things may not turn out so badly.' But there was to be no rest for us that morning, for scarcely had Will reached for the coffee pot when the silence was obliterated by the sound of a fist hammering on the apothecary door. A man stumbled in, his oilskin streaming with rainwater. I slipped the coffins into a sack and out of sight beneath the work bench.

'Beggin' yer pardon, Mr Quartermain, sir.' The man wiped mud off his face with a large meaty hand. 'But there's something you should see up at the churchyard.'

'What is it?'

'It's best you look for yourself, sir.'

'But can't you just say what it is?' said Will, irritably. 'I've just come from the place. What urgency can there possibly be?'

'A body, sir. A corpse—'

'There are hundreds of corpses,' said Will. 'All equally offensive to the eyes and nostrils. I'm sure it can wait.'

'There's hundreds, yes sir, but not like this,' said the man. 'None of 'em's like this.'

Chapter Thirteen

I had not visited the excavations in the churchyard for a couple of days and I could hardly believe what I now saw. Will had directed the proceedings with meticulous attention. The gravestones had been stacked like dirty dishes against the church, and a deep trench sliced into the earth following the line of the churchyard wall. It ran from one side to the other, six feet deep and ten feet wide. The occupants of the trench had been removed systematically, one layer at a time, as far as this was possible, as some disorder was evident the deeper the excavations went. They had been set out beside the trench to be loaded into carts and trundled away across the city. But it was clear that the number of bodies and bones were more than the carts could manage, and a great mound of rags and corpses had risen up on the greensward beside the excavated pit.

'Initially this mound comprised only the most recently disinterred,' said Will as we approached. 'But getting rid of them has involved one delay after another – carts, cabs, people, animals – the streets are choked with obstructions, and the rain has caused nothing but delays and accidents.' He sighed, and passed a hand across his eyes. 'The number of bodies removed from the ground far exceeds the number who might conceivably be taken away in one day. And so the corpse mountain grows daily in size, and disorderliness.'

'Surely the trench is almost empty,' I said.

'It's only one trench,' replied Will. 'We'll have to dig at least four of them to empty the earth. And the ground is little more than bones, with soil squeezed in between.'

I peered into the pit. The sticky clay walls were studded with human remains, like chunks of suet in a Christmas pudding. At the bottom, more bones, rags, skulls and bits of wood protruded.

'And we've not reached the bottom of this one yet,' said Will gloomily. 'The ground is clay. It's not sufficiently aerated to permit rapid decomposition, though now that everything is exposed to the air – not to mention the flies and the rain – what the clay had arrested is now taking place with horrible swiftness.'

'But there must have been quite a number of empty coffins,' I said. 'The resurrectionists will have been unable to resist the allure of so many fresh corpses so close to the anatomy rooms. St Saviour's was well known amongst the medical students for its ready supply of bodies.'

'Pity they didn't take a few more. It would have saved me from doing it. And not only that, but your medical students seem to have dumped back into the graveyard those body parts they had no use for. We found an entire collection of random legs and arms and skulls, all bearing the unmistakable imprint of knives.' He shuddered. 'Like the remains of a giant's banquet.'

'Fe, fi, fo, fum,' I said.

He did not laugh. 'And skulls with holes punched in them.'

'Trepanning,' I said.

'Over and over again in the same head?'

'Practice makes perfect,' I replied. 'Dr Magorian's anatomy school is famous. His students are the best for a reason.'

'Some of the men have left,' said Will. 'They refused to work amongst the dead.'

'Three more of 'em 'ave gone now, sir,' said the foreman. 'Since we found this.'

'Found what?'

'Down 'ere.'

We followed the foreman down the ladder to the foot of the pit. Boards had been laid across the bottom, so that those working in the depths were not wading through a soup of mud and corpses. As the pit deepened, so the boards were moved down. The mouldering coffins and their occupants were dug from the earth, loaded into tarpaulins, and hauled up to the surface by ropes. It was crude but effective, and progress had been brisk despite the number of men who had left.

The pit itself stank. Even I, so used to the stench of the city and the infirmary, was obliged to put my handkerchief over my mouth. Above us, the excavated remains rose against the thunderous sky in a great slag heap. On either side of the pit, dressed in oilskins glistening with water, the workmen had gathered. Covered in clay from head to foot, their faces invisible within the dark cowls of their hoods, they looked down at us like some silent brotherhood of muddy friars.

At the bottom of the pit, an oilskin lay on the ground beside a cache of spades, ropes and tarpaulin slings. The foreman pulled it aside.

Joe's face was white against the dark earth.

'Who found him?' I said.

'Me,' said the foreman.

'Here? Has he been moved? Was he lying like this?'

The foreman nodded. 'No one saw him at first. We were pegging out the next section, loading the carts . . . other things. No one likes coming down here. But then I came for a tarp, and I saw him.'

'Was he covered, like this?'

'Yes, sir.'

Was it concealment, or respect that had prompted the use of the tarpaulin as a shroud? But Joe was an urchin, a thief and a child of the slums; what respect would a murderer have for one such as that?

The area about the body was a mass of footprints and churned mud. It looked as though every workman on the site had filed past to take a look and no distinguishing marks were visible. I bent down. Joe's face was turned towards the sky, the rain falling upon it like tears. How young he looked. He had told me he was twelve years old, or so he reckoned, but he looked to me to be no more than ten.

'P'raps he fell,' said the foreman.

'Perhaps,' I said. It seemed unlikely. The boy's limbs were positioned neatly at his sides, and the tarpaulin had been drawn over him. Had the murderer climbed down into the pit with Joe's body over his shoulder? A man might perform such an undertaking. A woman might have to throw him down, and then climb down after him to arrange and conceal the corpse. I would have to examine him to be sure. Joe Silks might be small, but I'd bet anything he'd put up a fight. And he was fast too, and wary as a fox. The peelers had been after him more than once, and Joe could give all but the most determined of assailants the slip. How was it that he had been caught in the first place? Unless he had known or trusted his attacker.

There was little to be gained from leaving Joe where he was. I bent down and wrapped him in the oilskin that had formed his shroud. His body was limp, the flesh of his cheek cold as marble against my fingers, the muscles only just growing rigid. Had Will and I led the murderer to him, that day in Prior's Rents? I could not escape a terrible sense of culpability. And yet, weeping over him would not help us find his killer. I could not afford the luxury of guilt and remorse; I had to be calm, to think rationally and clearly.

'I would guess he's been dead six, perhaps eight hours,' I said. 'But it could quite easily be longer.'

'That would be between twelve o'clock and two o'clock in the morning.'

'Who on earth would be up in the graveyard at that time?' I muttered. 'What are the chances that anyone saw or heard anything?'

Will said, 'I can think of someone. Dick Wrigley. The sexton. The churchyard is his kingdom. Nothing happens here without him knowing about it. He watches the excavations every day. Poor old fellow can't understand what's going on – he's about a hundred years old and must have been here since the place was surrounded by fields. He talks about the past and the present as though they were both the same thing. It's a bit peculiar, but once one gets used to it it's not so bad.'

I knew Dick Wrigley, and I did not hold out much hope for a coherent discussion. I had not spoken to him for years. Occasionally, when I was weeding my mother's grave he had skulked into view amongst the gravestones. I had nodded, and uttered a word – 'morning', 'afternoon', 'evening' as the occasion warranted. The sexton always replied with silence, a creeping sort of bow, and a knuckle to the forehead. I could not remember ever having held a proper conversation with him. Would the man be able to help us? I was doubtful, but Will seemed positive.

'Dick's fascinated by the whole excavation,' Will went on. 'I went to see him before we started. I thought he might be upset at the desecration, but he seemed oddly excited. He appeared with his own shovel, in fact, though I can't think when he last had the strength to use it. Asked to help. I said surely he was more used to seeing bodies going *into* the ground than watching men take them out again. He said I'd be surprised what he'd seen in that churchyard over the years.'

'Let's hope for the best,' I said. 'Though it's quite likely the old fellow has lost whatever wits he once had.'

'Give him a chance,' said Will. 'Besides, who else do we have?'

❧

The sexton lived in a tiny cottage that looked as though it had risen up from the putrid ground like some giant fungus. Built in a corner of the churchyard, its walls were green with moss, the windows covered by rotten boards, the thatched roof slick with a slimy layer of wet soot. A crooked chimney pointed heavenwards, oozing thick black smoke. I knocked. The door felt soft beneath my knuckles.

'Dick!' shouted Will. 'Dick!'

The door opened.

Dick Wrigley had a face like a dried fig. He peered up at us from beneath a gigantic tricorn hat, his wrinkled throat wrapped in a grey ragged kerchief. He appeared to be shirtless, but wore an old blue military-looking coat, stiff with dirt and grease and evidently made for a much larger man. It was fastened up to the neck with bits of string and a motley collection of random buttons. His boots were hardly visible beneath the hem of his coat, though from what I could see of them they were held together with strips of cloth and tar.

Will greeted the old man cordially. They shook hands, Dick's face aglow with pleasure. I wondered when anyone but Will had touched his hand, or shown any interest in him at all, and I felt wretched. It would not have taken much to visit the old chap now and then, and yet I had never bothered to do so. I shook his hand too. The ancient bandages that bound his palms were damp and sticky. I tried not to shudder.

As soon as the door to Dick's hovel closed behind us, I wished we had stayed outside. The place was repulsive – filthy and low ceilinged, rank with mildew and smoke and the stench of burnt food. The table was fit only for firewood, and the chair (upon which Will sat as guest of honour) leaned drunkenly. The hearth was a blackened pit set into the wall of the cottage, the coals mean and brown and discharging a trickle of acrid smoke. I felt instantly unclean.

'Been here for ever,' Dick was saying in answer to something Will had asked. 'Born here too.' He jabbed a tortoiseshell fingernail at me. 'I know you. You're Jeremiah Flockhart's lass.'

'Lad,' I said.

'That what you tell 'em, is it?'

I slid Will a glance, but he was looking in disgust at something slimy on the table top that he had leaned in, and he didn't seem to have noticed. 'Were you out in the graveyard last night, Mr Wrigley?' I said.

'Who's Mr Wrigley?' cried Dick, suddenly looking fearful.

'You are, sir,' said Will. 'Your name is in the parish register.'

'But I'm Ol' Dick.'

Out of the corner of my eye I could see Will smiling at my exasperation. 'Well, Old Dick,' I said. 'Were you out in the graveyard last night?'

'I'm *always* out there.' He spoke as though my question was the stupidest thing he had ever heard.

'At night?'

'Course at night!'

'Did you see anyone last night?'

He grinned, revealing empty gums. 'I *always* sees 'em when they come,' he said. 'It's them young doctors. They come to dig 'em up. The ones I just put in the ground.'

'That was years ago, Dick,' I said. 'There are no resurrection men now. I'm talking about last night.'

'Frighten 'em with me lantern, I do,' said Dick. 'And me dog.'

'You don't have a dog,' I said.

'Don't I?' Dick frowned. 'But I always 'ave a dog.'

I glanced at Will. 'He's never had a dog,' I muttered.

'I'm eighty!' cried Dick. 'Ninety! One hunner! I've had plenty o' dogs!'

I sighed. 'Thank you, Dick.' This was useless; the old fellow was talking gibberish. I made as if to leave. But Dick was speaking again. His tiny eyes shifted from my face to Will's, his right eye dead and misted with cataracts, his left blinking in the candlelight, as bright as an apple pip.

'Used to watch 'em,' he said. 'Them what came from the 'ospital. Dug up anyone they could. Paid me not to see, but I always saw. Sometimes I took their money, sometimes I didn't. Up to me, ain't it? Took a stick to 'em once, chased 'em out the place. 'Ad my dog then.' He chuckled, and shook his head. 'In and out the ground they go. In and out and in again. No peace for 'em even here. Even now.'

'In *again?*' said Will.

Dick nodded sagely. 'Puttin' 'em in. They did that too. That's my job, ain't it, and I can't say as they did it right. But I left 'em to it. No one asks Ol' Dick nuffink any more, so why should I tell 'em how to do the job like it should be done? Why should I tell 'em where they should be diggin'?'

'*I'm* asking you,' said Will. 'You know this graveyard better than anyone, Dick. Did you see them last night?'

'Yes,' said Dick.

'Who?' I cried.

'Medicals,' said Dick. 'Always the same ones.'

I sat forward. 'Did you see who they were? Their faces? Can you describe them? How many did you see?'

'Nah!' said Dick, recoiling. He scowled at me. 'Didn't see *nuffink*!'

'Come along, man,' I cried. 'You said you saw someone, so who did you see?'

Will put a hand on my arm. He stood up, and coaxed Dick to sit on the chair, then crouched down at the old man's side. 'Now, Dick, just you tell us what you saw. You remember last night, don't you? Out there in the dark. Who did you see? Could you tell who it was?'

'Yessir,' Dick nodded, peering down at Will fondly. 'It's one to watch and two to dig, when they're takin' 'em out. Take it in turns, that's the way. But not when they put 'em in. When they put 'em in there's two of 'em – man and boy. Should o' taken my dog an' chased 'em.' He stroked his chin and looked perplexed. 'Didn't atcherly *see* 'em dig though. Not this time. Didn't hear 'em dig neither. Usually do. Must be me deafness.' He frowned. 'Used to be dark when they came. Dark as pitch, and the lantern movin' amongst the gravestones like will-o'-the-wisp. Even *that's* changed now. They come in the moonlight now.' He grinned. 'One big-small. Nine guineas, when it's the season for cuttin' 'em up! But I'll let you take 'em all if you give me a shillin'.'

Will smiled, and pressed a coin into the old man's hand. 'You drive a hard bargain, sir,' he said. 'But I *will* take them all.'

❧

'Two of them,' I said, as we walked back to the excavations. 'He said he saw two of them. A man and a boy. A boy! D'you think one of Joe's gang is a party to his murder?'

'Unless he was referring to Joe himself. Perhaps he meant Joe and his attacker.'

'Perhaps. And he said there was no digging. "Didn't see 'em dig, didn't hear 'em dig neither." That's because there *was* no digging, not last night.'

'What did he mean by "One big-small"?' said Will.

'It's resurrection men's talk for a large child,' I said. I had not heard the term for years. 'Nine guineas was the top price some anatomy schools paid. And Dick was surprised to see them putting the body into the ground rather than taking it out. "That's my job," he said. Pity he didn't see their faces,' I added.

We fell silent as we walked back towards the mound of bones. The rain drummed on the hoods of our oilskins and trickled down our faces. The men laboured in the pit, and around the bone pile, but they did so in silence, their faces turned to their grim work. From each hood a pipe projected, down-turned to keep the cinder alight, the clouds of smoke that billowed from between their teeth masking the stink of the earth. I had decided to take Joe to the dissecting room, and I gathered him up in my arms, still wrapped in his tarpaulin shroud. The men stopped in their work and parted to allow us through, their heads bowed.

As I carried Joe's body towards the gate, a curious feeling crept over me. It was an uncanny sensation, a contracting of the flesh, as though a raindrop had penetrated my oilskin and was oozing down my spine. I looked up, my gaze drawn to the windows of the infirmary – black, gaping rectangles in the great grey edifice of that ugly square-shouldered building. For a moment I could make out nothing but the rain pouring down from inky skies, rising up again in a miasma of dampness. It rendered the air opaque, as if we viewed the world through a curtain of dirty muslin. And then a breeze blew; the drizzle billowed and shifted. A face looked down at us, the ribbons of her bonnet blowing about her face like the heads of the hydra.

✦✦

We took Joe to the anatomy room. The morning was dark, even for the time of year, but the glass panes in the roof turned the place into a luminous theatre; the rounded bellies of glass vessels catching the light in glinting rows of watchful eyes. Dr Graves kept the place gleaming, and my face – red and white, like blood and bandages – was reflected back at me from the mirrored surfaces of bottles and knives. I laid Joe on the dissecting table.

'You're not going to cut him up, are you?' said Will.

'No,' I said. 'But we must examine him, to see what we can discover.' I pushed Joe's hair back from his face. He seemed to be watching me from beneath half-closed lids, wary, even in death. *One big-small*, I thought. *Nine guineas*. The lad would have been worth more dead than alive.

The tarpaulin had kept much of the rain off, so he was dry, more or less. This, I knew, was to our advantage. We removed his clothes, and went through the pockets. Apart from a ha'penny, they were empty. I examined him as gently as I could: his face, head and neck, his torso and limbs. I looked at his nails with the magnifying glass, and lingered over his palms, and the tips of his fingers.

'Well?' said Will. He was standing against the wall, his

271

gaze fixed upon his boots, as if he was afraid to look up. I knew the place unsettled him; the jars of preserved tumours and organs made him uneasy. As for the hiss of a scalpel against flesh, the grating of the bone-saw, or the squelching of fingers amongst viscera, those things, I knew, he would not be able to countenance at all. But I had no need of such drastic measures: my senses would serve us well enough.

'There is a gash to the back of Joe's head,' I said, my fingers probing gently. 'The skull is crushed. I can feel that the wound is rounded at the edges, as if caused by something heavy and blunt.'

'Dr Catchpole has a weighted stick,' said Will. 'And Dr Magorian.'

'All gentlemen have them,' I said. 'But I don't think this has been caused by a blow from a walking stick. I think it's been made by Joe's head striking the edge of one of the tools at the foot of the pit. There was blood on the shaft of an axe which lay beneath him, did you notice? The axe was wedged under a block and tackle, so it could not have been used as a weapon *per se*.'

'So he was flung down into the pit, hit his head, and that's what killed him?'

'It would be easy to claim he fell, easy to say that his death was nothing more than misadventure.'

'And yet he was covered by a tarpaulin. Concealed.'

'Yes. Though it would be possible to argue that he pulled it as he fell. More telling are the bruises on his wrists. The imprint of fingers is clear.'

'So he was held tightly, or dragged, by the wrist?'

'I think so. Joe's a slum child. His whole body is covered with bruises and weals, but I'm sure *these* marks are fresh.

They're red, not yellow or blue like the other bruises on him, so you may well be right. Still,' I sighed. 'It doesn't prove anything. Not when there are so many other, older marks of violence upon him.'

'There's a bruise around his eye,' said Will, stepping closer.

'And look at his fingers,' I said. 'The nails.' I handed him the magnifying glass.

'Recently broken. The dirt's not rubbed into the breaks.'

'Poor Joe,' I said. 'He must have put up quite a fight.' But there was something else; something I was sure would provide us with some answers at last. If I could only be certain. 'Look at the palm of his right hand, Will. Use the magnifying glass. What do you see?'

Will bent over the dissecting bench, the glass to his eye, his nose almost touching Joe's fingers. After a moment he said, 'I can't see anything.'

'Can't you?' I took the glass. I was hardly certain myself. And yet Dr Bain had said one must use *all* the senses. Sight was not the only thing we might rely upon to uncover the truth. I sniffed at Joe's hand, but it was hard to detect anything in the thick atmosphere of the dissecting room. I touched his palm with my fingertips, but the gritty sensation I was searching for was indiscernible. I licked the skin in the centre of his hand. I shook my head. 'I still can't be *sure*,' I said.

'What?' said Will, his expression disgusted. 'What can't you be sure about?'

'I'm sorry, Joe,' I murmured. And then I leaned forward, and put my mouth to his. I licked the tip of the dead boy's tongue.

'What are you doing?' cried Will. 'Jem!'

But now I *was* certain. 'Sugar,' I said, wiping my lips. 'The last thing Joe touched, the last thing he ate, was sugar. And he did so just before he died.'

∞

The coffins were our last hope to find the truth. That evening, in search of privacy and solitude, we took them to Dr Bain's laboratory. The place was eerily silent: the clock no longer ticked; the rats, which used to keep up an incessant rustling and squeaking, I had stuffed into a sack and flung into the Fleet Ditch. Since Dr Bain's death I had kept the shutters closed. I now added the precaution of pulling the curtains closed too, so that not a single thread of light might be visible from the street. It was clear that this was something Dr Bain never did – certainly, I had never seen him do it – and the ponderous drapes released choking grey clouds.

Tears stung my eyes. 'It's the dust,' I muttered. But it wasn't. I put my hand over my eyes, unable, for a moment, to bear the sight of that familiar place: the black marks on the fireplace where the doctor had knocked out his pipe; the greeny-brown blobs of masticated coca leaves that littered the hearth. How many evenings had I spent at Dr Bain's bench? His book on poisons lay unfinished; the notebooks in which we had written up our findings were in a pile on the corner of the desk. It was the custom at St Saviour's for a medical man to bequeath his papers to his successor; but to whom might I give Dr Bain's papers? Had he meant for me to keep them? Who would be appointed, now that he was dead? I did not want to think of it. Dr Bain could never be replaced.

Will pulled out the coffins. Both appeared to be cut from the same material. 'They are made from a pre-scription ledger,' I said. 'We have used the same kind for years. Anyone would be able to procure such a thing.'

I removed the lids. The handfuls of dried flowers looked like shreds of dead skin in the lamplight. We sifted through the petals, examining each of them. But it was the same combination – wormwood, rue, hops, black rose – as we had found in all the other boxes. We unwrapped the dolls, and pored over the wood, and the blood-soaked bandages, with the magnifying glass. Other than ascertaining that the fabric was a fine cotton, and that it appeared to have been cut with a sharp blade rather than simply ripped into strips, we could find nothing remarkable.

'It *must* be the boxes,' I said. 'We are thinking that it's the contents, the flowers and dolls, the things that were put inside deliberately. But what if it's nothing to do with those things? What if it's something that was put inside the boxes unintentionally?'

'The lining.'

'Yes. Each lining is crudely cut and pasted, with no thought and little skill to the execution. But each lining is different. We are racking our brains trying to work out the language of flowers, when we should be focusing on a language that we can actually understand. This one here,' I pointed to the box we had been given by Lily, 'This one we have already seen. Its words are written in blue ink, in a man's hand. *Elizabeth Maud. 18th July 1822.*'

Will picked up the box Dr Bain had left with Joc. 'Can you read the words in this one? They're small and daubed with paste. The box has been damp at some point too and the ink has bled.'

'I work in a hospital,' I said, reaching for the magnifying glass. 'I read bad handwriting all the time – frequently when it's been moistened by bodily fluids.' I hesitated. 'Are you sure you wish to pursue this? It may lead us into danger. Dr Bain is dead. Mrs Catchpole. Joe Silks—'

'And if I said "no" would you throw the boxes onto the fire and have done with it?'

'I would not.'

'Then I'm with you,' said Will. He squeezed my hand. '"Lay on, Macduff, and damned be him that first cries, 'Hold, enough!'"' and we grinned at one another like thieves in the lamplight.

I held the magnifying glass over the second coffin. The lining was a patchwork of fragments, some larger than others, stuck down to cover the seams of the lid, base and sides, and to bind the whole together. The writing itself was fragmented; truncated where the coffin-maker's blade had sliced clumsily. But there were letters, syllables, words distinguishable nonetheless. Would we be able to work out its meaning from so little? 'Write this down,' I said.

Will rummaged about the table top until he found a pen. He flipped open the ink pot. 'Yes?'

'rupt,' I said. 'transu . . . many trials I . . . plain water . . . udation, thrown in . . . umbilical . . . readily gets into the . . . thence into . . .'

At length we were done. 'The paper is the same in both boxes,' I said. 'And the handwriting. I'm familiar with the hand of every doctor at St Saviour's, but I don't recognise this one. And apart from its obvious medical content I can't fathom a word of sense from it either.' I groaned, and put my hands over my eyes. They were streaming with the effort of peering at the tiny faded scribbles. 'What on earth did Dr Bain *see* when he looked at these boxes?'

'Are they torn from patients' notes?' said Will.

'The paper is too thin to be from a ward ledger, though it's possible it's from private notes,' I replied. 'It looks to me to be foolscap. There is a slight perforation, or a watermark at the edge here. I'd say it was a part of a letter, or a draft of something.'

We sat in silence, gazing at the list of words, the fragments Will had written down. What else was there that might guide us? 'Your mother's name,' said Will. 'Can you confidently say that it is written in the same hand as the word-fragments from this second coffin?'

'I'm certain,' I replied. 'The "b", "a", "u" are all identical. And the tall stroke of the "t". There's no question about it.'

'So why might a doctor write her name? And her date of death?'

'For his notes.'

'And who was her doctor?'

'Dr Sneddon,' I said. 'She was a special case. An interesting case. She and my brother both died. He published a piece about it in the *London Chirurgical Review*.'

'When?'

'1823.'

'Oh.' He sounded disappointed. 'That's the year *after* the date we have here.'

'Of course,' I said. 'It takes time to get published.' And then, all at once, I knew. I looked up, up at the wall opposite, covered from floor to ceiling with shelves, each lined with leather-bound volumes. I took the lamp and went over to them. Midway down the second bay was a bound run of the *London Chirurgical Review*. I seized a chair. Still holding the lamp I stood upon the seat, so that my face was level with the volumes. 'It's fortunate that Dr Bain and I were such slap-dash parlour maids,' I said. 'One can put a book back, but not the dust. And the dust lies undisturbed along this entire shelf, apart from in front of the volume for 1823.' I pulled it out. 'Catch.'

Will caught the book in both hands. My own were shaking. My heart raced, and all at once I could hardly breathe with excitement.

'I think you should look for it,' said Will. 'It's about your mother after all.' He handed me the volume.

'Thank you,' I said. I took his hand and squeezed it. 'Thank you for being here. For helping. For being a true friend.'

He blushed. 'It's you who solved the riddle.'

I grinned. 'I know. Brilliant, eh? Let's just hope we're right.' I flicked through the volume. 'The notes in the coffins must have been written by Dr Sneddon.'

'Would he use his own notes for so macabre a purpose?'

'I suppose it doesn't seem very likely.'

'Besides, you say Dr Sneddon is long dead. Obviously he didn't kill Dr Bain, though it may well be someone connected to him who did.'

'And we cannot be certain these are his notes lining the coffins. Unless we find—' And there, there it was. 'Look!' I said. 'Look! Read that. It is his. And yet – oh!' All at once my heart seemed to stop inside me. Dr Sneddon would not have used his own notes as scrap paper, but someone else would have.

Will took the volume. '"rupture or transudation,"' he

read. '"By many trials I know that plain water, or any simple fluid fit for transudation, thrown into the umbilical arteries or veins—"'

'And the author?'

'*Observations on the Gravid Uterus* . . . Dr Henry Sneddon.'

'And look at this.' I handed him the words he had written, the words I had read out, culled from the scraps of paper that lined the two tiny coffins. *transu* . . . *many trials I* . . . *plain water* . . . *udation, thrown in* . . .

'It's the same,' said Will.

'It is his paper about my birth. The coffins are lined with his notes, the *Review* confirms it.'

'But why would he—'

'Use his notes for such a purpose? He didn't. Dr Sneddon died the year after I was born. I believe he followed the tradition of St Saviour's and bequeathed his notes and papers to his successor. It was *that* person who used Dr Sneddon's notes to line the coffins.'

'Then who was Dr Sneddon's successor?'

For a moment I could not answer. I tried to speak, but my tongue would not move. I knew well enough who it was. His name stuck in my throat even as the consequences of our discovery made my mind reel. I would not have chosen such an antagonist for the world.

We put the leather-bound volume back onto the shelf, and the coffins back into the sack. Despite the evening's discovery I was still hesitant: we could still not be completely sure who had murdered Dr Bain, Joe, Mrs Catchpole. Mainly, because I simply could not fathom *why*. But we were moving closer. The knowledge was unsettling. Will extinguished the lamps. Our candles were feeble in the engulfing blackness.

❀

Perhaps it was because I was glad to get out of Dr Bain's cold and cheerless house that my cautiousness deserted me. And, I had to admit, my mind was whirling and confused. I felt as though I was in a dream – walking through a parody of our once-ordered and mundane world; a world now filled with those who would take life rather than do all in their power to save it. Will too was silent and distracted. And so neither of us saw the dark figures standing in the shadows of the garden wall. They had sticks, and a dark lantern. I smelled the hot metal of the thing at the same moment that they came at us.

'Jem Flockhart?' the voice was rough. In the moonlight I saw his brass buttons glint, his tall hat gleam a dark blue-black. 'I'm arresting you for the murder of Dr James McCredie Bain; the murder of the vagrant known as Joe Silks, and the murder of Mrs Annabel Catchpole.'

Chapter Fourteen

～

They said I was a murderer, and that Newgate was my
destination. Newgate. The name is enough to strike
terror into the strongest heart. I was bundled into a
Black Maria and taken there directly. My manacles were
thick, heavy things, rough at the wrists, as though coated
with a rim of dried blood; the gyves about my ankles
chafed and rattled. I was alone – thank God for that
mercy, at least, though I could not see that I had much
else to be grateful to Him for. The wagon stank of piss and
fear, but I held myself firm; I would not allow my body or
my mind to betray me, not now. Nor would I sit silent. I
was falsely accused, and I would not go quietly into that
hellish place. And so I screamed my innocence at the top
of my voice, over and over again, till my throat was raw,
the streets rang and my ears buzzed.

Inside, I was brought along a narrow winding passage.
So many gates were locked and unlocked, so many
gratings and doors creaked and slammed before and

behind me, so incessant was the harsh jangling of the keys, that I was soon lost in confusion almost as deep as my despair. A dismal tarnished moon eased out from leaden clouds as we crossed a courtyard, bounded on all sides by high walls and black-barred windows. The air, even outside, was thick and choking, the flagstones slimy underfoot, the prison above us a dark, brooding hulk. From the right, on the other side of a tall, spike-topped wall, I could hear the screams and cries of the women prisoners – as hideous to the ear and as fearful to the heart as the howls from a pack of she-wolves. We entered the building opposite; it was broad and heavy looking, like St Saviour's. But whereas St Saviour's windows were large and bright, the windows of Newgate were small and thickly smothered with dark iron bars. Up ahead, the groans and horrid laughter turned my blood to water.

I was taken to a ward – one of many that we passed, all exactly alike – in which some twenty men were lying upon the ground. My shackles were removed; I was handed a stinking mat and a thin grey blanket, and told to lie upon the floor. I lay down as I was bid, my eyes staring, my body shaking. And there they left me, at the mercy of my fellow prisoners, in the darkness of the Newgate night.

As my eyes adjusted to the gloom, I could make out shapes; bodies lying, crouching, moving in the darkness. Beside me, a man's face emerged out of the shadows, as though conjured from the deep. His skin had a greyish cast, and was stretched tight across his broad flat face. He was thickset, muscular, with a bald head; his left eye pale and dead, his right eye cruel and glinting with desire. His lips curled – 'Hello, my pretty.' His breath was rank with decay.

I threw back my head, so that whatever dim light the place possessed might illuminate my features. My voice, when I spoke, was a snarl, my mask – that hideous scarlet stain I had despised all my life – lent my face such a villainous aspect that he recoiled from me at once.

'Have a care,' I hissed. 'I am not what I seem, and I can poison you so vilely that you will scream for my forgiveness. I can make your eyes melt in your head, your skin itch till you tear it off with your own fingernails. I can make your guts boil like tar inside you. I will cause you such pain, such torment, that you will beg for the hangman's noose.' I held up a finger, and pointed it directly at his one good eye. 'I am a man like none you have ever known. And I *will* kill you if you come near me.'

I lay there trembling, while whatever vile practices my fellow inmates indulged in went on around me. There was no sleep to be had – how anyone might sleep at all in that infernal place I had no idea. My mind was almost deranged with fear. I had not expected this, had not foreseen this at all. I screwed my eyes shut and stopped up my ears as the noises around me grew in volume and torment.

The next morning, the warders took me out to another, quieter place where the howls and debauches of the inmates were not so loud as to prevent communication. The bars upon the windows there were so thick as to admit scarcely any light at all. I sat on a wooden stool at a rough trestle table, my ankles and wrists in irons once more. After a moment, another warder brought in a candle. He was followed by a tall, thin, bespectacled man. I could see immediately that he was a man of the law, though I could not say what kind.

'Who is my accuser?' I said.

'You will know that soon enough,' said the man, sitting down opposite me. 'The evidence will be discussed in a court of law and you will have the opportunity to defend yourself. But I have some questions to ask you first.' He pulled out a sheaf of papers which bore line after line of close-written scribbles. The lies of my accusers, no doubt. He took out his pen and ink and positioned himself close to the candle so that he might amend his account as he saw fit. 'The night before the deceased, Dr James Bain, was found dead at his home on St Saviour's Street, it has been averred that you went with the aforementioned Dr Bain to the home of one Mrs Roseplucker, on Wicke Street.'

'Yes, I did,' I said. 'But can you not speak plainly? Are we to be here all day while you "aver" this and "afore-mention" that?'

He looked at me over his spectacles. 'It is averred that you and he were working on a book about poisons together.'

'So we were.'

'And that it was his intention to publish it without acknowledging your assistance.'

'We had a long way to go before it was ready for pub-lication. We had not discussed the matter of authorship.'

'But I argue that you *had* discussed it, and that you were most put out when Dr Bain said he was to publish the work without your name on it. His colleagues have con-firmed that he spoke of it to them the day before he died.'

'Lies,' I said.

'And I also suggest that you were jealous of Dr Bain – jealous of his professional abilities, his position at St

Saviour's, his popularity with the opposite sex. You were unable to perform the office of a man, were you not, when you visited Mrs Roseplucker's house?'

'I—'

He waved a hand. 'We have a witness.'

I thought of the girl who had come for the herbs, the girl who brought the coffin. 'You've twisted her words,' I said.

'I take them at face value. You did not perform. You never did when you went there, and you went there often, whilst in another room Dr Bain disported himself with vigour. You say it is because you *would* not? I suggest that it is because you *could* not. And yet Dr Bain was a man with no such peculiarities. What man would not be piqued by the hot-bloodedness of a companion when he himself was impotent?'

'Do you think impotent men often feel moved to murder their more priapic brothers?'

He did not look at me, but dipped his pen in the ink pot and wrote something on his paper. I felt sick. No doubt he had taken my words to be a confession of impotence, the fool. And if I admitted I was a woman would that help my cause? No. I would become an object of horror, a monster, a victim of suppressed hysterical urges, my mind undone due to the pressures of living a man's life whilst inhabiting a woman's body. Things would be far worse for me if I disclosed my true identity. That revelation, it seemed, must be saved for after the gallows.

He paused in his scribbles, and looked up at me. 'And so you killed him with tincture of bloodroot.'

'No—'

'Later, returning to the place, you pretended to find his body and raised the alarm.'

'I *did* find the body! There was no pretence—'

'And that some time later you likewise poisoned Mrs Annabel Catchpole—'

'Mrs Catchpole was killed by curare,' I snapped. 'Dr Bain, I strongly suspect, was killed by aconite.'

'I beg your pardon?'

'Curare. *Chondrodendron tomentosum.* A species of tropical liana, deadly only if it enters the blood. Aconite is a flowering plant widely found in Britain. It tastes bitter, but unlike many toxins can be absorbed through the skin. They were killed by *different* means.'

He peered at me over his spectacles. 'Aconite?'

'Aconite. Monkshood. Wolfsbane. Call it what you will.'

'I will call it murder, Mr Flockhart.' He stared at me as if I were mad. 'Your specialist knowledge of poisons is noted. As well as your ready access to it.'

'St Saviour's is full of men with specialist knowledge of poisons,' I said. 'Each of them has ready access to the stuff. You may as well arrest the entire medical staff of every hospital in the city.'

'As for the death of Mrs Annabel Catchpole—'

That, I had to admit, did look peculiar. Other than the attendant who had taken her clothes and locked her in for the night, I was the last person to have seen her alive. The salve was still in my room at the apothecary. Would they have looked for it?

'The pot of salve you left for Mrs Catchpole was found to contain enough poison to kill a cart horse—'

My face drained of blood. I felt his gaze upon me.

They had been to my room. 'But *I* didn't put the poison in that salve.'

'But you gave it to her. There are witnesses. And the constable found it in your apothecary.'

I closed my eyes. 'I didn't put curare in it.'

'How else did it get there? There is no mistaking it. '

I shook my head. I knew the adulterated salve had been placed there that evening at Angel Meadow, swapped for the one I had prepared myself, but as for who had done so—

'The salve is poison. Dr Graves has demonstrated its efficacy. He rubbed a quantity of the stuff into a wound on the leg of a dog and we saw the terrible effects for ourselves.'

I could imagine the spectacle: the grinning Dr Graves, the gasps of the assembled crowd, the agony of the beast as the paralysis took hold. How could sensible explanations possibly compete against such theatrics? But the man was talking again, and I was obliged to listen. 'An attendant at Angel Meadow has confirmed that the pot of salve found in your room was the same stuff you brought to Mrs Catchpole, which you then removed from her room as she lay dead on the floor. Why would you remove the stuff if it was not to conceal your crime?'

'And would I not throw the salve away, rather than keep it at home?'

'Perhaps you had other victims in mind.'

I could see the logic of his thinking, even though the conclusions he drew were mistaken. 'And Joe,' I said. It was hardly worth the asking. 'Why would I kill Joe Silks?'

'We don't yet know. But you were seen in Prior's Rents, looking for, and then talking to, the vagrant known as Joe

Silks. Witnesses say there was shouting. Threats were uttered.'

I said nothing. No doubt there were plenty of people in Prior's Rents who might be persuaded to testify to anything.

'His head was bludgeoned,' added the prosecutor.

'It was crushed by his fall,' I said.

'Oh?' He grinned, as though he had just tricked me into a full confession. 'Was it really? Do you admit that you were out in the full moon that night? The night Joe Silks was murdered? You might as well. We have a witness.'

'Who?' I cried, astonished. 'Who can possibly have seen me doing something I patently did not do?'

'The sexton of St Saviour's parish church saw you. You and Silks. Shortly before you clubbed the unfortunate child about the head and dumped him into the open graves in St Saviour's churchyard.'

I opened my mouth, but I could not speak. Old Dick had seen two people, certainly. 'Man and boy' he had said. It might mean anyone. 'It wasn't me he saw,' I whispered at last. 'I had no reason to murder Joe Silks.'

'I'm sure I can think of one,' said the man. 'Besides, it hardly matters. You're going to hang anyway. One of these will bring you to the rope, you can be sure of that.'

I sank to my knees in the filthy straw. How had I come to this? Not two weeks earlier I had been the apothecary at St Saviour's Infirmary, attending to the sick and making up prescriptions just as I had day after day, year after year for almost as long as I could remember. Now three people had been murdered and I stood to hang for it. Should I put my faith in the ability of the law to discover the truth? But the law was a stupid and arrogant beast, and I had no confidence in it, nor in the dolts that purported to practise it. The magistrates were drunks, the witnesses narrow-minded, and easily led. Evidence was sensational, and entirely subjective. And my bloody highwayman's appearance would do nothing to further my cause. *Does he not look like the very Devil,* they would say, *with his tall, thin scarecrow body and his crimson mask?* If my face was repulsive and devilish, was that ugliness not matched on the inside? No wonder one such as I might be capable of villainy . . .

'Who speaks against me?' I said. My voice was hoarse, my throat dry as bone. 'Dr Magorian, no doubt?'

The prosecutor nodded. 'Dr Magorian brought his concerns, and his deductions, to our attention last night. He is a man of great reputation,' he said. And then added in a more conversational tone: 'The magistrate was cut for the stone some years ago. If it were not for Dr Magorian's skill and precision . . . the magistrate has often said that he owes his health, and his happiness, to Dr Magorian.'

'I'm sure he's eternally grateful,' I said bitterly.

Dr Magorian. It could be none other. It was Dr Magorian who was Dr Sneddon's successor. Dr Magorian who had used Dr Sneddon's old notes to line the coffins, though why he might make such peculiar mementoes was still a mystery. Had he murdered Dr Bain? It seemed likely. And yet why would he do such a thing? They had known each other for years without evidence of any deep-seated animosity. It made no sense to me. Still, we were close on his heels. Ensuring that *I* was charged with the murders *he* had committed, merely revealed his guilt and desperation. But I could not prove it – not yet, and certainly not from inside Newgate.

I told the prosecutor to go. I had spoken recklessly, and I knew it. My own wits were all that might save me now.

⁂

Will came. I was taken to meet him in the yard, where I was permitted to speak to him only through the grating of a cage. The place was crowded with my fellow inmates. To the left, a tall thin man with one eye was muttering through the bars to a ragged old beldam with a pipe clenched between her gums. To our right a great towering hulk of a man was being admonished by a female visitor so small and filthy I thought at first she might be a child. But the profanities that issued from her lips were nothing I had ever heard, even from Joe Silks and his friends, and when she turned to look at us we saw a face so destroyed by gin and the pox, I could not begin to imagine what their relationship might be.

'Dr Hawkins is doing all he can to help you,' said Will. 'And I.' He had brought with him one of Mrs Speedicut's pound cakes and some small beer from the infirmary brewhouse. He passed them through the grating.

'Dr Magorian went to the magistrate,' I said.

'Yes. But I don't understand why. What does it matter if Dr Sneddon's notes were found in a foolish totem like a toy coffin?'

I gripped the iron bars. 'Will, we have to *think. Think.* Why would Dr Magorian murder Dr Bain? What is the connection between that murder and the words in the coffins? We must link the two.'

He licked his lips. 'I don't know.'

'Then let us think more generally and hope that

might lead us forward. Why would anyone commit murder?'

'Love?' he said. 'Hate? Greed? Jealousy?'

'Good,' I said. 'But Dr Magorian has plenty of money. I can think of no reason why he might be greedy for more.'

'Jealousy?'

'His reputation is extraordinary. He counts members of the aristocracy as his patients – I've always been surprised he bothered with St Saviour's at all.'

'And yet what if that reputation was threatened in some way? Would he not do all he could to protect it?'

'Quite possibly.'

'And what of Dr Bain's relationship with Miss Magorian?'

I had vowed to myself that I would say nothing about that to anyone. Even Will did not know the extent of it. But he was right. 'It cannot be discounted,' I said.

'That brings us to love,' said Will.

'The most powerful, irrational and destructive motive of them all.' We fell silent. 'I *have* to get out,' I said at last.

'Jem,' said Will. 'You were the last person to see Mrs Catchpole alive. The salve was found in your room. It does not look good for you.' He sighed. 'I'm sorry. I'm not making you feel any better, am I?'

'I need to know the truth,' I said. 'I don't expect you to come here and pretend that all's well.' I put my head in my hands. '*Why* did I take that salve?' We stood without speaking. 'How's my father?' I said after a moment. 'Does he know I'm here?'

'Yes.'

'Can he come to see me?'

'I doubt I'll be able to keep him away.'

'And how does he seem?'

Will shook his head. 'Your father is not what he was, Jem.'

I rubbed my face to keep the tears away. 'Dr Bain,' I said. 'He holds the key. We must ask ourselves what Dr Bain knew. When he looked at the coffins, that first time in the apothecary, he turned pale. I assumed it was because Dr Catchpole had just split his head open, but perhaps it was something else.'

'You think he'd seen the coffins before?'

'Possibly. But let's put that aside for now. Dr Bain takes the coffins. Why? To examine them? To prevent anyone else from having them? Whatever the reason, there was something familiar about them, something *wrong*, and Dr Bain knew – or at least suspected – what it was.'

'You knew him more intimately than anyone—'

'But there was plenty I did *not* know about him. You recall that night when we were at his house? When you uncovered the hook, the rope, the mattock? The tools of the resurrection men. He must have been one himself.'

'You had no idea?'

'None at all! Though many students were obliged to procure their own bodies for dissection – there was no other way to learn.'

'Old Dick said as much,' said Will. 'He said it was "always medicals" looking for bodies.'

And so it was. The resurrectionists had passed into history as reckless and uncouth men, but that picture was far from true. 'I don't judge Dr Bain too harshly if he became an expert in digging up the dead,' I said. 'But I do say that he most certainly had secrets, perhaps ones he too would have liked to keep hidden.'

'And there is also his second visit to Lily,' said Will. 'She was quite clear about what he said. "Not again. Not this again."'

'Which confirms that he *had* seen the coffins, or something similar, before. But *where?* And *when?*'

'Not recently,' said Will. 'It can't have been recently as the boxes were old. Perhaps before he came to St Saviour's?'

'He's always been here. His father was a scrivener on St Saviour's Street. He died when Dr Bain was a boy—' I stopped.

'What is it?'

'*Hoots toots mon,*' I murmured.

Will looked perplexed. 'I'm sorry?'

'Edinburgh,' I said. 'Dr Bain studied at Edinburgh Medical School before he came to London.' I gripped Will's hand through greasy bars of the grating. 'I must see my father. Dr Bain lodged at the apothecary – years ago, while I was with the wet nurse in the country, after my mother died. He was a student, and had just come down from Edinburgh. My father must know something about that part of Dr Bain's life – why he left that city. Edinburgh is the finest place in the world for a medical education. Why would one leave before one had finished, especially when one was as capable a student as Dr Bain?'

I ripped off a hunk of Mrs Speedicut's pound cake and took a bite. It was as dry as sawdust, as I knew it would be. But it tasted of home.

❧

In the afternoon, I was told I had another visitor.

'Special treatment,' said the warder. He grinned at me. 'He paid ten guineas for it too.'

I was taken into the ward where I had spent the night. A dozen men were sitting on benches before a smouldering fire, the sleeping mats and blankets rolled away. Against the wall, standing far from the others, was a tall, thin, old man. For a moment I wondered who he was, he was looking at me so strangely. And then I realised. 'Father!' I sprang towards him.

For the first time that I could remember, he held me to his heart. 'Ten guineas, Father?' I mumbled the words against his chest.

'I would give all I have to hold you without the impediment of bars and locks.'

He was skin and bone beneath my hands. I had seen him only two days previously, but in that short time he had aged. His illness, compounded by care and worry, had eaten him alive. Its progress had not been arrested by Dr Hawkins's efforts, and it was apparent that he had not slept for days. I could not blame him, or Dr Hawkins, for trying to find a remedy, but I could not find it in my heart to pretend that I saw anything in his countenance but death.

He took my face in his hands and kissed my forehead. His eyes were filled with tears. Then he said, 'Things are worse for you than you realise, my dear.'

'But I'm guilty of nothing but trying to discover who murdered Dr Bain.'

'I know.' He stroked my hair. 'I know.'

We sat together on either side of a trestle table. Around us, men gambled and swore, fought and shouted. The place was ill lit, and in the darkened corners shadows moved and grunted. My father looked about, appalled. 'How in Heaven's name did we end up like this? You to hang, me to go mad.'

'Let's not think of it,' I said. 'But I must ask you some questions.'

He rubbed his eyes. His skin was grey, papery dry and flecked with dark flaky patches. It cleaved to his skull as though all moisture had been sucked from him. His eyes seemed huge, pale and anxious in their dark-ringed sockets, the lids membranous above gaunt cheeks and lips puckered and drawn.

'Father,' I said. 'Can you remember when Dr Bain shared your lodgings? When he had my room at the apothecary?'

'Of course. He was a student. One of Dr Magorian's most promising.'

'And before he came to London he studied at Edinburgh, didn't he?'

'Yes. But he didn't finish his studies there.'

'Did he ever talk about the place? Did he ever talk about why he left and came to London?'

My father looked at me in silence. All at once his eyes were vacant. It was as if his spirit had left his body and walked away, leaving nothing but an empty husk. 'Father?' I said. He glanced from side to side, his features resolving into an expression of alarm and perplexity, and I realised that he did not know who I was or why he was there. I had never seen him look so startled, so afraid. 'Father.' I took his hand. 'It's Jem.' All my life he had been stern and self-assured, a tall taciturn man, austere, unforgiving, disappointed. But he had been strong; resolute and decisive. Over the preceding weeks I had watched those attributes slowly diminish; standing by hopelessly I had seen him become a different man – vague, undecided, lost.

'Fight it,' I whispered, holding his hands between my own. 'Do not give in to it.'

He blinked, I felt his fingers respond, and I saw in his eyes that he had come back to me – for the moment. 'I cannot,' he whispered. The tears ran down his face too now, dripping from his chin onto the filthy straw.

'You must.' I spoke sternly, the way he spoke to Gabriel. 'Father, you *must* help me. You *must* remember. Did Dr Bain talk to you about his time in Edinburgh? What did he tell you? What did he say? What happened when he was there? Why did he leave?' I took him by the shoulders. 'Father!'

My father swayed in my grasp like a reed. 'Dr Bain?' he said. 'He was only with me for a short while. After your mother died; while you were away.'

'When? When was he with you?'

He shrugged, too tired to speak.

'You were married in 1824. I was born in '25.'

'Then he was there just after that, '21 and '22. He helped in the apothecary while he completed his studies. He was very able, very knowledgeable. Hard working too. He helped me with the prescriptions, and I gave him food and lodgings. We were company for each other in the evenings. It suited us both well enough.'

'And you must have talked?'

'His parents were dead. His father had left him very little money and he used what he had to go to Edinburgh, and to pay for his studies. But he was very poor. It was a difficult time for him, he said. But he was an able student and he found work soon enough, in the anatomy rooms at one of the extra-mural schools. And better lodgings.'

'Who with? Who did he live with in Edinburgh, did he say?'

My father rubbed his eyes with his fists. I could hear his eyeballs squelch and squeak. The sound turned my stomach, but he seemed to have entered a trance-like state and on and on he went, his fists screwing into his eye sockets. I took hold of his hands and pulled them away from his face. For a moment, there was that look of confusion again.

'Who did Dr Bain lodge with in Edinburgh? What work was he required to do?'

He sighed. 'I'm sure he will have told you himself. You knew him better than anyone.'

'But I did *not* know him, Father, his past was a secret. He never mentioned it – and I had little reason to ask.' I hesitated. 'He was a resurrectionist, wasn't he?'

My father nodded. Suddenly his mind seemed to clear. His sentences became lucid and steady. 'You cannot judge him,' he said. 'They were not all Burke and Hare, you know. Many of the students were obliged to procure their own corpses, and there was a sore need for dead bodies in the anatomy schools. It's no use dissecting a dog and thinking it might prove a useful template for under-standing the human body. Books, specimens, wax preparations are of limited use. A man must dissect for himself if he is to comprehend, to value, human life. Dr Bain always knew the importance of that. He gave himself, his own body, to medical science. He always said he was to be given to the anatomists after death.'

I remembered the relish with which Dr Bain had been dissected – dismembered, unravelled, and pickled by Dr Graves. I doubted whether Dr Bain would have considered himself justly used.

'Which anatomy school did he work in?' I said. 'What caused him to leave?'

'He worked for Dr Magorian, and found lodgings there too.'

'Dr Magorian was in Edinburgh?'

'Yes.'

In all the years I had known him, Dr Magorian had never mentioned Edinburgh. At that moment I wondered why I had never asked before. 'Tell me about Dr Magorian,' I said. 'About Edinburgh.'

'Dr Magorian came down from Edinburgh, over twenty years ago now. He brought Dr Graves with him, and Dr Bain, though Dr Bain was only a young man and not qualified. Dr Magorian had already made a name for himself as a surgeon. Obstetrics was his interest, along with anatomy and surgery, and he had done well for himself in Edinburgh. Dr Graves had been his dresser.'

'And Dr Bain?'

'Dr Bain was still a student. He had begun his training in Edinburgh when he was little more than a boy. Dr Magorian had recognised his ability and had encouraged him, finding him work in his anatomy museum and as a demonstrator while he pursued his studies. But, naturally, there was something expected in return.'

'Subjects?'

'For anatomy, yes. Dr Graves had a certain relish for the activity, so Dr Bain told me. Dr Graves is strong and quick.

No one was faster at getting a body from the ground. It was not something for the weak or faint hearted, and they worked together – Dr Graves and Dr Bain.'

'And Dr Magorian, the great teacher in the ascendant, awaited their finds with his knives out and his students gathered.'

'I suppose he did,' said my father.

How blind and stupid I had been. If I had known about this I might have been able to stay ahead of the game; I would have been quicker to recognise the links between past and present. But then my father had never been one for talking – not to me, at any rate. 'Why didn't you tell me this?' I said.

'You didn't ask. Dr Bain and I often talked together, back then. He was good company. I knew that what he told me was not to be talked of. And I can keep a confidence – you know that better than anyone. Besides, I'm telling you now.'

'So what happened? Why did Dr Bain leave? And Dr Magorian and Dr Graves? They all came to London together. Why?'

My father shrugged. 'Dr Bain was never clear about it. There was something about those final months in Edinburgh, some details that he chose to miss out. Murder was implied. Dr Magorian, Dr Graves, Dr Bain were all implicated.'

'How? What happened?'

'I have no idea.' My father closed his eyes.

'Think, Father. Dr Bain must have said *something*.'

'He said it was all in the past, something not to be talked of, and that's where it would remain.'

But Dr Bain was wrong. It was not in the past. It was

there, now, amongst us. And it was about to lead me to
the gallows.

❦

I passed a fitful night. They moved me to a smaller cell,
darker than the first and strewn with filthy grey straw.
The ground beneath my boots crunched as I moved, as
though the boards were sprinkled with grit, though I
knew the sound came from the lice and cockroaches
thick underfoot. My fellow inmates, two surly, thin-faced
horse thieves destined for the hulks, wrapped themselves
in their ragged overcoats and went to sleep almost
immediately. No doubt they were accustomed to such
vile and wretched surroundings. But I was not, and I
trembled where I sat, looking up at the window, watching
that small smudge of grey high in the wall grow brighter
as the dawn approached.

In the morning the warder came. 'You can go,' he said.

My heart jumped. Had the real murderer been found?
It seemed unlikely. Had Dr Hawkins and Will managed to
persuade the magistrate of my innocence? That did not
sound plausible either. 'Why?' I said. The warder didn't
answer. Something was wrong, I was certain. 'Why am I to
be let out?' I repeated. 'Answer me!'

'Because we have our murderer now,' came the reply.
'And it appears it ain't you.'

'Who is it?' I said.

The warder grinned. 'You mean you don't know?'

'How would I know?' I snapped. 'I've been stuck in
here.'

'Because you were talkin' to him yesterday.'

'You mean Mr Quartermain?' I said. I could hardly believe what I was hearing. 'But that's absurd!'

'That young gen'leman?' said the warder. 'No, not 'im.'

'Then who are you talking about?'

'The old feller. Thin. Grey. Looks like the Reaper 'imself.'

'What?' I seized the warder by the arm. '*What?*'

The warder wrenched his arm away. 'Don't touch me!' His face was inches from mine, his breath rank with last night's ale and onions. 'Came in this morning. Confessed to everythin'.' He laughed. 'Folks love a hangin'. Should be a good crowd for it.'

❧

They took me to his cell. He was alone, for which I was grateful. At first, neither of us said anything. I took his hands and kissed them, waiting for him to speak.

'I'm dying, Jem,' he said. 'And before I die I will go blind. Then I will go mad. I will end my days raving in the darkness, and I will not know you, nor myself. I will have no memory of my wife, no conception of grace or beauty or love; there will be nothing for me but pain and torment.'

'Father—'

He held up a hand. 'Let me speak. Yesterday, after I left you, I went to see Dr Hawkins. There is no improvement in my condition, no diminution of this disease. I asked if I might see my brother.

'Dr Hawkins wanted to refuse, but he could not. I had to see my fate with my own eyes. Few men are permitted so clearly to see what the future holds.' He shut his eyes and covered his face with his hands. 'And it holds for me such a death as I would not wish upon anyone. You should not wish it upon me either.' He looked up at me with eyes red rimmed with sorrow. 'Only you can save me, Jem. Only you can save me from that.'

'But how?' I didn't understand. How could I save him when Dr Hawkins had failed? I could not think what he meant. 'I would do anything—'

'Then you will let *me* hang for these crimes, and *you* will walk free.'

'No!' At once his intention was clear. 'You can't hang for crimes you didn't commit—'

'And you should?'

'No—'

'But you *will* hang, Jem. For Mrs Catchpole, at least. And there's nothing I can do to change that. The evidence all points to you and no one has the wit to see otherwise. No one but *you.*'

'But Father—' I hardly knew what to say. To see my own father – an innocent man – condemned? To allow the real murderer to escape with his life? To leave judgement in the hands of God? It was impossible. My voice was a whisper. 'I can't allow it.'

'You *must*, Jem. You *must* allow it. You can clear my name after I am dead. I would not wish to die, and be thought a murderer – but only I can save you now. And I can use my own wretched life to do so.' He held me at arm's length and looked into my face. 'You are like your mother,' he said. 'She was strong. She never gave up. She was beautiful, in her heart and soul, as you are. And I see her in you every day. She never knew you, Jem; she died so that you could live. And now, it's time for me to do the same. You're dearer to me than my own life. I resented your mother for making that choice, for choosing you above herself, above me, but now I understand.' He kissed my forehead. 'So you must leave me here, and go away from this place.' He gave me a gentle push, and smiled. 'My reputation, Jem, is all that matters now that you're safe. What else does a man have if he loses that?'

Chapter Fifteen

❦

I went back to the apothecary. My father had left detailed instructions and Gabriel was working hard. The extent of the devastation around him was, for once, limited, and it appeared that only one glass retort had been smashed – and that swept aside. The air of resentful mayhem that usually surrounded the lad whenever he was left alone with a task to do was, for once, quite absent.

'Mr Jem.' He nodded at me, his expression serious, his nose smeared with white dust. Powdered mallow root, perhaps, or cornstarch?

'How're you getting on?' I said. 'You look as though you've the measure of everything. More or less.'

'Yes,' he spoke proudly. 'Your father left me in charge. He said he loved me like a son and that he knew I would do him proud.' The lad's chin trembled as he held up a sheet of paper and squared his shoulders. 'He said you'd be busy when you got back so he left me a list. An' I got some helpers. Mrs Speedicut, she's been on the pestle and mortar.' He lowered his voice. 'She got arms like a wrestler, or like one o' them what works on the docks, and she can grind like nuthin' I've ever seen!'

'I've no doubt she can,' I said.

'An' Mr Quartermain, he's out at the churchyard right now but he's helped too. And there's the girl that knew Joe Silks. Her name's Sally. Sally!' he shouted. '*Sal!*' Sal's blonde head appeared from behind a row of glass vessels. She stared at Gabriel admiringly. 'Sal's bottling,' said Gabriel. 'Made some iron tonic earlier, and there's some tincture of nettle leaf what wants decanting. She's got a steady hand. Mrs Speedicut got her bathed and scrubbed and found her some new clothes. Said she might stay on and help as we're short just now.' He frowned. 'Pity you're back, really,' he added. 'Not that I'm not glad to see you, Mr Jem—'

I reached for my apron and glanced at my father's list. 'He forgot out-patients,' I said.

I set to work. It would help to focus my mind and clear my thoughts. I tried not to think about my father, alone in that terrible place, nor of the fate that awaited him. Instead, I allowed my mind to rest, forcing myself to think only of tinctures, powders and pills, my hands working at tasks that I had performed countless times. For once, I cut corners. Most of the out-patients' prescriptions were for iron tonics, worming powders, purgatives. Blue Pill and black dose would do for most of them. Perhaps I might forgo attending the out-patients' dispensary altogether – was not Mrs Speedicut quite capable of handing out medicines? She had seen more furred tongues and costive bowels than I'd had hot dinners – so she repeatedly told me.

I prepared everything as quickly as I could, and then tore off my apron. The stink of Newgate was making me feel ill and I itched like the Devil. 'I need a bath,' I said.

'Want the nit comb and the lavender oil?' said Gabriel, helpfully. 'You'd better get 'em yourself, mind. I'm too busy now to be helping with baths.'

Will returned while I was putting the kettle onto the fire. 'Good to see you, Jem,' he said. For a moment I thought he was about to fling his arms about me, but etiquette prevailed and he merely shook my hand vigorously. 'Your father.' He could not meet my eyes, but looked down at our clasped hands. When he spoke, his voice trembled. 'God help him.'

I nodded. I could not speak. Tears filled my eyes, and I brushed them away with the back of my hand. Will thrust his handkerchief at me. I dabbed my eyes. The square of white linen stank of decay. Will himself reeked of it, and it seemed to ebb and flow about him in some invisible current. 'You smell even worse than me,' I said.

'I spend my days among the dead. The stench of the place is indescribable.'

'You don't have to describe it,' I said. 'I can smell it for myself.'

'The Company have seen fit to provide me with only three carts. Three! If they saw what I'm required to do they would realise – but never mind that. We have other matters to attend to. Your father.' He slid a glance at me. 'We need to think what to do. We don't have much time.'

'He cannot die on the gallows,' I whispered.

Will poured a cup of coffee from the pewter pot on the stove top and handed it to me. I sipped the black liquid. It was as bitter as wormwood on my tongue, but it did something to clear my head. Behind us, Gabriel clattered the weights on the scales.

'Dr Magorian,' said Will. His voice was quiet, guarded. 'The secret lies with him. The coffins, Dr Bain, everything. There is no other possibility.'

'How might we prove it? We have no evidence. And why would he do such a thing? To kill a colleague, and a colleague's wife!'

'We might speak to the sexton again.'

'Old Dick?' I said. 'His account is so vague, so confused that it might very well mean anything. Besides, it is his testimony that has me placed at St Saviour's churchyard at midnight with a bludgeon in my hand and a dead boy at my feet.'

'We could look at the coffins. Pull them apart.'

'They hold nothing more for us,' I said. I told him what my father had said about Dr Bain's time in Edinburgh, about his hasty departure from that city, and the events that had precipitated it. 'The coffins are an echo of something that happened in Edinburgh, back when Dr Bain procured bodies for Dr Magorian's medical school.'

Above the dresser the clock ticked, a sullen reminder of the unstoppable passing of time. 'You think it was murder?' he said.

I thought of those six tiny coffins we had once lined up on the work bench; the six bandaged effigies lying within. What else might they signify, but death? 'I think it was six murders,' I said.

❧

Will carried the tin bath up to my bedroom and put it before the fire. I emptied two kettles of boiling water into it. The room was warm, the fire blazing. The bundles of lavender that hung from the rafters filled the air with the scent of summer, the rosemary I grew in a plant pot on the window ledge added a stimulating, astringent woodiness. But Newgate had impregnated every part of me. My hair and clothes, even my flesh seemed to stink of the place, and I felt gritty and stale, as though my clothes were filled with chaff and my skin crawled with fleas and lice. Gabriel had brought up some cold water, and I poured this too into my bath. I added a few drops of geranium oil, some lavender oil, and a muslin bag of camomile flowers, rosemary and oatmeal. The steam grew fragrant, the water milky.

I lay there with the perfumed vapour rising about my ears. I sank beneath the surface, my knees raised, my breath held and my eyes closed tight. I could hear nothing but my own heartbeat. Was this what it felt like in the womb? Warm, safe and confined, the world outside muffled and soporific? Then I thought of my father – cold, alone, awaiting death, denied even the oblivion of sleep. I drew the nit comb hard across my skull, and tried to think what I was supposed to do.

The water grew tepid. A pale scum gathered at the edges. My shoulders, out of the water and resting against the back of the bath, felt cold. A draught blew under the bedroom door as someone came into the apothecary, and I shivered. I reached for the towel. At that moment there came the sound of hasty footsteps on the stair. The door burst open and Eliza rushed in.

'Jem,' she cried. 'Thank God you're—' She stopped.

I sank back, beneath the water. Had she seen? 'Can't you knock?' I said.

She did not reply, but stared at me in silent amazement.

'Close the door. You're letting all the heat out.'

She kicked the door closed with the heel of her boot. I had meant for her to be on the other side of it. What should I do? I could not remain where I was, half-submerged in a bath full of chilly water, for ever. Her hair was dishevelled, as though she had run all the way from her father's house to the apothecary (which, I discovered later, was exactly what she had done). Her cheeks were pink and her eyes wide. I saw her tongue dart against her lips. I reached for the towel, but she was there before me.

'I'll do it,' she said.

There was nothing for it but to emerge. I rose up, the water lapping about my knees, naked and dripping. She put the towel over my shoulders. 'Step out of the bath. Come close to the fire. Turn to face me.' Like a child ordered by its nurse, I obeyed. She rubbed the towel beneath my arms, over my breasts and stomach. She crouched before me, and stroked it against my legs. Would she betray me? I felt her fingers touch my damp skin and I closed my eyes.

When she stood up again, her face was inches from mine, her pupils dilated like a fox at bay. I could see a vein pulsing in her neck in time with the beating of my own blood.

She put up a hand to comb my hair off my face with her

fingers. 'Do you bind yourself?' she whispered. 'So that no one knows?'

I swallowed, and pointed to a length of freshly laundered muslin, draped across the chair on top of my clean shirt and britches.

She picked it up. 'Raise your arms.' She leaned closer, and passed the muslin around my back. She began to wrap it about me, folding it across my chest. She slipped a hand beneath, and held my right breast in her hand while she pulled the fabric taut. She did the same with the other, holding it close, pressing against me with her hand, my nipple a cherry stone in her palm. She pulled the muslin tight, and pinned it closed. My breasts ached beneath, until I realised I was holding my breath.

'Poor Jem,' she murmured. 'All this time and I never knew. How lonely it must be for you too.'

'Lonely?'

'To pretend. Always, forever, pretending to be someone you're not.'

'Yes,' I said. My voice seemed to snag in my throat. All at once I wanted to touch her, to taste her, to forget my sorrows with her even for a moment. At the same time there was something about her words that made me uneasy. But I could not think what it might be, my senses were distracted – how beautiful she was, how warm and vital, close enough that I could feel the heat from her, smell the scent of her hair—

'I know what it is to keep a secret.' She put up a hand, and traced the outline of my breast beneath my bindings.

'What secret?' I whispered.

'Mine,' she said. 'And now yours.'

'What will you do?'

'Do?' She smiled. 'Only this.' She put her hands to my face, and kissed me on the lips.

❧

We lay with our arms around each other. I told her about my twin. My brother. How I had taken his place. She listened in silence. Then, 'I had a brother too,' she said. 'Once. I never met him. He died before I was born.'

'I had no idea.'

'No one knows. My mother never speaks of it.'

'And your father?'

'Of course not. He lives with the daily disappointment of a daughter. It's the one thing that he and my mother disagree about. She loves me. He does not.'

I had guessed as much. But she was moving too quickly: a dead sibling? *That* I had never imagined. I had heard no rumours of such a child, not even from Mrs Speedicut. 'Your brother,' I said. 'Was he a baby when he died?'

'He was older. Perhaps ten, or twelve.'

'It must have been a long time ago.'

'I suppose it was. My mother never got over it, I think. She never mentions him, but she keeps mementoes.'

'There are no mementoes of *my* brother,' I said. 'Other than me. I have been brought up as though I were him.'

'But you cannot wish it otherwise, surely. You have such freedoms.' She sounded jealous, resentful almost.

'I don't know anything else,' I said. 'And I would make an ugly woman. I am so tall and thin. My birthmark too—'

She put her small, cool hands to my face. 'But you've always been special because of it. You are always concealed, always mysterious.'

311

'It's hideous.'

'It's you, Jem,' she said. 'Without it you would be someone else entirely, and what use would that be? Your Mr Quartermain would say the same.'

'Will?'

'Will, is it now?' She smiled. 'He's in love with you, I think?'

'How could anyone love someone so ugly, so disfigured?' I turned away. I could not bear for her to look at me. Instinctively, I put my hand up to cover my birthmark, as I always did. And yet I drank in her affection like a plant trapped in the barren earth. 'I've always hated it.'

'And I've always envied you for it. You're safe behind it. Safe from harm. No one sees you, they look at your mask, they marvel at it, then they turn away. They judge you for who you are, not how you look.'

'Everyone is judged by how they look. People look at me and see something horrible. It's a poor start to any acquaintance.'

'But you have lived your life as a man. It's a man's character that matters, not his beauty. Men accept you as one of them, as an equal, no matter what your outward appearance might be. You can be clever and witty, opinionated and confident. You can answer men back and speak your mind to anyone without being thought mad. You can walk with a stride, and eat off your knife, and go out alone at night and laugh loudly and spit into the fire—'

'Do you want to spit into the fire?' I said.

'I want to spit!' she cried. 'On my beauty, and on the fact that it's held in such high regard. What use is such a thing? To be valued simply because of the curl of one's hair or the redness of one's lip? My father hates me because of it, my mother fears me. I'm bred to be a wife, and nothing more. What servitude is *that*?'

'Your father hates you because you're beautiful?'

'He used to beat me because of it.'

I shook my head. 'I don't understand.'

'He said I'd been sent to tempt him, to test his lust and sinfulness, but that he was not a man to give in to such things, and that he would beat the whore's gleam out of my eyes.'

I felt my blood turn cold. What language was this for a gentleman to use against his daughter? Was he not supposed to be her protector, her champion and defender? But I could make no sense of my thoughts, and I tried to put them from my mind. And yet, how expert her lips and fingers had been, how skilled in finding those secret places. Had she mapped those desires upon her own body, or had she been taught by other, coarser hands? 'And did he give in to those . . . those temptations?'

'No.' She spoke quickly. 'But he often beat me for it.'

'Didn't your mother stop him?'

Eliza shook her head. 'In her eyes he's never wrong, you must have seen it. She said that he did such things for my own good. Afterwards she comforted me with fairy tales – she said I was a changeling; the baby of a fairy queen, swapped at birth.'

I remembered Eliza in the physic garden, prancing through the lavender with a crown of marigolds on her hair. 'You were Titania,' I said.

'And you were Oberon, King of the faeries, in your mask of autumn leaves. Do you remember when I found that fairy ring under the rowan tree?'

But I was not so mercurial, I could not flit through the conversation from one thing to another like a butterfly in a flower bed. And she had told me such things . . . such unexpected, terrible things – about herself, about her father. There was something rotten concealed behind the veneer of respectability so carefully guarded by Dr Magorian. It was something that connected everything – the coffins, Dr Bain, Mrs Catchpole – something that tainted all who knew of it, and it could not be left in the shadows of the past. 'Do you know your brother's name?' I said.

She looked surprised. 'No.'

'Have you asked?'

'Once. I asked my mother. She had no idea what I was talking about – or at least, she pretended not to. I assumed it was a topic too painful to acknowledge. I didn't tell her I'd seen her keepsakes. Another time I went to look for his grave in St Saviour's churchyard. I couldn't find it.'

'No,' I said. 'I don't think you'd find him there.' We were silent for a moment. Then, 'May I see them? The keepsakes?'

'Why?'

'Please,' I said. 'I can't say why. I don't even *know* why. All I know is that my father has taken my place in Newgate and I must prove his innocence. Nothing else matters. And I was imprisoned on the word of *your* father. What wickedness would drive him to engineer the arrest of an innocent man—' I stopped. Dr Magorian was her father, after all, no matter what he'd done. I expected her to object, to defend him, but she did not. Instead, she kissed my hand. 'I'll do all I can for you – and your father. But how might my mother's mementoes help you?'

I could not answer. I thought I knew all about St Saviour's, about the people who worked here, but it appeared that I knew hardly anything at all. 'I don't know,' I said. 'But there are too many secrets at St Saviour's and I need to know why. Why does your mother never speak of this dead child? Why does your father do all he can to keep the past away from the present?' She looked up at me, her arm behind her head, her face closed and serious. I stared at her hair, dark against the pillow, at the smooth curve of her breast, hip and thigh. What did she want from me? Why was she here? And I had so many things to do . . . all at once I saw myself for what I was – lazy, selfish, thoughtless. My father needed me and here I was, on my back. I turned away. 'There can be no secrets,' I said. 'Not any more. Only that can save my father now.'

Chapter Sixteen

❦

The Magorians lived in a square Georgian house. It was plain-fronted, but large, and set back slightly from the street behind a small apron of grass and a row of tall black-painted iron railings. It was not part of a terrace, but stood alone, dark and box-like, its upper windows shuttered, its walls black with soot. On one side it was separated from the surrounding houses by a narrow lane. On the other side was St Saviour's physic garden.

The front door was at the top of a short flight of steps. The windows below these were filled with frosted glass to thwart the gaze of the curious public, for the lower-ground floor of Dr Magorian's house had long done office as an anatomy school. It was at the back of the house that Dr Magorian prepared his vast array of anatomical specimens. The specimens themselves were exhibited in Dr Magorian's private anatomy museum which was housed on the top floor, beside the 'discussion room' in which Dr Catchpole had infected himself with venereal disease. A

316

narrow flight of stairs led from the lower-ground floor to the museum at the top. None but Dr Magorian and his medical friends – colleagues and students – were allowed to use those stairs, or to enter the medical rooms. The floors in between – the ground floor, first and second floors, were where Dr and Mrs Magorian lived with their daughter.

Eliza ran up the steps and vanished inside. We had decided that I should wait in the street until she reappeared at the door, having checked whether she might successfully get me into the house without being seen. The usual traffic of people, carts, cabs, animals, made their way up and down the thoroughfare. It made for a convenient place to wait without being noticed, and I stood beside a whelk vendor without appearing out of place.

The day was warm, for the time of year, the air still and close. The smell of brine and shellfish mixed with the stink of drains and horse dung. Beside a lamp-post a scruffy Italian boy exhibited a tortoise in a box for a penny-a-look. A fat woman in a tattered black dress squatted on the pavement, like a gigantic crow, selling flowers from a hand cart. A man lay drunk in the gutter at the head of an alleyway and a girl with a basket of watercress in each hand stood wearily against the railings on the opposite side of the street. I saw a pair of students, medical men from St Saviour's, strolling arm in arm towards the chop house on the corner of Prior's Lane. Cabs and carts rattled past and a boy herded a pair of bullocks down the street, his left eye showing the first purple marks of a black eye. He was a long way from Smithfield and the animals looked exhausted, their haunches dripping blood from the goad he had used mercilessly upon them. I stood back, so that I was half hidden by the whelk stall, and looked towards the infirmary, its clock tower still visible at the far end of St Saviour's Street.

And then I saw him. Dr Magorian! I drew back. Had he seen me? He was striding towards me, though he was still some distance away. My first instinct was to vanish, before he noticed me, into the physic garden. And yet, I could not. I could not wait for another opportunity, another chance to discover the truth. I had to continue what I had started. But how could I? How could I slip into Dr Magorian's house while Dr Magorian himself approached? Eliza had to open the door, or all would be lost. I saw Dr Magorian pull out his silver pocket watch and squint at its pale dial. *Now!* I thought. *It has to be now—*

At that moment the door to Dr Magorian's house opened, and I bounded up the steps.

❧❦

I was unused to such fashionable surroundings. The thick carpet on the polished wooden floor, the smooth white plaster of the cornice, the rich, gold-framed landscapes on the walls – how different Eliza's world was to mine. How warm and stultifying it seemed, hemmed in with overstuffed chairs, stifled by curtains and cushions as soundly as any padded cell at Angel Meadow. The rooms my father and I inhabited above the apothecary were simply furnished – if he was happy with an iron bedstead, an oaken bench and a ewer and pitcher, then so was I, and the only colours that brightened the drab palette of my daily life were found in the bottles upon the apothecary shelves and the neatly tended beds of the physic garden. I took a deep breath. How I longed for that place now, with its clean, sweet scents. In the corner of Dr Magorian's hall, on a tall spindly-legged mahogany table, a large bunch of white, flawless lilies burst from a Chinese vase. Their stamens had been neatly clipped, and their heavy aroma was clogging the air as thick as honey.

'Where's your mother?' I said. From the yard at the back of the house came the steady *'thwack . . . thwack . . . thwack'* of a carpet being beaten. The rattle of a coal scuttle echoed from the direction of the parlour.

'My father is at Dr Graves's,' she replied. 'My mother is upstairs, asleep.'

'And your mother's mementoes?' I did not tell her that her father was no longer at Dr Graves's, but was, in fact, approaching the house.

'They are in her room,' whispered Eliza.

'Where she is sleeping?' I heard the maid in the parlour pause in her labours with the coal scuttle. Eliza's face took on a pinched and hunted look. Her nostrils flared as if scenting danger. 'Quickly!' She put out her hand to me. 'You wanted to see them, did you not?'

'But your mother—'

'Is insensible with laudanum,' she hissed. 'You might dance a hornpipe on her washstand and she'd not wake.' Behind me, at the front door, there came the sound of footsteps, the rasp of boots being scraped clean. 'My father!' Eliza gripped my arm, her face set in an expression of terror. We heard the maid cross to the parlour door. Eliza vanished up the stairs. I bounded after her as, at my back, the door opened.

❦

Mrs Magorian's room was dark and stuffy. The curtains were drawn and the shutters closed. There was no light other than that given off by a pair of candles – one on the mantel, the other at Mrs Magorian's bedside. The embers glowed through the bars of the grate like a dragon's eye.

'She sleeps every afternoon until three,' whispered Eliza.

'What about the maid?'

'Dilys?' Eliza grinned, her teeth white in the gloom. 'She's gone out. She fancies herself a cut above now that she's a lady's maid. She takes a walk with one of the medical students while Mother sleeps.'

The ambitions of medical students were generally set high above anything a lady's maid might have to offer. 'No doubt I'll see her in the Magdalene ward before long,' I muttered.

We crept across the room. The air was heavy with the musty, sweetish smell of camphor. Beneath this, I could detect Roman camomile, rose water and citrus. But none of it could mask the thick, stale reek of exhaled laudanum. On the far side of the room Mrs Magorian's bed loomed. The sheets glimmered white in the glow of the bedside candle, the counterpane a rich midnight-coloured damask. Mrs Magorian herself was lying on the bed. For some reason, I had expected her to be inside it, trapped within the starched white sheets like a fold of paper in an envelope. To see her fully clothed, lying on her back as if laid out, her face a white mask in the sepulchral darkness – I drew back. Had her eyelids flickered? Had her hands, resting on her abdomen, trembled? Perhaps she had decided not to take her laudanum that afternoon and was not asleep at all. I recoiled into the shadows.

Eliza glided forward and took up the bedside candle. 'Mother?' she whispered. 'Mother?' There was no reply. Perhaps it had simply been the dark jumping as the coals shifted and flickered in the grate.

Eliza moved silently. She skirted a small table laden with medicine bottles and pulled open a door adjacent to the bed – a dressing room, no doubt. It brushed against the thick Persian carpet with a deep sigh. Behind the door the void was filled with dark shapes – a dress mannequin, a large wardrobe, a tower of boxes. I thought I detected a sudden movement, a tall thin shadow shifting warily in the darkness, and all at once I saw a face staring out at me – horrible, darkly disfigured, blinking in the gloom. He looked straight into my eyes, his mouth opening to shout out – and then I realised that I was staring at my own reflection in a tall dressing mirror. My cry choked in my throat.

Behind us, Mrs Magorian let out a sigh and shifted on the counterpane. 'No,' she murmured. Eliza licked her fingers and pinched out the candle flame. We stood without moving in the oily darkness. 'Please!' Mrs Magorian moved her head on the pillow. 'No more,' she said. 'No more.' Then, she was silent. Somehow, I knew she had woken.

We heard the rustle of her silks as she moved on the bed. 'Dilys?' she said. 'Is that you?' There was a sigh. 'Another candle, Dilys.' Her voice was sleepy again now. Her breathing deepened. Eliza relit the candle.

The walls of the dressing room were lined with shelves crammed with hats, muffs, scarves and furs. Eliza went directly to a small chest of drawers set against the far wall underneath a tower of hat boxes. She pulled open the bottom drawer and drew out a cotton bag, rather like a pillow case in size and shape. My heart struck hammer blows against my ribs, my eyes seeming to stretch in my head as I peered into the gloom. What relic would be revealed? Into my mind's eye rose the image of a coffin-shaped box, inside it that familiar kidney-shaped package, the rust-coloured rags, the handful of dried flowers. *These six things doth the Lord hate: yea, seven are an abomination unto him* . . . Eliza unfolded the end of the bag and pulled out – a shirt. There followed a pair of 'hussar' pantaloons, a pair of stockings, a short jacket of boiled wool, a cap, a pair of boots.

I stared down at the costume in surprise. What was this? 'She kept his clothes?' I said.

'Yes,' whispered Eliza.

I cursed myself for my fanciful imaginings. Nevertheless, the choice seemed an odd one – would it not have been more orthodox to have kept a lock of hair? A favourite toy? A photograph or miniature? I held up the shirt. It was made of fine linen, with ruffles; but small, as though made for a lad of twelve or thirteen. The trousers were the same. 'How peculiar,' I whispered. 'And yet no one ever mentions the boy. Not even Mrs Speedicut.' I held up the jacket. It was well made with silver buttons in the short 'Spencer' style that had not been fashionable for some twenty years or more. I picked up the boots. It was not possible to see much in the light of the candle, but I held one up all the same, squinting at it in the half dark.

Brown. Laced. Hardly worn. And yet, there was something else about it—

From the bedroom, all at once there came a faint knocking sound. Eliza blew out the candle and put her hand on my arm. 'It's Dilys,' she whispered.

'Mrs Magorian?' The voice was gentle, apologetic. 'Mrs Magorian, ma'am?'

Eliza put her lips to my ear. Her words were no more than breath. 'She'll open the curtains and then bring my mother a cup of tea.'

Sure enough, we heard soft footsteps cross the room. Metal hooks rattled like chains as one of the curtains was flung aside. The maid opened the shutters a few inches and the light split the darkness from top to bottom, illuminating a whirling cosmos of dust motes and smoke particles. 'Now, then, Mrs Magorian, ma'am,' she murmured. 'I'll just get your tea.'

'Thank you, Dilys.' Mrs Magorian's voice was heavy, drugged. The bedroom door closed softly as the girl went out.

Beside me, Eliza quickly stuffed the clothes back into the pillow case. I pushed one of the boots in on top, but the other, I rammed into my jacket pocket. If I were caught with it by anyone in that house, then all would be lost. And yet if I left it behind I would never know . . . I *had* to examine it properly. I did not think twice.

'Stay here,' Eliza whispered. She strode into her mother's room and went straight to the window, where she opened the shutters further. 'How are you, Mother?' she said.

'Oh!' Mrs Magorian gasped. 'Where did you come from?'

'I came in with Dilys,' said Eliza. I heard the mattress

323

creak as she sat beside her mother. 'It's the annual meeting of St Saviour's ladies' committee at three.'

'Oh, so it is,' Mrs Magorian sounded weary. 'Is your father home?'

'Yes.'

'Good.' Mrs Magorian sat up. 'I must change.'

'Shall I help you?'

'But Dilys will be here in a moment. She can help me.'

'I'll get your dress. Which is it?'

'The navy silk. It's on a chair in the dressing room.'

Eliza appeared again in the dressing room. She pulled open the shutters that covered the window and flung up the sash. 'It's so stuffy in here, Mother,' she said loudly. 'I think Dilys has been rather heavy-handed with the camphor.'

'But the moths are so trying.' Mrs Magorian sighed.

Eliza pushed me towards the open window. 'Climb,' she hissed.

'I beg your pardon, dear?' said Mrs Magorian

'I said "fine", Mother,' cried Eliza. 'But spike lavender would do just as well, and would smell much better.'

I stared out of the window. The ground looked far away. We were only on the first floor, but there was no drainpipe to assist my descent, no balcony to swing down from. Did she really think I was going to jump? I would surely break my neck! Eliza rustled the dress to mask the sound of my movements and gestured impatiently at the open window. I began to ease myself out of it, like a crane fly emerging from a crack in a garden wall. I looked left and right. Up and down. There was no means of escape at all. I clung to the sill. Eliza's face was at the window now, furious to see me still squatting there like some giant spindly pigeon.

She flapped the dress at me. Perhaps if I eased myself down, I thought, I might hang from the sill by my hands and drop the last twenty feet. I might land in the middle of the large mound of grass cuttings, sticks and nettles the gardener had left against the side of the house in readiness for burning. Somehow I twisted round. I rested my buttocks on the sill, my legs dangling over the abyss. Perhaps it would be better to face forward and just *leap* . . . The easterly wind brought with it the smell of Smithfield – dung, and rotten meat.

'Oh, dear, close that window!' I heard Mrs Magorian say. 'Whatever are you thinking of letting the smell of the abattoirs in like that?'

I felt a sharp kick to my arse as Eliza helped me off the window ledge with the tip of her boot, and I plunged downwards, my arms windmilling. Above my head, the window slammed closed.

❈

I burst into the apothecary. 'What happened to you?' said Will.

'Eliza Magorian threw me out of her mother's bedroom window.'

Will raised an eyebrow. He did not pause in his labours, but continued wiping the rounded belly of a giant retort with a chamois. The squeak of the soft moist leather on the glass set my nerves on edge. I caught sight of myself in the mirror that hung between the coat pegs – my shoulders and lapels were stained, my collar awry, my hair matted with wet grass and laced with bindweed. But in my hand, I held my prize.

Will and I sat at the bench, Mrs Magorian's dead son's boot before us. It was brown, well made, and hardly worn. It was no bigger than something Gabriel might wear, though the workmanship was of a finer quality: the upper and sole a smooth Italian leather, rather than the thick hide of the coarse boots Gabriel favoured. 'Pick it up,' I said. 'Tell me what you see.'

Will turned the boot over in his hands. 'It's not new. But it's had little wear – look at the soles and the heel. And it's been worn recently.'

Even in the darkness of Mrs Magorian's dressing room I had felt it. The leather was cold, soft and pliable to the touch. Unmistakably damp. I ran my finger around the edge of the sole. 'Smell it,' I said. I held the mud under his nose.

Will recoiled. 'It stinks of the dead. I should know, I spend my days amongst them.' He pointed to his own boots, drying on the hearth. The soles were rimmed with the same thick, hard crusts of yellowish clay.

Chapter Seventeen

〜

St Saviour's had become a place of fascination. News of my brief imprisonment, and of my father's confession, had spread through the city, and by the end of the day it was as though we were under siege. On St Saviour's Street, crowds of people gathered outside the infirmary, jeering and pointing. The porter locked the gates, only opening them to allow doctors or patients in and out. The apothecary, mercifully, was inside the hospital precincts, so we were at least spared the discomfiture of having crowds of ghoulish sightseers pelting our door with mud or trying to peer in at our windows. I had never been so grateful that we lived within the hospital as I was during those days. It seemed not to matter that many of those in the crowd had known my father all their lives, that he had often given them medicines paid for with his own money. All they could think of now was that a murderer had been in their midst; he had killed a good doctor, an innocent woman and a poor, helpless slum

327

child. I knew they felt duped, deceived into liking and admiring a man who, it appeared, had wished to harm them, and I could hardly blame them for it. Many of them had known Dr Bain. Still more claimed to know Joe Silks, and whereas the boy had had few friends when he was alive, when he was dead it seemed as though the whole of Prior's Rents wished to claim him as their own. And so they gathered at our gates, angry and violent, their voices a furious howl echoing off walls and windows as though the day of judgement was upon us.

As for the apothecary: once the bustling hub of the hospital, it was now eerily silent. The door did not bang open and closed all day, doctors did not come in and out, the lady almoners stayed away. People only came in when they had to, but they said little, and would not meet my gaze. Doctors sent in students, men unknown to me, rather than come in and have to speak to me themselves. No one but Mrs Speedicut came to see us, but I could see in her face that even she doubted my father's innocence. He had confessed, had he not? What innocent man would do such a thing? But she said nothing, and for that I was grateful.

'We have to get out,' said Will. The noise of the crowd out on St Saviour's Street was a dull angry murmur. 'We can do nothing from in here, and we need to speak to Old Dick. Is there another way out?'

We left St Saviour's via a narrow underground thorough-fare. Low-ceilinged and no more than three feet wide, it was known as the Prior's Hole. The entrance – or exit – began in the sub-basement under the mortuary; the air there was dank and chilly, and our candles burned less brightly as we entered, as though the flames themselves were crouched and shivering. In the far corner of this place, a low, iron gate gave out onto the drain-like Prior's Hole. We floundered through a dark pool of standing water. Neither of us spoke. The Hole was a thoroughfare that did not encourage talking, but at least we were able to leave the infirmary without having to pass through the mob.

We found the sexton in the churchyard, sitting on top of one of the gravestones, cross-legged like the Devil himself. He was watching the excavations, his greasy, blue-bottle coat spread about him like a pool of spilt oil. He was chewing on an old clay pipe, his tricorn hat pulled down low over ears bristling with wiry hair. Beside him was his spade, though the hands that rested in his lap were too twisted and misshapen with rheumatism to use the thing. But it is hard for a man to abandon the tools of his trade, and Dick carried the spade everywhere, as if hoping he might one day come across a patch of earth soft and yielding enough for the final dig.

'Afternoon, Dick,' said Will. He unwrapped a currant loaf he had bought from the baker's on St Saviour's Street and held it out. Dick sniffed at it suspiciously, though what he possibly had to fear from a currant loaf, I had no idea. But the loaf, it appeared, was acceptable. Dick stuffed it into his coat, out of sight and protected from the rain.

He turned back to the earthworks and pointed a horny finger. 'There's not as many as there was,' he remarked.

'Bodies?' I asked. I looked up at the great mound of corpses, stacked one on top of the other, which reared up beside the pit. There seemed to be a prodigious quantity of them.

329

'Men,' said Dick. 'I been watchin' 'em. They don't like the work much. Can't say I blame 'em.'

'No,' said Will. He drew his oilskin closer about himself. The mountain of bone glistened, washed white by the rain. Hanks of hair clung here and there like weed at low tide, the remains of shrouds hanging in grey rags from the sagging sides of broken coffins. A cart stood beside the corpse mountain, its axle resting on a pile of bricks, its front left wheel missing. 'And now that we have only two carts, progress is slower than ever.' He gazed dejectedly at the bones. 'So there they stay.'

'Might as well 'ave left 'em where they was,' said Dick.

'I suppose so,' said Will.

'What you goin' to use to fill that pit?' The hole in the earth which had once contained the bodies was cavernous.

'I had no idea there was going be so many,' said Will. 'But there is plenty of rubble to be got. And some of St Saviour's itself will go into the hole when the place is demolished.'

Dick threw Will a look of deep suspicion, and sucked on his pipe. It gurgled emptily.

'Dick,' said Will, handing him a tin of tobacco he had bought especially for the purpose, 'how long have you worked here?'

'Always,' said Dick. His apple pip eye vanished in a mass of wrinkles as he scowled up at us. 'I told you that already.'

It was not a good start. 'Perhaps he doesn't want to talk today,' I said.

Will ignored me. 'You must have seen some changes.'

Dick fingered the tobacco, examining its quality. 'Like what?'

'At St Saviour's. In this graveyard.'

'Like what?' said Dick again.

'This is getting nowhere,' I muttered. I watched the three corners of Dick's hat dripping water like gutter ends. He seemed unperturbed by the recent downpour. No doubt he was used to being wet: from what I had seen of his home he had spent his entire life in dampness and moisture. I would not be surprised if he had webbed fingers and toes. My glance strayed to his hands. They were large, twisted with arthritis and bound up with rags. 'You know, I have some salve that might help your hands,' I said. From my pocket I pulled a small pot of fresh salve – comfrey and camomile – which I had picked up before we left the apothecary.

'No one can help 'em,' said Dick, but he held them out to me all the same.

Before he could draw back, I took one of his hands in my own. The skin was black and weathered as old leather, the ridged nails the colour of amber. The strips of coarse canvas he had wrapped about them were shiny with grease and filth. I peeled off the wrappings. Dick stared at my fingers, mesmerised.

'Your mother used to look after my 'ands,' he said. 'Back when they was first gettin' stiff.'

'My mother?'

He nodded. 'She were like you. Just like you.'

'But I look like my father.'

'Not to me you don't. You got 'er eyes. An' 'er touch. She were gentle. No one cares about my 'ands, but your mother did. She were an angel. There's not many like she was, not round here. Most of 'em's devils.'

'You never said a truer word, Dick,' I said.

But Dick was not listening. 'I sat next to 'er grave ev'ry

331

night till I knew she were no use to 'em. Them medicals! Said it were fer the good o' mankind. Fer the sake o' 'natomy. But I'd not let 'em dig 'er up and chop 'er into bits.' He shook his head, his gaze still fixed upon my pale slender fingers moving over his dark stubby ones, gently rubbing the salve into his swollen knuckles. The joints burned like fire.

'How hot your hands are,' I murmured. 'They must be so painful. But the salve will help. The camomile is good for inflammation, the comfrey helps the bones.'

'Helps the bones,' repeated Dick. He sighed. 'The bones is all we have left in the end. And even them's not left in peace.'

'Why not?' I asked. I stroked his fingers. 'Who disturbs them?'

'I ain't never told what I saw.' He screwed his eyes closed. 'But I can remember it all right, even if it were a long time ago. I'd not thought much about it till I saw 'em again.'

'Saw who?' I said.

'The man and 'is boy. Used to see 'em all the time. First time was not long after I were sitting by your mother's grave with my dog and my lantern. But then there they were again, the night that young lad were found in the pit over there. Last week.'

'Can you describe them?'

'Black hood and cloak. Tall. The lad carried the lantern.'

'His face, Dick. Did you recognise his face? Or the boy's?'

'How would I see his face?' said Dick. I felt his fingers stiffen. I thought he was about to snatch them away, but he didn't. 'It were dark. An' I weren't about to go over an' ask to see it. The Abbot's what they used to call him out in the streets, on account of his hood.' He gave a snort, which turned into a terrible rattling cough, and hawked a giant blob of brown phlegm onto the ground. '*He's* no abbot. I knows *that* much.'

'And the boy?' I said. 'What was he wearing? A cap? And pale trousers? A short jacket?'

'Pr'aps,' said Dick.

'And what did they do?'

Dick shrugged. 'The boy? Sat on a stone an' 'eld the dark lantern, like I said. It were always the same. Same pair, same place, same things.'

'Same things?' I said. 'What things?'

'Sack, shovel, body,' said Dick. 'Puttin' 'em *in* the ground, not takin' 'em out. But them doctors were always up to it. I seen 'em. And 'eard 'em. Drunk as lords, sometimes.'

'We found some of the remains of the anatomy subjects,' said Will. 'Mostly against the far wall near the infirmary. Bones with saw marks. Skulls with holes.'

But Dick was not talking about the human refuse from the dissecting tables, I was sure. His eyes were fixed on the northern wall of the churchyard, away from the hospital. 'What about "place"?' I asked. 'You said "same pair, same place". What "place" d'you mean?'

'Over there,' said Dick. He jerked his head. 'At the foot o' that wall.'

We looked over to where Dick was pointing. The excavation of the churchyard stopped about ten feet from the northern wall. 'We stopped digging at the edge of the grave plots,' said Will. 'Where the ground slopes downwards. Beyond that there was nothing. The ground was hard. Empty. It's clay mostly; the worst kind, too.'

'The ground's not much use anywhere at St Saviour's, but it's no use for *nuthin'* over at that wall,' said Dick. 'You'd never put anyone in there. Not if you want 'em gone.'

'Gone?' I said.

'Rotted.' Dick grinned, revealing empty gums and a brown tongue. He pointed to the bone mountain with the stem of his pipe. 'The dead want air. Fine, dainty soil full of air, not clay. It's the air what lets 'em rot. Clay's no use for buryin'.' He took a deep breath, filling his lungs with the smell of putrescence. 'You can smell it good an' proper now. But not over there.' He pointed again to the northern wall – cold and black, mossy with perpetual shadow. '*I* never put *no one* in there.'

⚭

Will and I took a spade each from beneath the tarpaulin. We started directly against the foot of the northern wall. The grass was tightly matted, but we dug it out in a thick shaggy layer. Beneath, the ground was hard – a dense, sticky brown mass that cleaved to the blades of our spades like cold fat.

They were not far below the surface. Six of them: one for each tiny coffin, lined up, head to toe, along the very edge of the wall. Unmarked by any headstone, they had been crammed into the vile earth and hastily covered over; the ground stamped down, the sod carefully laid back.

The clay had preserved them well. They had not rotted, but instead had turned waxy and hollow, their faces black and sunken, but recognisable – eyes closed, mouths open as if in a scream of fear and pain. Each was clothed only in a simple chemise – once white, but now ragged and blackened with water and dirt, dried blood and time spent underground.

We laid them side by side, some distance apart from the mountain of bones. I could tell from the way their filthy underclothes clung to their bodies that something was amiss. I crouched down and lifted the hem. I cut it with my knife, an incision from ankles to sternum, and peeled it open. Beneath, where the skin should have been taut across their shrivelled womb, was a great dark hole. Within, the blackened cavity was empty, the pale bones of the pelvis clearly visible. But this was no butchery: there was no ripped and ragged flesh. Instead, I could see that the skin bore the signs of the knife – the neat cut from hip to hip, from pubis to umbilicus, the uterus removed cleanly from its moorings. Who were those six girls? For girls they were, their long hair clinging to their skulls in matted locks of brown and yellow; their skin blackened like the skin of a raisin; their once-young flesh now dried and cleaving to their bones.

What had we learned? That in his four score years as sexton Dick had repeatedly turned a blind eye to the activities of the resurrectionists? That someone had put six bodies into the ground – at night, in secret, all of them young women, each of them with their wombs cut out? There was no evidence of foetuses buried alongside them. Had they been pregnant? We could not tell. I could not work it out, and I could still prove nothing. Everything was connected; it had to be, but how? I remembered Mrs Roseplucker's story . . . *for the Abbot of St Saviour's was as wicked as the rest of them, and he was lookin' for a young girl to slake his appetites* . . . No one would miss a street girl, a prostitute. No one would ask where they went or care what had happened to them. And there was something else too, something else Mrs Roseplucker had said about one of the girls who had vanished. *Fanny Bishop . . . Pretty girl. Leastways she was till she got her teeth bashed in one night* . . . I was not mistaken: one of those empty, butchered corpses had no front teeth.

Perhaps it was the Abbot, I had said, my manner impertinent. I had been right. If only I had realised it at the time. And yet we had unearthed nothing but more mysteries, more questions. Who was to say that those six bodies were not simply the corpses of six paupers, or six cadavers no longer required by the anatomy school? We still had nothing concrete; we could accuse no one. We were so close, and yet the truth, whatever that might be, still eluded us.

Time was running out. I went to Newgate every day: I could not leave my father alone there, waiting in the condemned cell without love or comradeship. And I could not persuade him from his purpose. 'I cannot kill myself,' he said. 'I cannot forfeit my immortal soul for the sake of my own peace. But I can save you, and I can be spared from madness.'

I did not tell him that someone had thrown a stone through the apothecary window; that Gabriel had been pelted with mud on St Saviour's Street, and that crowds of curious onlookers gathered every day at the infirmary gates to catch a glimpse of me, the heir of a murderer. But he was no fool. He knew we would have our own troubles.

'You must not stop me, Jem.' Always, it was the same thing. Often, he said nothing, just stared into the candle, rocking to and fro.

I brought a soft cloth and a bottle of rose water, and I wiped his face and hands. The smell of the roses mingled briefly with the stink of sweat and drains, rotten straw and stale food, before being consumed by it completely. It was like a garden glimpsed through a charnel house. I wondered whether it reminded him of a world he would never see, or smell, ever again. How could he be so calm? It was clear to me that he never slept; day after day he became more gaunt and wraithlike. Often I would go and he would look at me with no recognition in his eyes. He stared into the candle without flinching, as though he saw no light at all, only a black abyss.

I could not bear the place – the rattle of the keys, the cruel scrape of the locks seemed like nails driven into my brain. I would sit beside him and hold his hand. Neither of us spoke – what was there to say? But he would repeat over and over in a whisper: *You must not stop this from happening. You must clear our name. You must find out who did these things once I am gone.*

'I will, Father,' I replied.

Sometimes his gaze was as sharp and keen as ever, his brain focused, his attitude as abrasive as always. 'Why are you here?' he cried then. 'Go! Go away from here. I don't need your company. I need you to take action. Come along, Jem. I have taught you to be bold, have I not? Now is the time to act, and to do so without fear.'

Sometimes his mind was lucid and calm, fixed on the

mundane activities he could no longer attend to. 'Have you changed the leeches' water?' he said. 'Make sure Gabriel dusts the bottles on the top shelf. You must stay at the apothecary, you and he. He is a good boy, and there's always been a Flockhart at St Saviour's.'

I did not tell him that the Secretary of the hospital had already asked us to leave. 'Yes,' I said instead. 'Gabriel is working hard.'

The warders told me that Dr Hawkins had been. I did not see him. I did not want to talk to him. Not then. Later, I was to wish I had sought him out straight away. Even now, I cannot dwell on the subject without pain.

And so, what had once been a week vanished as quickly as a nightmare. Will still slept on the truckle bed in my room. He could easily have used my father's bed, but I had grown used to his company, and I found comfort in the sound of him breathing, as I lay and stared up at the whitewashed ceiling, the wooden beams hung with bunches of lavender and rue. I thought I could not sleep, but then I would feel Will shaking my shoulder, and he would thrust a hot mug of tea into my hands. My dreams were like waking – filled with dread, memories of the past mixed with the worries of the present and fears for the future. I dreamed I saw Eliza arm in arm with Dr Bain, their lips stained crimson with bloodroot. I saw a woman in a green dress sprigged with flowers walking away from me. I called out to her, 'Mother!' But she did not turn around. I saw her vanish into St Saviour's churchyard. I dreamed that I ran after her, only to find her lying in a ditch of clay against the wall of the graveyard, her face cold and sunken. When I awoke I was crying. I felt Will put his arms about me in the darkness.

And the questions remained unanswered. The women we had disinterred were added to the bone pile. What else might we do with them? We took some of the fabric from their chemises to compare to the fabric that was swaddled about the wooden dolls, but the stuff was too dirty, too dark and impregnated with moisture to allow us to draw any useful comparisons. Had Dr Magorian killed the girls? Had they died of natural causes and simply found their way to the anatomists' classroom by the usual means? In my dreams their eyes stared up at me accusingly. Their leathery fingers pointed up at a dark hooded figure; the boy at his side had the face of Mrs Magorian.

I did not see Eliza again, though I looked out for her. I thought of the hour we had spent together and it seemed lost in a haze. What game had she been playing? Did she love me? I could not fathom it. Will came and went, working first in the apothecary, then, as dawn broke and the thin grey drizzle became visible in a veil of grey, he pulled on his boots and his oilskin and vanished into the graveyard. I did not know how I would have managed without him. How dear he had become to me in so short a time, always to be relied upon, his loyalty and affection the one constant and good thing in a dark and miserable world. In the depths of my heart I dreaded the day he might leave us. As for the others, Mrs Speedicut moped at the fireside, Gabriel worked at every task in grim silence. His hands grew raw. He asked to come to Newgate with me but he could not be spared, and besides, in those final days my father had deteriorated to such a degree that I did not want Gabriel to see what had become of him, did not want him to see the terrible surroundings in which my father now lived.

And then, all at once, it was too late. Now I would not even be able to tell my father that yes, I had discovered who had murdered Dr Bain, Mrs Catchpole, Joe Silks. I would never be able to tell him that I knew who had done it, why, and by what means. I could tell him nothing – nothing but my suspicions, and they were no use to anyone.

'We *will* find out,' said Will.

I could not answer.

❦

On the morning of the hanging I could not get out of my bed. I lay there, cold as bone beneath the sheet, my eyes staring, dry in my head. How had this happened? What had we done, my father and I, that we found ourselves here, now, like this? And yet in those last few days he had seemed serene, pleased that he was soon to be reunited with my mother. I could not be so sanguine. If being a good man meant one had to decide between the ignominy of madness or the notoriety of a public hanging, if it meant a choice between the disgrace of a felon's death or to be sent, raging, into the night, how could God be merciful? Our sufferings seemed like the cruellest kind of sport. There was no logic, no coherence, no justice or fairness in the world. At that moment I hated God for his malice and wantonness. And what of Dr Magorian? Would he have to wait until judgement day before he received just punishment? It was no consolation.

Will brought me some tea. He toasted a slice of bread for me, but I could not swallow it.

'You must eat, Jem,' he said gently. I hid the toast in my

pocket when he turned away so that he might not worry about me.

I went to my father's room. I had not been in there since he had gone to Angel Meadow with Dr Hawkins. How little time had passed since then, and yet how much had changed. I sat on the bed. Outside, I heard St Saviour's clock chime the quarter hour. The scaffold would have been up for some hours already, the hammer strikes echoing through the streets even before the crowds began to gather, measuring out the passing of time with their cruel blows. I closed my eyes and pressed my palms into the sockets. Had I loved him? Even now I could not be sure. I feared him and respected him. But he had been a difficult man to love – distant, aloof, humourless. He had neither touched me, nor shown me any affection as a child. I had tried hard to please him, to be as he wanted me to be, but always I knew he was disappointed. I stood at the window, looking out over the city but seeing nothing. The sky was the colour of blood.

At eight o'clock, Dr Hawkins came to see us. We made a sad group, Gabriel's face raw with crying, Will silent and subdued. I was gaunt and dazed, my eyes bloodshot in my red mask, which had turned an ugly greyish colour, so sickly and ashen had I become. Mrs Speedicut sat on her chair, an empty mug in her hand. Tears stained her flabby cheeks. Dr Hawkins shook my hand. 'I'm sorry, Jem,' he said.

'He's innocent,' I said. 'You know that, Dr Hawkins?'

He nodded. 'It's against my judgement to applaud his chosen course of action, but I cannot find it in my heart to stop him.' He rubbed a hand across his eyes. He too looked as though he had been up all night. 'Nathaniel is

341

dead,' he said. His expression was bleak, and he looked at me strangely, with a mixture of sympathy and horror I had never seen before. I knew, then, that he had seen the future: my father's and mine. 'You slept?' he said.

'It hardly matters today,' I replied.

He did not look at me but allowed his gaze to rest on his hands, his fingers smoothing away the creases in his white buckskin gloves. 'I wonder if I might – that is, if you would allow – I hardly know how to ask—'

'You wish to anatomise him,' I said.

Dr Hawkins nodded. 'If it's not in the blood, then we must look to the mind – the brain. The connection between the two is little understood. If we could—'

'You have Nathaniel.'

'Yes, but a comparison would be most instructive—'

'Of course,' I said. 'Though I imagine Dr Magorian will be there before you.' In my pockets, I balled my hands into fists. Would I watch my father die on the gibbet, and then have to wrest his body from the medical men crouched like scavengers at the foot of the gallows? They would be sure to be there, waiting for their prize, and a felon was accorded no choice in the matter.

'I have paid the hangman to ensure my prior claim,' said Dr Hawkins. 'It's all settled. Your father was adamant that his remains should come with me, but I wanted to speak to you too.'

'You'll take him to Angel Meadow?'

Dr Hawkins nodded.

'May I see him there?'

'You know he may not . . . he may not look himself.'

'All the same—' I did not want to discuss the matter. Dr Hawkins inclined his head. He shook my hand once more.

I had witnessed hangings before. Any corpse was worth fighting for and more than once I had accompanied Dr Bain, when he and Dr Graves had sought to secure a body for St Saviour's dissection rooms. But how murder could be made into entertainment and spectacle I could never understand. I knew what to expect: the crowds that filled the streets, faces at windows and peering from rooftops, people climbing up lamp-posts and onto window ledges, all eyes turned towards the scaffold, and the rope. And so it was for my father's hanging. I stood with Will, amongst the crowd. Should I have stayed away? My father had told me not to come, but I could not leave him to his fate, alone, without anyone there to think well of him as he died. I closed my eyes as a man appeared beneath the gallows, but I knew what was taking place: in my mind I could see the rope, the man examining it, testing its strength and evaluating the drop. I looked up. The rope had been approved. And now here was the Ordinary, come to say a prayer with the condemned man. His appearance was the cue for silence, and silence there was. How extraordinary a thing it is, for whole streets filled with people to be completely without sound. How strange it was to hear it, to feel it, the presence of so many, but all of them, for a moment, holding their breath.

I saw Dr Hawkins, at the foot of the gallows, nod to the Ordinary, and the hangman. And then my father was brought forward. His hands were behind his back, his white head bowed. He was so thin that it was as though a puff of wind might blow him away. Would he be heavy enough to make the drop a fatal one, or would he dangle there, kicking and thrashing until someone had the heart to pull on his legs – I could not bear to think of it. I let out a moan, and almost crumpled to my knees, but Will was there. He put his arm about me and held me up.

'Don't look, Jem,' he whispered. 'I will tell you when it's done.' But I shook my head. I would not look away, I would not desert him. For, as long as I was looking at him, I was with him; I was there beside him upon the scaffold and, somehow, I was certain he would know it and would take courage from it. And so I turned my gaze to my father, up there beneath the noose, and I did not flinch.

I heard the Ordinary recite the Lord's Prayer, my father's head still bowed. At the end of it, my father looked up, out across the crowd, and despite the hordes of people, the thousands of faces, he saw me instantly. He looked at me for a moment – looked at me and no one else – and then he smiled. He closed his eyes and I saw his lips move. Was he thinking of me? Was he saying a prayer to the God who had taken so much and given so little in return? But he would die with my mother's name on his lips, I knew. And I? I would be left behind, alone, uncertain, counting the days until my own fate became clear.

The clock began to chime; the final moments were upon us. They tied his hands and covered his face. The crowd began to shout and hiss; there was laughter and hoarse cries; the air prickled with excitement, and a curious ripple of energy passed through us all. I shivered as it touched me and I felt instantly filthy, sullied by the repulsive enjoyment of the crowd, and as though all the water in London could not wash me clean. As the clock

struck ten, the air thrummed with expectation. A hush
held the city, as if it were sealed in a bubble beneath a
great silent ocean. And then came the harsh rattle of the
drop as the trap opened, the gasp of the crowd as ten
thousand onlookers drew breath at the same moment;
and then the gentle groan of the rope, the rhythmic creak
of its burden. There was a moment of silence as we all
watched the body, my father's body, swing . . . swing . . .
swing . . . and then still.

As if from some distant place I heard the roar of the
crowd. I clapped my hands to my ears and sank down
onto my knees, leaning forward to retch. It was over. He
was gone. He had made me who I was, and now, without
him, I did not know how I was to live. Nothing could be
the same. He had left me no guidelines, no set of
instructions, no list of things I must accomplish. I was lost
and alone, and I did not know what to do.

❦

Somehow, Will dragged me through the crowd. They had
been distracted by the spectacle, but now it was over they
were free to look again at one another. When they saw me
they knew straight away who I was. A boy threw a stone
and it hit my forehead. The warm blood running over my
face brought me to my senses, and I began to push my
way back towards the infirmary. Ahead of us, in the middle
of the crowd, a carriage blocked the road, positioned
sideways so as to command the best view of the scaffold. I
recognised it straight away, and before Will could stop me
I bounded forward and wrenched open the door.

There, perched on plush maroon cushions like a crow

in a boudoir, was Mrs Magorian. She was sitting upright, her pale blue eyes fixed upon me, her mouth pursed in a bitter smile. Across from her sat Eliza, dressed in black from neck to toe, her face stony. I stared at her, at her face stained with tears, but at that moment I could think of no one but my father, dead, disgraced; murdered, just like Dr Bain, Mrs Catchpole, Joe Silks. My voice, when I spoke, was raw with rage and sorrow, so that I hardly even recognised myself.

'Six coffins. Six effigies. Six girls buried beneath the churchyard wall. Buried by your husband, madam, and by *you*!' I knew people had stopped to listen, I could feel them at my back watching, muttering amongst themselves, and I was glad. I raised my voice to the volume of a street vendor. 'You think no one knows what you've done? You think it's all in the past? Well, I will drag it into the present and then I will drag you to the gallows, and the world will know what you are!'

Her eyes flickered, as if she had blinked, though I had not seen her eyelids move.

'He was seen, madam,' I shouted. 'In St Saviour's churchyard. And you with him.'

'I?' Her lips curved slightly, as if she were amused by my accusations.

'Oh, don't trouble to deny it,' I cried. 'Don't insult me. It was *you* who accompanied him. It was you who flung Joe Silks into the pit.'

Eliza put out her hand to me. 'Jem, please. Can't you see she's frightened—'

I shook her off. 'Frightened?' I spat the word out. I did not look at Eliza now but kept my eyes fixed upon her mother's face. I could not weaken, and I would not feel pity. 'Twenty years ago your husband killed six girls. I don't know why, but I'll not rest until I find out. And there will be no escape for you in this world, or the next, until I do.' I raised my hand, my bloody face fearful to look upon, and I pointed at her heart. 'I will follow you wherever you go. Wherever you look, I will be there. In your nightmares you will see me, and I will worry you and haunt you, and I will uncover every one of your secrets. Make no mistake, but I *will* find out. And when I do—' My hand was shaking with fury, and it was all I could do to stop myself from reaching in and dragging her off her cushions, out of the carriage and into the mob. 'When I do, you will watch *him* hang, as I have watched my father hang. And then you will follow him to the gallows and you will die, alone, in shame and fear, with nothing but a felon's grave and an anatomist's knife awaiting you.'

Chapter Eighteen

❧

Dr Hawkins took my father's body directly to Angel
Meadow. He used one of the hospital's carriages. I
made my own way there, with Will for company.
I could not speak. I felt as though I could hardly move,
and if it had not been for Will I might still be standing,
staring up at the gallows.

Dr Hawkins was in his room at the top of the building.
There was a tray of tea waiting for us. I wanted nothing,
but Will forced me to drink a cup of the stuff, hot and
sugary, and my mind began to clear. I forced myself to
attend to what was going on. I had not been to Angel
Meadow since Mrs Catchpole had been found dead. I had
to be alert.

'He's downstairs,' said Dr Hawkins. 'Would you like to
see him?'

I nodded.

'But first . . .' Dr Hawkins was standing with his back to
the window, so his face was in shadow. 'Your father loved

you, Jem,' he said. 'Though I know he did not always show it.' He turned to his desk and picked up a box. 'He asked me to give you this.'

It was a box of polished yew, smooth to the touch and coloured a rich amber. I had never seen it before, though I could tell before I opened it that it had been well-handled – the catch was discoloured with the repeated pressure of a thumb, the hinges loose from opening and closing. But it was oiled and cared for, as though what was inside was too precious to be left untouched. Somehow I knew, even before I opened it, what would be inside.

It was a miniature, a small portrait of a young woman, no older that I. She was sitting on a chair, wearing an olive-coloured dress sprigged with summer flowers. Her eyes were green, her face pensive but happy, her hands resting on the bulge of her pregnant belly. I looked at her, in silence, for a long time. Then I put the picture away. 'Thank you, Doctor,' I said. I held the box to my heart. It was all I had of them now.

In a daze, I followed Dr Hawkins down the long, winding flights of stairs to the basement. My father had been stripped and washed and wrapped in a sheet of white cotton. His end had been swift. Dr Hawkins, up on the scaffold, had ensured the rope broke his neck as he fell. And so, in death, he looked very much as he had in life – joyless, austere, with a scornful, pinched look about the nostrils. I did not touch him, or kiss him. I did not cry. In fact, I felt a peculiar sense of detachment.

'Take what you need from my father, Dr Hawkins,' I said. I thought of the small plot where my mother lay against the church wall, and into which I would lay my father's earthly remains. South facing, the honeysuckle and rosemary grew ever-green upon it, the daffodils dancing in the cold spring breeze, and I was glad he had found peace at last.

But he had abandoned me to my troubles and they were as numerous as ever around me. I had still to prove his innocence, and mine. There was no time to sit about. I had publicly accused Dr Magorian – and his wife – of the most terrible of crimes. As I had finished my speech to Mrs Magorian I had smelled the doctor's sugary breath and felt a shadow fall cold across me; I knew he was behind me and had heard everything. He had not said a word. Instead, he had pushed me aside, climbed into his carriage and driven away, slowly, through the seething crowds. But he had failed to see me hanged, and he knew I would not remain silent. Well, let him come for me, I thought. Let him seek me out, for I was ready for him. He would betray himself and I would be there to cut him down when he did.

❧

Will and I marched across the lawn between the wings of the asylum, towards the dark perimeter wall and the tall heavy gates.

'Mr Flockhart.' The voice came from behind us. 'Mr Flockhart?' I turned. A woman dressed in the black and white uniform of the ladies' attendants was hurrying after us across the grass. She came up, panting, her hand to her side. She looked familiar, though I could not place her, and my mind was too full of sorrow and despair to pluck from it any useful recollection. 'I heard you were sent to prison,' she said. 'And then your father after you.'

I nodded. What did she have to say to me? Everyone believed my father was guilty of the crimes he had confessed, and I had no wish to discuss the matter with the gossip-mongering servants of the asylum. I opened my mouth to tell her so, but she spoke first.

'I knew your father,' she said. 'He was a kind man, always good to me, and to my mother when she lay dying. He gave her the medicines she needed out of his own pocket.'

'He had a good heart,' said Will. I knew he was watching me, trying to protect me, and I was grateful for it. He took my arm. 'But if you would excuse us—'

'Wait a moment, Will.' There was something else, I was sure. The woman was wringing her hands, a look of concern shadowing her features. 'Yes?'

She said, 'I know he didn't do those things. Those things everyone says he did. He's not the first innocent man to hang and he won't be the last, but he didn't kill anyone. Nor you.'

Was that all that she had to say? Suddenly, I felt furious. Did she expect me to be grateful? To thank her? Did she think her vague platitudes, her feeble ruminations on loss and death were of value to me? I knew Will could sense my annoyance, for he put an arm about my shoulders and made as if to steer me across the grass to the doors. 'Thank you for your kind words,' I said. My voice was flat and insincere, even to my own ears.

'If you would excuse us,' said Will.

'You don't recognise me, do you?' she said.

I shook my head

'I was Mrs Catchpole's attendant, the night you came to see her.'

'Oh?'

'Yes. But I was called home that very night. My mother was ill, so I wasn't here to see to Mrs Catchpole the next morning, and I didn't know she was dead till I came back yesterday.'

'It must have been a shock,' said Will.

'I'm sorry you weren't told sooner.' I murmured the bland sentiments dutifully. But my mind now felt as clear as a glass. Something was coming, I felt sure of it. Something that would help us move beyond groundless accusations at last.

'Well, it wasn't really much of a shock,' she said. 'The people here do all sorts of things to themselves during the night, though I'd not have said Mrs Catchpole was likely to harm herself. But they said it was you who'd poisoned her, then they said it was your father, that he'd admitted everything, and I couldn't believe that either. Never heard such nonsense! I said as much, but no one listens to me.'

'*I'm* listening,' I said.

The woman continued, as though I had not even spoken. 'Your Mrs Catchpole said something to me the evening before she died, the night you came to see her, when the other ladies were there too. You remember? And then I saw you coming out of Dr Hawkins's office just now and I thought it was my duty to tell you—'

'Yes?' I felt my skin prickle.

Will gripped my hand so tightly that I nearly cried out. 'What did she say?'

'Well, I was brushing her hair, the way she liked me to. She was in her nightdress, sat before me. She seemed happy enough, less melancholy than she had been when she was talking about that Dr Bain every minute. She was humming a song, in fact, in time with the brush strokes. And then she ups and stops, just like that, and she says: "Cartwright, I've just remembered something. Mr Jem was asking me about it earlier and I couldn't recall a thing, but all at once I can see what it was quite clearly." "What's that, ma'am?" I said. "Well, he asked me what was different about the room, about Dr Bain's room, and I couldn't think. All I could see was Dr Bain in his chair, and my husband bending over him." And she started up with her hands again then, rubbing them over and over like she were washing them clean.'

'Yes?' said Will. 'Then what?'

'Well, she frowns and bites at her fingernails and then all of a sudden she says: "I remember there *was* something different." Of course, I asked her what it was. "A bonnet," she says. "It was a bonnet. On the table top. A wide one, pale blue with a little veil."

'To be honest, sir, I thought she was a bit confused, what with all the visitors and Dr Catchpole taking on so in front of everyone. But she was quite certain. "I know what I saw, Cartwright," she says. "I saw a blue bonnet." "Well, whose might that have been?" I said to her, and she looked at me all peculiar-like and her voice was all sharp and angry, she says: "I know *exactly* whose bonnet it was, Cartwright. It was Miss Magorian's." Well, I tried to persuade her, sir, but she wasn't having it. "Who else's bonnet might it have been?' she said. "I know Eliza Magorian's blue bonnet when I see it." And she was angry, I could see it, so I said nothing more. I didn't want to set her back, sir.'

'Of course,' said Will. I could see him looking at me,

but I did not move, or speak. I felt my skin turn cold and my heart seemed to have stopped within me.

'Well,' said Cartwright, 'she was silent after that. Thoughtful, like, but she'd not let go of it, and she kept saying to me: "I must tell Mr Jem tomorrow. I must be sure to tell him," as though she couldn't get it out of her mind, or at least didn't want to forget it. But of course, she couldn't tell you, sir, could she? She couldn't say anything to anyone.'

❦

I knew he would come for me that evening. Would she come with him? It was quite possible. I was not afraid; I would face them and draw the truth from them even if they killed me for it.

'I'll stay with you,' said Will.

'No,' I said. 'This is my business. Besides, you have your own work to attend to.'

'But who knows what will happen? Four people are already dead; will you be the fifth?' He raised his hands, as if in surrender. 'I won't interfere. It's a precaution, that's all. You'd be wise to take it.'

He would brook no argument, and in the end I relented. In the meantime, I took my mind off everything with work. There was plenty to do: the herb drying room had to be cleaned out and reorganised, especially as the governors insisted that I was to leave St Saviour's as soon as possible. All the herbs in the drying room and the apothecary had been bought by my father and me. I would be sure to take them, wherever I went. Besides, the infirmary was already being emptied in readiness for its removal and eventual demolition. The mound of corpses in the churchyard had hastened the process, as the governors were concerned that the miasma was injurious to the health of us all. The world was in turmoil. The scandal that hung over the place – the murders, my father's confession – had given St Saviour's a terrible notoriety. Crowds of onlookers still gathered outside, pointing and staring; the physicians and surgeons, the hospital governors, still arrived with the blinds drawn down on their carriages. The patients muttered together, looking at one another fearfully. When I entered the ward, the place fell silent, as if I carried in my pockets poisons to be randomly administered. Out-patients was no different. It appeared that people were prepared to remain ill, or to walk for miles to go to another hospital, rather than be attended by someone by the name of Flockhart.

Our work in the dry and dusty space of the herb drying room made us thirsty, and at five o'clock I sent Will out for some beer. I knew he would go to Sorley's, and that Sorley would keep him talking, and I was glad to think of him safe. But there would not be another chance. I stood at the window and looked out across the city, at the darkening sky and the familiar crooked vista of rooftops and chimneys. I heard the stair creak, the scrape of a boot upon the treads, and I knew the time had come.

I learned later that Dr Magorian had seized poor Will as he left the building, bludgeoning him with the weighted head of his stick, and dragging him into the chapel, that cold, junk-filled place where we had found those six small coffins so many weeks ago. But it was not Dr Magorian who came to me that evening.

I had wondered whether she would wear the cream

hussar trousers, and the short Spencer jacket, but she was dressed as she always was, neat and tidy in her navy blue wool coat; her hands sheathed in white kid; her bonnet pinned to her shiny hair. She clasped her hands, holding them tight beneath her breast, the fingers moving over one another in a repetitive motion, as if trying to rid them of the sticky filaments of a spider's web. Hooked over her arm was a bag. It swung against her skirts, slow and heavy. She stood in the doorway, her face bone-white in the lamplight, her eyes darting back and forth, searching the shadows for eavesdroppers.

'Will you take a seat, Mrs Magorian?' I indicated the chair before the stove. As Dr Bain had done on the night he died, I moved a pile of books onto the table top so that the woman might sit down. But whereas I was sure that Mrs Magorian's appearance at Dr Bain's house had been unexpected, all that day I had been waiting.

I sat opposite her. Mrs Magorian looked at me in silence. Had she expected a bustling show of bourgeois courtesy? Tea and cakes? Inquiries about the weather, the state of the roads and the reliability of servants? She wrung her hands together, her gaze still restless. I lounged in my chair, my legs stretched out before me. How well she played the game! But I was as skilled as she. I had acted a part all my life and I could recognise a fellow player when I saw one. There would be no secrets at St Saviour's, not now. I would hear her confession, and then I would decide what punishment she deserved.

'Where's your husband?' I said.

'This is not his concern,' she replied. Her hands stopped moving. She watched me now as a snake might watch a mouse.

'My father's dead,' I said. 'You killed him as surely as you killed Dr Bain.'

She shook her head. 'That's none of my doing.'

I felt rage flame inside, as though my blood had been set alight. But anger would not serve me now. I must stay calm and clear headed. And so I swallowed my fury and answered flatly: 'It's no one else's.'

Mrs Magorian clicked her tongue, as if bored by my stupidity. *Let her think me stupid,* I thought. *She will soon learn otherwise.* 'I'm here,' she said, 'to explain.'

All at once the trembling bird-like woman had vanished. She looked at me without flinching: the downward gaze she usually had, the subservient bobbing of her head, the slight cant of her body, had all disappeared. Her voice, usually so soft and apologetic, was brisk and commanding. 'Your father sacrificed himself for you,' she said. 'Perhaps that will do something to help you understand the love a parent has for their child. And, given what you are, maybe you can also understand how much a woman longs to be a mother – and the pain of realising that that can never be.' Her lips twitched in a knowing smile. But I would not let that distract me, not now.

She had put her bag beside the chair. Now, she took it up and rested it on her knee. 'I have something here that will explain everything,' she said. 'It's easier if you read it, than for me to try to put it into words.'

'What is it?' I said.

'A journal, of sorts. I kept it during those . . . those difficult years. It explains what took place and why, far better than my own colourless narrative might, especially after so much time has passed.' She pulled a heavy, hardbacked book from her bag and handed it over. 'You'll understand, after you've read it, that I can't let you keep it.'

'You expect me to read it now?'

She smiled. 'You have something more pressing to attend to?'

I held the book tightly in my hands, my eyes fixed upon the white gloved fingers that had passed it to me. It was some ten inches high, and bound with brown morocco. The cover was worn, stained with mould spores and splashes of ink. I opened it, but there was no inscription on the fly leaf, no acknowledgement of ownership. The pages were thick and yellowed, corrugated here and there, as though it had once lain somewhere damp. A floury, dust-like residue was faintly perceptible on my fingertips.

'Will you not read it?' said Mrs Magorian, when I showed no sign of turning the pages. 'Do you not wish to know what you stumbled upon? Why so many have died?'

'If I might ask you—'

'No, you may not,' she said. 'Everything is in this book. Read it, and you will find the answers.'

But still I waited. 'Dr Bain saw the coffins and he knew it was your handiwork, didn't he?' I said.

Mrs Magorian pressed her lips together. Her eyes flickered to the book in my lap. 'Yes,' she said. She spat the word out, as if it had lodged in her throat for years. Again I waited. The desire to explain, to confess, was a powerful one. If I could curb my urge to step into the silence with questions then she would tell me everything. I held my breath.

'Dr Bain lived with Dr Magorian and I in Edinburgh,' said Mrs Magorian. 'Dr Bain was a gifted student, and an excellent anatomist. But he had no money. Everything he had he spent on fees for the medical school. When we first met him he lived in rooms in some draughty garret in the Old Town. And so my husband took him in as his assistant.' She stopped. She seemed to be recoiling from me, withdrawing into herself. 'It is in the journal,' she said. Her voice was soft, hopeful. 'Will you not read it?'

But that would never do. Perhaps if I provided her with some mistaken information: could she resist the desire to correct me, to point out where I was wrong and tell me what had really happened? 'Dr Bain excelled, did he not? He soon put your husband to shame—'

'He did nothing of the sort,' she cried. 'He helped my husband at the anatomy school. He prepared specimens and gathered subjects in exchange for board and lodging, and his medical education. He had much to thank my husband for.'

'He was a resurrectionist?'

'An excellent one, my husband said. Fast. Strong. Willing. He had a way with the resurrection men too. They were a rough lot, but Dr Bain got along with them well enough.'

'Dr Graves too?'

'Dr Graves.' She shivered. 'He was a different matter. He relished his work amongst the dead. Dr Bain merely did what was required.'

'And your husband?'

'What of him?'

'He was interested in the physiology of the *gravid uterus*?'

'Yes.' Her voice was as sharp as a mouse trap. She heard it, and fell silent. But I had her now. She could not back

359

out, though she might wheedle and coax all she liked. I smiled to myself. She had started her confession. She would not stop till she had finished.

'Why the *gravid uterus*?' I said. 'Men midwives are not something the profession exalts. I am surprised your husband was prepared to settle for a branch of medicine so despised by his colleagues.'

She was unable to let the insult pass. '*Why?*' she cried. 'It was for me, of course, that's *why*. He chose that specialism for me. I could not have children. And yet if he could understand the way the womb functioned, if the process of conception and gestation could be fathomed, perhaps there would be some hope.' She smiled, but there was a glint in her eye that I did not like. 'The way Dr Hawkins will dissect your father, in the hope that what he finds will somehow explain the poor man's suffering, and will provide *you* with answers, with hope.' She sighed. 'For the future is bleak for you, is it not, Jem? We're not so different, you and I. Always hoping, always searching for a cure for our affliction. But Dr Hawkins will find nothing, as you well know. How will you bear it?'

But I did not want to talk about my father. I did not want to think about his illness – my illness. To think of such things would rob me of my rationality, and that I could not allow. I closed my eyes. 'What happened in Edinburgh?'

She licked her lips. 'My husband wanted a pregnant female subject. One was procured.'

'Murdered?'

'Saved from the evils of the world is a better description.'

'Who was she?'

'A prostitute.'

'Dr Bain brought her?'

She laughed. 'How I wish I could say "yes". "Yes, your precious Dr Bain killed a whore and she ended up on my husband's dissecting table."' She shook her head. 'Dr Bain did not kill anyone. But my husband could see my need, my longing. He found the girl. He did what was necessary and he did it without hesitation. Naturally, without its mother to sustain it, the babe in her womb died too.' She looked down at her hands, her expression troubled. 'I was sorry. Not for the girl, you understand, she was as full of vice and sin as any of them and had no useful purpose other than to show us the mechanisms within a woman that support life. But her child was quite innocent. And for that I *was* regretful. And so I made a small coffin and a doll – the same as those you found – as a token. An acknowledgement.' She was wringing her hands again now, twisting the rings beneath her fine leather gloves. 'Somehow, Dr Bain must have seen it. Perhaps I left the box out in the library; perhaps he saw me hide it in Greyfriars kirkyard that Sunday, I don't know. But Dr Bain suspected the means by which the girl had come to the dissecting table; he was aware of the talk of the resurrectionists; he had heard the rumours about the town and he knew my husband's professional interests intimately. He said nothing about it at the time.

'But Edinburgh is a small place and it is impossible to do anything without an acquaintance finding out about it. Even the most secret of acts cannot remain a secret for long. It appeared that the girl's mother had seen her with a man shortly before she disappeared. No one knew who the man was, but inquiries were made. In the course of these it transpired that Dr Graves was one of her regular

. . . *visitors.*' Her disdain, for Dr Graves, and for the girl, was clear and she said the word with a sneer, as though even the euphemism was worthy of contempt. 'And so the gossip started. Dr Graves had nothing to do with the girl's disappearance, but the scandal followed him nonetheless, and from there it reached Dr Bain, my husband, the anatomy school. Nothing was proved, of course. The girl was gone, and no one knew where she had ended up. But people make up what they cannot prove. We could stay in that city no longer.'

She lowered her gaze to her hands, her fingers restless in her lap, and there, before me once again, was the passive, cringing Mrs Magorian I had always known. 'Poor babe,' she said. 'I had to mark its passing, to acknowledge its life.'

'Rue for regret, wormwood for sorrow, the petals of the black rose—'

'Yes. So you knew their meanings? Well, well.' Her voice was sharp again, her mouth pursed in irritation. 'My little *memento mori* was neither here nor there. Dr Graves, Dr Bain, my husband, all of them had too much to lose from the affair. We knew what had happened to Dr Knox. Burke and Hare had ruined a great man's reputation; I was not about to see the same thing happen to my husband. So we left Edinburgh and came here. The medical world is small, but not so small that we could not escape the rumours.'

The book lay in my lap. Mrs Magorian's gaze rested upon it, but she seemed no longer to see it. She did not urge me to open it, but waited, silently, for me to speak. Did she expect absolution from me? Did she hope I would understand that what had taken place had been done in the name of scientific inquiry? Did she believe such worthy objectives put murder beyond the commonplace morality of men?

'So you came to St Saviour's,' I said.

'Yes.' She smiled. 'They were delighted by my husband's reputation as an anatomist. And his speed and skill as a surgeon were widely acknowledged. They recognised his value immediately. Dr Sneddon was instrumental in getting him the post. Dr Graves also found a position easily enough, thanks to my husband, and Dr Bain was able to resume his medical education.'

'But Dr Bain did not work for your husband again?'

'He did not.'

'And Dr Graves?'

'Continued as before. Bodies were needed. He was well acquainted with the manner of the resurrection men and soon found out their haunts. He ensured a steady supply. The graveyards of London are more numerous than those he was used to.'

'And your husband's research continued? He took Dr Sneddon's position after that doctor died. He carried on Dr Sneddon's work too?'

'Yes. We've known about you all along.'

I did not respond. 'And you?' I said. 'What was your role?'

'I was his wife. I supported him in his work. He is a brilliant man.' Her face was illuminated with pride. 'And he wanted me to be happy. A baby would make me happy, but we needed to understand more. I conceived, yes, but it came away. So much blood.' Her face turned pale. She pulled a handkerchief from her sleeve and dabbed her lips with it. 'He said he could help me. I knew he could find a way if the process itself, the creation of life, could be understood.'

The creation of life, I thought. What could he possibly know about such a thing? It was not for Dr Magorian to decide who should die for the sake of medical understanding. 'Dr Magorian found his own subjects, didn't he?'

Mrs Magorian sat back in her chair. Her face was stony. 'This city is unlike any other,' she said. 'Edinburgh was small. Everyone knew everyone else. But here—' She held her arms wide. 'Here is all the world! A great teeming dung heap. So many people, so much noise and chatter and vice. Such want and poverty. The poor are everywhere. They thrive and breed like vermin in those great filthy rookeries. Why are they allowed to get children when I have none? Why would God favour a drunken slattern over me?' Her hands were clenched in her lap. 'The girls were easy to find. They would ply their trade no matter what their condition, no matter what the weather. He brought them home. He preserved what he needed from their bodies, wrote up his notes and findings, and then together we put them into the churchyard.'

'You were dressed as a boy.'

'So much easier. *You* know that much.'

'Six times,' I said. 'And, for each one, a coffin, a doll. Each doll wrapped in a bloody fragment of their mother's chemise.'

'They were pregnant, each of them. They were no use to us otherwise. But I could not let them go into the ground without some kind of memorial. My husband thought me foolish, but I would not be persuaded. I was sure they would never be found. And if they were, who could possibly guess their meaning?' She twisted her handkerchief into a rope. 'I didn't guess that Dr Bain would do so.'

'And Eliza?' I could hardly bear to hear what might follow. 'What of her?'

'I love her as if she were my very own,' said Mrs Magorian. Her voice was tense, her eyes ice-blue gimlets.

'She's – she's not yours?'

'She's not my flesh and blood, though she *is* mine. In the end, though he could not provide me with our own baby, my husband gave me what I craved, what I longed for above anything else. Can you understand that longing, Jem?'

She spoke my name tenderly, as if we were somehow in accord, as though I too could comprehend what it meant to bear the pain of childlessness. But I would not be drawn into an endorsement of murder. And who was Mrs Magorian to assume that a woman's fulfilment might come only through motherhood? Who was she to assume she might prove a better mother than the girls her husband had murdered? My questions caught in my throat.

But Mrs Magorian anticipated me. 'Eliza *is* mine,' she cried. 'I was at her birth. I saw her mother's pain. I felt it as if it were my own.'

All at once, I became conscious of a movement at the door; a change in the shadows. I did not look, did not shift my gaze from Mrs Magorian, but I knew, at that moment, that we were no longer alone. Mrs Magorian was oblivious, sitting forward, her white-gloved hands spread like pale starfish, clutching the arms of the chair. Her voice was high pitched, her words tumbling out, sharp and urgent. How long had she kept that knowledge to herself? How long had she been unable to speak about it to anyone? I knew what it was to keep a secret: the desire to talk, to let it go and feel the relief of being free of it, even for a moment, was so profound, so all consuming . . . and now, here was a chance to confess, to explain, to unburden. I knew she would seize that chance as a drowning man might seize at a rope end.

'There was a girl. My husband tried to take her, but somehow she escaped him and she ran – faster than I thought possible for someone so far along in her pregnancy. She ran through the fog and out into the street, almost under the wheels of a cab. But it was dark and the fog was thick, the cab man must have felt the jolt, but he didn't stop. When my husband reached her, the girl was unconscious but breathing. He took her in his arms and brought her round to where I waited, at the end of Wicke Street, in the carriage. He drove us home. In the carriage, I cradled the girl's head; I stroked her belly and soothed her as she lay there. But then she regained consciousness. She was frightened, and she was strong. She had no idea where she was and she would not be calmed. Her front teeth were missing and I knew she had lived a violent life, that she was used to fighting; I would be no match for her, even in her condition. Suddenly she leaped at me, scratching my eyes and screaming, clawing at me as if she would tear a way through me and out of the carriage. I cried out for my husband to help, but he couldn't hear and he didn't stop.

'And then just when I thought she would overpower me, just as I thought she would kill me with her bare hands, she crumpled to the floor.

'I thought it would happen slowly, I understood

366

childbirth to be a great protracted affair, and yet it was not. Something was wrong. She was screaming and holding her belly, rolling her eyes at me, her mouth wide and red, her face bloodless, her hands cramped and twisted. She crouched down before me, her face twisted in pain. And then she gave a great cry and fell silent. She lay on the floor of the carriage where I had pushed her.

'I fell to my knees beside her. There was blood – on my face, my clothes, my hands – everywhere.' Mrs Magorian's eyes were lost in shadow, her voice a whisper. She held her hands out, as if seeing them for the first time, her face fixed in an expression of such horror that I could hardly bear to look at her. 'Who'd have thought she'd have had so much blood in her? So much blood for one as small and thin as that? Her skirts were soaked with the stuff – it coated my arms and my dress; I could feel it sticky beneath my shoes.' She closed her eyes, passing her tongue across dry, cracked lips. 'She looked up at me, and I could see the fear in her eyes. She gave birth right there, before me, and I took the child into my arms.'

Mrs Magorian sat back. 'Well.' She shrugged. 'I left the girl where she was on the floor of the carriage. And then my husband took her inside and did his work – we could not let her go to waste, and the womb directly after birth was something he was keen to examine. But the baby, she was mine – a gift from God. From my husband. I went immediately to the country. And when I returned, some months later, I returned with my baby daughter.'

I watched her, my mind going over all she had said . . . and yet something was not right. Something in her account did not quite fit with what I knew. I frowned. 'But there were six coffins,' I said. 'The coffins marked the dead babies, the innocent. And yet the sixth, Eliza, survived.'

'But her brother did not.' Mrs Magorian smiled; but her smile was wild now, as lopsided as a torn pocket, the eyes above it a pale, empty blue. 'Eliza was a twin. We didn't know until my husband cut the girl open. The other child was dead, its skull crushed, perhaps by the girl's fall beneath the hansom. But it's all in the journal,' she said. 'Will you read it now?'

'No,' I said. I forced myself to concentrate. I could hardly believe what I had heard. Such pain and horror. And Eliza, like me, a twin . . .

'Why not?' She frowned. 'I hand you my confession, and you ignore it?'

'I will not read it because you have painted the leading edge of these pages with monkshood,' I said. 'And then loosely stuck the pages together with flour and water paste. You hope I will lick my finger to get a purchase on the paper, or at least worry at the pages and the stuff will be absorbed through the skin. You would poison me exactly as you did Dr Bain. Anyone who turns these pages must wear gloves, as you do, Mrs Magorian.'

She lunged forward to seize the book from me, but I was taller and faster. 'You killed Dr Bain to prevent him from discovering what I have discovered,' I said. 'That you and your husband murdered seven women, including Eliza's mother, and you buried the remains of six of them in St Saviour's churchyard.'

'I could not lose her,' cried Mrs Magorian. 'She is my daughter. No one will ever say that she is the daughter of a common prostitute.'

'Far better that she might be the daughter of a murderer?'

I said. 'And what about Mrs Catchpole? You replaced the salve with poison when my back was turned, didn't you?'

'You were easily distracted.'

'Curare,' I said. 'It entered her body through the cut on her forehead.'

'It was only a matter of time before she remembered what she had seen.'

'I know what she saw. You killed her for nothing.'

Mrs Magorian shook her head. 'She said nothing to you!'

'But she told her attendant and her attendant told me. Mrs Catchpole saw your bonnet. You'd left it on Dr Bain's table when you hid behind the screen while Dr Catchpole was there. Mrs Catchpole saw the bonnet and she assumed it was Eliza's; she had seen Dr Bain with Eliza that night and, like you, she thought the worst. She jumped to the wrong conclusion. But it was *your* hat she saw.'

Mrs Magorian recoiled. 'She told you? But *when?*'

I did not deign to answer. 'And Joe Silks?'

'That boy? He would not give up what Dr Bain had entrusted to him. Such misplaced loyalty. But he could not resist a lump of sugar.' She smiled. 'It was an accident that he fell.'

'Was it?' I said. But it hardly mattered now.

Again, at the doorway, I saw a movement. Out of the corner of her eye, Mrs Magorian must have seen it too, for she leaped up and cried out, 'Charles, thank God!' Her expression dissolved into relief and she took a step towards the door. But she fell back again almost immediately, the cry dying on her lips as her hands flew to her mouth.

Eliza stood before us. She was soaked with rain; her hair

plastered to her head, her dress leaking water onto the floor. She was shivering, but whether it was from cold or anger I could not say.

'Dear girl.' Mrs Magorian held out her hands.

'Don't.' Eliza stepped back, 'Don't come near me.'

'But I'm your mother—'

'You're not my mother.' Eliza's face bore that closed, pinched look. Her gaze crossed to the boot I had stolen from Mrs Magorian's dressing room which now lay on the table beside my chair. And then she looked at me. 'Did I help you to bring us to this?' she said. 'Was that why you asked for my help, so that you might come into our home and take our secret things?'

'I would never do anything to hurt you.' My words sounded hollow, even to my own ears. Had I not taken the boot in the full knowledge of where it might lead? Did I not know that by doing so I would bring forth the truth, and with that cause her the most terrible pain? 'It's the truth, Eliza,' I said. 'The truth at last.'

'Well, I don't want it.' Her eyes were dry of tears, her face cold and hard. 'I don't want the truth – not any of it!'

'Oh, Eliza,' cried Mrs Magorian. She stepped closer.

Eliza backed away. 'You murdered her. You murdered my . . . my mother. My brother.'

'They died,' said Mrs Magorian, 'in childbirth. I took you and brought you up as my own. You would have died too without me.'

'You don't know that.'

'Would you have been happier in the poor house? Or living in some dirty corner of Prior's Rents? Or on the streets?' Her voice was sharp now. 'You'd be a drunkard and a whore, just like your mother – if you'd lived that long. But instead you're a lady. You've no cause to recoil from me.'

Eliza was silent for a moment. 'And those other girls?'

'Street girls.'

'And their babies?'

'We had to know. We had to understand *why*. Those girls were doomed. If the gin didn't get them, then the pox would. Your father—'

'He is *not* my father.'

'He loves you as if you were his own daughter.'

'He hates me.' Eliza's eyes were dark and furious. 'He hates me because he wants me. He has always wanted me.'

Mrs Magorian frowned. 'I don't know what you mean.'

'Don't you?' said Eliza. 'Don't you know what I mean? Perhaps I'm not so far from the gutter as you think, for it is he who's dragged me into it; he who's made a whore of me. He loves me like a husband, not as a father. He's done so since I was a child. Do you understand me now?'

Mrs Magorian gaped at her. She could not comprehend it. I closed my eyes, trying to shut out the horror of the world. I had guessed as much, but my mind had revolted to accept it. She had denied it when I had asked, but there had been something hasty in her refutation, and her confidence, her knowledge of intimacy had given the lie to it.

'Oh, he hated me for it – for tempting him – and I was duly punished with a beating. But I am a whore, and my true nature cannot be beaten out of me any more than it can be smothered with silks and fine manners.' She stood there for a moment. 'That's what he used to say to me. I always wondered what he meant.' She looked down at her hands, the neat nails, and clean, starched, white cuffs of her dress, and a tear ran down her cheek. Her small upright figure seemed to dwindle, to grow smaller. Her face darkened and her lips drew back over her teeth. 'I owe you nothing, *Mother*,' she said. 'And I will tell the world what you have done.'

'Eliza!' Mrs Magorian sprang down the stairs after her, the poisoned book forgotten in my lap.

❧

Outside, the rain was falling again. I emerged just in time to see Mrs Magorian vanish through the gate that led to the churchyard. I raced out after her. There was a glow in the sky to the west, but the place would soon be as black as a glove. Ahead of me, I saw Mrs Magorian's pale blue bonnet, darkened with the rain, bobbing amongst the graves. I heard her voice, faint against the roaring darkness. 'Eliza! Eliza!' But I could not see Eliza at all. Beneath my feet, the ground was uneven, sagging and mounded with bodies that had yet to be exhumed. Up ahead the great flanks of the bone mound were silhouetted against the inky sky. The stink of it filled the air. The men had stopped work hours ago, and the place was deserted. The night was growing wilder; I saw the tarpaulin that covered the tools billow like a great flap of skin as the wind caught it. I had to find Eliza, to explain – what? That all would be well? That I would save her from the cruelty of the world and the judgement of men?

At that moment a dark shape detached itself from the surrounding blackness. I saw a white face, sunken eyes beneath a shadowy brow, the dark wings of a cloak caught in the wind. I took a step back to brace myself, to throw him aside . . . But he was too strong. In an instant I was on my back. Above me, his face was tight lipped, his eyes invisible in shadows. I thrashed beneath him, my legs kicking impotently, but he sat astride me now, pinning me to the ground. Was this what he had done to Eliza? Had he pinned her down and forced himself upon her, or had he wheedled and coaxed – I felt his hands about my throat, squeezing. The rain poured into my open mouth, my staring eyes. I squirmed beneath him, the ground churning to sludge and rising up about my face as he pushed me into the earth. There was a roaring in my ears and the darkness that closed in upon me was the colour of oxblood.

As if from far away, I heard shouting. Above me I felt Dr Magorian jerk. His hands slackened and my vision cleared, though I could not move. My breath rasped against my bruised and bloody throat.

There were two of them now: one in a black cloak, the other in a brown oilskin. They wrestled with one another, plunging this way and that, rearing up before me, locked together as they struggled to bring each other to the ground. I tried to stand, but I could not. And then the oil-skinned one fell sideways, flung against a tombstone. He lay there, unmoving, twisted upon the rain-soaked earth like a rag doll, while his adversary, dark and terrible in his great billowing cloak, vanished into the night.

I crawled forward, the rain drumming on my skull. My voice was raw, my neck torn and bruised, my throat swollen.

It was Will, dear, loyal Will. I cradled his head in my lap. At his temple, a bloody gash told where he had smacked his head against the stone. *Not Will,* I thought, *please, not*

Will. I threw my head back and screamed my grief and despair against the wind. What hope, what chance of redemption could there be if he too was taken from me? I pressed my fingers to his throat with hasty imprecision. But the mud and rain, cold and slippery, defeated me, and I could feel no pulse. I bent over him and kissed his face. How lonely I had been before he came. And now? Now I had no one. No one at all.

'Jem?' his voice was a whisper, as close as a lover's in my ear.

'Oh!' I held him tight then, tight against the rain and the darkness. 'I'm here. You're safe.'

'And you? Are you safe?'

'Yes.'

'What about Eliza? Where is she? Where is Dr Magorian?'

I looked up. Ahead, against the shadow of the mountain of bones, I could see movement. I pointed.

'Go,' he whispered. 'Gabriel is coming. I sent him for help.' He squeezed my hand. 'Don't worry. He'll find me.'

Faint and far away, snatched by the wind, I heard a voice. I made Will comfortable against a gravestone, and then, with a last glance back, I abandoned him, following the sound, heading north across the graveyard. I stopped and listened, peering into the rain, hoping to catch a glimpse of something. My head throbbed and my breath came in sharp, raw gasps; I felt sick and dizzy, and I staggered forward onto my knees, holding onto a crooked headstone for support as I vomited onto the ground. My throat blazed.

I heard the cry again and I wiped my lips and stumbled on. And then, there, in front of me, were the bones, and the pit from which they had come. I stared up, shielding my eyes with my hand as the rain stung my face like nettles. They gleamed white, skulls and ribs glistening with rainwater; amongst them, slimy strips of flesh and hair, fragmented coffins, tattered winding sheets and streaks of dark, sticky earth. And all about was the sound of gurgling, bubbling water, as though the ground itself was laughing. As I looked, the bones seemed to move. I dashed the water from my face and blinked. There it was again. I could not make it out . . . and then I realised. There was somebody there, on that great mound, climbing.

Eliza.

I tried to call out, but the sound was no more than a rasp. At the foot of the mound stood the tall, hooded figure of Dr Magorian; beside him, the small, boy-sized shadow of his wife.

'Eliza!' I heard the call once more, a high-pitched keening sound, followed by a terrible anguished sob. Mrs Magorian sank to the ground at her husband's feet. I watched as he raised her up with both hands. She tried to pull away from him, but he held her close. He bent his head and whispered something to her; he smoothed the tears from her cheeks with his thumbs, and kissed her face. And then he too began to climb. Eliza stopped and looked back. I saw her start. Her foot slipped and she slid back towards him. The doctor put out a hand to seize her boot but Eliza scrambled away. I heard her shouting, screaming, but I could not hear what she said. If I followed them, I might bring the whole heap sliding down. And yet, if I waited – what then?

Even as I watched, the bones began to shift and

fragment, arms projecting, legs extending, as if the Trumpet had sounded and they were compelled to rise up at once. I stood, transfixed. What could I do but watch? They moved out, and down. Slowly at first, but then faster. Mrs Magorian cried out. I saw her raise her arms, calling to her husband. He turned and reached out to her. But the landscape was changing, bones grinding upon bones, jostling, plunging, surging, down towards the hole from which they had come.

I saw Eliza standing tall, silhouetted against the dark glow of the vanished sun; and then she was gone.

'Eliza!' I sprang forward. But mud was upon me too now, and my feet were swept asunder. I tried to stand, but I could not. Ahead, I saw Dr Magorian leap towards his wife. He put his arms about her as if to lift her clear, to throw her out of harm's way, but instead he held her close. For a moment they stood there, unmoving, clasped together as the bones seethed and rolled, and then they vanished from sight.

I cried out, but the rank earth stopped my mouth. And then all at once I was being pulled; someone was hauling at my arms, dragging me free. I choked and gagged, too weak to do anything but try to thrash my legs clear. The air was filled with an immense roaring sound, like a great shovelling of coals. And then there was only silence, and the sound of the rain pouring down upon a sea of bones.

❧❦

I opened my eyes. Above me, I could see that the mound of excavated bodies had collapsed, surging towards the pit from which they had been removed. I turned my head.

How it throbbed! Beside me, Will lay, unconscious. His temple bore a great dark bruise, his right eye swollen shut. But I could see that he was safe, and alive. For a moment, I watched him breathing, in and out . . . in and out. He had done so much for me that evening. I stretched out a hand, and wiped the dirt from his face. Some distance away, Dr Magorian was also visible, half buried beneath rags and mud. I saw his head move from side to side, and his arms rise up. His wife was nowhere to be seen. Someone would come, soon, and get us out. Someone would find her. I tried to shout for help, but my voice was gone.

I heard her before I saw her: boots floundering, slipping, slithering as she clambered across the wreckage; the slap of wet fabric as her heavy skirts dragged at her legs. I did not see where she had come from, and she had not noticed me lying there, covered in mud and unable to speak. But I saw her. I saw her run towards Dr Magorian. He was calling his wife's name now, his voice desperate, frantic. He turned his head from side to side, trying to see where she was, trying to sit up, to pull himself free. He saw Eliza, coming towards him across the wreckage as quickly as she could, and he gave a sob and held out his arms.

She knelt down beside him. Once again I tried to call out; I tried to pull myself up, but my strength had deserted me. The moon slipped out from a break in the clouds and I saw her look down at him. Her hair was bedraggled, her dress torn at the neck so that both shoulders were exposed, her skin streaked with brown. She smoothed the dirt from his face with tender fingers, her expression unreadable.

'Eliza,' I heard him say. 'My dear—'

And then, as I watched, her face resolved into an expression of such fury I could hardly believe that I was looking at the same person. She did not speak, did not make a sound, as she cupped her hands about the back of her father's head, and forced his face into the mud. He gurgled and heaved beneath her, writhing this way and that, but he was trapped from the waist down in the grip of the graveyard and he could do nothing to escape. His arms flailed. I saw Eliza's knees part beneath her soaked skirts, both hands now pressing hard upon her father's head. I saw her arch her back, her eyes closed, all her weight bearing down upon him as he bucked again, and then again . . . and then was still.

Chapter Nineteen

❧

I hardly know what happened next. Beside me, Will groaned. I could not move to help him, could not move to help myself. I turned my head and tried to whisper something encouraging. When I looked back, Eliza was gone.

I heard the sound of voices echoing up from St Saviour's, the porters' lanterns bobbing towards us as they ran to see what had happened. We were dug out, and carried home. I can remember little but the touch of hands, the lights of the apothecary, Mrs Speedicut's face rising up before me like a baleful moon.

Eliza had vanished. At first, it was assumed that she had perished, along with her mother and father. But I knew better. Only Dr Magorian and Mrs Magorian were unearthed, and a verdict of accidental death recorded. After that, events followed a logical sequence: the poisoned book was found in the herb drying room where I had left it. I gave it to the magistrate, along with a pair of gloves,

and in its pages the truth was made clear. My father's innocence, and mine, was established beyond doubt, and he
was buried with little ceremony, beside my mother, in that
undisturbed stretch of sunny earth at the southern wall of
St Saviour's church.

And I? Like Gabriel I too was now an orphan. I looked
after Will while he recovered from his ordeal with Dr
Magorian amongst the gravestones. The scar from that
evening would stay with him for ever, a peculiar heart-
shaped patch of raised, pink flesh at his temple.

'You're lucky not to have contracted septicaemia,' I
said. 'Or brain fever. Or lockjaw.'

'But I have the best doctor in you, Jem. And the best
nurse. I have every confidence.'

I patted his hand. 'And yet, I could poison you in fifty
different ways, if I chose.' It was true, it was in my power to
preserve life, and to bring death. How omnipotent I was!
And yet the one simple thing I could not do was forget –
my father's murder, Eliza – and the pain of their loss ate
into my soul.

Once he was recovered, Will stayed with us at the
apothecary while he completed his work at the graveyard.
The hospital governors asked me to stay, to come to St
Saviour's new site across the river. And yet my heart was
no longer in my work. I tried to carry on as usual, but
every day I watched the crowds on St Saviour's Street for
Eliza's face. I listened out for her voice, her laugh, though
I knew, in my heart, that I would not hear either. In the
herb drying room I looked down into the yard hoping to
see her walking across it. But, of course, she was never
there. I had told Will everything. What had happened
between Eliza and I, what I knew of her past, how I had

seen her force Dr Magorian's head into the earth. How
could I not have seen how unhappy she was? Why had she
not come to me earlier? If I could but find her . . .
Questions circled my mind like lazily flapping crows, dark
and ragged. I would look up and see Will watching me.
'There are some people who cannot be saved, Jem.'

The weeks lengthened to months. The graveyard was
emptied. St Saviour's, gradually, was emptied too. The
railway company would not wait; the foundations for the
new hospital were laid already, and St Saviour's was to
move to temporary accommodation out to the west.
Would I follow them? I could not. Gabriel would manage
well enough without me, and a new apothecary might be
found easily enough.

Will alone seemed to understand. He had acquitted
himself well amongst the corpses and his Master had
decided he was to work on a less grisly project: the
rebuilding of Brixton Gaol, out to the east.

'Well done,' I said, shaking his hand. 'And well
deserved.'

'Perhaps you might think of a new beginning too,' he
said.

'With St Saviour's?' I shook my head. 'You know my
thoughts.'

'No. Not with St Saviour's. With me.'

'You?'

'We are both alone in the world. Do you not love me?'

'As a brother?'

He smiled. 'If that's your wish, that's what it shall be. As
a brother. You might open an apothecary. Gabriel will be
sure to come with us, and you don't need to be part of a
hospital to peddle your potions and pills—'

I shook my head. 'Perhaps one day,' I said. 'But not yet.'

He put his arms about me then and held me close. 'Well, Jem,' he said, 'then I will just have to wait.'

I had never had a friend, not truly, and Will's loyalty amazed me. Every day, I walked down St Saviour's Street to the physic garden, though I knew I was not going there to tend to the place. Will came with me. My mind was no longer concerned with physic, and plants and poisons held no savour for me. The gardener and his boy I laid off – if there was to be no hospital, what use was a physic garden? How quickly the place went to seed! We sat on the iron bench and watched the wind blowing the dandelion clocks over the wall and into the city. Would any of them take root in that unfriendly place? No doubt there was a welcoming dung heap somewhere.

Next door, Dr Magorian's house stood empty. It could not be sold, as Eliza had vanished. She was the sole inheritor, but her death could not be proved, even if the fact that she was alive could not be demonstrated either. One day we saw some workmen boarding up the windows. Nothing had been removed, and the place remained full of furniture, specimens, books, surgical equipment. I looked over the wall, standing on the rusting garden roller at the foot of the physic garden. Dr Magorian's lawn had become a meadow full of couch grass, nettles and dandelions; the beech hedge was a bristling monstrosity, the flower beds now wild clumps of weeds and overblown perennials. I thought I caught a glimpse of something; the flicker of a brightly coloured summer dress amongst the apple trees, but when I looked again there was no one. Out of the corner of my eye, I thought I saw a movement at one of the windows of the house. I shaded my eyes and peered up at that great black villa, but my mind was playing tricks and there was nothing to see. One of the panes had been smashed in the window to Mrs Magorian's dressing room. No one would be coming to fix it. At length, the men boarded that one over too, and the entire house was closed off to the world.

We went back to the infirmary. The place was silent, the familiar noises – the coughing and hawking of the patients, the rattle of doctors' carriages, windows opening and doors closing – all had gone for ever. Rooms I had been familiar with all my life, which I had always known as bustling, noisy places, were now shabby and silent. The operating theatre, where once Dr Bain had appeared with his spray pump and his white smock, was cold and dilapidated; the dissecting room nothing but an ugly brown chamber. One of the panes in the skylights was already smashed and the glass littered the floor in long shards, reflecting the grey clouds overhead as if the heavens themselves were falling in.

We walked the cold, silent wards. The wind blew through the building, gusting in at the open windows as if, having been denied access for so long, it was determined to reach every corner of the place. The fireplaces, which had burned constantly, summer and winter since the place was built, were now no more than ragged black holes, the grates and mantels torn out to be used elsewhere. I had not realised quite how filthy the place was, how stained and damp the plaster, how bowed the floors, how cracked and dirty the window panes. When the wards had been filled with noise and activity, these things had gone unnoticed. Now they were all the place had left.

I insisted on walking past Eliza's house every day. One

day I thought I saw her face, but it was only the girl selling watercress. On another day I thought I saw smoke rising from the chimney, but when I climbed over the ivy-twisted gate and ran across the wild meadow of the front lawn, the door was still boarded up. We walked the streets about the infirmary – up and down the length of St Saviour's Street, past Prior's Rents, along Fishbait Lane. I moved as if in a daze, following blindly where Will led, thinking of my father, of Eliza, of that night among the bones. All at once I realised he had turned into Wicke Street. At the steps leading up to Mrs Roseplucker's front door, Will stopped. I looked up. The place was even more decayed than I remembered it: the gutters more bowed, the plaster more scabrous and soot-smeared.

'I wonder how Lily is,' said Will.

I shrugged. I was about to turn back when the door opened. Mr Jobber stood there looking down at me.

'Go on then.' Will did not look at me. 'I'll be here. I'll be waiting.'

Mrs Roseplucker's parlour was the same as when I had last seen it. The place was warmer than ever, and as damp as breath, as if somewhere a kettle was perpetually boiling. 'She's upstairs,' said Mrs Roseplucker. 'You know what room.' She grinned, and held out a scrawny claw. 'Knew you'd come. That's ten shillings to you.' She pocketed the coins and turned back to her penny blood. 'Don't expect much,' she said. She licked her forefinger and reached for the corner of the page. 'She ain't what she was.'

I climbed the stairs slowly. I don't know why I went. It was unlikely that Lily would be pleased to see me, and I had little to say to her. I shook my head. That I had come to this . . . I knocked, and pushed open the door to her room. There was the bed, that great sagging mattress on its crooked iron bedstead; the awful prints on the walls; the crimson drapes at the windows; the cracked ewer and pitcher on the washstand. Wrapped in a blanket, huddled in a chair before the dismal coals of a brown, smouldering fire, was Eliza.

'Hello, Jem,' she said.

Her voice was flat. She had grown thin, her hair hung dull and lank about her shoulders and across cheeks that were pale and hollow. I stared at her, unable to find the words that might make her look up, make her come to me. I put out a hand to the wall to steady myself, my knees suddenly barely able to hold me up.

'I came here after that night,' she said. She did not look at me as she spoke, but kept her eyes downcast. 'Mrs Roseplucker gave me some clothes, a bath, a room. She knew my mother – my real mother – years ago. She was happy to take care of me in the only way she knew how.' She pulled the shawl tight about her thin shoulders. 'There's no more to tell. No more I *want* to tell. So here I am; where I belong and no better than I deserve.'

'It's not your fault,' I said. I remained where I was, at the door. I hardly dared to draw closer, hardly dared to move, or to take my eyes off her in case she disappeared. Was I dreaming? I had been sleeping badly, and could not be sure . . . I rubbed my eyes, but when I opened them again she was still there, in that chair before the mean, smouldering fire, still unable to meet my gaze. It was the hardest thing of all to bear, to find she could no longer look at me; she who used to wink at me like a boy, whose eyes used to sparkle with mirth at the absurdity of others. Into my mind flashed an image of her in that room, on that bed, with man after man, crushed beneath them, their hands tearing at her, pulling her this way and that, stuffing themselves into her wherever they could. I closed my eyes. That was not who she was. 'None of it was your fault,' I whispered.

She shook her head. 'This is where I should be.'

'Of course it isn't. I can't believe you didn't come to me.'

'I killed him.'

'Yes,' I said. 'I would have done the same thing.'

'You would?'

'Undoubtedly.'

She seemed to shrink into her chair, then; drawing in on herself. She said, 'I don't believe you. You're better than I, Jem. You would have given him a chance. But I'm not like you. There's nothing in me that's good. There never was. Whatever you saw, whatever you *think* you saw in me, you were wrong. *This* is my place. My fate.'

I went to her then, and took her hands. She was cold to my touch, as cold as any corpse. I rubbed her fingers between my own. 'And so you will stay here, or will you come with me? It's your choice.'

Her face was expressionless. Still she did not look at me. 'The things they have done to me.' Her voice was a whisper.

I bent my head, my tears running over her hands. 'Oh Eliza,' I said. 'Eliza.'

❧

I never saw Eliza again. She did not remain at Mrs Roseplucker's, and I have no idea where she went. I think of her often, and I hope she found some sort of peace. As for me, I had no choice but to leave her where I found her, for she would not be persuaded. What else could I do? And so, that part of my life, that part of my heart, is closed off for ever. But I have much to be grateful for, and my position is unique amongst women. I have my father to thank, and my mother, who died without giving him the son he wanted. I work as an apothecary, alone amongst my herbs and powders – save for Gabriel, who still makes a mess, and Will, who helps us from time to time, when we are busy and he is back from his work for the evening. He shows a surprising aptitude with the pestle and mortar, and has perfected a recipe for aniseed balls. We are no longer at St Saviour's Infirmary – we have had our fill of that place – instead, we have taken a shop on Fishbait Lane. Will chose the place wisely: we are south facing, and the sun shines through our windows, the tinctures and syrups we have made glowing warm, like lanterns. The room beyond is full of welcome, the stove with its pot of coffee, the wing-backed chair beside it, the polished glass of my flasks and retorts winking brightly from the high shelves. We are safe here in our clean and ordered world, surrounded by the scents of hops and lavender, sage, citrus and cinnamon. And I am not afraid, as my father was. Why? I am not afraid because I am not alone. And when I can't sleep, which happens sometimes, I sit beside the fire, reading and thinking. Or I work on my treatise on poisons. When it is finished, I will dedicate it to Dr Bain. Upstairs, as dawn breaks, I hear Will moving about. I have an idea for an experiment involving a possible test for the presence of arsenic that I am keen to explain. I fill the tea pot, and listen for the clatter of his boots on the stair.

Acknowledgements

❧

A number of people have been instrumental in the genesis of this book. A few of them deserve special mention. For the suggestion that I try my hand at crime fiction, I am grateful to Alison Hennessey – what a good idea! For support and encouragement in all my writing efforts, and especially in the early stages of this novel, and for her kindness and hospitality over a number of years, I'm indebted to Jane Conway-Gordon.

For corrections, suggestions for improvement and steadfast enthusiasm for the book and its characters, even from its beginnings, I owe a debt of gratitude to the elite writers of Helen Lamb's Saturday morning writing class. In particular, the comments on early sections and drafts made by Michelle and Kirsty, Denice Percival, Olga Wojtas and Margaret Ries were invaluable.

I must also thank my mother, for her unwavering belief in me, and my lovely sons who have heard the words 'I'll

389

just finish this bit and then I'll come . . .' more often than I care to remember.

Special thanks and a round of applause go to Adrian Searle, friend, supporter and my favourite lunch-time companion; Jenny Brown, my fabulous agent without whom this book may never have seen the light of day; Al Guthrie for his judicious and intelligent edits, as well as Krystyna Green and the lovely people at Constable for their belief in Jem and her adventures.

Finally, to John Burnett, friend and fellow writer, I owe the most heartfelt thanks. He has read various drafts without demur, has offered the best of advice, and is always the most diplomatic, interesting and entertaining of companions. John, 'thank you' just doesn't cover it.

Author's Note:

I tried to be precise with dates and events, but must admit to some poetic licence here and there. In particular, the test for blood carried out by Jem (Teichmann's test) was not actually common currency before 1853. Any other liberties I have taken with history are entirely my fault – the result of a novelist's exuberance outweighing a historian's desire for pin-point accuracy.

BROCHURE